. . . And The

Whippoorwill Sang

by

Micki Peluso

Light Sword Publishing

Timeless Tradition; Word by Word

First Edition

Edited by:
Shawn M. Guideau, *MA, LPC, NCC*
Kimber Lee Cole

Formatted by:
Linda Daly
Kimber Lee Cole

Cover designed:
Sean Dickey

ISBN: 978-0-9792030-4-6

PUBLISHED BY LIGHT SWORD PUBLISHING

www.lightswordpublishing.com

Printed in the United States of America

To the one I loved and lost . . .

I kept my promise

The author would like to thank . . .

Linda Daly, my wonderful and gifted publisher, for making this book happen; Margaret Kelly, my long-time editor and friend. The wonderful editors at Light Sword Publishing, who said, "Tell your story and we'll worry about the rest." Special thanks to my personal editor, Shawn M. Guideau, who patiently corrected all my errors, never pulling out her hair in frustration. Without her editing skills this book would not have the special polish that makes a book stand out to the reader.

My husband, who stood behind me, refusing to read the book until it was published. Hopefully, there will be no lawsuits, divorce, or murder. I did warn him.

My daughters and daughter-in-law, who typed, formatted, encouraged, laughed and cried with me. Special thanks to my oldest daughter who spent many weeks putting the book together--working tirelessly through days and nights. To her talented husband, Al Cole, who helped with the technicalities and made my picture presentable.

My sons, who gave me time lines and lost memories. I think they felt it was finally safe to admit to their childhood antics.

My friends, Pat Guthrie and Bob Kocher, who patiently critiqued, read and offered needed advice.

All my friends, online and off, who read, typed, edited, and prodded me to keep new chapters coming to them. Each of you knows who you are--my utmost thanks.

Bonnie Golightly, deceased, my Writer's Digest School teacher, mentor and friend. Without her talents, warm wit and strict yet gentle writing lessons, this book would never have been written.

Michael Boyes, mentor and friend, the first one to insist I had talent and helped polish my skills, which led to 25 years of publishing success in newspapers and magazines.

Prologue

September 2, 2005

"Oh, Mom! There she is," Brandon says with a big grin on his face.

"Really? Where?" his mother, Kelly asks.

"Right there in the clouds--can't you see her?"

"Brandon, I can't see anything but the sky."

"Never mind, she's sitting right in the seat next to you . . . "Duh," And she says you never listen to her, so I hafta tell you that she doesn't want me to play in the street with the big boys no more.

Table of Contents

Dedication
Acknowledgments
Prologue

Table of Contents

To Weep . . .

To Laugh . . .

To Grieve . . .

To Dance . . .

~ *One* ~

August 23, 1981

The doctors stride into the emergency waiting room, nodding curtly to neighbors and friends, indicating that they want them to leave. The door swishes shut, entombing me with these harbingers of death, who sit in a semi-circle about ten feet from me--as if getting too close might somehow contaminate them. They introduce themselves, one by one, but their names wash over me unheard. It is the looks on their faces that I will always remember.

"I'm sorry," one of them says, "there's nothing we can do."

The room begins to close me in.

"You may as well let us disconnect the life support machines," another one adds. "The spinal cord is completely severed."

"No," I say, my voice sounding calm and detached--someone else's voice. "No, I want the machines connected."

"Mrs. Peluso, why don't you come with us now and look at the x-rays," says the third doctor, sitting closest to the door.

The room seems to grow dimmer and dimmer and the faces of these men who choose to mandate life and death are a blur.

"I don't want to see the x-rays. I want to see my child."

They flinch slightly at the cold fear inflecting my voice, then shake their heads in agreement. Glancing furtively at each other, they rise in unison and leave. People slowly filter back into the room, and someone places a jacket over my shoulders to stop the uncontrollable shivering. Finally, a nurse comes to lead me to my child.

When I reach the cubicle in the emergency room and pull back the gray curtain, I lose all remaining sense of reality. This cannot be the child who had run out my front door only an hour ago, too excited to give me a kiss goodbye, calling out, "Bye, Mom." What I am seeing is some stranger, bloodied and swollen beyond comprehension, fighting for life within a mass of human destruction; shattered jaw, broken nose, missing teeth. My tears mingle with the blood that slowly trickles down an alien face that does not even vaguely resemble my child.

"Please God," I pray. "I'll do anything you want if you just fix all this."

An orderly comes and wheels the gurney into the elevator and up to the Intensive Care Unit; and I follow.

Someone contacts my husband and he calls the hospital. I try not to scare him, but he knows me too well, and is driving the five hour trip back from New Jersey in apprehensive terror. Two of my children are with me; numbed into a silence they seem incapable of breaking. Shock, maybe, but I can barely console them. My thoughts are linked with the one in the room next to us. Ten-year-old Nicole is with a neighbor, and the other two cannot be located.

I feel so cold and so alone--like being in a dream where something terrible is about to happen which I can avoid if I run; run fast away from it. Instead, I drift in slow motion as my senses struggle to obey my mind to hurry, to escape from here, back to the safety of a time that now seems an eternity away.

~ Two ~

February 11, 1959

The office of the Justice of the Peace had barely enough room for all of us to stand. If I fainted I would have had little chance of hitting the floor, which was cluttered with old furniture and a huge desk overflowing with legal paraphernalia. But I wouldn't faint. The prospect of eloping to Elkton, Maryland at the questionable age of seventeen, was an adventure I found both exciting and more than a little frightening.

What would my mother say? Probably "congratulations," since it was her idea to remarry in a double ceremony. The bizarreness of a double elopement with my own mother wouldn't occur to me until years later.

My husband-to-be, eighteen years old, looking sixteen, turned to me, a smile lighting up his handsome, dark face; beaming reassurance that I didn't share. I never stopped to wonder whether he felt as confident as he looked; such was his personal power and charisma, or maybe love really is blind. He reached for my hand and squeezed it.

"Are you sure you want to go through with this?" he had asked the night before, as we sat nervously preparing to spend the night in the back seat of my mother's Buick, in the vacant parking lot of the A&P, waiting for the courthouse to open.

"Do you think we should?" I had answered, well past the point of decision-making, and not wanting to take responsibility for something as enormous as this.

"All I know is that if we don't get married tomorrow, your mother will take you out of school and drag you off to Florida with that gigolo she's marrying."

"Be quiet, my mom and Sal will hear you."

He turned on the seat to face me, taking both my hands in his. His face was deeply shadowed, highlighted only by the parking lot lights, but I could still see the intense shine in his olive brown eyes.

"You are the epitome of my life's dreams, and the only hope in my future." He had a sincere flair for poetic rhetoric, which both amused and moved me. I had to drop my eyes, unable to bear the raw emotion reflected in his.

"I know you're right. It's just so scary." My nerves were frayed from the long wait and my voice hoarse from the effort of whispering. There was so much I had to say, so many questions to ask. My doubts and fears battled against the intense love I felt for this man/boy and the conflicting emotions tearing at me left me speechless.

The moon had set over the A&P before we finally relaxed and nestled into each other's arms. Butch moved my hair away from the nape of my neck and kissed me behind the ear.

"It'll be all right," he'd said. "I promise I'll always try to make you happy."

The tension had drained from my body as I lay against his. He seemed so strong, so much stronger than me, and so safe. A small voice inside me countered, *maybe it won't be all right and if it isn't, remember that this was your choice.* I surrendered to the strong male scent of him, melted into the warmth of his body and nothing else mattered.

My mother planned on moving to Florida soon after we all returned to Easton, taking Sal and my younger brothers with her. Stevie, at twelve years old, would not mind the move, nor would Billy, who was only ten. Their lives had been so traumatized by the messy divorce that moving to a new life could only be a welcome change. My mother would be relieved to leave me in Pennsylvania, a married woman no longer her responsibility.

The Justice of the Peace pronounced us man and wife; all four of us, and my life on that bright and cold February morning took a turn that would forever alter whatever course was set in another direction. I walked out of the courthouse, blinded by the dazzling sunlight of a brilliant day, as a different person . . . a married woman.

Our elopement had to be kept secret, because I was graduating high school in June and in 1959, school officials frowned on married students. If a girl became pregnant she was automatically expelled from school. The education system was strictly totalitarian and rules were not made to be broken and rarely bent to fit the needs of individual students. Butch's parents could not be told due to the real fear that they would have the marriage annulled.

We had taken on the mantle of lifetime commitment, but had no place to live together, no full time jobs and no real future. My attic bedroom became our honeymoon suite, with the sounds of my brothers horsing around and Sal's hearty belly laughs wafting up through the walls.

"Doesn't that guy ever shut up?" Butch complained, as he perched on the edge of the narrow daybed where I had slept for the last four of my seventeen years. I sat on the other side of the bed, busily fluffing up my two pillows and picking imaginary lint off the quilted comforter overflowing with stuffed animals. Butch kept glancing over at me, expecting me to do something. I kept fidgeting, wondering how I would tell him that we couldn't make love.

"Since I didn't get to carry you over the threshold, do I at least get a kiss?" He looked so young and so dreadfully hopeful. I slid over to him and gave him a peck on the cheek.

"We um, what I mean is . . . well it's just that we can't do this tonight. I have my um . . ." My cheeks flamed red as I struggled for the words.

"Oh. Oh, I know. I get it. No, no, it's okay. We don't have to do this tonight. We can wait. We have our whole lives to make love." He put his arms around me and we snuggled under the soft blankets, both of us uttering a barely audible sigh of relief. All at once we were the best friends of a few days ago as we giggled over the absurd imagery of short, fat Sal making love to the statuesque beauty that was my mother. Much later, Butch left for his own home as if nothing unusual had happened that day.

~

During the following weeks, I helped my mother pack for her trip south. Sal spent most of his time on Long Island, where he was from originally; doing whatever it was he did. Business, he always said, expecting that statement to satisfy everyone's curiosity. My mother never seemed to notice that Sal's life was about as open as the gates to Sing Sing. She hadn't known him very long before she married him, but he had sweetened the sour taste of the divorce and made her happy.

After they left for Florida, I felt a twinge of abandonment. I had never been separated from my family before and it caused an unsettling sensation in my stomach. My father lived in the next town, not ten minutes from me, but when my mother divorced him, he broke all contact with his children, as did all the members of his family. I didn't miss him. He was often cruel and I bore a lump on the side of my once-broken nose as proof of it. He was my mother's second husband and had adopted me at the age of five. He treated me exactly the way he treated his own sons--harsh and uncaring much of the time. I took comfort in the fact that he wasn't my real father. Still, I felt truly orphaned, with no one to call my own, except my new husband. After my mother left, I moved into the spare attic bedroom of my boss's married daughter, who worked with me at her parent's pizza parlor. I tried not to notice that I had spent most of my life sleeping in attics that were freezing in the winter and stifling in the summer.

~

Graduation was four months away. It couldn't come soon enough for me. I worked late every night after school which stifled any motivation for arising at six a.m. and walking several blocks in the cold to catch the school bus. Being married had set me apart from school life, even though no one knew about it. The ordinary locker room chatter between girls, seemed childish to me now. After all, I was doing the things my friends snickered and whispered about. Almost. Butch and I were afraid to consummate our marriage. We were not well-versed in birth control, which, except for the packets carried in boy's wallets, but seldom used, was a taboo subject. I was busy working and going to school. Butch, having graduated the year before, was too exhausted working days as a stock boy for a men's store and nights as a busboy, for either of us to worry much about our lack of a sex life. We made time for sock hops and quarterly teen formal dances, as if we were ordinary teenagers unshackled by the bond of matrimony.

June finally rolled around and two important things happened. I graduated high school and realized I was pregnant. Passion had finally overcome fear and ignorance and while it was only one time--one time was all it took.

The graduation party was held at the Easton Hotel. I finally told my friends about the elopement and consequent pregnancy. Most of them were stupefied, yet excited by the tinge of naughtiness about it, but Jeanie, my best friend since the sixth grade, was appalled at our lack of responsibility.

"How could you do something so stupid? What about college? You've ruined your future! You know that, don't you?"

"Look Jeanie, what choice did I have? My mom would have taken me to Florida if I hadn't got married and then I'd never see Butch, you or any of my friends again."

"Don't give me that crap. We could have thought of something. Anything would have been better that what you did," she said. She stormed off to the ladies room, ignoring me throughout the rest of the party. Her intense reaction startled me. I reflected again on the reasons behind my elopement; true love or cowardice at the thought of being totally on my own? For I never would've gone with my mother. I found no answer and resented Jeanie for the twinge of shame I felt on a night that had held the promise of fun and short term notoriety. Jeanie knew as well as I did that I couldn't afford college, although we shared the dream. Grants and student loans were not easily attainable then and my grades, which had always been high, had slipped dramatically, due to my work schedule. I wondered if it was her voice inside my mind that night in the car. She didn't speak to me for several weeks, but I suspected it was more for not telling her than for the dastardly deed itself.

Becoming pregnant moved up the problem of telling Butch's parents that we were married. We told them as gently as possible in late June. It was all we had expected and more. His parents had always liked me, at least up until that night. The fact that I wasn't Catholic, a big fact, and that Butch dared marry outside his church, condemning him to excommunication, was inconceivable to his parents.

"How could you do this to me, Ormond?" his mother wailed, sinking down into the kitchen chair, her hands covering her stricken face. No one in his family called him by his nickname, which he'd acquired in school after joining a gang of nice boys who wanted to sound tough. His father, noticeably upset, also had quite a bit to say, but most of it was angrily muttered in Italian and I wasn't anxious for the translation. After the shock wore off and the tears subsided, they offered their home to us, realizing that the act could not be undone. Being gracious people, they were willing to make the best of what they considered a deplorable situation. We were not in a position to refuse and we both knew it. Morning sickness had struck like the Black Plague and I knew my working days were numbered.

~

Within the week, I moved into Butch's home and was treated like a member of the family. I shared a bedroom with his two younger sisters. Butch slept in his room with his brother. His mother, like a Crusader of God, monitored the hallways at night to make certain we didn't get together in the biblical sense. No matter what time of night I got up to use the bathroom, a compulsion brought on by the pregnancy, she was up, too. She could not accept a marriage outside the Church and told me repeatedly that my baby was illegitimate. In spite of my indignation and anger over what I believed to be religious fanaticism, much of the time I felt like a wanton sinner, a Mary Magdalene.

In order to marry her son "legitimately" I had to attend Catholic indoctrination by the priest. One of the stipulations was my promise to raise our children as Catholics. The priest who instructed me in the ways of Catholicism was young, barely out of the seminary; and I was a feisty Baptist, raised on fire and brimstone. We argued constantly, mostly over theology, but in order to marry Butch and finally get some order back into my life, I conceded my own beliefs and agreed to the dogma of the Church. The young priest, after four weeks with me, was sent to a rest home for frazzled priests; a just reward, I thought.

~

On July eleventh, an unusually hot and sultry day, we were married in the eyes of God (who apparently wasn't watching the first time). On this auspicious occasion, someone did faint. Butch went down for the count, either from the heat or the fact that this time he was "really married." The family reception was held at his parents' home, a day I spent alternately retching and smiling. Butch's relatives descended upon us in droves, all talking at the same time as they wished us well. They resembled each other to the point where I gave up trying to tell which aunt from which and married to which uncle. They were boisterous and loving, enveloping me in that love as if they had known me all my life. The air was charged with warmth and genuine caring. I thought how strange I must look to them, a tall, Scotch-Irish girl, standing five feet nine among these shorter, compact Italians. Butch was the first person in his family to marry both outside his nationality and his religion.

After showering us with hugs and kisses, giving new meaning to the term, "kissing cousins," family and friends got down to the important business of the day; eating. There was more food set out on the twelve-foot dining room table than I had ever seen at one time. Italian dishes of every variety, some that I couldn't even pronounce; roast beef, ham, turkey, salads, vegetables, crisp Italian bread and dessert heavy enough to weigh down the table.

"Eat! Eat!" Butch's Uncle Hubert insisted. "You're too thin. You want that baby to starve?" He put his arm around my waist and laughed when he realized that his head barely reached my shoulder.

~

The day mercifully came to an end and Butch and I were more than ready to embark upon our honeymoon. We planned to drive to Florida to visit my mother and if jobs were good, maybe stay there for a while. I was uncomfortable living with my in-laws. I was pregnant and I wanted my mom. The old '52 Studebaker that we had pooled our money for was packed to the brim with all our belongings. We said goodbye, were kissed and hugged a hundred times more and set off for the 2200 mile journey, alone for the first time in our marriage--well almost alone. We were returning Judy, my family's ten-year-old dachshund that Butch's mom had taken care of when my mother left.

We started off, the three of us in the front seat, the back seat filled to capacity with all our belongings. We had hopes of driving four or five hours and then stopping at a motel and initiating our honeymoon. After three hours on the road, I noticed that the landscape looked increasingly familiar. The truth became evident. We had driven in a complete circle and were only a few miles from Butch's home. Exhausted as he was, Butch was not about to drive home and admit this to his family, so we started off again.

"How are we going to find Florida if we can't even get out of our own state?" I asked Butch, who had grown quiet.

"Don't worry, we'll find it all right," he muttered sheepishly. He was more tired than he would admit and we ended up pulling into a motel just off #309, fifteen miles from Easton. On the inside the motel was shabby, but the bridal suite was available. At least that's what the night clerk called it. To our tired eyes it was the Waldorf Hotel. Within half an hour we'd unpacked our necessities and were snuggled beneath the cozy, well-worn comforter . . . just the two of us and Judy.

~

The drive south was interesting and relatively uneventful, until we reached the border between Georgia and Florida. It was late evening and we had been traveling all day. Instead of stopping where there was civilization, Butch decided to log a few more miles while it was still light. Before we realized it, darkness fell and the winding road became treacherous, cutting through misty swampland. Dense, eerie fog rolled in like low clouds, lifting only sporadically.

"We better stop somewhere soon, before I fall asleep at the wheel," Butch said. "I can't see more than six feet in front of me."

A few miles down the road, we passed a small, dimly lit diner called "Ma's Place" and backed up to it.

"What do you think?" Butch asked me.

"How bad can it be?" I answered, my stomach rumbling from hunger. "It's probably family run with home-style cooking. Let's go in. We might not pass another place for hours."

We ordered our food and while we waited, I made a hurried exit to the rest room; a glorified outhouse sitting behind the diner in the midst of dense trees and weeds. I flipped the light on as I entered, too anxious to use the facilities to notice that I wasn't alone. When I saw them, I stood motionless and screamed. I was surrounded by hundreds of large black spiders that looked like they'd stepped out of a horror movie. Butch heard my screams and came charging in like Sir Lancelot on a quest, followed by Judy, whose genes were geared for the hunt. The spiders, previously stationary, began to scatter in all directions. I screamed again and bolted out the door.

"That was really bright," I said to both my saviors, one of whom was about to get kicked if he didn't stop laughing.

"What are you so worked up about?" Butch asked, trying to keep a straight face. "They were probably only harmless Clocks. Wouldn't hurt a fly. Hmm, maybe a fly but not you."

"Is that so?" I asked. They sure looked like National Geographic photographs of black widow spiders to me."

He put his arm around me to stop my shivering as we walked back to the diner. Our order had arrived. I noticed a huge black fly floating feet up in my milk. That was the final straw. I ran back to the car, followed by Butch, who found the fly in the milk much more horrible than the spiders in the rest room. While we were in the diner the car had filled to capacity with vicious, hungry mosquitoes, delighted by our arrival. The fog had lifted and we sped at 80 miles an hour with the windows open, but didn't lose the last of them until we crossed the border into Florida; the land of sunshine and things that go bite in the night.

~

We arrived in Fort Lauderdale shortly before dawn and were welcomed enthusiastically by my mother, brothers and Sal. Judy, happy the trip was over, showed her joy at seeing my mother by peeing on her carpet. My mother was renting a rustic country home just outside Fort Lauderdale. The house stood a few hundred feet from the shore of a small lake, flanked by tall coconut palms, with lemon and orange trees right outside her kitchen windows. It was a veritable Garden of Eden, and like Eden, housed serpents; not only in the form of snakes but scorpions, black widow spiders, (curiously resembling the "Clocks" of Georgia) as well as chameleons, those strange little lizards that can change color to match their environment. The local mosquitoes made the ones who'd ridden with us seem harmless. The palmetto bugs, large, hard-shelled cousins of water bugs, two inches long and half an inch thick, could only be killed by stepping on them, causing a sickening crunch as they met their just rewards. I spent a lot of time in the bathroom.

There were many parts of Fort Lauderdale that were spectacular. Most of Florida was beautiful, the beaches taking priority in the order of loveliness. The ocean was a calm blue-green, so clear that you could see through the water. The beach sand was pure white, unmarked by the debris of constant tourism, and the breakers in the ocean hardly broke at all, cresting like the gentle waves of a mountain lake. The tall palms were majestic, even when bent nearly to the ground by sporadic summer storms that blew up from nowhere and were over almost before you got wet. But beauty notwithstanding, Florida's insect population gave me nightmares.

~

Butch found a job in a nearby gas station and came home tired and reeking of motor oil, which hampered our sex life. The smell of him, which I could perceive even in another room, sent me running to the bathroom. His usually optimistic attitude was being flagged by my constant complaints, the intolerable humidity and the futility of our situation. Both my mother and Sal worked, so I passed the days babysitting my brothers and doing light housework, very light, careful not to disturb anything with more than two legs.

My brother Billy spent his days fishing in the lake behind the house, while Stevie, who hated the sport, whiled away the hours with me, coloring with crayons, reading or playing cards. One afternoon Billy came home with a large, ugly, unusual-looking fish in his bucket. He decided to keep it as a pet and hand-fed it daily. Several days later, a neighbor walked over to the backyard and nonchalantly asked us why we were keeping a barracuda. *Oh God,* I thought to myself. *Please help me leave this jungle of poisonous bugs, lizards and man-eating fish.*

~

I cried often that torrid summer, feeling sorry for myself and puffed up with righteous indignation, angered that no one understood me. No one did, myself included. My outbursts surprised even me, and while Butch was always moved by tears, his patience shortened and the tension between us grew faster than the baby inside me. I couldn't help it. I missed the Pocono Mountains rising above my hometown, the serenity of the valley, and summers that were hot but not unbearable; and most of all, familiar.

Butch and I knew that as much as we hated Florida, we were trapped. All of our traveling money was gone and Butch's job paid for food and little else. He had stringently managed to save up two hundred dollars in the hope of leaving for home, but Sal had borrowed it from him.

"How could I say no?" Butch asked, when this news infuriated me. "We're living in his house and only kicking in money for food."

"You're right, I know it," I answered, tonelessly. "It's just that I want to leave this place so bad and Sal will never pay you back."

"Don't you think I know that?"

"Keep your voice down," I warned, shifting my body in an effort to get comfortable on the double mattress lying on the floor of the sun porch that was our bedroom.

He turned his back to me and I knew the subject was closed.

~

One afternoon, in my usual fit of melancholy, I decided to browse through all our wedding cards, hoping to take my mind off the weather. To my amazement, I came across several cards that we must have overlooked in our rush to be off on our honeymoon. Cards with checks and cash in them. There was more than enough money to get us back to Easton, and I could hardly wait for Butch to get home so I could surprise him with the news. Within two days we were packed, in the car and driving north on I-95, heading back to civilization.

~ *Three* ~

It is silent in the waiting room, a silence that is unworldly and strangely deafening. Only the occasional words spoken by passing nurses assure me that this is really happening. Friends and neighbors come and go, offering heartfelt condolences that strike a hollow note. I cannot be consoled.

Two policemen call me out into the hallway to ask if they can talk to me. I nod, as they say something about local jurisdictions and the wrong police taking the accident report. I've no idea what they're talking about and don't care. They tell me that the person responsible has been apprehended. I don't care about that either. At last they register my dazed stare and leave me alone.

A woman walks up to me and starts asking me about donating body organs. I look at her in horror. *My child is not going to die.* She keeps right on talking, oblivious to my state of shock, like a magazine salesperson refusing to take no for an answer. A friend quickly pulls me away from her and leads me back into the waiting room. My children have fallen into a deep sleep, one sprawled across two vinyl chairs, the other curled in a fetal position on the couch. Another friend tells me that while I was speaking to the doctors, Kelly had raced out of the hospital. Dante had chased after her and tackled her to the ground. The kids had run out of the hospital in anger and hysteria, thanks to the bumbling of the hospital chaplain. He sat with them and told them all the ramifications of the accident, including the vegetative state of their sibling, which he stressed, would be worse than death. Until that point, they had no idea as to the seriousness of the situation. Several of the neighbors still in the waiting room, had brought them back.

Our local parish priest was on his way to his vacation when he heard the accident report on his police scanner. He turned back and came to the hospital. One of the doctors stopped by a few minutes ago, pressuring me to disconnect the life support systems, assuring me again that there is no hope. Again, I refuse. The priest supports my decision which helps convince me that I'm doing the right thing.

The room is dark now, the only light coming from the antiquated soda machine which greedily swallows the loose change of neighbors and friends anxiously waiting outside the ICU door. I am exhausted, but sleep eludes me. Instead, I slip into a hazy trance, grabbing on to the past in an effort to block out the future.

~ Four ~

1960 heralded the beginning of a new decade, both for the country and me. I was about to bring a new life into the world, a life that would become my responsibility, not just for the eighteen years of childhood, but for as long as we both lived. The cold war was an ever-present reality that my generation lived with. Would my child face the same future? We were the children of the bomb, a daily threat made real through media propaganda. Cuba, armed by and allied with Russia, was eight minutes by jet to the Florida coast. At any given moment the dangerous, fanatical Fidel Castro could launch a nuclear missile at the United States, devastate major cities, initiating global war.

Living under the constant threat of annihilation made the children of the late fifties and early sixties aware of their fragility, causing them to adopt a tendency to live day by day. Tomorrow might never come. Even my brother Billy, eight years younger than me, often commented that he would never live to manhood. *The world would end before then; the Russians would bomb us.*

Many teenagers and young adults were plagued by suicidal thoughts or death wishes. They couldn't imagine what it would be like to leave the relatively ambivalent safety of childhood, and move into the tenuous world of adulthood where the problems of a discordant world would fall to them.

Butch was one of them. For several years he'd suffered dreams in which he drove down a particularly dangerous hilly curve in Phillipsburg, New Jersey, a small town along the Delaware River across from Easton, and plunged into the river. His recurrent nightmares were precise. On the day of his eighteenth birthday, he would drive his car around the treacherous curve, go off the side of the road, plunge into the Delaware River and be killed or paralyzed. He believed the dream, and like most of the fatalistic children of the time, intended to meet his fate with bravado. On the day of his birthday, he drove his car around the curve, speeding to his pre-ordained destination. Nothing happened, except that he scared me to death with worry. I was a pragmatist. If I dreamt of my own death on a given day at a given place, I would've spent that day in bed, covers over my head--no sense in tempting fate.

Children of the fifties, living under this cloud of death, accepted its promise and baited it in various ways. There were death-defying drag races on deserted highways; sometimes racing to the edges of cliffs, testing who could stop closest to the edge. That and gang fights in the ghettoes of the cities, where it was considered noble to die protecting your turf, were the sad legacies of the past decade. Would 1960 be any different?

On the first of February, it didn't seem likely. Four black students in Greensboro, North Carolina, took seats at the luncheonette in a Woolworth store and ordered coffee. The first of many black sit-ins. Woolworth's, a nationwide chain, served them and the movement quickly spread across the country. Negroes throughout the South, led by the charismatic Martin Luther King, were awakening from their long slumber of subservience and answering the call of freedom; the beginning of a bloodbath that would eventually insure their inalienable rights, constitutionally, but never fully stifle the inherent bigotry of mankind.

Living in the small community of Easton, Pennsylvania gave me a sense of disdain and horror over the bigotry of my country. I hadn't yet realized that there was no racism in rural Easton, because there were no blacks living there. Or if there were, they kept themselves inconspicuous from the mainstream population.

~

Still, nothing could mar the excitement of the presidential election that year. John F. Kennedy, a charming forty-three-year-old Massachusetts Senator, beat Richard Nixon by a narrow, even questionable, margin and introduced Camelot to a country desperate for change. Even those who disagreed with his politics, and there were many, liked the man. He brought new meaning to the word, charisma. The young president with his thick mop of dark hair and smiling, babyish face, often appeared hatless and in his shirt sleeves, to address a public that identified with his dreams. He made us believe we were part of the government, and together with him, nothing was impossible. Even the threat of the bomb dimmed somewhat. Kennedy, our hero, would make everything all right.

His wife, the haughty but strikingly beautiful Jacqueline, stirred the admiration of women everywhere, and their young children, five-year-old Caroline and two-year-old John, put the final touches to the love the country felt for its first family. The Kennedy's brought to the White House a sense of rebirth, youth; perhaps an end to the hated cold war and the ongoing threat of death at the hands of the power-hungry evil Communist regime.

On January 20th, less than a month before the baby was due, John F. Kennedy was sworn in as president, promising his voters a "new frontier" of wonderful new developments. It was snowing hard on Capitol Hill, with strong wind gusts bringing disruption to his inauguration, possibly an omen of things to come.

On February 6th, the birth of our first child took precedence over the developments in the world. It was a uniquely momentous experience, at least for me. I had an old obstetrician, well past retirement, with a grandfatherly attitude that helped keep me calm during the most frightening time of my life. No woman, no matter how well-informed she is, ever expects childbirth to be as painful and traumatic as it is. I was no exception.

"When will it end?" I moaned to Butch as we walked up and down the hospital corridors in a futile effort to hurry the baby along. Eighteen hours of labor wore my endurance down.

"It's got to be over soon," he said, worry creasing his brow and paling his usually ruddy complexion.

"Easy for you to say," I said, grimacing through another contraction. "The next time we decide to have a baby, you have it!"

As the pains escalated to unbearable, nurses moved me to the delivery room. The doctor nodded after examining me, and chuckled.

"I think I just might make it home in time for the fried chicken my wife's cooking for me, after all. Yep, I just might."

I was humorless at the time and couldn't imagine anyone thinking about fried chicken while trying to deliver a baby. Suddenly my body took on a life of its own. No longer wracked by pain, I was shocked by the intense pressure forcing me to bear down and push. As the baby's head poked through, it seemed as if I was losing a vital part of myself, and when her body slipped out, rubbery and quick, I experienced something close to resentment over the loss of a togetherness that had been shared for so many months. The baby was placed upon my newly flattened stomach while the doctor detached the placenta. I lay still, feeling awed and godlike, overwhelmed at my part in creating life. I loved her at once.

Kimber Lee was over eight pounds and had a ridiculous curl, a cowlick actually, right in the middle of her forehead. The nurses fawned over her, especially when she raised herself up on her arms and complacently eyed her surroundings just minutes after her birth.

Easton Hospital was small, lending itself to a warm and caring atmosphere, which compensated for the shabby rooms and worn hallways. I was in a ward with five other women, most of them near my age. We sat up late into the night, discussing the astounding thing we'd accomplished, our husbands, and the perfection of our babies. We were like college girls huddled in our dorm, except that by becoming mothers, we entered a new dimension in our young adulthood, distancing ourselves from the carefree actions of most girls our age.

~

Two months after Kimber's birth, spring crept in, quietly revitalizing the barren, damp cold of late winter, until the countryside was painted with blossoming plants, trees and shrubs. As Mother Nature rejuvenated the earth, I felt a restless urge to move forward into a home of my own, and a family life not contingent upon relatives.

Living with my in-laws held some wonderful moments, but I wasn't a child anymore. I had borne a child of my own and felt the natural inclination to go off and build my own nest.

The family doted on the baby. Kimber strongly resembled her fifteen-year-old aunt and godmother, Marie, who strongly resembled the rest of her sisters and brothers. Lynn, shortened from Michaelyn, was a comical, puberty-ridden twelve-year-old, prone to clumsiness and mismatched outfits. Lynn fervently believed that bright plaids and colorful stripes had an affinity for each other; a fashion queen before her time.

The baby of the family, Donald, was a handsome, quiet eight-year-old, hopelessly in love with me. He had soft, dark brown eyes and he loved to have me run my fingers through his thick, nearly black hair, much like his older brother. Whenever the baby wasn't in my lap, Donald was.

I was taken with my young sisters-in-law. Being raised with brothers, who soon became my responsibility, I often wondered how it would be to have sisters. Butch's older sister Gerry was away at college on Long Island, but she returned home for holidays, and the playfulness of a large, loving family became a distinctly pleasant experience.

I was considered the maverick of the family, especially by the kids, who watched as I subtly, but without malice, converted my mother-in-law's strict regimen to fit my own. She served health food at the time and I wondered if the mountainous feast served at our wedding had been a figment of my imagination. She prepared and served the family nutritious foods, such as fresh squeezed orange juice, oatmeal, steamed vegetables devoid of salt or butter, and lean steak and lamb chops that she broiled to the consistency of beef jerky. I slipped in contraband like mayonnaise, whole milk (something my mother-in-law insisted was only good for calves); plus chocolate donuts, cookies and candy, and the biggest taboo of all--the dreaded white bread. My mother-in-law, too polite to reprimand me, pretended not to notice.

There were times when the togetherness was too much, leaving little privacy to covet the pleasures of solitude. I was like a lioness where Kimber was concerned. Armed with the latest childcare manuals, I made visitors and family alike wear surgical masks to prevent any stray germ from landing within a mile of her. She was breastfed, which gained me points with my mother-in-law, but nursing was not a relaxing experience for the baby or me with so many people around; all of whom enjoyed watching the process. After two and a half months of tension, I broke out in hives, the milk in my breasts dried up and the baby screamed in protest. I had no choice but to place her on a formula of boiled water, corn syrup, and canned milk. Kimber thrived on it and calmed down immediately, making me feel like a complete failure.

It was becoming more apparent that the big old house on Fairview Avenue wasn't large enough to house two families, especially when one member was a high-strung new mother.

Butch worked swing shifts at the dye house that his father managed, but by spring he was laid off. Being the boss's son didn't help, for my father-in-law would never stoop to giving his son deferential treatment. It was the perfect time to drive to Long Beach, Long Island to visit my mother, who had not yet seen the baby. She left Florida with Sal and my brothers shortly after we did and settled near Sal's family; something to do with Sal's "business." The job situation in New York would be better than Easton, whose industry was limited mostly to rock quarries and factories producing paint, crayons, shoes and clothing.

~ Five ~

Long Beach in 1960 was a rural town, situated between the ocean and the bay; parts of it resembling a quaint fishing village. It was a long finger-shaped island, connected to Long Island by bridges at either end. Along the narrowest part, the West End, the land area was only two blocks wide. Rows upon rows of one story bungalows, with only a few feet separating them, stretched between the two bodies of water. The main street, running parallel with the water, was cluttered with small stores of every variety, most in need of major renovation. Every other block sported a tavern. It was picturesque and antiquated, a far cry from the looming mountains and spacious valleys of Eastern Pennsylvania.

My mother was thrilled to meet her first grandchild, and Stevie and Billy were sufficiently awed by their niece.

"She looks just like her daddy," Sal remarked, making a big fuss over the baby one of the few times he was home. I asked my mother again what it was exactly, that Sal did.

"He's in business, you know," she answered.

"What type of business?"

"I'm not sure, honey" she said. "Just some sort of family business."

Sal was always bragging about his ties and contacts with the Mafia, which Butch and I only half believed. We figured with his con man tactics, he was probably in some sort of sales, because he made his own hours and often popped in during the middle of the day to take Billy fishing or both boys to the beach. He carried a black gun, resembling a German Luger, but Butch found out one day that it was only a C02 powered pellet gun. Sal was pseudo-macho, charming, good-looking in a dark Italian way and extremely mysterious, which my mother seemed to dismiss as normal. But then, my mother wasn't exactly normal herself. Either she really didn't care what Sal did, or was afraid to find out.

During the first few weeks at my mother's small bungalow, "Grammy" took over Kim's care, getting up for middle of the night feedings, giving me time to catch up on long-lost sleep. She cooked all my favorite meals; fried chicken with mashed potatoes smothered in gravy, breaded pork chops layered in fluffy white rice, and casseroles filled with sinfully fattening ingredients. I ate like a starved child.

During the day Butch pounded the streets looking for work while my mother and I took the baby and toured Long Beach or spent lazy afternoons sun tanning on the broad sandy beach, not yet crowded with summer tourists. The ocean was a roiling dark blue-green, not transparent like the gentle waters of Florida. Stone jetties were spaced at block-long intervals, breaking up the vicious undertow that threatened to erode the shoreline. The breakers were high, angrily rushing inland with an urgency untamed by the massive jetties. In spite of its fierceness, the ocean had a calming effect, as huge waves lashed forward and back, mesmerizing in their constancy, backed by a crimson, benevolent sun that seemed to beam approval. I quickly picked up a golden tan while Butch acquired blisters on his feet and a bout of depression. If he didn't find work soon, we would have to return to Easton.

One overcast afternoon, too chilly to brave the beach, Butch burst through the door in exceptionally good spirits.

"Well, Mick, if you like it here and want to stay, I think we can do it. I just got a job at Benny's Steak House. You know that restaurant on Beech Street with the logo of the fat, mustached chef? Well, Benny, the boss, looks just like his sign. He seems like a nice guy and he said I can work as many hours as I want." He was out of breath, but smiling.

"That's great!" I said, and after hugging him hard, I ran to tell my mother, who was bathing the baby.

"What does it pay?" I yelled over my shoulder.

"Mostly tips, but Benny said the tips are pretty good. Oh, and I'll need some white shirts, black pants and a black bow tie. I start tomorrow."

He dressed for work the next day, excited and apprehensive. His prior busboy job had been at a busy diner, while Benny's was one of Long Beach's most prestigious restaurants.

"Don't worry," I said, adjusting the bow tie that bobbed up and down over his Adam's apple when he spoke. "People are the same everywhere."

His taut, muscled body did justice to his uniform, giving him an aura of confidence, even if he didn't feel it. It was after midnight when he returned, the first of many sixteen hour days. He was exhausted, filthy, splattered with food, but happier than I had seen him in weeks. Now he could begin to support his family.

My mother's small bungalow seemed to be getting smaller and smaller and we were all getting on each other's nerves. The baby was growing quickly and demanded more attention, and my brothers, resenting the time spent with the baby, vented their jealousy on the rest of us the way that only preteen boys can.

"It's high time we got a place of our own," I told Butch, after his late Saturday night shift. "We can't go on living with your parents or mine forever."

"We'll look tomorrow. I don't have to be at work 'til five o'clock," he said, and was asleep before I could answer.

We took the first apartment we saw. It was within our means and sat across from Benny's, an asset, I thought at the time. Our apartment was one of six, situated over a row of stores. The entire building looked like something out of the Depression Era. We thought it was wonderful.

The front and only door to our apartment opened into a small kitchen, which had an old sink propped on rickety, wooden legs on one wall, with a chipped, white enamel gas stove next to it that nearly blew up every time it was lighted. Adjacent to the stove stood an old, mammoth refrigerator with black mold running up and down its gaskets. The kitchen table in the corner of the room was painted black and white, although most of the paint was fading and peeling as were the three unmatched chairs.

Off the kitchen was a tiny nook, designated as the master bath. Gray and maroon tiles layered with the scum from previous tenants lined the walls and floor. A rusty toilet, small sink which dripped constantly, and a scratched aluminum shower stall, tinted green from mold, completed the decor.

The kitchen faced two rooms, one small and the other smaller. A large iron bed dominated the larger room, which would be our bedroom. The only other furniture was an old wooden dresser, painted white with missing knobs. Two tall, grimy windows faced the street and when I looked outside, after rubbing away layers of greasy dirt, I could see the entrance to Benny's. The other room, not much bigger than a walk-in closet, was for the baby, whose possessions consisted of a crib and dressing table.

"We can fix this place up to look adorable," I told Butch as I plopped down on the old bed, which creaked loudly in protest. My mind raced with decorating possibilities.

"Sure," he agreed. "It'll be no problem at all."

My mother-in-law drove up to see our new apartment. I remember she wept.

"Oh, how can you live like this?" she asked, her face unable to mask her horror. "This is terrible. Please come back home and stay with us. You'll live rent free and be able to save your money."

"We can't, Mom," we told her firmly, wondering what she found so bad about the apartment.

She left for the three hour drive back to Easton that afternoon, with her rosary beads entwined tightly around her fingers, clacking against the steering wheel in time to the fervent chant of her prayers.

~

Summer arrived in heated fury, turning the tiny apartment into a sweat box. Taking advantage of the beach, I carted baby, stroller, beach umbrella, sometimes the playpen, and lunch for both of us down the one block to the ticket booth, dragged everything across the hot sands, and stayed until sunset. Butch continued his sixteen hour days, giving us about an hour together each night before we both slipped into exhausted sleep.

Butch had been working for Benny for about two months, when he asked me if I wanted to work there, too. Not even caring for a demanding infant and painting and fixing up the apartment could fill the hours I spent alone. I had worked in food establishments since I was fourteen, and waitressed three years at the pizza restaurant, but Benny's intimidated me. Customers there were rich, mostly Jewish, and paid well for the good service that they demanded.

"C'mon, you can do it," Butch said. "You're a good waitress and you said yourself that people are the same everywhere."

"Yeah, well that was to make you feel better. I never believed it for a minute."

The window fan hummed monotonously, doing little more than moving the hot, sticky air around. The vibrations from the old refrigerator joined in every few minutes. "But think of the tips," he said. "You'll make almost five dollars off every table."

"All right, all right. I'll try it; but if I don't like it, I'm quitting."

"Fine," he said. "I'll tell Benny tonight and he'll probably want to talk to you. He might even put you on this weekend, since one of the girls quit last night."

~

Benny's was decorated in red and black; red rugs, black vinyl upholstered chairs, red linen drop cloths over white tablecloths and white linen napkins. Standing nervously in the entrance foyer in my black nylon uniform and apron, I blended right in. I was the youngest waitress, duly noted by the head waitress, who happened to have the same name as I did.

"That just won't do," she said. "It'll confuse the cooks. What's your real name?"

I should have lied and said Monica or Michelle, or even Mary. I hated my given name. It caused me years of torment by taunting young children and even more vicious teenage peers. It was an old Scotch-Irish southern name and had belonged to my mother's favorite aunt. The pain of bearing such an appellation probably contributed to her untimely death at the age of nineteen, an age I was fast approaching.

"Well, what's your real name?" Mickey asked again. She reminded me of Rumplestiltskin and I was considering whether I could get her to jump up and down before I finally told her, but other waitresses and customers were beginning to stare.

"Mallie."

"What? Speak up!"

"I said it's Mallie. Mallie Faye."

"Mallie," she said, and as I saw a flicker of amusement cross her face, memories of junior high school passed before me. "Hey, hey, Mallie Faye. What da ya say, Mallie Faye?" Torturous rhymes by torturous upper classmen, who recognized the lack of confidence in a tall, gangly thirteen-year-old, who wore a Prince Valiant hairdo and hand-me-down clothes. Didn't my mother like me? Who would gaze into a newborn's face and say to herself, 'I think I'll call her Mallie?' And if she liked the damn name so much, why did she always call me Micki? I had asked my mother many times, and she insisted that Mallie was for her aunt, the hated Faye was for Fayetteville, North Carolina, where I was born, and Micki was in honor of her best friend. Good reasons, bad choices.

"Mallie. Mallie!"

I jumped. I wasn't used to answering to that name, but I was going to have to get used to it.

"I'm sorry," I said. "I was daydreaming."

"Well, this is no job to daydream at. Pick up your waitress pad and go see Edna. She's the old, dark-haired woman standing in the corner by the kitchen. She'll show you what to do. Oh, and Mallie…try to smile a little more. People come in here to enjoy their meals, not be dragged down by a sour face."

"Right," I said without smiling, and walked over to Edna.

The rest of my first night at Benny's was total chaos, but my customers were wined and dined, seemingly unaware of my shaking hands and trembling legs. The head waitress studied me in quiet appraisal as the male customers fawned over me; attention I could only assume, was usually delegated to her. Mickey had washed-out red hair, a splash of freckles, and narrow, hazel eyes that only brightened around men. I was almost certain by the end of the night that she disliked me.

"Well, how did it go?" Butch asked when I limped in the door after midnight on blistered feet. The blast of heat emanating from the apartment was a sharp contrast to the air conditioning I'd worked in all night.

"Okay, I guess. I made good tips, but they only gave me four tables--a half shift until I get better."

"Four tables is a full shift," Butch said.

"Not according to Mickey. She says if I can't handle four tables, I'll never be able to handle a full load."

"She's nuts," he said. "What did you think of the rest of the crew?"

"Benny terrifies me. He struts around the dining room with that big belly and stern face and never speaks to me. And Buddy, that dwarfish maitre d', looks like he escaped from a carnival."

"Nah, Buddy's all right," Butch said.

"He's not all right. He's mean, probably perverted, and he followed me around all night, saying 'smile, smile.' Edna's great, though. She had so much patience with me and covered for me every time I got buried. But Butch, she's too old and frail for that kind of work. She couldn't weigh a hundred pounds. I carried trays tonight heavier than Edna."

"I think you're exaggerating a bit," Butch said, laughing.

"Maybe a little, but you know what I mean. Anyway, I didn't like that tall, big-boned one named Hannah. She looks like the Wicked Witch of the West, in the Wizard of Oz. She smirked at me all night. But the rest of the crew was really nice to me and so were the customers, especially when they found out it was my first night. How was the baby?"

"The usual. Up all night 'til about a half an hour ago, chattering in my ear. I think this kid's an insomniac."

"I think she's just spoiled rotten. When did you change her diaper last?"

"Was I supposed to change it? You changed her before you left. You know I don't do diapers."

"That was seven hours ago, you idiot. She's probably drenched. Just go on to bed. I'll be in after I take care of Kim."

At the end of my second night at Benny's, I was fired. Mickey went to Benny and told him I just couldn't handle my station. Throughout the entire night, she'd hovered over me like a vulture, rushing up to a table I was headed for, grabbing the condiments off it, then yelling at me for not doing it. I made over a hundred dollars that night and thought when Benny called me over, that he was going to congratulate me for catching on so fast. I walked out the back door of the restaurant into the alley, stunned and humiliated, knowing in the back of my mind that Mickey had me fired out of pure jealousy. I lacked the confidence in myself to believe it, much less defend myself. Butch believed it too, when I tearfully told him what had happened; more so when he spoke to his coworkers, who were all shocked that I was let go. He couldn't say or do anything, because we couldn't afford to jeopardize his job. I had never been fired before and it had a profound effect on me.

~

The rest of the summer dragged on, each day hotter than the one before, bearable only on the wet, cool sands of the beach. Kim had been weaned from the breast for several months, but I took no note of my missed periods, because I had read that breastfeeding disrupts the reproductive system indefinitely. If you didn't menstruate you weren't ovulating and therefore could not get pregnant. I must have read it in "Grimm's Fairy Tales."

I cried, but Butch held me close and said, "Look, honey, we always wanted a son and I know this one's a boy. Now they'll be close in age. If we can handle one kid, we can handle two."

"What do you mean, we, paleface?" I asked. I dried my eyes, put a cold rag on my swollen face and tried to make the best of a rotten situation. His sympathy quickly waned when I began to get all day and all night morning sickness.

"All I need," I whined, "is some dry toast and a cup of tea in the morning before I get out of bed and then maybe I won't get sick. But no, that's just too much trouble for you. I bet if my name was Benny, you'd jump to wait on me."

"Yeah, well Benny pays me and I pay for your rent and food. If you don't like it, why don't you go back to your mother?"

"Maybe I will," I said, and stomped off to the bathroom. I didn't speak to him all night, difficult as it was to ignore someone in three small rooms.

The next morning he left for work before I woke up. Sitting on the floor next to my bed was a cup of lukewarm, grayish-white tea and two pieces of burnt toast. It was a start.

Michael was born on a brisk, cold day on the second of March, thirteen months after his sister. As we headed for the hospital, gusting winds blew white cottony clouds across a clear, blue sky; a wonderful day to be born. Butch's mom came up to watch Kim and stay a week after the baby was born to help me.

Once I reached the labor room, the beautiful day became a fuzzy, distant memory. Butch left after depositing me with the nurses, because Benny refused to give him the day off.

"What for?" Benny had asked. "What are you, a doctor? You can't do anything 'til it's over so
get back to work. We got three parties this afternoon."

Butch didn't argue and I made a mental note of both the power Benny held and Butch's priorities.

Long Beach Hospital, streamlined and coldly modern, lacked the warmth of my hometown hospital. I was placed on a bed in the labor room and virtually ignored until the birth was imminent. During the delivery, my mouth was covered with a noxious substance that did not kill the intense pain, but left me frustrated and disoriented. I remember no birth, no warm, wet baby across my stomach, no feeling of accomplishment in teamwork between my doctor, me and God. Eight hours later, I awakened, drugged, still in pain and was told that I had a son. To complicate a miserable experience, a candy striper, who shouldn't have been dispensing medicine, walked into the small, two-patient room and gave me pills to induce labor, instead of painkillers. In spite of the trauma having him, Michael was a gorgeous baby, certainly the most beautiful baby in the nursery of two.

We took Michael home and jammed the new crib that his grandma brought with her into his sister's tiny room. He was a sweet, placid baby, unlike Kim, who was a demanding little minx who thought sleep was a waste of time. Each bedtime she screamed, knowing we would have to let her up before the other tenants banged on our door for quiet. Both children had large brown eyes. Kim's sparkled with devilment--Michael's were the kind you see on deer. My mother-in-law only stayed a few days. The apartment was too small and I felt confident that I could handle both babies myself. Butch was relieved. He'd suffered three days of two women nagging him over his work hours.

"He was never like that at home," his mother noted, shaking her head as she moved about the apartment straightening things up. I said nothing, but the tiny seed of thought that maybe Butch just didn't want to be with me was firmly implanted in my mind.

~

"We've got to get a bigger place," I said to Butch late one night in August, as the three of us tried to get some sleep. Two drunks were having a fight under our window, and Kim was squirming around, trying to get the largest share of the bed. By coincidence, the drunks were named Frankie and Johnny, like the country western song.

"Frankie," the man bellowed, "Come back to me. I need ya', Frankie."

"In ya dreams, Johnny, in ya dreams," the woman screamed back, slurring her words.

"Why does this kid have to be in our bed every night?" Butch asked, ignoring both the drunks and my statement about moving.

"Because she keeps waking up the baby. I'd like to get a little sleep now and then, too."

"Yeah? Well you're not on your feet sixteen hours a day, every day."

"Oh no, I toss the kids a bottle every few hours and watch TV all day. We were talking about a bigger place, remember?"

"We can't afford a bigger place and you know it. We haven't paid off the doctor and hospital bills yet."

"The apartment across the hall in the corner has the same three rooms as this one, but they're much bigger, and it's only twenty-five dollars a month more. The tenants are moving out soon and we can have it."

"We'll see," he said and curled up in the triangular section of the bed that Kim allotted him and fell asleep. Frankie and Johnny had taken their argument to another block and could only be heard faintly. Kim fell asleep, stretched across the center of the bed and I lay there wondering how much longer we could live like this. Of all the thousands of words spoken throughout our marriage, some in love and some with anger, those two words, "we'll see" rankled me more than any other. It was Butch's way of stalling.

We moved into the larger apartment a few months later. It was in the back of the building, facing the parking lot, and sat over a dry cleaning store, whose owners ate in the back and were less than fastidious in cleanliness. Because of this, I was able to add a new bug to my hate list. I had never seen a cockroach before, nor ever hoped to see one, and spent the next year and a half trying to outsmart them. Anyone living in New York or any big city can attest to the fact that cockroaches are the most devious bugs alive. We finally formed a truce. If I didn't turn on the lights in the middle of the night, they wouldn't scatter across the kitchen.

~

My mother came over one morning in tears, visibly upset over something. At first I thought it was nothing more traumatic than a new wrinkle.

"What's the matter, Mom?" I asked. "Are the boys okay?"

She was starting to scare me.

"Billy and Steve are fine," she sobbed, narrow trails of black mascara streaming down her face. "It's Sal."

"What happened? Is he hurt?"

"No, he's not hurt. That son of ah bitchin' bastard is ah bigamist!" she cried, lapsing into a deep southern accent that always signified anger or distress.

"Ah bigamist! He's got ah wife in Brooklyn. Ah hate the slimy, fat little bastawd! Oh, Ah feel like such ah fool. Ah just spoke to his so-called wife and she's been trying to track him down for ovah ah yeah."

"Why would he marry you if he was already married?" I asked.

"Because he's ah son of a'bitchin', miserable, Italian bastawd, that's why."

"Well, Mom," I said as gently as possible. "You didn't know very much about Sal when you married him. Butch and I tried to warn you, but you wouldn't listen."

"But Ah loved that lousy, fat creep. You don't know what it's like to be in love." The sobbing increased. "Ah'm married to ah bigamist."

I hugged her close to me until she stopped crying. *I don't know what it's like to be in love,* I thought, *but the grandmother of my children does.* Some things never changed. My mother's problems were always more important that anyone else's. At least the mystery of Sal was over. At last we knew exactly what Sal was; his "business," however, remained a mystery. Later, when I recounted the story to Butch, we burst out laughing. It wasn't that we didn't feel sorry for her, but my mother had a way of getting into the kinds of trouble that ordinary people manage to avoid. Within a few months, she was back to her old self, working for a major cosmetic firm and dating practically every night. Sal was forgotten, and if he was missed by anyone, it was by my brothers, who were once again without a father.

~ *Six* ~

September, 1962

In mid-September one of my friends phoned and invited herself up to Long Beach for a few days. Shirley and I had been close friends throughout high school, although we didn't see much of each other outside of school. She lived at the other end of Easton, closer to Bethlehem. During the fifties, two-car families were not the norm; forcing kids to walk, or else take the local buses. The distance between Shirley's house and mine was almost ten miles and I only attempted to walk it once.

Butch liked Shirley as much as I did, and gave her explicit directions on how to get to the Long Beach. She arrived late in the afternoon on a Friday night, with Hurricane Diana snapping at her heels.

"Gee, you guys," she said, laughing as she burst through the door, drenched from the heavy downpour. "You didn't have to go to all this trouble. A cup of coffee and a home-cooked meal would've done just fine."

"Hey," I said, grinning. "You brought this hurricane with you! Long Beach hasn't had a storm like this in twenty years."

As we helped her unload her car and drag her suitcases up the narrow flight of stairs to the apartment, I realized with a sharp pang how much I missed Easton and all my friends.

"Shirl," I said as we plopped down on the new sofa that doubled as our bed at night, "you look wonderful! But you haven't grown any, have you?"

She gave me a menacing look, followed by an impish grin.

"Nope, but I'm still working on it. When I hit five feet in my stocking feet, you'll be the first to hear about it."

Shirl missed it by a quarter of an inch and we never let her forget it. She had dark brown eyes that complimented a wide, constant smile, and thick black hair that she always wore short, framing her oval face.

"You guys look great, too," she said. "Marriage seems to agree with you. Where are those babies? It's too quiet around here."

"Sleeping, and we're keeping it that way. They only take one nap a day and when it's over, you'll know why I never cut it short."

The hurricane arrived in full force, with the howling winds playing background music to the rain pelting against the windows. We sat around the kitchen table, drinking coffee and catching up on the backlog of gossip--who got married, who got pregnant without being married, who was cheating on who's boyfriend; all things from a life I'd left behind me.

Butch left for work at five o'clock, since Benny firmly believed that even in a state of emergency, hungry people still craved red meat. Shirl helped me feed and bathe the kids. Kim preened for Shirley in her new floor-length red flannel nightgown, and proudly exhibited how adept she was at combing her dark, shoulder-length hair all by herself. Mike toddled around in Kim's wake, with unbiased adoration.

"God, they're growing fast," Shirl said, when we finally got them both tucked into bed, much to Kim's objections. "It seems like they were both babies when I last saw them in Easton."

"Well, that was over six months ago, and babies grow fast. These guys can really wear me out, and the apartment is so small that sometimes I feel like they're my second skin. You know?"

"Yeah, but you're really lucky. The kids are beautiful, and you and Butch are good together. Look at me. I work for the phone company, live at home and go out once in a while with some of the guys who haven't gone away to school or joined the army. The pickings ain't too good, I can tell you that."

We talked late into the night, curled up on the open sofa bed. Butch came in long after midnight, and slept in his sleeping bag on the floor next to the kid's cribs. The wind continued to screech as the rain streamed down in torrents. We were only catching the tail end of the storm as it blew itself out over the ocean, but the moon was full and the tides, dangerously high.

The next morning the storm was only a wet memory, as the sun shown bright through a veil of swift-moving white clouds. The tides had come in so far during the night that the ocean met the bay. The wind-tossed waves lapped together, aimlessly carousing up and down the narrow streets of the West End, taking lawn furniture, boats that had broken loose during the night, garbage cans, and anything else that wasn't tied down, with them. It was an eerie sight. The streets had become canals. Looking out the bedroom window, we could see huge, white-crested waves breaking at the ticket booths, two hundred feet inland.

Benny's had been sand-bagged during the night by Butch and the rest of the help, so damage was minimal, but hundreds of cars parked along neighborhood streets were destroyed by the salt water. Our own car, and Shirley's, were parked on higher ground in the back of the parking lot and suffered no permanent damage after drying out. The water came up to the third step of the apartment house staircase, causing Butch to wear hip boots to get to work. Benny's was open to whoever had the courage to wade to the restaurant and didn't object to soggy carpeting. By the end of the day, the waters finally began to recede.

Shirl and I weren't able to leave the apartment because of the high tides, so later that evening, I asked my brother Stevie to baby-sit the kids who were both sound asleep, while we set off to explore the area. We walked up to the ticket booths where the waters had ebbed somewhat, but were still breaking halfway up the beach. Shirl took out her camera to photograph the phenomenon and promptly dropped it into the swirling waters. It went out to sea with the next wave.

"Damn it," she said. "No one back home is going to believe this and now I have no proof. What should we do now?"

"Let's walk down Beech Street and see how far we can get without drowning," I said. We walked about two long blocks and came to the Irish House, an adorable little pub that resembled a gingerbread house. I had always wanted to see the inside. But Butch refused to take me there, claiming that it was nothing but a dive. By New York law, we were both old enough to drink, so we stepped bravely into the dimly lit barroom. There were a few non-descript people inside--most people were safely inside their homes, since the tides were due to roll back in within the hour.

We both ordered a drink and were just about to sip it, when the doors to the pub swung open and a familiar figure loomed menacingly in the entranceway. It was like a scene from a spaghetti western movie.

"Hi, Butch," Shirl called out. "Did you get off work early tonight? Come on over and join us."

He stomped over to our table, wearing ridiculously large wading boots, and glared at us.

"No, I didn't get off work early. I called home to see how you were doing and Stevie told me you two idiots were out wandering around. I've been searching for you for over an hour. Get up. We're going home."

"But we just got here. We haven't even finished our drinks," I said. "Besides, there's no danger. The tides won't be in for another hour."

"You're going home now," he said in a menacing voice. "Don't make me make a scene."

The few patrons scattered about the bar were taking a keen interest in us--I could hear snickers from one end of the room. Shirl and I were too embarrassed to do anything except push back our chairs, rise with as much dignity as we could muster, and follow Butch out the door. He didn't speak on the walk home and we both had to run to keep up with him. Once we got inside the door he launched into a long lecture on the stupidity of being outside when the tide was due back in, and an even longer tirade on the diverse reasons why nice girls don't frequent bars. Then he slammed out of the house, stomped down the stairs and went back to work. I didn't speak to him for several weeks.

"That was an interesting evening," Shirl said, as I helped her pack her bags to leave the following morning. "I think maybe I'm better off single than subject to the orders of a domineering husband." For the moment, I agreed with her.

After Shirley left, boredom hung over me like an oppressive weight, as each mundane day seemed identical to the next. The kids were cute, time-consuming, and I worshipped them, but spending an excessive amount of time with toddlers leads to brain drain in young adults. I was becoming acutely aware that life was passing me by.

~

My mother moved into the apartment building in October. The beach house was too expensive for her now that Sal was gone. She took the vacant apartment at the opposite end of the hall and began redecorating the drab three rooms with the ardor of a high priestess adorning her temple. I shuddered in apprehension. My mother had an obsession with certain colors, particularly pink, black and gray; heavy on the pink. My childhood homes were inundated with those horrid colors, every room without exception. She wasn't alone. Those colors were popular in the fifties, but my mother took the fad to extremes. I hated pink so much that I refused to buy clothing, even baby clothes for Kim, or household furnishings that bore any hint of the putrid color.

"Now Baby, I don't want you to see the apartment 'til I'm all finished," Mom said, lugging her supplies down the hall. "It's going to be a surprise. Your momma's gonna turn this hovel into a palace."

It's going to be worse than I thought, I said to myself and willingly stayed barricaded behind the walls of my own apartment, dreading the day when her artistic endeavors would be completed.

Two days later, Billy knocked on my door.

"Mom says come see the apartment," he said, a whimsical smirk spreading across his freckled face, his hazel eyes trying hard to look innocent.

"How bad is it?" I asked.

"You'll see," he said, grinning.

I had to admit as I gingerly moved throughout her small apartment that my mother had surpassed my wildest expectations.

The ceilings were painted jet black with sparkles glued to them. Mom flipped on the glaring overhead florescent light fixture and the ceiling became a starlit night sky. The walls were various shades of pink, ranging from rosy mauve to hot fuchsia. The old enameled stove shone a glossy black with iridescent pink knobs, and the refrigerator radiated hot salmon. The floor tiles, which were pale gray to begin with, did little to tone down the gaudy ambience of the room.

Since pink was strictly a feminine color (something my brothers may have pointed out), my mother did the boys' room in red and black, with lots of stripes. Her own bedroom continued the pattern of pinkness, and included a starlit ceiling.

"What do you think, honey?" she asked proudly.

"There are no words to describe it," I hedged.

"I know," she sighed. "It's better than even I could have imagined. But wait. The bathroom is the best yet."

I steeled myself and followed her to the bathroom. As I walked into the tiny cubicle, I fought the impulse to cover my eyes with my arm. The sink and toilet were painted in slick black, the walls shocking pink with decals of gray swans attached at random. The ceilings were, of course, sparkled black, and the shower curtain, partially concealing a bright purple shower stall, was a nauseating shade of light lavender with zigzagging stripes of black and gray. A fluffy purplish-pink rug hugged the floor and matching towels hung from the single towel bar behind the door, topped with black wash cloths.

"Mom, you've outdone yourself," I said, edging toward the outer door of the apartment, fighting a wave of vertigo.

She nodded. "I knew you'd love it."

"But you know, Mom, I don't think enamel fixtures are supposed to be painted."

"Don't worry, Baby," she said. "By the time the paint starts to chip off, I'll be long gone. I'm not staying in this dump forever."

"What do you suppose the landlord will think?" I called down the hall as I headed home.

"Honey, he's gonna love it!"

I had my doubts about that. Our landlord was a short, squat, grumpy man in his sixties, with thinning white hair and quick, darting eyes that seemed to constantly evaluate whatever they fell upon. He had a tendency to spit when he spoke, and we soon learned to stand at least six feet away from him, preferably not downwind. He was always dressed in threadbare, gray suits when he visited the apartment house each month to collect the rent, and was notorious for popping in unannounced. His wife was about four and a half feet tall and almost as wide, and had the largest thighs that I had ever seen on a human being. From the knees down, her legs resembled tree stumps, with no definition at her ankles. She had small, beady eyes placed too close to a hawkish nose which nearly met her thin, bitter lips. Her hair, what there was of it, was a wad of steel gray that matched an unyielding personality.

Their names were Mr. and Mrs. Miller, and we had immediately dubbed the apartment building, "Miller's Landing". Aside from charging exorbitant rents for a run-down hole of a building that they were not inclined to maintain, their major vice was nosiness; particularly Mrs. Miller. They had master keys to all the apartments and thought nothing of entering our home during our absence. This really annoyed Butch.

"I'm sick of this nonsense," he said one day, after we returned home from shopping in time to see Mrs. Miller leaving our apartment.

"We'll have to get a bolt lock and a chain for across the door," I said. "I want one anyway for the kids. They're tall enough now to open the door and leave."

"Right," he said, thoughtfully. "But first I'm going to teach that ugly old bat a lesson."

"What are you going to do?"

"You'll see," he said, refusing to say anything more.

The first of the month rolled around and the Millers came for their rent. I had taken the kids for a walk down the five-mile boardwalk that ran along the beach. I was on my way home when I spotted Mrs. Miller charging down the long staircase faster than I had thought it was possible for fat people to run.

"Good afternoon, Mrs. Miller," I said, lifting the kids out of the stroller. "Is something wrong?"

She sputtered something unintelligible at me and hurried out of the building, her face beet-red and small venomous eyes blazing furiously.

What has he done now? I thought. He probably insulted her and now we're going to get evicted. I carried the kids upstairs, leaving the stroller in the doorway, and called out to Butch.

"In here," he said.

I walked over to the bathroom. He was sitting there, buck-naked, reading the Reader's Digest.

"You didn't," I said.

"Yep, she walked right in on me. I bet she never sneaks in our apartment again."

It was unlikely that she would. She purposely avoided us both after that incident, but we put the chain across the door anyway.

When I told my mother the story later that day, I asked her what the Millers thought of her apartment.

"They never said a word," she said. "They just walked around the apartment and stared at it for the longest time."

Understandable, I thought. They were probably in shock.

~

Winter passed slowly. Stevie was fourteen years old and mature enough to baby-sit for short periods of time, if the kids were asleep. This left me free to see an occasional movie with Butch on the rare days that he was off from work, or go shopping with my mother. Mom was on a serious manhunt and often took me to bars and restaurants, in the hope of finding her one true love. Butch resented these outings, but as my mother was quick to point out, she had been taking care of me for a lot longer than he had.

The wind off the ocean was too bitter most of the winter to take the kids for walks. Our biggest outing was to the laundromat on the next block where I did mountains of diapers each week, along with the regular laundry. Humanity's greatest invention was not the wheel--it was disposable diapers.

Christmas broke up the monotony of the season. For the third year since we had moved to New York, we drove to Easton to spend the holiday; packing up bottles, diapers, both kids and all their presents. Butch worked Christmas Eve, which gave us a late start, so it was around one-thirty in the morning when we pulled into Easton. Everyone was still up. They had just returned from midnight mass and were feasting on all the goodies they forfeited until the fasting period before mass was over. There was very little edible food on Christmas Eve as far as I was concerned. There were dishes like boiled eels, something I preferred not to even think about, much less sample.

"I don't eat snakes, Mom," I explained to my mother-in-law. "Or anything with scales, fangs or fins."

"Oh, they're delicious," Mom said. "C'mon, just try it and you'll be surprised."

I made a face and refused the eels, as well as the Baccala soup, a nasty concoction of tomatoes, codfish and vegetables. There was also thin pasta tossed with garlic, olive oil and anchovies, another fish not on my list of delicacies. My only experience as a fish eater had been canned tuna and baked swordfish. I filled up on fresh Italian bread, salad, and the mountainous trays of homemade cookies, pastries and pies.

Kim and Mike had perked up after sleeping through the trip and attacked their Christmas presents with unrestrained excitement. Traditionally, Butch's family opened their presents on Christmas Eve, which seemed strange at first to me, but I quickly saw the merit of it. Everyone got to sleep in on Christmas Day; except my mother-in-law, who always went to 6:30 morning mass. Dinner the following day was nearly as lavish as our wedding feast; no health foods on holidays, thank goodness. And no nasty fish. By late afternoon, it was time to start home, bracing for the inevitable holiday traffic. It was a hectic Christmas, but preferable to our lonely three-room apartment, with no real friends or relatives.

~

The spring of that year brought a familiar queasiness to my stomach. I kept it to myself as long as I could, but Butch was beginning to catch on to the fact that unexplained nausea usually signified pregnancy. He turned a sickly shade of greenish-gray when the doctor confirmed my fears. Kim was two years old and talking like a Supreme Court judge. Mike had just turned one, still the most beautiful baby I had ever seen--almost too beautiful to scold when he got into anything and everything that he could find. We had the perfect family; two lovely, healthy children, one of each sex.

"I don't know what we're going to do now," Butch said, holding his head in his hands, trying to digest the news.

"There's nothing we can do," I said.

Abortions were illegal in 1961, not that we could have afforded one, or considered it as an alternative. Butch was more closely tied to his Catholicism than he cared to admit. While I didn't relish being pregnant again, once the baby was a reality, I protected it with a maternal fierceness that I couldn't explain.

"We sure can't fit three kids in this apartment," he said, after minutes of silence. "We're overcrowded with the two we've got. Mick, we can't afford another baby. We just paid off the bills from the last one. And we bought the new car, which cleaned out our savings. I don't know what we're going to do."

"I know," I agreed and sighed. "But we're beyond the point where we can do anything. We'll have the baby and we'll manage somehow, just like we've managed before." I had nothing further to say. I was too busy calculating whether or not I could make it to the bathroom before I threw up. I would have made it if I hadn't tripped over Michael's toy truck.

When Benny heard the news about the baby and saw, by Butch's downtrodden attitude, that we were in deep trouble, he called him into his office.

"There's a small bungalow for sale a few blocks down the street. Only $8500.00. You want it?" he asked.

"It sounds good, Ben, but I don't have any money for a down payment. I just bought the new Chevy."

"Didn't ask if you had any money. Don't worry about it. You want it or not?"

"Let me ask Micki," Butch said, and walked out of the small room behind the kitchen that served as Benny's office.

"Don't take too long," Benny called after him. "At that price it'll be sucked up quick. Think of it as my gift to the baby."

Later that night, Butch came home all keyed up.

"What do you think?" he asked, after explaining his conversation with Benny.

I was nestled under the covers on the sofa bed, hoping that Butch wouldn't plop down on his side of the bed and set off another bout of nausea. My hopes were soon dashed.

"I don't know," I said, gagging. "It sounds too good to be true. What do you suppose the catch is?"

"I don't know, honey, but I'm sure there is one."

That was one fact of which we were certain. Benny was generous in every way but his money and time off for Butch. But after hours of discussing the pros and cons of accepting Benny's "gift", we fell asleep, knowing that we couldn't refuse his offer. Anything would be better than trying to stuff five people in a three-room apartment. And it would be a long time before we could afford a down payment for a house.

Soon we were caught up in the excitement of it. Our own home. It made the summer, hot and muggy, pass by quickly. It made the small three rooms bearable. Our problem had a solution; our troubles would come to an end. Even the nausea that plagued my pregnancies seemed of shorter duration and less intensity. Things were going to work out all right. I almost liked Benny; almost trusted him.

The closing for the house fell during the second week of September. Benny told Butch, who was scheduled to work that day, that he didn't need to attend it. The catch was made painfully clear. The title to the house would remain in Benny's name until the down payment, Benny's "gift", was paid off. This protected Benny's investment, ensured a profit by the interest accrued, and ensured that Butch would continue to work for him as long as we lived in the house. As much as I despised the man, I had to admit that I was impressed. Butch, who was developing a father/son, love/hate relationship with Benny that would have fascinated a psychologist, seemed genuinely hurt. Nonetheless, we accepted the house.

The house was on Nebraska Street. All the streets running parallel between Park Avenue and Beech Street were named after American states. The house was typical of most of the beach bungalows, except that it was heated and had a basement, which doubled as a swimming pool every time there was prolonged or heavy rain. The outside shingles were painted white, with the tediously overused, popular, sea-foam green paint as trim for the windows and doors. The small, cemented front yard was enclosed by a faded, peeling fence, with most of the pickets broken off or missing. There was a large, beautiful white birch tree on the left side of the yard, a rarity, since the West End had few shrubs, trees or grass lawns. In spite of the underhanded catch to our home ownership, we were thrilled with our first real home.

The front of the house was enclosed by a sun porch with rows of small-paned French windows opening out into the yard. Inside, the house had a small living room off the sun porch, a medium sized medieval kitchen in dire need of renovation, an average sized bathroom and two fairly large bedrooms. The smaller bedroom, which would be ours, encompassed the entire back of the house, with a tiny laundry room next to it. The back door opened out onto a small, square cement stoop and two feet of back yard. A trap door at the opposite end of the bedroom had steps leading to the low-ceilinged, overly damp basement.

Because the house remained empty for several months, we were allowed to clean it up before we moved into it. Each morning, I stuffed both kids into the stroller, laden with cleaning supplies, diapers and food, and wheeled it down the eight blocks to the new house. I stayed all day, working feverishly to have it ready by the time of the closing. Kim and Mike followed me around, chattering in my ears, or played outside in the closed-in front yard, breathing in the fresh, clean air of late summer.

Moving day arrived finally. The house was now thoroughly scrubbed, painted and ready for human habitation. I had planned in advance where each piece of furniture would be placed, even where the few pictures that we possessed would hang. We rented a small U-Haul trailer, loaded it up and hooked it to our new 1962 silver Chevrolet and set off for Nebraska Street. It only took one trip. By the day's end, we were settled into our new home and quite proud of ourselves. It looked as if we had lived there for years.

Only one flaw marred an otherwise perfect day. When I had cleaned out under the kitchen sink a few weeks before, I never noticed what I presumed to be a water pipe was actually a sawed-off broomstick, and the sole support of the sink. That fact was made evident after I filled the sink with dishes and it caved in, sinking to the bottom of the old wooden cabinet. Washing cartons of dishes and glasses in the bathtub was no easy task for a woman who was seven months pregnant. This marked the onset of problems with the fifty-year-old house. The more we fixed it up, the more it broke down.

On December eleventh, I went into labor with Dante. This time I insisted on having the baby in Easton, in the same hospital where Kim was born and moved down to my in-laws several weeks before I was due. My old obstetrician had retired, giving his practice to his son and two other doctors. Delivery and doctor's fees were cheaper in Pennsylvania, and the hospital was across the street from Butch's parents. It saved his mother from having to leave her home and come to me after the baby was born. My own mother was always too busy working to take time off to help.

The birth was difficult, convincing me I had made the right decision by coming back to Easton. The labor droned on for over two days before Dante finally made his entrance into the world, wailing with fists clenched and his eyes furiously shut tight; perhaps upset over the delay.

My best friend, Jeanie, was working in the nursery during her midwinter break from Penn State, and slipped Dante into my room in the middle of the night.

"Micki, I can't believe this kid is yours. I even double-checked the identification bracelet to make sure. Kim and Mike were so gorgeous, but this kid's a mess," she said, handing me the small, swaddled baby.

She was right. During the two days of intense labor, my body was procrastinating, but Dante was fighting and pushing in his struggle to be born. And it showed. His head was pointed, casting an elfin look to his red, wrinkled face. His chin was smashed in and his nose looked like a blob of uncultured clay. Only his bright, dark eyes, which were already focusing on his environment, were unscathed by his perilous journey.

"He's mine, all right, Jeanie. Give the poor kid a break. He's had a rough trip, that's all," I said, hugging Dante close to me, marveling at the fresh, sweet smell of a newborn. Jeanie nodded, but didn't look convinced. Christmas was spent in our new home, with our own resident elf-baby, whose face still bore the trauma of his birth. For the first time, we felt like a real family, a regular "Father Knows Best" family; although Kimber was not overly impressed with Dante, and Michael noted that his face was too wrinkled to be presentable.

Dante was a difficult baby, finding little to like in either his new home or the members of his family. He cried constantly, was colicky and managed to scream himself into a ruptured hernia at six weeks old. I took him in for his first medical checkup and we had to wait for what seemed like hours in the tiny cubicle off the doctor's office. Dante was not only loud, but opinionated. He had definite likes and dislikes. One thing in particular that he hated, was reclining in the nude. Some babies, like most adults, feel insecure and exposed when naked and Dante was one of them. The doctor insisted that I remove all the baby's clothes and he would return shortly, a word that apparently means different things to different people. The doctor disappeared, doing whatever it is that doctors do while patients wait in small rooms devoid of their dignity. Dante bellowed in rage, would not be consoled, and twenty minutes later, out popped a walnut-sized rupture.

"It's a hernia, all right," the wandering doctor confirmed. "It would have happened sooner or later. Better now than when he's a fifty-year-old man."

If you hadn't made me wait forever with a naked baby, it might not have happened at all, I thought. I was furious. But I said nothing.

Dante underwent a double hernia operation the next day. He only weighed nine pounds. His father and I were terrified. The recommended surgeon who performed the operation had hands nearly as big as the baby and we couldn't imagine him cutting into our child. It was over in two hours and Dante, too groggy to voice any objections, slept throughout his hospital stay. We took him home the following day. *I don't ever want to go through anything like this again,* I thought on the drive home, nestling

Dante close to my breast. The fragility of life had been presented to me in a most frightening way.

~ *Seven* ~

A few months after Dante's birth, my back, which troubled me since his birth, gave out completely. I got out of bed to give the baby a bottle, took two steps, and my legs buckled out from under me. After some practice, I found that I could sit or stand, but couldn't make the transition, at least not without a yelp of pain. I was afraid I might collapse taking care of the kids.

"Butch," I moaned, walking stoop-backed over to the kitchen table, where he was reading the paper and drinking coffee, unaware of my predicament. "Please stay home today and help me take care of the kids. I'm in a lot of pain and I'm afraid I might fall with the baby."

"You know I can't stay home today. We're having a Bar Mitzvah and Benny needs me."

Michael was sitting next to his father drinking his "pretend" coffee from his milk cup, solemnly absorbing every word.

"Sure," I said, letting out a long sigh. "What else is new? Go on to work. I've managed without you before and I can manage without you again."

Guilt trips never worked on Butch. He got dressed for work and left. My hurt feelings overcame my anger and I was sniffling in self-pity before he got off the block. I called my mother.

"Now, honey," she said, her voice dripping with sympathy, "You know Mother would love to help you, but I've already taken too many days off this week. I really have to work today."

"Fine, Mom," I said, and hung up.

I couldn't believe it. The two people who supposedly loved me thought nothing of leaving a virtual cripple home alone in a house with three small children. I managed to put Dante in the playpen, not his favorite place, and spent the rest of the day on my hands and knees; crawling back and forth to the kitchen to warm his bottle--and using Kim and Mike to fetch whatever else I needed.

Dante, always ready to take advantage of any given situation, flipped over in the mesh playpen and got his toes caught in the netting. By the time I managed to free him, he was screaming, the other two were crying, and I was sobbing incoherently. Butch came home to a cold silence that lasted a month.

~

Winter dragged slowly into spring. My time was occupied with redoing the bungalow and entertaining the children, although they provided most of the entertainment. At five months, Dante had decided the world wasn't such a bad place after all, becoming almost pleasant toward the rest of us. Butch still worked long hours, leaving me with time on my hands after the kids were in bed. Somehow, I developed a guilt trip over not contributing my share of the work. After all, Butch put in sixteen-hour days and worked on the house in his spare time and all I did was care for three kids and keep the small house adequately clean. I felt Butch subtly supported this notion.

Desperate to make up for my lack, I threw myself into crafts, figuring it would serve two purposes; occupy my time and contribute needed items for the home. I forgot for the moment that I had nearly flunked home economics in high school, except for the cooking segment. My first project was crocheting a two-foot bath mat. I taught myself the basic stitches and used an easy pattern. The bath mat took on a life of its own and grew to be twelve feet long. I was optimistic and decided it would become a lap robe instead, despite the fact that it was only eighteen inches wide. The kids had little laps. The orange rug with white footprints placed along the length of it kept growing even after completed. I finally stuffed it into a closet, hoping the confinement would stunt its growth.

Butch, impressed with the growth potential of the bath mat, bought me a sewing machine. Remembering the sewing machines in Home Economics, I was a little intimidated, but after weeks of jamming, snarling and thoroughly confusing the machine, I learned to put it through its basic functions. I tackled making curtains, which were never the same length, but since I tied them back anyway, it didn't matter. Soon I was making my own clothes, as well as outfits for the kids and most of the time I did quite well--for a novice. I sewed a shirt for Butch out of suede-like material and proudly presented it to him. The nap went the wrong way in places and the cuffs were on backwards, but he said it was beautiful. Strangely, he never wore it out of the house.

The only other breaks in the monotony of my life were the nights Butch got off work early and brought home some of his co-workers. Gene and Olga were older than the rest of the crew, and emigrated from Germany when Hitler began his maniacal rampage. They spoke with thick German accents and lived in the East End of Long Beach. Gene worked all year round, while Olga, who had a heart condition, stayed at home. Charlotte also worked year round and kept the rest of them jumping with her quick Jewish wit and outrageous antics. She was fortyish with blonde hair, a plain face and the body of a twenty-year-old.

Sometimes Clarence, the tall, handsome chef, with skin the color of burnished eggplant dropped in, or Edna, the old waitress who had trained me. David, the short-order cook, who had recently moved up from North Carolina, was Benny's brother-in-law. We didn't see much of him after his wife Fran followed him north with her four children. Fran moved into "Miller's Landing," in the apartment my mother had long since abandoned. She never mentioned the decor of the apartment and I never had the nerve to bring it up. David and Fran were separated, so we never had both of them at the same gathering. Even Hannah, the witch of the west, came by now and then, since she was part of the crew, but our dislike for each other never changed. No one else really liked her either, but at Benny's, "family" was family.

~

Late one evening I was walking home from the corner candy store where I had gone to buy some milk. It was a cold, raw night, with a misty breeze coming off the ocean; one of those

nights when winter tries to make one last grandstand play before spring establishes itself. Someone called out to me from one of the winterized houses.

"It's too cold to be out walking. Why don't you come up and have a brandy with me to warm up?"

The voice was coming from the second story window.

"I'll be right up," I called back. I had no idea who I was talking to, other than that it was a woman, but on that bleak deserted street, a friendly voice drew me like a magnet. I walked through the downstairs of the two-story bungalow and up the narrow staircase to the second floor.

A smiling gray-haired woman met me at the top of the stairs and handed me a large decanter with brandy in it.

"Come on in and sit down," she said. "My name is Ann Eunice MacVeigh and I was hoping we would meet."

I took the brandy, sat down on her old, overstuffed sofa and took a sip from the glass. The brandy burned all the way from my throat to my feet, but she was right. I warmed up immediately.

"I was beginning to think we were the only people alive on this block," I said, smiling at her open friendliness.

"Nonsense," she answered in a matter of fact tone that I would later find to be her trademark. "I, for one, am very much alive. I've just been too busy with my kids to run down and introduce myself. I must apologize."

I stayed at Ann Eunice's home for over an hour, sipping my way through two more brandies; a drink that I had never tasted before, but found to my liking. By the time I left, I felt as if I had known her all my life. When I got home, relaxed and a little tipsy, Butch was furious.

"Where the hell have you been?" he yelled. "I've been crazy with worry and I couldn't leave the kids to go and look for you."

"I found a new friend," I said, and started to explain, but he was in a black mood, so I went directly to bed and savored my enjoyable evening.

Ann Eunice was thirty-five years old, the mother of three children; ten-year-old Charles, eight-year-old Donna, and six-year-old Diane. She had been widowed six years ago when her husband accidentally plunged to his death from a high-rise apartment building in Manhattan, while working as a maintenance engineer. Ann Eunice stubbornly refused help from family and friends and insisted on living in her bungalow and raising her children alone. Her husband had it literally moved from one of the islands in the bay and placed it on Nebraska Street. She was cheerful, energetic, and possibly the most optimistic woman I had ever met. Thanks to her friendship, the confining walls of my home expanded and I branched out into a new relationship. We went shopping together, leaving Butch to babysit, while we walked a mile into town and then back. Neither of us could drive a car. A few times a week we exercised in her downstairs den, huffing and sweating over the Canadian Air Force exercises, then collapsing until we found the strength to drag ourselves upstairs and sip a brandy or gorge on cookies and tea.

Now that my homemaking skills had improved and a new friend had entered my life, I had little time for boredom. I had braided several wool rugs by hand, sewed curtains for every window in the house and was working on Easter outfits for the kids. My life was full and I was happy.

~

In early May, I realized that unless I had the flu, I was pregnant again. Birth control had failed me once more. The Pill had just hit the market, proving to be 100% effective, a margin of safety later challenged. The Catholic Church rose up and issued warnings of hell-fire and damnation to any woman who partook of the blasphemous sacrilege. Nevertheless, thousands of women, Catholic and non-Catholic, grasped eagerly at the chance to avoid unwanted pregnancies. But it was too late for me.

This time Butch took the news better than I did. Maybe it was the doomed expression on my face.

"Look, Micki, it's not so bad. Now that I'm working the bar, the money's good and our bills are paid. We'll have another girl and it will round out a perfect family. And we're young enough that we can grow up with them."

I could never figure out how he could always accurately predict the sexes of his children, but he was never wrong.

"Are you crazy?" I asked. "We've lived in the house less than a year and now it's going to be overcrowded again. Do you really think we can keep four children, two of each sex, in one bedroom?"

"No, but I think that room's big enough to make into two bedrooms. Give me time to think about it."

I gagged and ran for the bathroom.

By late November I was more than seven months pregnant and enjoying a pleasant autumn afternoon enhanced by a lazy Indian summer. The tranquility of the day was shattered by four words that would forever change the course of history: the president has been shot! The words were blasted across radio and television stations, causing a stab of pain in the hearts of all Americans. Newscaster Walter Cronkite cried, I cried, my friends and neighbors cried; not only for the man, but for the loss of a new era, over, almost before it began. The president was dead; the flame of

Camelot snuffed out before it could blaze a path of new awareness across a country barely recovered from the realities of war and depression.

The entire nation was glued to television sets as a team of huge Clydesdale horses clopped slowly, pulling the wagon with the body of the young president to his final resting place in Arlington Cemetery. Kim, at three years old was in tears, Michael, barely interested. John-John and Michael were the same age and looked remarkably alike--both staunch, proud, handsome little boys with large brown eyes and thick, dark, Buster Brown hair.

The kids were not watching television when Lee Harvey Oswald, arrested for the sniper attack on the president, was shot in cold blood by Jack Ruby. But Butch and I were. We were horrified by both the incident and the miracle of technology that brought the hideous event into our living room, live and unabridged. *What's going to become of us now*, I thought, with nuances of the insecurity of the fifties slipping into my mind.

~ Eight ~

Butch was true to his word and converted the children's large bedroom into two smaller ones. He knocked down half of the wall between the kitchen and what had been part of the kids' bedroom, creating a small dining room, and installed a marbleized countertop over the divider. The remaining half of the room was converted into a bedroom for the boys. What had been the dining room off the living room became a second bedroom for Kim. The new arrangement not only accommodated our growing family, but enhanced the old house and made it more modern. With the help of his new radial-arm saw that I had recently bought for his birthday, Butch built bunk beds, dressers, desks, recessed closets, and toy bins for the children. Not an ounce of space was wasted. We often worked late into the night, spurred on by the kids, who couldn't sleep through the noise. When it was completed, we were proud of our accomplishments.

~

In the latter part of August, my brother Stevie came over to my house after supper. He was carrying his duffle bag and I knew by his face that something was terribly wrong. He was almost sixteen years old and had run away from home.

"Micki," he said, wiping his reddened eyes with his sleeve. "Can I stay here for a while? Mom's on the warpath cause she found a book that I carved a hole in with my knife. Now she thinks I'm on drugs."

"Calm down, Stevie, and start all over," I said. From his disjointed statements, I finally deduced that he had fashioned a hole in one of his books to hide things that he didn't want his brother to find. He had seen it done in a television movie and it seemed like a neat idea at the time. Stevie was the same quiet, gentle boy that he had been as a child, although he now stood over six feet tall, with the lanky clumsiness of adolescence. He was more beautiful than handsome, with straight fine features, serene blue eyes that changed hues with whatever he was wearing, and thick, chestnut, wavy hair. I thought that my son Michael resembled him.

"You don't know what it's like at home," Stevie went on. "Ever since Milt broke up with her, Mom's been acting like a maniac, nagging at me all the time, screaming, and swearing. I can't take no more. I'm bleeding from my stomach."

Milt was the previous bartender at Benny's and my mother had fallen in love with him, even though she knew he was married. She fully believed he would divorce his wife and marry her, but he had no such inclinations. My mother went through men faster than I did underwear, but this time, she had fallen hard. This is the real thing, she had told me. It didn't seem much different to me than any of her other affairs. But then, what did I know about true love?

"Stevie," I said, hugging him until he stopped shaking. "You can stay here for as long as you like. I'll talk to Mom."

"No, no," he begged. "Don't tell her I'm here. She said she'd call the police and throw me in jail."

"She didn't mean that. You know Mom. She loses her temper and says horrible things, and then she calms down and forgets what she said."

When the phone rang later that evening, I was proven wrong.

"Micki, have you seen Stephen? When Ah get mah hands on that son of ah bitch, Ah'm gonna kill him!"

Her accent was in full swing. She was really mad.

"Ah already called the cops, and told them if they find him on the streets to pick him up and throw him in jail."

"Mom, you didn't really do that," I said. "What could he have done that's so horrible?"

"Your brother's on drugs. Ah saw the hole he carved out in ah book. The little bastawd. Aftah all Ah've done for him."

Not that again. Every decision or change my mother ever made was always for one of her children. Privately, she would tell each of us that we were her favorite child, not realizing that siblings who are close tell each other everything. For some reason, it was usually for me that she married, divorced and remarried; looking for the perfect daddy for her fatherless little girl, or so I assumed. I had lived with her tantrums all my life, but this time she seemed out of control and I wasn't about to test her to see if she would really put my brother in jail.

"Well, Mom," I said. "Stevie's not here. Why would he come here when he knows that this is the first place you'd look for him?"

"Don't you lie to me, Micki," she warned. "You're ah mother yourself and you know how it feels. Just tell me the little bastawd's there and Ah'll come and get him, so ah can beat the living hell out of him before ah send him to reformery school."

"Mom, I haven't seen Stevie in days," I lied. "If he shows up here, I'll have him call you. I don't believe he's on drugs, and if you were thinking clearly, you wouldn't either. And it's reform school, not reformery."

She slammed the receiver in my ear. I turned to Stevie, who was sitting on the couch, shaking uncontrollably and knew that I had done the right thing. I called Butch at work and told him what had happened. He came home early and made some phone calls. My mother actually did call the police, who put out a warrant for my brother's arrest. Long Beach's police chief, a favored customer at Benny's, told Butch, after hearing the story, that as long as Stevie stayed at our home the police wouldn't bother him.

None of us got much sleep that night. Shortly after dawn, I was awakened by the phone. It was my mother, no calmer than the night before. She insisted that Stevie was with me, although I continued to deny it. She screamed, she cursed and when that didn't work, she begged and cried. I was torn--unsure of what to do. I hated lying to my mother, but she was so over the edge that I didn't dare let my brother, who had all the symptoms of a stomach ulcer, return to her. I couldn't help but notice how thin he'd become in the past few weeks. The phone rang throughout the day, until finally I took the receiver off the hook and told the kids, who looked at me strangely, to leave it that way. They were irritable, sensing the tension in the house, but unable to understand what was happening.

Right after supper, I heard the squeal of tires out front and had a sinking feeling my mother had arrived. She had, and was enraged beyond belief. Stevie saw her first and took off to hide in the basement. I was grateful that Butch was off from work that day, hoping that he could calm her. When he saw the condition she was in, and realized that she'd been drinking, he quickly locked the front screen door.

"You give me mah son!" she screamed through the screen door, loud enough to spark the interest of the entire neighborhood, which was filled with summer residents.

"Micki, you're ah mother. How can you take mah baby and let me worry mahself sick ovah him?"

"You were going to put him in jail, Mom. You didn't sound too worried to me."

"You're goddamn right Ah was gonna put him in jail, and when Ah get mah hands on him, he's going to reformery school!"

She embarked on her usual tirade about all she had done for us and how could we be so cruel to her. I shooed the kids into their bedrooms and shut the door. Even that small act fueled her temper.

"Yeah," she said, screaming. "Put your kids away. And you better keep them away, because if Ah see them on the street, ah'll run them down with mah car."

My mouth dropped open in shock. She had to be out of her mind to say such a thing. My thirteen-year-old brother, Billy, stood at the bottom of the steps leading to the house, white as a sheet, his eyes filled with tears.

"Lee," Butch said to my mother, with a quiet steeliness to his voice that always scared me, "Why don't you go on home now, and calm down and we'll talk about this tomorrow?"

"Ah'm not leavin without mah baby. Butch, how can you do this to me? Ah've loved you like mah own son."

"Go on home, Lee. I won't say it again."

"C'mon, Mom, please!" I heard Billy call up the steps.

My mother only got angrier, kicking and banging the door.

"Ah'll kick this goddamn door down if ah have to. Ah'm not leavin' without mah son."

And then Butch took action. He went out the back door and a few seconds later he was rapping on the window screen in the living room, motioning for me to open the screen. He handed the end of the garden hose in through the window to me, and then returned to the living room from the back door.

"Don't do anything to her," I begged him. "Just shut the front door and maybe she'll go away."

I knew he wasn't listening. He opened the front screen door, turned on the hose and literally washed my mother, sputtering and yelling, down the front steps and onto the patio. Billy tried to wrestle the hose from him, but

Butch just shoved him aside and continued to hose down my mother. She finally backed away and went out the fence gate and stood by her car.

"Y'all be sorry for this!" she screamed. "As for you, Micki, Ah hope that baby you're carrying is born dead or deformed."

I didn't hear anything she said after that. Something within me died with those words. Mom got into her car and spun away, taking Billy with her. Butch came back into the house and we just looked at each other, too shocked to say anything. Stevie unpacked his duffle bag and spent his second night on the daybed in the sun porch. We all slept fitfully that night, wondering what my mother had in store for us next.

It was only a few days until we found out. Not only had she filed assault charges against Butch, she was taking us to Family Court to get Stevie back. The court date was set for October, and until that time, we had no contact with my mother, which was frightening, since we never knew what she might do at any given time. I kept the kids in the house, remembering her threats, and Stevie, still a walking disaster, never left the house either.

Court day arrived, and I was feeling nervous. Butch, with all the political clout that Benny offered, didn't seem worried. Ann Eunice watched the kids and I stuffed my eight months pregnant body into something presentable and climbed into the car. The court house was in Minneola, and stood tall and imposing as we drove up to it. We'd been briefed by our lawyer that I would be the primary witness, which did little to quiet my pounding heart. The courtroom seemed similar to the one on the Perry Mason series. So did the third degree I received from the District Attorney. I was sure we were wasting our time and that Stevie would have to return to my mother.

Then Mom took the stand and our lawyer, craftily sensing which strings to pull, managed to goad her into a tirade. She swore, she said horrible things, called everyone terrible names and completely threw away any chance at regaining her son. Not for the first time in my life, I was embarrassed and ashamed of my mother. The court awarded custody to Butch and me, instead of his natural mother and dismissed the assault charges against Butch. The judge remarked that after listening to her mouth, he would have liked to hose my mother down himself.

The only stipulation made was that Stevie's father would also have custody rights. We all went home elated, except for my mother. She placed one more venomous call to me before she disappeared from my life; and added a final touch of vengeance, although I didn't know it at the time. Months later, when I was looking for the shoe box containing my baby pictures, to prove to Ann Eunice that the kids did resemble me a little, it was missing. I never knew if she actually took it and destroyed it, or how she managed to do it, but she was the only logical suspect. As far as pictures were concerned, all tangible remnants of my past were gone.

After the trial, we tried to get our lives back to normal. I tried to contact Billy, but he was forbidden by Mom to communicate with any of us. Poor Billy, definitely Mom's favorite child now, was too young to understand. He loved us all, but he was his mother's son and his loyalty remained with her. I understood that, although I worried about him and most of all I missed him terribly, as did the kids.

~

Kelly was born in January, thirteen months after Dante. It was an easy birth and she was a quiet, placid baby like her brother Michael had been, contented and serene. She looked remarkably like my mother, which I thought was a subtle touch of irony enacted by a Higher Power with equitable justice. Stevie was still living with us and working at Benny's as a busboy. He had tried to help while I was in the hospital by rearranging my living room furniture. I had a penchant for moving my furniture around whenever I was depressed, or just plain bored. If I couldn't change my life, I could alter my immediate environment and feel like something was accomplished. Stevie was proud of his new arrangement. I was furious. I went into the house, carrying an infant cranky from the long drive from Easton and was pounced on by three excited children, all jabbering at once. After hugging them all and nearly bowled over by their enthusiasm, they finally settled down and I had a moment to survey the new furniture arrangement. I became irrationally upset and snapped at my brother, hurting his feelings. For the rest of the day, my mood was black and even though I knew I was acting like a jerk, I could not snap out of it. I went to my bedroom to lie down until the baby's next feeding.

The next afternoon, while Butch was at work and Stevie was in school, I rearranged the furniture the way I had left it and sunk exhaustedly onto the couch. By the time Butch came home from work, I was bleeding heavily and terrified that I was hemorrhaging. I felt stupid, knowing better than to move heavy furniture a week after delivering the baby; although my black mood had lightened considerably. I was not aware of the term 'postpartum depression' at the time. My father-in-law drove my fourteen-year-old sister-in-law, Lynn, up to stay the weekend. I was put to bed, with threats from Butch that if I got up, I might be bleeding in other places.

It was the beginning of 1964. We were feeling safe and content. We owned our own home, a new car and had four children. Most of our friends were about to graduate from college in the spring. It seemed like we were ahead of them in entertaining our dreams, but years later when the degrees they achieved led them to positions of power and money, we would find that time had stood still for us. But at that moment, we were confident that we were well on the way toward prosperity and good fortune.

That spring, Stevie migrated to the basement where Butch had built a partition, creating a small room for him; albeit a damp one with ceilings so low that Stevie had to walk in a stooped position. Butch had postponed the final alterations for so long that I felt forced to take matters into my own hands.

"How hard can it be?" I asked my brother, after telling him that I planned on doing the renovations myself, if he would help me. I called the lumber yard that we dealt with, and ordered a bunch of two by four pieces of wood, wallboard, and nails, and then gathered up all the tools that I had seen Butch use when working on the house. When the order arrived, Stevie and I carted everything down into the basement and I was ready to begin my first home improvement project.

The first thing I did, after having watched Butch do it so many times, was hang the plumb line from the ceiling to the floor, to see if something was level. The trouble was, I couldn't remember what it was that was supposed to be level. The line looked straight to me, so I let it hang there and went on to the level. When I laid the two foot level on the cement floor, the yellow liquid floating in the tube in the center of the tool, wobbled back and forth. I took that to be a good sign and proceeded to lay one of the two by fours in the spot where the level was. So far, so good. I laid all the wooden studs in a line, cutting the ones that were too long with Butch's hand saw. Sawing wood was not as easy as it looked and an hour passed before I was ready to nail the wood to the floor. With great foresight, I had purchased cement nails. Nevertheless, as I attempted to hammer them into the wood and concrete, sparks flew, nails broke, including those on my fingers, yet I couldn't nail those miserable spikes to the floor. Stevie was no help. His mechanical skills ended at hanging his artwork on the walls with straight pins.

By the time Butch came home, I was hot, sweaty, frustrated and on the verge of tears. Watching him stand at the bottom of the cellar steps, laughing uproariously, did little to improve my spirits.

When he could manage to speak, he said, "One of the guys at the lumber yard called me at work the other day and said you had placed a large order of building supplies and he thought I might want to know. I told him to go ahead and deliver it, so I could see what you were up to." He started laughing again when he noticed the plumb line hanging from the ceiling.

"I don't believe the lumber yard called you!" I said, hoping that he would choke on his laughter. "How dare they assume that I don't know what I'm doing, just because I'm a woman." The fact that I didn't was quite beside the point.

I stomped through the sawdust, kicked a sawed off two by four out of my way and stomped upstairs; but not before giving Stevie a withering glare for what I thought was the beginning of a grin spreading across his face. Adding to my humiliation was the sound of more laughter following me. Stevie's basement room was finished within a week, although I staunchly refused to help.

~

"The Feminine Mystique," by Betty Friedan had just been published that year and while I hadn't read it yet, I knew what it was about--women like me tied down with kids, and married to husbands who considered them possessions. I seemed locked into my own destiny; too many kids, too little money, and no education beyond high school to change my situation. Mine and Butch's roles were fixed. He was the breadwinner and master of the house and I was the caretaker.

"But I give you everything you ever ask for," Butch said, when I tried to explain my feelings. "Everything isn't yours to give me," I said. "It's supposed to be ours."

I didn't really know what I wanted. I just knew that I didn't have it.

He didn't and couldn't understand. There was a virus of malcontent spreading across the country affecting many women, and as I felt the slowly rising fever of my own discontent, I didn't yet realize that I wasn't alone.

~

During the next two years that my brother stayed with us, Butch and I probably saw more movies than we did throughout our entire marriage. We both loved the movie "Hud." Me, because Paul Newman was in it, which was enough reason for any woman, and Butch, because Paul Newman was playing a macho he-man. But halfway through "Who's afraid of Virginia Wolf?" Butch insisted that we leave the theatre. The language was bad enough, at least for the times, but when Elizabeth Taylor started chomping through food like a starving animal, that was too much for Butch, who detested bad table manners.

"If I wanted to watch this crap, I could have stayed home and ate dinner with the kids," he said, getting up to leave, with or without me.

Luckily for the children, he worked through dinner time, except for the dreaded Mondays. Mealtimes on his days off were a horror. He nearly gave the kids indigestion with his black looks and cutting remarks when what he deemed rules of etiquette were repeatedly broken. All the kids quickly learned how to chew celery, lettuce, apples and potato chips without making a sound. Years later, they would tell me that the trick to it was to slowly suck the offending food until it could be quietly swallowed.

While movies and songs, such as "Blowing in the Wind," with Peter, Paul and Mary, and the first three singles from the Beatles, including, "She Loves You," were hits that year, politics were in a slump. Accepting Lyndon Baines Johnson as President was a culture shock for all of us caught up in the Kennedy charisma and still in a state of mourning. Johnson was boorish, outspoken and was constantly putting his foot in his mouth--antagonizing people still nursing memories of their slain President. Following in the footsteps of a glorified President shot down in his youth, was an impossible task for any man, much less this arrogant, boisterous Texan.

By the middle of Johnson's second term, most of the patriotism promoted by John Kennedy began to dissipate, as the Cold War continued to nurture fear, and the Vietnam War, then considered an unpopular skirmish, escalated. The media showed newsreels of the fighting, focusing on blood and gore, depressing the nation even more. After a while, people became apathetic. Watching young boys die on the evening news took away much of the war's credibility; it seemed like a movie, too orchestrated to be really happening. It wasn't even a real war, never having been declared by Congress; just a never-ending police action, with more young men and women dying each day for a principle never clearly defined.

One of the busboys who worked at Benny's was the first casualty of the war that we knew personally. Charley was a good natured, immature boy, who had no business being in a war, much like the thousands of other boys sent to a strange country to play a deadly adult game. He was trusting and optimistic and that trait killed him. Showing his usual lack of good sense, Charlie showed his loaded gun to a young Vietnamese boy, who promptly shot him with it.

Stevie would not be drafted because of a scar on his shin bone the size of a fifty-cent piece. While living in Florida, he and my brother Billy had suffered allergic reactions from the prolific mosquito bites, which festered and oozed and left terrible scarring on their bodies. The scar tissue on Stevie's leg would break open and bleed if he did any strenuous exercise or took long walks. The bug population of Florida proved to be good for something after all. It kept my brother from becoming one of the 45,865 casualties that would occur in Vietnam over the next nine years. Butch, of course, was exempt from the draft, as sole support of his family, although he wanted to go more than he dared admit to me. The war would surely end before my sons were old enough to serve. I thanked God daily, that the Vietnam War could not touch my family.

Fifteen years later, I would be proven wrong.

~ *Nine* ~

The summer that Kelly was eighteen months old, I was going crazy trying to handle four small children, plus a teenager who saw little reason to listen to myself or Butch. Stevie had turned eighteen and was, in his own eyes at least, a man.

My sister-in-law, Lynn, who had recently turned sixteen, came up to stay for part of the summer. She was having trouble at home, too; due, in part, to her mouth, which was always open when it should have been shut, and too sarcastic for her parents to tolerate. She had lost the clumsiness of puberty, as well as her penchant for mismatched clothing; and become a lovely teenager, with an outrageous sense of humor--humor apparently lost on my in-laws.

With both Stevie and Lynn living with us, we were never without a willing babysitter, and it was a relief to be able to walk down to Ann Eunice's house in the evenings and relax, unburdened by the sounds of little people disturbing me. And an even bigger relief not to have to drag four children through the supermarket, and then take out the dozens of items that they had dumped into the basket when my back was turned.

Lynn slept in the sun porch during her visit and our little house rocked from morning to night, overrun by children, the gray pewter cat, Cinder, which had condescended to live with us and two teenagers who didn't get along particularly well. Secretly, I was delighted. I'd found that when in the midst of uncontrollable bedlam, it was best to join it, rather than fight it.

Lynn, unlike my brother (the slob), was a meticulous housekeeper, and took on my home as a challenge. I didn't believe in wasting time cleaning anything above my line of vision. Since I was tall, that worked out fine; except for the times when Butch, after hearing me complain about how hard I'd worked, would reach up and run his hand along the molding above the door and then show me the dust.

"But, nobody can see it up there," I would tell him, annoyed that I could never seem to do anything perfect in his eyes. "Besides, I do clean it twice a year."

"Yes," he would answer. "But it's there, and you know it's there, so why not just clean it when it needs it?"

I don't know what irritated me more; his finding the dust, or his smugness.

Anyway, I gave Lynn full control over my home, and even with so many people crammed into the little house, the floors were always shiny and the dishes done; although even Lynn drew the line at cleaning door moldings.

One evening, an extremely pleasant one following a day at the beach, Lynn and I walked into the center of town and saw the movie, "Help," starring the Beatles. Lynn went wild for the oddly dressed, mop-haired English boys with their cockney accents, and was screaming at the top of her lungs with the rest of the kids in the theatre. I had read recently that half of the population of the country was under thirty. In that packed movie house, ninety percent were well under twenty, making me feel old and out of place. I found the Beatles, as actors, lacking and obnoxious, although I was still young enough to pretend to Lynn that I was wild about them, too. Their music was a different matter. It was great then, and would prove to stand the test of time.

~

That fall, Kimber went to afternoon kindergarten and Stevie moved back to Pennsylvania to live with his father. He became increasingly hard to handle, which was in direct proportion to Butch's lack of patience with him. My stepfather, exercising his custody rights, had visited once or twice during the past summer. He'd remarried and brought his new wife and piles of expensive toys for the grandchildren he'd never seen. Dad was at his charming best, winning over the kids immediately. I found myself forgetting how it had been to live with him; remembering instead the good things from my childhood. Surprisingly there were many; renting a beach house on the shores of Kitty Hawk, North Carolina, taking day trips up into the Pocono Mountains, and camping by frigid mountain streams, or searching the night skies for the planet Saturn with the telescope bought for my father with my babysitting money. I wanted my kids to have relatives from my side of the family and like a child anxious to do anything for love, I was willing to trade the bad times for the good. Butch was more skeptical.

After a family conference, in which my father pointed out the advantages of Stevie living with him, the decision was made, and Stevie went back to start a new life in Allentown, Pennsylvania.

~

The day Kim climbed on the school bus and sat near a window so I could take her picture, I cried. She didn't, and I was both proud and resentful of her bravery, which wasn't feigned. My baby, a firstborn child who would forever hold a special place in my heart, was entering the outside world without me.

She didn't return from her first day in school as cocksure as she was when she left. The ride to her new school took thirty minutes and the bus fumes made Kim, who was prone to carsickness, ready to throw up. Long Beach, like many communities, was doing its bit to combat racism by integrating the school system; putting the cart before the horse.

"I don't believe this," Butch said, waiting for Kim to get home before he left for work. "We move into a neighborhood where our kids only have to walk a few blocks to go to school, and they bus them a half hour away."

"There's nothing we can do about it," I said. "I've gone to three school board meetings, watched a packed room of people swear, yell and nearly riot over this. I even wrote to the school board president, remember? Their minds were made up and the meetings were just to pacify the public into thinking they had some control. Even Washington, D.C. isn't as powerful as the state school board in Albany."

"Yeah, well, they're not going to solve the racial crisis by busing kids out of their neighborhood," he said, and headed for the front door.

"If they really wanted to fight bigotry, they'd integrate neighborhoods. Kids aren't prejudiced, their parents are," I called after him.

"Bull. All I know is my kid has to get sick every day riding a bus when she could walk to school. What's going to happen if she gets sick in school?" He slammed the door after him before I could answer.

I remembered the day, a few years ago, when a tall black man had walked by our house. Kim perked up at his appearance and I could tell she was going to say something. *Oh no*, I thought, *she's never seen a black person before and she's going to say something embarrassing. I just know it.*

"Mommy!" Kim called up the porch steps where I was sitting. "Did you see that man? He's wearing white sneakers."

Kim hadn't given the color of his skin any notice, but the fact that he was wearing white sneakers, when her father only wore black dress shoes, caught her attention.

With Stevie gone, Lynn back at her home, and my mother and Billy out of my life, it was lonely that autumn. The kids kept me on my toes, but I got tired of interacting with people who were under four feet tall; except for Kim, who was growing taller every day, well out of her age group. I had Ann Eunice, but she was busy working. Her insurance money from the death of her husband had run out and she was forced to clean houses to support herself and her kids.

There was one highlight that fall. On November 9th, we thought for a moment that the end of the world, as predicted in the bible, had arrived. The lights went out throughout most of the Eastern Seaboard and the world as we knew it, was plunged into eerie, dense blackness. It was a cold day, never climbing much above 46 degrees, and the gas furnace, ignited by an electrical switch, shut down. It happened right after I fed the kids supper. Butch was still at work. The kids screamed and I groped for the candles, thinking only that a fuse had blown. Butch got home before I had time to call him and helped me calm and reassure the kids. By now, we knew it was a major blackout, but not how extensive. We bundled the kids up in all the extra blankets we could find and settled them into bed. They had quieted down, but were still frightened, especially Kim, who hated the dark.

There was a bright moon that night, and as I stepped outside to survey the neighborhood, I was amazed by the silence. Nothing seemed to move or make a sound, not even the wind usually blowing off the shore. It was as if the world had suddenly been sucked into a vacuum. Dogs didn't bark, the hundreds of cats that prowled the streets of the West End didn't screech or fight. There was only the silence and the heavy blackness.

Butch had to go back to Benny's to secure the place and put the food on ice. Benny's was open, of course, but business was slow. The people who had been there when the blackout hit hurried to their homes and few, if any, ventured out. I was annoyed that Butch left us alone, since I was also afraid of the dark, but he promised he wouldn't be long and kept his word.

Later we would hear of people stuck in elevators, or trains, and trapped in subways throughout New York City. Thousands of babies would be conceived that night by people feeling an instinctive need to procreate when tragedy strikes. Happily, I was not among those who became pregnant during the great blackout. Sometime in the middle of the night the power came back on and we awoke to a dawn that had never looked so good

~ *Ten* ~

I have decided this is only a bad dream. I am not really sitting in the waiting room of the Intensive Care Unit, with my child hovering in a limbo that is neither life nor death. I've suffered nightmares before, throughout my childhood. Many times, in the middle of a disturbing dream, I would awaken, sit straight up in bed, open my eyes, and watch the dream unfold around me. It seemed as real as life. Like this. But it was only a bad dream.

Sometimes, as a young child of nine or ten, I would lie in my bed and see a two inch dark shadow outlining the entire edge of the bed. *It must be the devil*, I'd thought, and forced myself to stare fixedly at the illuminated cross on my dresser; one of those crosses that you held up to a light for a few seconds and then it would glow in the dark. It was terrifying to a young girl to be facing the devil, and my heart pounded with fear and dread. But I knew that if I stayed motionless in the middle of the bed, with my arms at my side, and concentrated on the ivory-colored cross, the devil would leave me alone.

God must be mad at me, I reasoned, and prayed hard for forgiveness, promising to be a good girl. No more squirting the aerosol can of whipped cream directly into my mouth when my parents were away. No more stealing walnuts from the uncovered bushel basket standing near the door of the little grocery store across from my home. No more smacking my brothers for losing the ball to my best set of jacks. I would become a perfect little girl, too good for the devil, much too good for God to consider punishing.

I slept in an attic bedroom of sorts, with slanted walls randomly stuffed with insulation; a room of your own, my mother said. But when the trap door, which was part of the floor, swung shut, condemning me to total darkness, I trembled and shook. The unfinished attic space was unbearably hot during the summer months and freezing in the winter. It was poorly lit, with dim, scant, light coming through the tiny windows at each end of the room. There was only a small bedroom lamp on the dresser across from my bed and my illuminated cross to light the large, sparse room, half of which was used for storage; storage which created frightening shadows when the room was dark. There was a bare light bulb, hanging at the top of the stairs above the trap door, but the switch was on the downstairs wall. As soon as the trap door slammed shut, my stepfather turned out the light. He was a firm believer in saving energy; both electrical and the energy of a wide awake child tucked away in an unfinished attic before the sun went down.

There was no flooring in the attic, except for the sheets of plywood nailed down where my bed and dresser stood, so if I wasn't careful, I could miss my footing when stepping across the wooden studs, and crash through the ceiling into the living room below. My stepfather wouldn't be happy about that. He sent my brothers and I to bed at seven o'clock each night. He needed his privacy with my mother, he said. My mother never defended us. She was afraid of him, too.

That's what I'll do now. I'll promise to be a better wife and mother. I'll have more compassion for Butch having to work out of town and only coming home on weekends, worrying less about myself and my own deep loneliness. He's the one forced to live out of the back of a small camper attached to our pick up truck. He's the one that wakes up covered in bugs, courtesy of the New Jersey swamplands. He's the one that suffers total isolation and deprivation. I have the kids. And I'll be more patient with them from now on. I'll find something good to say about my teenagers, who collectively attempt to drive me insane. I won't carp about their clothing, even though some of them look like rejects from the Salvation Army. I won't complain about their hair, their messy rooms, and their smart mouths. I won't treat them the way my mother treated me, so caught up in her own problems, that I was more an accessory to her home than a living child with hurts and needs.

I've forgotten how special my children are, how beautiful, and bright; really good, nice kids. When they were small, I seemed to have more control, more patience, and understanding. Surely they're not so different now. It must be me who has changed. It will be different from now on. Yes, I'll promise all these things and my nightmare will end. I'll wake up and everything will be normal again.

The night nurse nudges me gently and hands me a fresh cup of coffee.

This time the nightmare is real. If only I could transport myself back in time, back to when my biggest problem was four children in night time diapers simultaneously.

~ *Eleven* ~

The kids were growing fast. Their ages ranged from two to six years old, each a year apart, except for the boys, who had twenty months between them. Sometimes I felt cheated about not going to college and resented being tied down to a house, husband, and children. Most of my friends were out in the world doing exciting new things. Yet, I had only to look at the children as they slept to realize how fortunate I was to be the caretaker of such treasures. Sleeping children are angels in disguise, changelings for the night; the picture of harmony and perfection. An exception was Michael, who had a tendency to sleep flat on his back, hands folded across his chest and eyes open in a death-like trance. I often held a mirror to his mouth to reassure myself that he was breathing. He was weird, but he was breathing.

With so many children close in age, the household had to be run like an Army barracks, to prevent chaos from reigning supreme. Kimber was the straw boss. The others listened to her better than to me and almost as well as they obeyed their father. She was articulate, bright, pixie pretty, with dark expressive eyes and thick, nearly black hair. Her brothers and sisters feared as well as worshipped her. If Kimber told them black was white and the sun only shone at night, they accepted her words as gospel truth. I never found out the secret of her success, but years later, she admitted that she simply bribed them.

Michael was still remarkably beautiful, with tremendous brown eyes, fringed with lashes so long and curled that they often intertwined and stuck together. He had a petulant full mouth, usually turned down at the corners, a tiny, turned up nose and a perfectly formed chin that was almost always set into a mode of stubbornness.

Michael mystified me with his strange sense of values. If it were possible to be born with chauvinistic genes, this child was a prime example. He refused to eat lunch if his father made it, because, "Daddies aren't supposed to cook."

"Why aren't you out riding your bike with the rest of the kids, Mike?" I asked him one day.

"Because it's Monday," he said. "Monday is my day off."

"Today isn't Monday, Michael."

He gave me his usual complacent stare and continued building with his Lincoln Logs, as if it was obvious that this did not merit further conversation. Michael seemed to carry a handbook for living around in his head and God help the person who broke one of his rules.

I came home from shopping one day to find all my roses that had just bloomed to perfection, uprooted and lying across the sidewalk in a neat row. None of my offspring seemed to have any idea as to how this phenomenon might have occurred. I grilled them one by one, but I was pretty sure who the culprit was. I recognized the work.

"Michael, how did my roses get uprooted?"

Blank stare.

"I won't ask you again, Michael."

Blank stare with tears forming.

"You know, I loved those roses, Michael. You helped me plant them, remember? And they had just bloomed. They were so beautiful. This really makes me sad, Michael."

"You shoulda taken me with you," he said, with more ice in his voice that I would have thought possible in such a little boy.

"But Michael, I didn't know you wanted to go with me. Why didn't you ask me and maybe I would have said yes?"

"You shoulda known," he said.

That was Michael, my enigma; a boy who spent a great deal of his time deep in thoughts that he shared with no one, except his sister, Kim, and then only occasionally.

Dante was the house clown. Still comical looking, he was beginning to show signs of becoming a very handsome little boy--if he lived beyond his third birthday. Dante instituted a "search and destroy" mission from the time he woke up in the morning until bedtime, and sometimes well beyond. The boy either had no innate sense of right and wrong or simply didn't care. He caused more mischief and endangered himself more than all the rest of the children combined. Yet, when he was severely scolded, which was often, or, God forbid, spanked on his firm, little bottom, he became instantly dejected--took his bedraggled teddy bear and put himself to bed. It seemed unnatural for a toddler to make himself take naps, but it was in my own best interest not to interfere with his bizarre habit.

Dante also had the nose of a bloodhound.

"I have the smell of you, Ma," he would tell me, which made me a little paranoid about my choice of deodorants. He was capable of tracking down any odor, such as onions gone bad, or snacks I had hidden away.

Kelly was the baby of the family, the last child, I thought with certainty. She was the epitome of sweetness, with rounded eyes of brown flecked with yellow, and light brown hair, long and thick, that turned golden in the sun. But like the little girl in the nursery rhyme, "when she was good, she was very, very, good, and when she was bad, she was horrid." She far surpassed Michael in stubbornness and nearly matched his hot temper. When Kelly flew into a rage her siblings gave her a wide berth. She was apt to hurl whatever she could lift and her aim was always perfect. After she threw the small rocking chair (that had been mine as a child and since handed down from child to child) at me, I decided to have a talk with her. I was still nursing a bruise.

"Kelly, we don't throw things at people. Not even when we're angry," I started.

Kelly nodded solemnly and looked around, as if wondering who "we" were.

"It's just not ladylike," I added. She perked up at my words.

"But I yam a yady, Mommy. A yady is what I yam."

"Well, Kel, ladies never hit people and never, never, throw things, because ladies don't want to hurt the people they love. Do you understand what I'm saying?"

"Yep," she said, nodding. "Mommy hits and frows things. Mommy is not a yady!" She marched out of the room with a smug, self-satisfied toss of her head, and I resolved for the thousandth time, not to try and use child psychology on my kids.

With the beach practically in my back yard, it was tempting not to pack up the kids and spend our days there. But after lugging the stroller, (because Lady Kelly's legs got tired) diapers, toys, lunch and the beach umbrella down the beach to the water, having them play for an hour and whine to go home, (now wet, sandy, sunburned and cranky) my enthusiasm waned. I probably saw less of the beach during my years in Long Beach than people living hundreds of miles away. The rare exceptions were when my best friend, Jeanie, a true sun worshiper, came out for a visit, or my sisters-in-law came up for a week long stay.

~

Now that Butch had become the bartender at Benny's, his work schedule was almost normal. He didn't leave for work until early afternoon and was home not later than one or two in the morning. He utilized his time by working on the house and playing with the kids, who were thrilled by his presence. It was a nice change to have late breakfasts, which he usually cooked, and then laze the morning away with cups of coffee, while the kids played in their rooms or out in the front yard. I noticed how much better behaved the kids were when Daddy was home, but I was grateful for any reprieve.

Summers offered great times on Nebraska Street. Our house caught the ocean winds, backed by the breezes off the bay. Unless a heat wave knocked out the wind, the weather was always pleasant, and the nights, balmy and cool. The long narrow block filled up with "summer people" after the Memorial Day weekend. The wives and children stayed all summer, and the husbands either came for the weekends, or commuted back and forth to the city on the Long Island Railroad. It was a cluttered, noisy, tumultuous time, a three month vacation, but definitely a welcome change from the seemingly endless winters when there were only five occupied houses on the block. Parking on the one-way street was a nightmare, but it was safer for the large groups of children playing on the sidewalks. Just about the time that the bedlam and close proximity became a burden, Labor Day arrived and the summer people packed up and returned to the city. A comfortable silence settled over the block and was welcomed until February, when the doldrums of winter made the few occupants of Nebraska Street again yearn for human contact.

That summer all of the kids were old enough to play outside with moderate supervision. As usual, Kim was the overseer and had permission to come to me if they got into trouble. She took her position very seriously.

"Mom!" Kim called out on one unusually muggy day, as she ran through the kitchen looking for me. "Michael is doing it again."

"Doing what, honey?" I answered from my bedroom, my voice muffled from the pile of warm laundry nearly burying my face.

"It's so disgusting," she said, plopping down on my bed and upending a tall pile of folded clothes. "He's begging for ice cream at the custard stand again. He always does it."

The ice cream stand was at the end of the block and it was nearly impossible to keep the kids away from it. It seemed that they gained some secondary pleasure from watching other people enjoy the soft frozen cones, even if they couldn't have any themselves.

"Tell him I want him right now," I said, continuing to fold the mountains of laundry that I suspected of propagating during the night. Some time later, Michael came strolling into the room, making each step count, as if he were expecting a land mine to go off under his feet.

"Well, Michael?" I said. "Is it true what Kim tells me?"

He stood with his head down, chin nearly touching his chest and shook his head slowly.

"Then you tell me what happened."

A long silence passed before he spoke.

"I onwy asked one wady for a widdle wick. Just one widdle wick," he said, sniffling.

"That's what he always does, Mom," said Kim, who had returned a few minutes after her brother. "And then the people give him money to buy his own ice cream."

"All right, Kim, you can go back outside now."

Michael started to trail after her.

"Not you, young man," I said. "I'm not finished with you, yet. First of all, what is a "widdle wick?" I thought we decided that you were going to try harder to pronounce your Ls."

"Mommy," he said, with great impatience at my stupidity, "A widdle wick means just a bite, not too much."

"Mike, go on outside and play and if I hear about you asking anyone for ice cream, even a bite, you're going to stay in your room all day. Do you understand me?"

"You're mean to me, Mommy," he said, sobbing as he ran out of my bedroom. "You're always too mean to me."

Dante and Kim never begged for ice cream. They just slipped into my room and stole their father's change off the dresser and bought their own.

~

Aside from going to the supermarket and the Times Square Store in the neighboring town of Oceanside, my trips away from home were spent running the kids to the doctors for colds and shots, or out to the emergency room for strings of accidents that never ceased. Today, I would probably be accused of child abuse. Mike loved to put things in his mouth, and throughout his young life, he had swallowed pennies, (which Dante threw up into the air and dared him to catch with his mouth) ate rocks, small toys, and once got a twig stuck between his tonsils. The doctor at the hospital had wondered aloud, as he worked the twig loose, how this might have happened. I had no idea. Another time, for reasons known only to himself, Michael picked up a gum ball ring out of the gutter and seconds later it was up his nose; another hospital trip. He was a "pica" kid, the doctors realized after running blood tests on him. After treatment with iron supplements, his cravings for strange inedibles diminished.

Dante's self-destructive bent could not be so easily cured. One afternoon, in the middle of the summer, we had all just returned from shopping and Butch and I were having a cup of coffee at the kitchen table. We both realized at the same time that we hadn't seen Dante for a while. That was not a good sign. There was no end to the list of things that Dante could accomplish during unsupervised time. We finally found him lying in his bed, whimpering softly. He was holding one of his rectangular shaped blocks to his face, and upon removing it, we saw blood stream down his cheek and neck. He had climbed up onto the bathroom sink and reached above the medicine cabinet where Butch kept his razor and decided it was high time he started to shave. If more time had elapsed before we found him, and if he hadn't instinctively held the block tight against his face, he could have easily bled to death--not ten feet away from us. Fortunately, the doctor was able to butterfly the two inch slash, instead of stitching it up, which would have left a terrible scar. Dante was sufficiently traumatized by the incident for the remainder of the day.

"You know, Mick," Butch said, as we lay in bed, reliving our close call, and trying to savor what was left of his day off, "I was thinking this morning as I shaved, that I should lock my razor in the medicine cabinet, because that little monkey was getting too curious about it and was asking me when I thought he was old enough to shave."

"Nothing in this house is safe from him," I said. "I'm not going to survive him, or at least not with my sanity intact. He's already gone over, under, or through every gate we've put up on his door, and he's busted two locks on the medicine cabinet. Yesterday, I heard him call out to me, "So long, Ma, I'm going now," from his room. When I ran in to check on him, he had opened the French window and was about to step out."

"Great; that's a one and a half story drop, Mick. He could have killed himself."

"Well, all I know is that he's killing me," and turned to the wall so Butch wouldn't see the tears that sprung from nowhere and were wetting my pillow.

He reached for me at once.

"Don't cry, Micki," he said, holding me tight against his chest. "It was a close call, but he's all right."

"You just don't know how hard it is to handle these kids all the time," I gulped between sobs. "It's such a big responsibility and if anything ever happened to one of them, I couldn't live."

"Nothing will happen, Mick, nothing will happen."

We fell asleep in each other's arms and stayed that way until the combination of the morning sun bursting through the windows and a rather bawdy song coming from our youngest daughter woke us up.

Michael was marching up and down the hallway, like a wooden soldier, chanting, "Fee fi fo fum, I smell the blood of an English Muffin," and Kelly was marching behind him, singing "Mudderfudder, Mudderfudder," at the top of her lungs.

Butch was almost too stunned to react.

"Where in the name of God, would she hear language like that?"

"Well don't look at me," I said. "You know I don't swear. She must have picked it up from the summer people."

Meanwhile, Kelly was still vocalizing her new found song, raucously, but on key.

"Do something," Butch whispered.

"Kelly!" I called out. "Come in here, now!"

"I comin', Mommy," she said, and toddled down the one step into our bedroom.

"Kelly, where did you here that word?" I asked, quietly.

"What word, Mommy?"

"The one you were singing about in the hall just now."

"Mudderfudder," she said, proudly.

Butch winced.

"Sweetie," I began. "Mommy doesn't want you to use that word anymore, because it's not a nice word."

"I yike it," said Kelly.

"I don't care if you like it or not. You are never to use that word again. Remember last week when Dante said a bad word? What happened to him?"

"He hadda eat soap."

"Right, and if I hear that word in this house again, the person who says it will have their mouth washed out with soap. Understand?"

"Okay, Mommy. Dante yikes ta eat soap."

She went back to her marching, but changed her repertoire to "Mary had a yiddle yamb."

"Your daughter is really something," Butch said, standing up and stretching before he got dressed.

"My daughter? My daughter? Why are they always your children when they do something cute or clever and my children whenever they're in disgrace?"

"Because no daughter of mine would ever say 'mudder fudder,'" he said, and got out of the room seconds ahead of the pillow I hurled at him.

I crawled out of bed, unrested as usual. There was rarely a night that Butch and I got to sleep straight through. Kim was still an insomniac and afraid of the dark. She would wait until she thought we were asleep and reach down from the top bunk and wake up Kelly. The two of them would start to giggle, softly at first, but soon loud enough to drift into our back room. Butch would mutter to himself a while and then stomp off to their room in his colored bikini underwear. Apparently, the sight of their father in his underwear only set the girls off more, in spite of his threats to smother them with their pillows if they didn't stop. Eventually, I had to get up and settle them down. Other nights, one of us would wake up in the middle of the night to find all the lights on and the television blaring, sometimes playing the National Anthem; signifying the end of the day's broadcasting. Dante and Kelly would be sitting in front of it, calmly munching on cookies, cereal, or whatever they could find to eat, while Kim, blessed with an acute sense of ESP, would have already sensed one of us coming and be back in her bed feigning sleep. Michael slept like a zombie, and was always refreshed and raring to go as soon as the sun came up.

~

Dante gave us another bad scare that summer. Butch had been nagging him to give up his teddy bear, even though Dante was only three and a half. None of the other kids had attached themselves to a favorite stuffed animal or blanket, and Butch took it as a sign of weakness.

"You're a big guy now, Dante," his father told him. "Why do you need to carry a stuffed animal around?"

"I need him, Daddy," Dante said.

"C'mon, be a big boy and throw it away. You don't need it."

"Then you throw your cigarettes away, Daddy," Dante said, clever enough to think that he had his father now.

"It's a deal," Butch agreed. "You put your teddy bear in the garbage can and I'll quit smoking. Okay?"

Dante nodded solemnly and walked slowly over to the garbage can, holding his beat up teddy bear by the ear. He lifted the lid to the can and looked in. Then he closed the lid and looked back at his father. Butch nodded encouragement. Dante lifted the lid off the can again, and gently laid the stuffed animal on top of the pile of garbage, patted the bear on the head and closed the can. As I observed this drama from the porch steps, I was convinced that Butch was undoubtedly the cruelest man in the world. Dante started to walk away, then stopped and turned back. He lifted the lid once again, straightened out the bear a little, then closed the lid to the can and walked slowly into the house. I was crying, but Butch was proud of his little man.

Later that morning, I called Dante in for lunch. Only minutes earlier, he had been playing by the side of the house with Robbie the Robot, a mechanical toy that talked. He didn't answer and I couldn't find him anywhere in the house. We searched the neighborhood, checking next door with the people he had decided to live with the last time he ran away from home. They hadn't seen him. We checked the phone booth at the end of the block, next to the custard stand, where we had found him the month before in his underwear, clutching his large blue sailboat. He wasn't there either. We were on the verge of panic.

Even though my children were threatened with the most severe punishment if they ever went into the street, we couldn't help but think of the treacherous bay across from Nebraska Street, or even the ocean, if he was brave enough to venture that far from home. All of our neighbors joined in the search, but Dante was nowhere on the block. Now we were terrified. We went back inside the house to call the police, and decided to check his room one more time. For some reason, I bent down and looked under the bed. There he was, fast asleep, curled up with his pillow and the straggly teddy bear he had rescued from the bowels of the garbage can, and didn't want his father to know. Butch, relieved to find Dante safe, never again mentioned the teddy bear. And he kept on smoking. I just headed for the Alka Seltzer and tried to reassure myself that close calls only counted in horseshoes and hand grenades.

~

Most of the crew from Benny's stopped over during the week nights when Butch was off from work, or on an early night when business was slow. Jim and Sally Cameron preferred to also stop by early in the afternoons to see the kids. They drove up each year from Florida to work the summer season in Long Beach. They were in their early fifties, with children long since grown and on their own. Jim fell in love with all the kids, but he was particularly smitten with Kelly. The two of them had a love affair from the time Kelly was six months old and reached her little arms out to Jim, who was completely overwhelmed. The more Jim tried to woo and win her with toys, candy and dolls, Kelly, acting like the little vixen she was, would pretend to be mad at him and throw his gifts back in his face. This only made Jim worship her all the more. As I watched this exercise in female domination I wondered how a two-year-old baby girl could know instinctively how to keep and hold a man. She must have inherited my mother's genes, I thought.

"Kelly's going to be a handful when she's in her teens," I told Butch one night as we lay in bed doing our favorite thing; recounting the cute or clever things that the kids had done that day.

"Have you noticed how she treats Jim?"

"C'mon, Micki, she's just a baby. She has no idea of what she's doing. You always read into things that aren't there."

I just shook my head and let the subject drop. If men were so blind to the wiles of even such a miniature little woman, it was not my job to try and educate them.

Russ and Gloria Styer came from Reading, Pennsylvania, not too far from Easton, and they, too, followed the seasons and worked up and down the coast. They were saving their money to buy a restaurant of their own one day, and for the past few years worked each summer at Benny's. They were in their late forties, and were both friends and surrogate parents. I often wondered if Butch would have preferred a life like that, working the resort circuit, instead of being tied down with a wife and children. One of his customers had recently asked him to spend six months traveling Europe with him, and I knew that Butch was sorely tempted. He took a different view of the matter when it was rumored that the young man with the generous offer was interested in him on a romantic level.

"That's the price you pay for having such a slim body and firm, tight rear end," I remarked, when he related the story, with embarrassment. "It's a cross you'll have to learn to bear." He was not amused.

Waiters and waitresses came and went at Benny's, but over the years a steady crew of about a dozen people, for various reasons, decided to stay and work for Benny. Even though he was less than an ideal boss, Benny had the knack of getting the most amount of work from his employees, while letting them think that they owed him something. My own life would have been a lot easier if I could have discovered his formula for manipulating people and making them enjoy it.

~ Twelve ~

Michael went off to kindergarten in September, stoically brave like his sister Kim had been the year before. Their father drilled it into his children that Pelusos never cry. Like Kim, Michael came home teary-eyed and frightened from the long bus ride, certain that the bus had "lost me."

Kim enjoyed walking to her elementary school, especially since she had to pass Benny's on her way home, and was always invited in for a soda and some pretzels. The school system had only bused the kindergarten students. She sat on the high bar stool before opening time, acting like the little princess that she was. Her daddy was Prince Charming, doting on his little girl, showing her off to the help, who agreed that she was perfect. Father and daughter were both egomaniacs.

It should have been easier with just two children at home for half of the day, but somehow it wasn't. The newly acquired mixed breed puppy was part of the problem. One morning, after sending the older kids off to school and walking the puppy, who thought it was nice, but had no idea of what was expected of her, I crawled back under the covers and snuggled up to Butch. I couldn't really sleep with Dante and Kelly loose in the house, but I was savoring a dreamy trancelike state close enough to sleep to be delicious.

Kelly came rushing into my room and shook me.

"Mommy, Mommy, Wendy's eatin' up all the garbage. Come see!" she said, as if it was the most exciting thing that had ever happened in her young life. When I saw the disaster in the kitchen, I thought she was right. The miserable little reddish brown mutt had all of the garbage out of the can and strewn across the entire kitchen, and was munching selectively, as if she was at a smorgasbord.

"Dante!" I screamed. "Did you take the lid off the garbage can? And who let the dog out of the dining room?"

No answer and no sign of Dante. The puppy stopped browsing long enough to give me a look that seemed to say, *I certainly couldn't have done it. I just came in to help.*

"Kelly, get in your room and stay there until I clean up this mess. And if you happen to see your brother, tell him he's in big trouble," I said, all vestiges of dozing brutally shattered.

Getting angrier by the second, I walked across the kitchen a little too quickly for the conditions there, slipped on something extremely mushy, and landed spread eagle across the waxed tiles. Unless I was bleeding, I was covered in something that might have been lasagna from the night before.

"Damn it," I muttered under my breath, and tried to grab the dog that had stopped eating only long enough to ascertain that I was all right.

"Bad word," Kelly yelled from her room. "Gonna hafta eat soap."

By the time I picked the puppy up by the scruff of her neck and shoved her none too gently into the dining room where she was supposed to be barricaded, Butch, awakened by the chaos, walked to the edge of the hallway and surveyed the mess. He mentioned, drolly, that the floors needed to be cleaned anyway, but could I keep the noise down a little? I shot him a black look, and went over to check on the now whimpering puppy. Wendy acted like she was in real pain.

"I think her leg might be broken," I said to Butch, who was still considering going back to bed.

Her leg was broken all right, and I soon had the sixty dollar vet bill to prove it. Throughout the day, the kids looked at me with horror, as if there was a murderer in their midst, and whispered things that I was sure were about me. And Wendy, acting as if she was up for an Oscar, walked daintily through the house, parading the stark white cast on her front leg for all to see. The dog even managed to cast a few martyred looks in my direction, followed by heavy sighs.

Butch was quick to relate the story to the crew at Benny's, noting that I was such a tyrant that I had broken an innocent animal's leg. As for Dante, he stayed in his room all day long, "busy," he said, and the subject of how the lid to the garbage was removed, and how the puppy got out of the dining room was never resolved.

~

Days of diapers, wet spots on the floor from Wendy, who never quite grasped the concept of housebreaking, children fighting and general calamity rolled into each other, until I could barely remember what week it was, much less what day.

Signs of strain were appearing in our marriage. Butch spent his little time at home sleeping, renovating the house or watching television. We had no social life outside of entertaining the crew from Benny's, and that was dominated by shop talk. We rarely had extra money to go out, and without Stevie living with us, we had no one that we could trust to baby-sit. Lynn could only visit during the summers, since she was in school. Most of our money went to doctor bills and house repairs. The old house was drafty and damp in the winter and the linoleum tile floors were always cold. Rarely a week went by that one child wasn't sick, Kim with chronic bronchitis, Dante and Mike with bouts of tonsillitis and Kelly with stomach viruses.

I was becoming a virtual shut in, never leaving the house except to go grocery shopping. I didn't drive, and it would have made little difference if I did since we only had one car. It never occurred to me that if I had my license, I could have driven Butch to work and kept the car all day. But where could I have gone, dragging four small children with me? I remained safely tucked inside our little dream cottage, fostering the seeds of agoraphobia, which would sprout in years to come when I could easily leave the house, but was no longer able.

Neither Butch nor I were good at verbalizing our feelings. When I was growing up there never seemed to be anyone around who cared to listen. The hurt and resentment over being left alone so much would build up for months before I could voice my emotions. If Butch was aware of this, he either didn't understand or didn't care.

"We can't go on like this," I started up, one night after the Johnny Carson Show had ended. "I just can't live like this anymore. I might as well be widowed."

"You can't live like this anymore!" Butch shouted, jumping up off the couch to turn off the television. "My life is no picnic. I have to work sixteen hours a day to support four kids and a wife who does nothing but bitch and complain!"

I was taken back by his sudden anger.

"That's not true. I rarely complain and you know it. And you don't work sixteen hours anymore. Ten or twelve at the most. If you're going to be a martyr, at least get your facts straight."

"Oh no, you don't complain," he said. "But you let me know just what you think of me by not speaking to me for weeks at a time, and when I ask you what's wrong, you say, 'nothing'."

"And when *can* I speak to you? You're either at work or glued to the TV, telling me to be quiet every time I open my mouth. All I've ever asked of you is a little of your time. It seems you don't care to share your life with me. Or with the kids either, for that matter."

"Fine, make me out to be the heavy," he snapped. "If you don't like your life with me, then leave. I am the way I am and I can't change."

"That's ridiculous," I said. "Anyone can change if they really want to. You just don't want to. I don't even know who you are, and the day will come when I won't want to."

"That's fine with me. Either accept me as I am, or go and live with your mother. You're just like her, anyway."

"That's the rottenest thing you could have ever said to me," I said, softly, close to tears. "And I'll never forget it."

"Yeah, I can believe that," he said. "Everything I do, you store up in that unforgiving, coldhearted mind of yours. You better make up your mind what you want and then just do it." He stomped out of the living room and went to bed.

I slept on the couch because real men don't, and let the tears, which had been building fast, stream down my face. I went back to my usual routine of not speaking to him, and he ignored me, conveniently working longer hours to avoid the tension in the house.

All of our fights were the same. Eventually one of us would break down, usually me, for in spite of what Butch believed, I couldn't nurture a grudge for long. I was often annoyed with myself for not remembering why I had been mad in the first place. When he noticed that my attitude toward him was friendlier, he would bring me roses or a bottle of my favorite brandy, and we would continue our relationship as if nothing had ever happened. The fights and issues causing it would never be mentioned again, until our next fight. The theme of my discontent was always the same. Butch had no time for me or the kids and placed his work before us.

And it wasn't like he was a scientist working on a cure for cancer to save humanity. I felt that he didn't really love me. He thought I was ungrateful. Working and making money was the only way he knew of showing his love.

~

The January that Kelly turned three, I began to get physically sick. It was a long, cold winter that year, and the kids and I were cooped up for months with little or no reprieve. I went to several doctors, who could find nothing wrong with me. My strength weakened, until I could barely get off the couch to care for the children. Easter came early that year, and I had spent the previous months sewing Easter outfits for the kids and myself. Holidays were always traumatic, because Butch had to work during each of them; except for Christmas Day, when the restaurant closed. On Easter mornings, he stayed home long enough to see the kids attack their baskets and find the hidden eggs, then take pictures of them in all their finery. I walked the six blocks to the church with them, then home for Easter dinner, which none of them ate after gorging on candy all morning. I came to hate Easter.

That Easter was the worst of all. Kelly came down with pink eye (conjunctivitis) a few days before the holiday and on Easter morning all the kids caught it and generously passed it on to me. We spent the miserable day huddled on the couch under blankets--curtains drawn because the sun hurt our eyes--unable to enjoy the chocolate bunnies popping up from all their baskets. To make matters worse, either Dante or the puppy ate the medicine salve for our eyes, and I couldn't afford to refill the prescription until payday. Butch gave us all a wide berth, treating us like lepers and pointing out that, strangely, he never got sick. *No*, I thought, *you bring home all the diseases from work and deposit them here and then leave before you catch anything*. I wished many a sickness upon him, in spite of the money he would lose, but to no avail. The man was perpetually healthy.

I grew steadily weaker and during the kid's spring break from school, I went to my mother-in-law's home. I couldn't care for the kids, and even Butch was worried. I was positive I had a fatal disease and my children would be motherless. Mom took one look at me and put me to bed, taking over care of the kids. But bed rest wasn't the answer. I had been resting for weeks and only getting worse. I made an appointment with my childhood doctor, whom I had not seen in years and geared myself for the worse. I had decided, since poring through Reader's Digest Medical Encyclopedia that it was either tuberculosis or heart disease, with an ulcer thrown in from worry.

"Micki," the doctor said after examining me. "No one can look as healthy as you do and be organically sick. I don't think you have an ulcer, although you may have given yourself gastritis from the built up stress. I'm going to prescribe for you what I call the poor man's psychiatrist. Take it for a few months and if you don't feel better, we'll run some tests. And Micki, please try and get out of the house more."

I went back to my mother-in-law's home feeling better already. It had never occurred to me that the sickness might be all in my head. It made me angry and embarrassed to realize that my mind could have such control over my body without my knowledge or consent. I was determined to overcome it. What the doctor had prescribed was small doses of Valium, but I didn't know that it was a tranquilizer, or I might have balked at taking it. Butch drove down to Easton and took us home, and I threw myself feverishly into belated spring cleaning, not omitting the dreaded and dirty door moldings. My strength returned quickly, even though nothing had really changed in my life except my attitude.

A few weeks later, a phone call from my sister-in-law cheered me up even more. Marie asked me if I wanted to become a godmother. She had married the year before to a tall, handsome red-haired Irishman, and was pregnant with their first child. I was honored and thrilled. Baptists never had godparents and I liked the thought of playing a special part in my nephew or niece's life. I wasn't Catholic and that was a major requirement for godmotherhood. The thought of becoming a godmother to a new baby overcame my reluctance to embrace Catholicism. After all, I reasoned to myself, if the kids had to be raised as Catholics, the only one who could instill lasting moral and religious beliefs into them was their mother.

Within a week, I set up semi-weekly appointments with Father Christopher, our local parish priest. He was a young priest, one of seven sons in an Irish family, and all his brothers were priests. For some reason, he neglected teaching me the basic catechism that I needed to know in order to participate in the church, probably assuming that I had learned that segment of church dogma during my first sessions with the priest who'd married us. He was much more interested in theology and we went rounds arguing heavy church theories, with Butch sometimes joining us and acting as Devil's advocate.

The one thing that the young priest was definitely adamant about was birth control. My own view was simplistic.

"If God, thousands of years ago when the earth was under populated, said, 'Go forth and multiply,' surely when the earth was overpopulated he would advise the opposite."

"Oh no, no, you're absolutely wrong, as wrong as you can be," said Father Christopher. "It's against God's laws and the laws of the church."

"But Father," I said, reasonably, "following that premise, I'll end up becoming pregnant every year of my life until I'm past childbearing age."

"No, no, you don't have to be pregnant," he said, looking somewhat aghast, and not directly at me, but somewhere off towards the massive dark drapes that dominated the windows of the small rectory. "All you have to do is abstain by using the rhythm system. It's worked for millions of Catholics all over the world."

"Sure, Father, that's easy for you to say," said Butch, who had come a little early to pick me up. "Do you really think you could lie in bed with someone who looks like my wife and not touch her?"

The priest turned a deep shade of crimson and shook his head resolutely.

"Then you must be strong and sleep in separate bedrooms."

"Then you must be crazy," Butch said as we rose to leave.

Eventually, the priest's arguments started to wear me down. If I was serious about becoming a Catholic, I should be willing to abide by the laws of the church. After all, when I was a bible toting Baptist, I obeyed the laws of that church without argument.

One afternoon, when Ann Eunice stopped by for coffee, I asked her opinion.

"Well," she said, with a wise look on her face that I had come to rely on, "I would never presume to tell you what to do; but I, personally, have used the rhythm system in planning all three of my children and found it to be simple and effective. But, of course, only you can decide what's right for you."

I hated it when she said that. I wanted her to presume to tell me what to do. I was tired of having to make all my own decisions. Even Butch, when I mentioned the subject to him that night in bed, just shrugged and said, "Do whatever you want. Just don't get pregnant," and promptly fell asleep; leaving me to wrestle with my dilemma.

After much soul searching, I decided to try the rhythm system. The first month was a success and the second. What Ann Eunice had neglected to tell me was that the method required some rudimentary math skills. While the method simply entailed marking off certain days of the calendar, the third month I counted wrong and became pregnant--unless it was an immaculate conception, which I somehow doubted.

Ann Eunice shook her head in disbelief when I told her the devastating news, amazed at both my stupidity (although she would never infer it) and my good luck. She had married six months before and was trying desperately to have a child while she still could. After much stalling, she had finally agreed to marry John Flannigan, a happy, always joking, handsome Irishman, who had lived on the block for twenty or more summers; and had been in love with her for years. After they were married, Johnny moved into Ann Eunice's home and commuted to the city, where he worked as a book printer.

Ann Eunice's children adored their new stepfather, and all the happy couple needed to make their near perfect lives complete was a child of their own. Instead, Butch and I were about to become parents for the fifth time in seven years. I was not only terribly upset by this pregnancy, but felt guilty as well, for not wanting something that my friend wanted so badly.

I was furious with the priest. When the next lesson was due, I stormed into the rectory and blamed the entire thing on Father Christopher, threatening to name the baby after him if it was a boy. The priest gave me a blank look, seeing no irony in my choice of names, and perhaps felt relief. There was no longer any reason to argue about birth control. The damage was done.

~ Thirteen ~

Knowing that I would have to tell Butch that I was pregnant again, I kept putting it off. He was in high spirits lately and the household was in harmony. Somehow he set the mood for the entire family. If he was happy, I was happy and consequently the kids were happy. And throughout his sporadic black moods, always work related, the whole household reacted as if there was a dark, ominous fog enveloping us. I tried not to let Butch see how sick I was, for the nausea accompanying this pregnancy was severe; but he noticed.

"What's wrong, honey?" he asked one night after the kids were in bed and I had slumped onto the couch in a wretched heap. "You're pale and tired all the time, you snap at the kids for no reason, and last night I thought I heard you crying in your sleep."

His face was full of genuine concern, which broke through my reserves and I started to cry.

"Promise that if I tell you, you won't be mad," I said, wiping my eyes and turning to face him directly.

"You know that there's nothing that you could ever tell me that would make me mad, unless you said that you stopped loving me. And that wouldn't make me mad. It would break my heart."

"All right, but remember, you promised," I said, and drew in a deep breath. "I counted wrong on the rhythm system and I'm pregnant again." I started to reach for him, but the minute the words were out of my mouth, he jumped up, swearing under his breath and rushed out of the room. He broke his promise. He was angrier than I had ever seen him.

Butch didn't speak to me for the rest of the night and stayed in our bedroom, reading. When I went to bed, he moved as far away from me as he possibly could without falling off the bed. I tossed and turned 'til morning, filled with guilt and self-pity.

Butch didn't get out of bed the next morning. When I finally swallowed my pride and went in to remind him that he had to go to work, he was thrashing and moaning from a migraine headache. He told me to get out and leave him alone. You would think he was carrying the baby and throwing up around the clock, I muttered to myself--angry that I now had to bear the guilt of both the pregnancy and giving him one of his dreaded migraines.

Benny stopped over that afternoon, concerned because Butch had never missed a day of work for any reason. The heavy man strode into the house, his huge domineering presence soaking up the entire living room, making me feel small and insignificant. He never said a word to me, acted as if he didn't see me, and walked right through the house to the bedroom where Butch was trying to sleep.

"What's wrong, Buddy?" I heard him ask, his tone suddenly warm and full of concern. I strained to hear their conversation, but their voices were drowned out by the sounds of the kids playing in the next room. "Damn him!" I said aloud. How dare he come barging into my home with no invitation, butting into my life? If Butch's relationship to Benny was love/hate--father/son--the feeling between the man and me was pure dislike. He ignored me whenever he could, and I countered his outrageous lack of good manners with sarcastic barbs that sounded innocent to anyone listening; but he got the message. Benny seemed to feel that I kept Butch away from him, although how much more of his time could he have hoped for? Competing with a woman for Butch's attention would have been hard enough, but trying to keep my husband from the clutches of a "Big Daddy" was beyond my scope.

Now this obnoxious man was in my house and Butch was probably telling him that I was pregnant again, with Benny was offering his heartfelt condolences. I was getting madder by the minute.

When Benny brushed by me to leave, giving me a halfhearted glance of feigned pity, I turned away and left the room. He sent his own doctor to the house later that afternoon, who gave Butch a shot of something to knock him out. The next morning his migraine was gone, but my resentment lingered.

Between the stress that hung over our house and the dreaded morning, afternoon and evening sickness, I decided to take the kids out of school and stay at my in-laws for a week or two; long enough to get my thoughts together. The day after we arrived, I started to lose the baby. My feelings were torn. A miscarriage would be the ideal solution; yet, though I knew we shouldn't have another child, I didn't want to lose the baby.

"Just go about your regular business," my obstetrician said, after examining me. "If you're meant to lose the baby, then you will. The fetus is probably defective."

His attitude served to make me more determined not to lose the baby. I was certain that the problem was with me, not the baby.

"Mom," I said to my mother-in-law when I returned from the doctor's office. "I think he's wrong. I don't believe that there's anything wrong with this baby."

"Oh Micki, I think you're absolutely right. Just stay off your feet for a few days and see what happens. I'll take care of the children. And don't worry. I'll pray for you every hour. God won't let anything happen to this baby."

After several days of bed rest, the bleeding stopped, only recurring if I walked around too much. The kids and I stayed for almost two weeks, but the day arrived when I had to return home. The kids couldn't afford to miss any more school.

~

That summer, Butch worked a lot of extra hours because Benny had opened up a cabana club at one of the beach hotels in Atlantic Beach. But I was sure that the sight of my fat belly and straggly hair, usually tied up in a pony-tail to be cooler, repelled him so much that he would have worked in a coal mine to be away from me. I still tried to stay off my feet as much as possible so the few times we saw each other, I was lying on the couch with my feet propped up, a resigned look on my face.

The kids tried to help and they were well-trained in taking care of themselves. Poor Kim took on the most responsibility and I felt guilty inflicting it upon her, but I was determined not to lose the baby. In my own defense, Kim was born to rule. With school over for the summer, the household was much more relaxed and there were fewer set rules. The kids could play outside all day and the piles of never-ending laundry were smaller. Kelly still wore diapers at night and Kim, Mike and Dante had occasional lapses. I had managed to potty train all the kids by the time they were eighteen months old, but I was never successful at training them through the night. It was probably my fault. I couldn't housebreak the dog completely, either.

One day, when I had finished changing the sheets on four bunk beds, I threatened the three older kids with having to wear diapers again. Mike became angry, throwing an immediate temper tantrum, but Dante was secretly relieved, I think, because it took the responsibility away from him. Kim just grinned, confident that the conversation certainly didn't include her.

"Someday, Mom, when I grow up, I'm going to put you in jail if you make me wear a diaper and I'm never letting you out," Michael told me sternly.

Nice child, I thought.

"All right guys," I said, "you all have one more chance and then it's back to wearing diapers." But my compassion for their dignity only created more laundry.

~

By late September I was almost into the seventh month of pregnancy and the bleeding stopped completely. I was over the hump. I could relax now, secure in the knowledge that if I went into labor, the baby had a fighting chance.

Since most of my catechism classes had been postponed, I hurriedly made them up in the hope of being baptized before Marie's new baby, Carl, was christened. The night before I was due to be baptized into the Catholic Church, Father Christopher called to ask me something.

"I just wanted to clarify one small thing," the priest said. "And then I feel that I will be able to baptize you in good faith."

"What is it, Father?" I asked.

"You must promise me that you are not using birth control devices that are against the laws of the Church."

"But Father, I'm pregnant. I don't need to practice birth control and after the baby is born, I probably will use birth control pills. In fact, I know I will."

"No, no," Father Christopher said. "Just promise me that you won't use it now. You can't be held accountable today for what you may or may not do in the future."

I was appalled by the hypocrisy of the young priest and the Church that he represented. We argued for a while but he would not budge his warped line of reasoning. Any joy I might have experienced in embracing

Catholicism was destroyed that evening as I caved in to his wishes, disliking myself as I did so. I would play by church rules and be baptized, to become godmother to my nephew, but from that moment on, there would be no love or allegiance for a religion so devious in attaining its goals.

The next morning I was baptized, with Ann Eunice and Johnny standing up for me as godparents. The kids thought it was neat to see a grown woman leaning under the baptismal font. After it was over, we all went back to the Flannigan's for a party. A few months later, I heard that Father Christopher had ended up in a rest home for priests. Rumor had it that I may have contributed to his nervous breakdown. All I know is that I never saw him in the parish again, and felt no remorse for his condition.

~

Much to the amazement of my doctors, I carried the baby nearly full term. My due date was December twenty-fifth, Christmas Day, but I had no intention of being in the hospital away from my children over the holidays. Butch, having seen me make my own delivery dates before, didn't argue when I asked him to take the kids and me down to his parents the second week of December. Dante's third birthday was on the thirteenth of the month and we planned a large party for him.

As with my other births, I communicated my desires to the baby and labor started the morning of Dante's party. I labored all day, through the night and into the next day. Nothing happened. I walked the length of shopping malls, up steep sidewalks and up and down stairs. Still nothing. All I got for my efforts was exhaustion.

Finally, late in the evening on the day after Dante's birthday, Noelle made her entrance, slowly and peacefully, with no wails of fury like her siblings. The most harrowing moment was when the doctor thought he heard two heartbeats. *Oh no*, I thought, as another pain tore through my body. *Not twins! That would not be funny, God.* But the other heartbeat turned out to be my own.

Noelle entered the world covered in a cheesy vernix, the "angel's veil" of legend, a sign of a gifted or special child. And so she was--the miracle child that the doctors had thought was defective. Instead, she was perfect.

The day we left the hospital, the nurses were decorating the halls for Christmas, and one of them sprayed "See You Next Year" on the elevator doors, in liquid snow.

"Oh no you won't," I called out to them, laughing. "This is absolutely the last time you'll ever catch me in a maternity ward!"

Earlier, I had said goodbye to my best friend Jeanie, who was spending her days outside the nursery, but not as a nurse's aid this time. She had just borne her first child six weeks before Noelle was born. Christian was due months later, but Jeanie went into premature labor, while alone in her New York City apartment.

For the past six years she had been working in the city as an assistant buyer, on her way to becoming the fashion designer she had dreamed of most of her life. And it was in the city that she'd met Nucho, a handsome young man from Italy, who spoke with a sensual, continental accent. Jeanie fell hopelessly in love for the first time and with the wrong man. They were divorced a year after marrying at the Justice of the Peace office in Long Beach, with Butch and I standing up for them as witnesses.

Nucho was charming, but irresponsible. Somehow, Jeanie found the strength to leave him and struggle on her own. The night her water broke, she called us, terrified and alone. Butch drove into the city to get her and then to Easton where she had planned to deliver the baby. Poor Christian weighed a mere two pounds, ten ounces at birth, with lung complications, and was barely alive. He was allergic to every type of baby formula and had to have special concoctions mixed for him. Months after he was born, he finally went home and Jeanie began the arduous task of raising a child alone in New York City. He gained weight quickly, and soon surpassed Noelle. Years later, Noelle and Christian would tell their friends that once they had spent five nights together, naked.

~

My sister-in-law Lynn had gone up to Long Beach to watch the kids while I spent the mandatory five days in the hospital with Noelle. Lynn was nineteen, lovely, and capable of watching her four nephews and nieces. She did a remarkable job, considering that the kids did everything in their power to undermine or override her authority. Kim made up new house rules, especially concerning bedtimes and snacks, and almost convinced her aunt that they were legitimate. Michael slipped into his famous stubborn mode and reminded her that he was not required to take orders from anyone except his mother, father, and God. Dante saw the visit as an opportunity to connive his godmother, Lynn, into giving him everything he wasn't normally allowed.

"But Aunt Yinn," he said, on the first day that she was there. "Mommy always lets me have the Pway Doh. Sometimes she even says, "Dante, why don't you get out the Pway Doh and pway? She says it all the time. Wight, Kimba?"

Kim never lied outright, and shrugged her shoulders, claiming that while she couldn't remember me saying that, it was possible. Kelly laughed loudly, called her brother a 'wotten liar', and told him that he had "better ship up or he was going to shape out." Lynn had spent enough time with the children to doubt her godchild's story, and the Play Doh remained on the shelf in the highest kitchen cabinet, out of Dante's reach. Lynn spent a harrowing five days, but when I returned home with the new baby, there were no signs of her turmoil.

We spent that Christmas in our own home, with another Christmas baby. There was something special about having a baby at Christmas. It seemed to make the holiday more meaningful. On Christmas Eve, Noelle lay in her tiny cradle next to the wooden manger her father had built, surrounded by two sisters, two brothers, a dog and a cat. Above the cradle the Christmas tree looked especially festive with the hundreds of homemade ornaments that I had crafted while pregnant, including the rows of fresh popcorn beads that the kids and I had tediously strung with needle and thread. Butch and I looked at each other and without speaking, agreed that we had the world in our hands.

~

The house on Nebraska Street was too small to house five children. Poor Noelle, a sweet, uncomplaining baby, had to sleep in the tiny laundry room next to our bedroom. There was room for the washer and dryer, her crib and dressing table and nothing else, except standing room. When her first sounds began to mimic the sounds of the washing machine's cycle, Butch and I knew that it was time to consider moving to a larger house. By the time she was five months old, Noelle's repertoire included the entire washing machine cycle and a few sounds from the dryer: "Whish, whish, glup, glup, ummmmm".

Noelle was a comical baby. She was cute, and would have been even prettier, if she didn't insist on making ridiculously funny faces. The other kids doted on her. The girls mothered her and the boys treated her like the china doll she was. Loud noises always made the baby jump, and our house was never without loud, sometimes indefinable noises.

Ann Eunice and Johnny worshiped Noelle and took their roles as her godparents with the utmost seriousness. Right after Noelle was born, Ann Eunice became pregnant and Johnny, being the Irishman he was, insisted that Noelle had brought them their long-awaited good fortune.

That summer was not a summer for spending time at the beach. It was bottles and diapers and strollers all over again. We did brave the trip a few times when Jeanie brought Christian to visit, but most outings turned into disasters. Two infants, sand, sun and four cranky children to watch turned the day into a disaster. Dante would head for the water, causing my heart to stop, and Michael would wander up and down the beach, until a lifeguard found him and returned him to me. Kelly hated getting wet sand on herself and Kim was simply bored. Only Jeanie seemed to enjoy herself.

~ *Fourteen* ~

In late August, my mother called and asked if she could see the kids. I hadn't seen her in nearly four years, although Billy had started sneaking over to see us without her knowledge. My mother had married again to a man she met while working at a cocktail lounge, another sweet-talking Italian. Butch didn't want me to see her, but I felt guilty depriving my children of a grandmother. I justified the terrible things that she had said and done, blaming it on the temper she couldn't control. She came over one afternoon, nervous and high strung, bringing Lenny with her. They both made a big fuss over the kids and the new baby. I was warm and cordial to her, which she gratefully accepted, but inside, my heart was still like stone. I realized that I would probably never again have feelings for my mother that were more than the respect she deserved for bringing me into the world. There would always be an empty place in my heart, cut away by the cruel words she had hurled at me when I was pregnant with Kelly.

~

Right before school started Kim had her hair cut in the newly fashionable pixie style. She hated it although the rest of the family thought it was cute, if a little drastic. Kim came home with me from the beauty parlor, stomped into her room, slammed the door and refused to come out. It was her father's day off. In an effort to cheer her up, but with a touch of sadism, he walked into her room and picked her up. She kicked and screamed, but he ignored her and carried her outside, dumping her unceremoniously into Michael's red wagon. Then to her utter chagrin and indignation, he wheeled her up and down the block so that the entire world, as she knew it, could view and appreciate her new haircut. Before this, Kim was embarrassed and angry over her hair. Now she was outraged! When the ordeal was over, one that only her father and brothers seemed to enjoy, Kim once again stormed to her room.

After supper, while Butch ran an errand, Kim came up to me and somberly informed me that she was going to run away from home, and she was taking Michael with her. Remembering what my mother had told me when I attempted the same thing at five years old, I felt I had the matter well under control.

"Well," I said. "I'll really miss you both, but if that's what you have to do, then go ahead. But you can't take anything that your father and I have given you, not even clothes. You came to me naked and that's the way you're going to leave."

Michael looked appalled, but Kim just stared at me, not saying a word.

"And I don't know why you're leaving, Michael. You didn't even have your hair cut."

He just shrugged and gave me that secretive smile of his that never told me anything and followed Kim back into her room. I thought I had handled the matter with expertise and was feeling quite smug, until I happened to overhear them talking in Kim's room.

"Look, Mike," I heard Kim say. "We'll only take the clothes that Grandma gave us. We can even take the money that she sent us for Easter."

"But Kim," Michael said, complaining. "I don't have any underwear that Grandma gave me."

"Never mind, Mike," Kim said. "You can wear some of mine."

I walked outside and sat on the lawn chair and was still out there, crying, when Butch came back from the store.

"It worked with me," I said. "Why didn't it work with them?"

"Because they're smarter than you are," Butch said, trying to hide his smile. Besides, when your mother tried it on you, you probably didn't have anything from your grandmother."

"No, you're right," I said. "It just wouldn't have occurred to me. What are we going to do now?"

"Stay here," he said. "I'll be right back."

He went into the house and spoke to Kim and Mike. He refused to tell me what he said to them, but they never made another attempt to run away from home.

~

Sadness struck us in late fall. Jim and Sally had left for Florida right after Labor Day, to work the tourist season. We got a call one afternoon, telling us that Jim had died of a massive heart attack. We were stunned, and dreaded having to tell the kids, who at this point had not been introduced to death.

We mourned Jim, yet we were angry at him. The man refused to listen to his doctors. He was diabetic, markedly overweight, and smoked a dozen cigars a day. He drank soda and ate too much candy and sweets. Yet, he loved life and preferred to live as he did rather than suffer restrictions.

We couldn't put off telling the kids. We gathered them together and gently told them that Jim had gone to live with God. All of the kids became upset, but Kelly went ballistic. She screamed, she raved, threw everything she could reach and finally ran to her room and threw herself onto her bed. For weeks, she refused to say grace at the dinner table, or her nighttime prayers, because God had taken Jim away from her. She was only three and a half.

~

Winter passed, long and bleak, but with an exceptional amount of snow. One snowfall literally buried Long Beach, knocking out power lines and causing five and six foot drifts. It was the most severe blizzard in years, and broke the monotony of a flat beach town in winter. The kids talked me into letting them go outside the next day after the snow stopped and the winds had died down. It was a wonderland outside and I shared their excitement, bundling them up in snowsuits, boots and gloves. Kim, Mike and Kelly were cautious in the deep snow, but Dante attacked the deep drifts with more enthusiasm than brains, and soon disappeared for what seemed like a lifetime, in a steep drift by the back porch. I dug him out and made them all go back inside, in spite of their pleas. Later we heard that one of Kim's classmates was killed during that snowfall, when a drift that he had burrowed into, collapsed in on him.

The highlight of the winter was the birth of John Andrew. Ann Eunice and Johnny were excited, especially Johnny, because it was his first and only child. Noelle had just turned a year old and although she still slept in the tiny laundry room, she had long since exchanged her washing machine routine for human words.

~

Spring arrived none too soon that year. With Noelle toddling around, it seemed that the house was wall to wall children. Butch and I spoke more often of moving. By this time, I didn't just want a bigger home; I wanted to move away from New York. I was sick of the long, dreary winters, and yearned for Pennsylvania, where everything was green, where huge mountains defined the land, and the streets were clean, and uncluttered with debris; too empty in the winter, too crowded in the summer. More importantly, I wanted Butch to leave Benny's and look for a job with a future. Benny was becoming even more possessive and I was tired of struggling with him over Butch's time. I sensed that if Butch didn't leave Benny's soon, he probably never would.

~

In the middle of April, Kelly became seriously ill. At first it seemed to be an ordinary stomach virus, and I wasn't too concerned. Kelly rarely complained when she was sick, and several days passed before I decided to play it safe and take her to the doctor. The pediatrician also thought it was a virus, but because her white blood cell count was slightly elevated, she sent us to a surgeon on the off chance that it was appendicitis. The surgeon wasn't sure either and wanted to hospitalize Kelly for tests. Meanwhile, her white cell blood count was getting higher, she was complaining of pain, and Butch and I were getting scared. The surgeon was old and not the most reputable one in town, which added to our fears.

Butch stepped outside the doctor's office and found a pay phone. He called the office of the children's surgeon that had operated on Dante years before. His partner, Dr. Bronster, was covering for our doctor. This doctor didn't like the sound of the symptoms and advised him to get Kelly to South Nassau Community Hospital as fast as possible and he would meet us there. Now we were really frightened. Kelly was listless and running a high fever.

When the doctor arrived, he examined Kelly and said that she needed an emergency appendectomy. Within minutes, she was in the operating room and we were left to pace the waiting room in fear. None of our children had been seriously ill before, yet worried as we were, we thought it was a routine, if hurried, operation.

Four hours later, the surgeon came out; a huge, heavily bearded man with large hands and a deep voice. We rose in unison to meet him.

"Well," he said, obviously exhausted. "It's going to be touch and go, but I think Kelly might make it through the night."

"What do you mean, Doctor?" Butch asked, turning pale. I sank back down into the lounge chair. He told us that Kelly had been walking around for several days with a ruptured appendix and peritonitis had spread throughout her small body. She was critically ill. The surgeon added that he would keep watch throughout the night and if she was still alive by morning, she might have a chance.

He left us numb and fearful. Butch found a phone and called Ann Eunice, asking her to take the kids to her house for the night, and then called his parents, who said they were leaving at once to join us. We were allowed to see Kelly for a few minutes when she came down from surgery. She was unconscious, but she was thrashing and tossing so violently that the nurses could barely restrain her. I thought that was a good sign. Kelly was fighting to live.

"Please God," I prayed, *"Please let her live."* Butch hugged me tightly, worry and grief written across his face. We sat in the waiting room throughout the night, clinging to each other for support. I kept talking to Kelly in my mind, willing her to live. I couldn't conceive of a life without my little girl.

By morning, Kelly was still unconscious, but she had made it through the night. The doctor offered us little hope, saying that she was critically ill and we would just have to wait and see. Kelly remained unconscious for four days and nights. Butch and I took turns sitting with her, which allowed us some time at home with the other children, who were frightened. My mother-in-law took care of them and ran the household.

In the early predawn hours of the fifth day, I was home getting some sleep and Butch was sitting by Kelly's crib. She opened her eyes, smiled at her father and said, "Hi Daddy, I was just talking to Jim." The crisis had passed. Kelly would live.

During the following three weeks of post-surgical care, Kelly was not an easy patient. She hated the hospital, especially the doctor, who must have seemed like a giant to such a small child. This gifted man, with his gigantic, hairy hands, did open heart surgery on infants, often for no pay. After saving Kelly's life, under near impossible circumstances, the man was a god in our eyes.

Kelly refused to eat the hospital food, even though it was delicious. She threw my mother out when she came to visit her, as well as Olga and

Gene, the old German couple who adored her, and just about everyone else who came to visit. She wouldn't hang her "get well" cards on the wall or keep any of her presents with her. She had no plans on staying and didn't want signs of permanence around her. She insisted I stay with her every moment and thought that I spent the nights there. I would stay until she fell asleep, and then go home. Early the next morning, I would slip back into the hospital before she awakened. My sweet little girl was becoming a tyrant.

The day Kelly came home from the hospital, I decorated the house with party favors and balloons and invited friends and neighbors for a welcome home party. The minute we entered the house, Kelly marched into her room, slammed the door, and refused to come out. Still angry over her ordeal, she made our family life a hell for some time. She had to stay on a special diet, excluding all refined carbohydrates, which were her staples, and continued to have recurring stomach problems. Yet, she survived and I was grateful to God, who let me keep my child.

~ *Fifteen* ~

August 23, 1981

As time ticks slowly away in the ICU, I feel as if I'm watching a movie or play. Sitting in the overstuffed chair--hard, wooden arms worn from use, the upholstery sagging from the weight of those who had sat here before--I vaguely observe the scene around me. It helps keep my mind off the horror of why I'm here.

Hospitals have an urgency about them, as if the process of birth, death or recovery must be kept to a strict schedule. Nurses scurry about, doctors stride through the corridors outside the waiting room, and the room is filled with the electric sensation of high drama. I am numb, unable to make more than the most rudimentary movements.

I sense that people are watching me--nurses, friends, and neighbors. Do they think that I will faint or jump up and scream hysterically? Pelusos don't behave like that, although I might. I want to faint dead away and wake up in yesterday's world. Scream? Oh, I'm screaming all right, with every fiber of my being. But no one hears me.

God, why have you forsaken me? Didn't I pray all my married life, asking nothing of you, except to keep my children safe? If I have done something to offend you, then take me instead. Please God, take me.

I remember another time when I pleaded with God to take my life. I was nearly sixteen years old, and had just experienced the bittersweet pain of a first love. I couldn't eat or sleep when the love wasn't reciprocated and fell into such a state of emotional exhaustion that I developed pneumonia. It was 1957 and a severe form of Asian flu had swept the nation, killing thousands. I didn't catch the flu, but the pneumonia nearly killed me. I spent over a week in an oxygen tent, hovering between this world and the next.

I remember, before I lost consciousness, seeing a young woman in the bed next to me, deathly ill from the flu, struggling for her life. She had a worried husband leaning over her. From the muted conversation, I learned that they had several young children. *Save her*, I implored my maker. *Take me. She has children and a man who loves her. I have nothing.* I wasn't being particularly altruistic; I just no longer cared to live. When I regained consciousness, the crisis passed, the first thing I did was turn to the bed next to me. It was empty. I cried then, for the young woman and for myself and vowed never again to try and bargain with God.

Now here I am again, bargaining, begging, pleading, while knowing with a certainty that the die is cast, and there is nothing I can do.

I hear familiar heel-stomping footsteps coming swiftly down the corridor. The swinging doors to the waiting room burst open as my husband rushes into the room. All of the emotions I have felt throughout this hellish evening gush forth--fear, desolation, heartache--as I rise to greet him. He falls into my arms and cries out, "Oh, my baby." We are one in our sorrow. I remember nothing more.

~ Sixteen ~

During the summer of 1968, we sold the house on Nebraska Street. Kelly had recovered from her brush with death and Noelle was eighteen months old. After Benny took the interest off his "gift," we still made a profit, more money than we had ever seen at one time. Butch went to Benny and told him that he was quitting and moving the family back to Pennsylvania. Benny, barely hiding his shock, begged Butch to reconsider. The end result was an extended leave of absence. I had to give Benny credit for being an optimist--he was confident that Butch would be back. I was positive that once we crossed the border into Pennsylvania, Benny's magnetism would fade. This was the first real power play between Benny and me and I intended to win. The man, I had to admit, was genuinely hurt by Butch's leaving. He was born into the wrong century and would have made a wonderful land baron or even a king, smiling benevolently down upon his subjects while subtly controlling their lives.

We moved into Butch's parents' home and stored our furniture and belongings in their basement and garage. Wendy and Cinder had to be given away, which broke the kid's hearts, and mine, but it would have been unfair to inflict my in-laws with two animals. Their grandchildren were "animals" enough. My mother-in-law and brother-in-law, Donald, who was sixteen years old, were thrilled to have a family of seven invade their home. My father-in-law seemed a little apprehensive--with good reason. His young grandchildren would spend the ensuing weeks wrecking his house and driving him crazy.

We almost bought a lovely farmhouse situated on seven acres of rolling green hills, crossed by a tiny, rushing brook, in the Pocono Mountains. Butch almost accepted a position as a restaurant manager in Allentown, twenty miles from Easton. That summer was full of almosts. But when Butch was faced directly with the finality of what we were doing, he couldn't go through with it. Benny, keeping in contact by phone, played his final ace by offering him a substantial raise and elevating him to the position of General Manager. None of the jobs in the Easton-Bethlehem-Allentown area could come close to matching Benny's offer.

"What do you think we should do, Mick?" Butch asked one night as we lay in his parents' bed in their master bedroom.

A huge picture of St. Theresa of the Roses hung on the wall facing the bed and the saint watched us intently as we talked. It was one of those pictures whose eyes followed you wherever you went and it made me shiver. There was never any chance of our making love under the watchful, stern, disapproving eyes of the pious, young saint. Butch's face was twisted with worry and indecision as he awaited my answer.

"You have to do what you can live with," I said. "As for me, you know what I want."

He sighed heavily and turned over in an attempt to lure a sleep that would not embrace him that night, or many nights to come. I lay awake, too, mourning the decision that I knew he'd already made. The battle to get out of New York and away from the constricting clutches of Benny was lost to me. The fat man had won again.

~

The kids and I spent the rest of the summer in Easton, and Butch returned to Long Beach and stayed at Johnny and Ann Eunice's home. He had until school started to find a new home for us. I was so depressed and disgusted that I refused to help him house hunt.

"Buy whatever you want," I told him over the phone. "Just make sure it's big enough."

"Well, I found one that I kind of like," he said, with forced enthusiasm. "How about if I drive down and pick you up so you can see it?"

"I don't want to see it," I said, hating myself for the chill in my voice. "Call me when you've bought it and I'll come up when it's time to move in."

"Goodbye," he said quietly, and hung up.

I knew that I was hurting him, but I was so disappointed that I couldn't help it. When would the day come, when what I wanted mattered?

I kept my word and did not see our new home until the moving truck pulled up to the front door. I had been suffering pangs of curiosity, but was too stubborn to admit it. As we moved our furniture into the house with the help of Butch's brothers and sisters, I could voice no objection or opinion on what I thought of his choice. A severe case of laryngitis had reduced my voice to a whisper. Sometimes I marveled at the sense of irony or sick humor inflicted by whatever fate it was that shaped our lives. I hated the house on sight, which was obvious by the morose, sullen look on my face. The kids loved it and Butch was proud of himself. I was still so angry to be relocating back to New York that moving into the Governor's Mansion wouldn't have pleased me. By the end of the warm, sultry September day, everything had been unloaded and everyone was exhausted.

The house was on Knickerbocker Road, in Island Park, a small village that lay just over the Long Beach Bridge, with lovely tree-lined streets running parallel to the canals. It was only a three-bedroom bungalow, small bedrooms at that, but the living room was twenty-five feet long and had a red brick, working fireplace. The dining room was formal and a good size, the kitchen average, and the one bathroom very small, just big enough to house the tub, sink and toilet. To add to my aggravation, the entire bathroom was pink--tub, tiles, toilet and sink.

The house had a full basement with low ceilings, but was partially finished into one long playroom for the kids. Outside the playroom was an antiquated bathroom that resembled an indoor outhouse with a dilapidated toilet and shower. The basement floors were cement and smelled of mold, and the back door led to a cement patio with plastic sheeting for an awning.

The yard was beautiful, in spite of the foot-high unmowed grass. There were three apple trees and two plum trees in the large backyard, and two stunning mimosa trees side by side in the front. The mimosa trees were in bloom, bursting with feathery flowers that resembled exotic birds sitting amidst the palm-like branches. Even I could not help but love the yard. I kept my appreciation to myself, refusing to yield to inevitable acceptance.

"How do you figure this house is big enough?" I whispered hoarsely, as Butch and I prepared for bed in a room that was too small for our furniture.

"Look Mick, this was the best I could do with the money we had. I'm sick of your attitude. If you don't like it, leave with my sisters tomorrow. I don't know what else I can do to please you."

He turned off the lamp on the nightstand and rolled over on his side. *Why do I always get thrown out of my house whenever we have a disagreement?* I asked myself. In the books I read, the television programs I watched and the personal experience of some of my friends, the woman always kicked the man out. I was definitely doing something wrong. I should go back to his mother's, I thought. But I knew that would serve no purpose.

In spite of myself, I soon became caught up in arranging the furniture and decorating the house. The rugs in the living room and adjoining dining room were a deep royal blue, which showed every minute piece of lint that fell upon it and had to be vacuumed almost daily. Still, the pile was lush and deep, and the color cast warm shadows across the walls. The three girls had to share the larger of the three bedrooms and the boys, the smaller one. Butch planned on renovating the basement and putting some of the kids down there. The kids, used to small, cramped sleeping quarters, were so thrilled with their huge backyard that nothing else mattered. Noelle, happy to be out of the tiny laundry room she had called her own for almost two years, thought her new house was wonderful.

In spite of my sour disposition, I couldn't help but consider the possibilities for expansion readily available in the house. Butch, encouraged by my improving frame of mind, came up with new and innovative plans.

~ *Seventeen* ~

Butch's sister, Lynn, got married a few weeks after we moved in. She had been engaged to Bob Mohr, who had served in Vietnam as a medic, and returned home safely. Before the wedding, he had built a house for them beneath the Pocono Mountains on the outskirts of Allentown; a beautiful ranch home perched on a hill and flanked by endless mountains and fields. It was hard not to feel envious.

I was a bridesmaid and Kelly was the flower girl, just as Kim had been a flower girl at Marie's wedding. Noelle, dressed in a beautiful pale green dress that Grandma had sewn for her, thought she was Cinderella and the reception given solely in her honor. She danced and preened throughout the entire evening, long after the rest of us were worn out from the festivities.

"Nice party, Mommy," she said again and again. "I yike parties." Her bright, dark, almond-shaped eyes sparkled with pleasure.

Her father remarked that when she grew up she was destined to become either a socialite or a caterer.

~

The winter in the new house seemed endless. I never saw a single person in the neighborhood. New Yorkers like to hibernate during the winter, tucked safe and snug within their homes until the first signs of spring. Many nights, I took walks through the neighborhood, depressed by the lack of any apparent life and wondered how a densely populated area could be so desolate.

We settled into our old routine. Kim entered fourth grade, Michael, third, and Dante, first. Kelly went to morning kindergarten, which she hated, pretending to be sick every day. Noelle stayed home with me. She was a timid, quiet child--except at parties, and until Kelly came home to play with her.

Butch and I had long since patched up our differences, mainly because I was able, if not willing, to adapt to any given situation. My dislike for Benny festered into something close to hatred. Now that he had what he wanted he was magnanimous to me and superficially friendly. I vowed to myself that the battle had just begun. I did not like losing.

In spring the unthinkable happened. Early one morning, Butch nestled close to me in bed, just as the sun and moon were fighting for dominance of the coming day. He whispered, nuzzling my neck. "Is it safe?" and continued kissing my ears, a particularly erogenous zone for me. I recall, half asleep, mumbling "no" and he remembers me saying "yes." The result was wonderfully warm lovemaking which I thought that I dreamt.

One month later, I realized I was going to be the mother of six. Feeling justified that I was not at fault this time, I told Butch at once, rebuking him for his lack of common sense. He should have remembered that I was comatose in the mornings.

"I don't believe this crap," he said, pacing up and down the long living room. "What's the matter with you? Don't you have any brains?"

"Me?" I said. "How could you possibly believe that any time of the month is safe for us, with the brood we already have?"

He shot me a look of pure venom, rushed out the front door, jumped into our new station wagon, revved the motor, and spun out.

"Bastard," I said, glancing around to see if the kids had heard, but not giving a damn. I reached for the ceramic owl that my brother Billy had given me for my birthday, took it from the fireplace mantel and smashed it to pieces on the tile floor of our bedroom. But it wasn't the owl that I wanted to smash to pieces. *I loved that damn owl,* I said to myself, not bothering to stem the tears running down my face. *Why didn't I break something of his--like his thick skull?*

The nausea was unbearable. I had come to the conclusion the sickness was in proportion to the mental and emotional state of my pregnancies-- always stressful and traumatic. I spent the next three months on the couch. It was a comfortable red velvet, two-piece Italian provincial sectional that curved at one end. We had bought it a few months after moving in. I slept on it every night, too furious to have even one hair of Butch's body brush against mine. He never understood that when I was angry I wanted him far away from me, preferably on another planet.

In the mornings I dragged myself up, and sometimes got the kids fed before running to the small pink bathroom to throw up. Cold cereal was the best I could manage, which was fine with most of the kids, but two-year-old

Noelle felt that breakfast wasn't breakfast without her favorite--eggs. Just the thought of a fried egg would start me retching.

School finally let out for the summer and after breakfast, the kids dressed and headed outside to play, while I dragged myself to the red couch and plopped down on it, as tired as if I had put in an eight-hour day.

One morning I noticed Noelle toddling past me with something yellow covering half of her face.

"Noelle," I mumbled, trying not to move any parts of my body that would trigger the nausea. "What's smeared all over your face?"

"Yeggs, Mommy. Jo makes me good yeggs. I yove yeggs," she said, continuing on her way.

"What are you talking about? Who's Joe and where have you been?"

"Cross da street at Jo's house. She make me good yeggs. Alweady told you dat," she said, her eyebrows lifted in impatience.

Later that afternoon, when I had a thirty minute respite from heaving, she took me by the hand, crossed the street in front of our house, which was sparsely traveled, and led me to the infamous egg maker. Jo Romano introduced herself and said that yes, she had been cooking eggs for Noelle all week. The other kids had told her that I was sick and Noelle was insistent upon having her eggs.

In the midst of my misery, I met my first friend on the block. Jo, in her early twenties, had three girls: Donna, a lovely blond child, the same age as Kelly; Paula, a dark-eyed, waifish little girl, was the same age as Noelle; and the chubby, black-eyed baby, Tina, was almost a year old. They lived in the upstairs apartment of a large, two-family house, with her father renting the apartment downstairs. Jo's husband, Paul, worked as a chef at the Italian restaurant across from the train tracks on the other side of Long Beach Road. We talked over tea, until the building nausea sent me hurrying home to be near the bathroom. But I had met a new friend and was considerably cheered. Noelle, in spite of threats and admonitions, continued to breakfast with the Romano's, but only on the days she could convince Jo to make fried eggs.

~ Eighteen ~

Jeanie called me from Manhattan one afternoon with a proposition. I was three months pregnant now, feeling better, and the relationship between Butch and me had gone from hostile to guarded.

"Micki," Jeanie said, with an enthusiasm that I knew meant she wanted a favor. "You remember that *little* Saint Bernard puppy that Nucho bought for Christian?"

"Yeah, I remember. The one that defecates all over your apartment while you're at work. The one that causes all your babysitters to quit within a week. What about her?"

"Ah, she's so sweet, a real doll-baby, Micki. You'd love her."

"Jeanie, spell it out. What do you want from me?"

"Well, ya know, the apartment's just too small for a dog, and I'm too tired at night to bundle up Christian and take Luna for a walk. Would you keep her for me, just until I get a bigger place? You've got that big yard and your kids would just love her. She'd be no trouble at all."

"No way, Jeanie. Butch would kill me. He's already said no more animals, after Kim slipped that black kitten in and he didn't find out for weeks. He'll never agree. We're barely speaking to each other as it is."

"Let me talk to him," Jeanie said. "I can handle him, and if he says yes, will you take her?"

"Okay, but he's not going to say yes."

Somehow Jeanie talked Butch into driving into New York City to pick up the dog for her intended short stay. I was impressed. Jeanie called me that afternoon to tell me that the dog and Butch were headed home. The kids were excited and could hardly wait. I got caught up in their enthusiasm and found myself delighted over the prospect of a new puppy in the house.

About four in the afternoon, Butch walked purposefully into the house, looking rather pale, I thought, and stared me right in the face.

"Your dog is in the station wagon. Go get it."

I didn't like his tone of voice, or the menace that lurked beneath his words. But I gave it little thought and hurried out to the car, the kids running behind me.

Then his attitude made sense. The puppy, which was the size of a full-grown medium-sized dog, started jumping up and down, excited by our arrival. She growled in apprehension, while wagging her tail at the same time. I was a little nervous approaching her. When I got a better look at the back of the station wagon, nausea returned full force. The dog had thrown up and had diarrhea throughout the entire car, then slid in it and was covered from head to toe in excrement of the worst kinds.

It took me hours to clean the car, intermittently running back to the house to throw up. Then I attempted to bathe the dog and realized she had a terror of water. Butch was morbidly delighted over my plight. He told me later that the dog had started heaving a block away from Jeanie's apartment and then had the runs, causing him to drive all the way home in rush hour traffic with the windows down and his head out the window. He'd fervently wished that the "damn mutt" would leap out the window and he didn't intend to retrieve her. I had recovered enough by now to laugh hysterically, forming the mental picture he described--a grave mistake. He sulked for days.

The dog was banished to the basement. Jeanie had neglected to tell me that Luna, Italian for moon, suffered from food allergies. Every morning I went downstairs with a shovel, mop and bucket of ammonia and water and shoveled up the mess, then raced upstairs to heave my breakfast. It was like owning a small horse. Luna, who did possess a remarkably sweet personality, tried hard to win me over those first few months, but she didn't have a chance. The dog was a full year old before she was housebroken, and that was mainly because she was kept outside on a long chain, except during the nights. Jeanie feigned total innocence and claimed that the dog had never displayed such traits when living with her.

The baby was due around Christmas and, as usual, I didn't intend to be in the hospital over the holidays. I think that I may have conveyed that wish to my body and the baby inhabiting it a little too strongly.

We were enjoying Thanksgiving Dinner with the Flanagan family when the familiar cramping of early labor started.

"I'm not ready for this," I complained to Ann Eunice. "I'm not even packed."

"Well the baby is ready, so you had better get down to Easton quickly."

"Quickly?" I asked, laughing. "When have I ever had a baby quickly?"

Another reason for my annoyance by this unexpected event was that resentment still festered over Butch's reaction to this pregnancy. I had been making tentative plans to take the Long Island train to Grand Central Station and then a bus to Easton, when the baby's due date neared. That would fix him, I had thought, indulging in my usual tendency to cut off my nose to spite my face. Now it was too late.

Ann Eunice kept the kids and Butch drove us home to grab some clothes for myself and the baby. We headed for Easton, Butch noticeably nervous, me put out by both the pain and the timing. He stayed with me all night and halfway into the following day. Then he had to leave to cater a party for Benny, and took his sister Marie and her three-year-old son, Carl, my godchild, with him. Marie would care for the kids while I was in the hospital.

The next few days were a nightmare. I labored day and night, the pains coming three to five minutes apart--nothing happened. Every day, after a pain-wracked, sleepless night, I would get dressed and go to the obstetrician's office. And every day the doctor would say, "Sorry, you're not dilated. It's false labor." Butch kept calling, asking if he should drive back to Easton, but I saw no reason for it.

This doctor was covering for my regular obstetricians, who were on a hunting trip. He was very young, inexperienced, and in my opinion, not too bright. Partly, his attitude was my own fault. Pride dictated that I force myself to fix my hair, put on make-up and look presentable before I went to see him. As a result, since I didn't look like a young woman in severe pain, he assumed that I wasn't.

By the end of the third day, I was bleeding, leaking amniotic fluids, dehydrated, and had dropped fifteen pounds. Yet the doctor kept sending me back to my in-laws with my false labor. By the beginning of the fifth day, I was exhausted, running a fever, and Butch, anxious by now, drove back to Easton.

"I've got to go to the hospital," I told him, when he rushed in the front door of his mother's house. "I can't take any more of this. Maybe they'll at least give me something for the pain."

I lay secluded in the labor room for the next eight hours, alone most of the time. The baby showed no signs of making an appearance. The labor room nurses relented and let Butch in the labor room with me, something that wasn't allowed in 1970. He silently rubbed my back, his face as twisted with pain as my own, while I attempted to cope with the relentless contractions. I tried breathing the way I had watched our cat when she delivered her kittens, but it only helped a little. The few times the young doctor checked me, I begged him for the labor-inducing drug that I had needed for most of my past birthings.

"Just one drop of that medicine," I said, gasping between contractions, "and I promise you that the baby will catapult out before you can get me to the delivery room."

"Sorry," he said.

Sorry seemed to be his favorite word.

"I can't give it to you. You've had five children already and it could rupture your uterus."

He made a quick exit to avoid further argument. Funny how a well-used uterus could withstand five days of continuous assault, but not one drop of the drug to bring on instant delivery.

The agony went on. I lost track of time. *Was it night or day? What day was it?* As I became more delirious, Butch became angrier and more scared than he had ever been in his life. He tried to find the doctor, who had conveniently disappeared. Just as well--Butch was ready to inflict serious bodily harm upon him.

I gave up. I could no longer take the brutal ravages to my body.

"I quit," I said to Butch. "I'm not having this baby."

A strange thing happened then. All pain stopped. The contractions continued as strongly and often as before--the nurses could see and feel them. But no pain. My body felt calm, relaxed and quiet. I started to turn over on my side and slip into the first real sleep in five days and nights, when I felt a sudden, quick movement.

"I think the baby's coming," I said to one of the nurses.

"Let me take a look," she said, and gasped as the top of the baby's head became clearly visible.

"You're right," she said. "Let's get out of here. And whatever you do, don't push."

As if I had the strength. We barely made it to the delivery room where the "missing" doctor was waiting. The baby slipped out as if sliding down a park slide; no pain, no pushing, no feeling as if I had passed a watermelon. It was over at last.

Nicole Jean was eight and a half pounds, content and pleasant, unaware of the last horrendous days of her journey. Her head was perfectly shaped. After all, I had done all the work. She had lain at the bottom of my womb as if she was waiting for an elevator door to open and let her out. She was beautiful, and as always, the trauma of bringing her into the world faded from my memory.

~

Marie said that the kids and the dog and cat were all well-behaved during my absence. *Not likely*, I thought. I could read Mike and Dante's faces, in spite of their feigned innocence. They were older now, ten and eight, but no less impish and troublesome. Seven-year-old Kelly and three-year-old Noelle were thrilled with their new sister, but Kim, an eleven-year-old with more responsibility coming to her, just sighed.

Butch became concerned that the usually happy baby always seemed to cry whenever he held her.

"Of course," I said, snidely. "Babies are sensitive. She knows you didn't want her."

His face fell as he handed her back to me and quietly left the room. It was a cruel thing to say, but he deserved it. Once again, I was amazed at the male mentality. He never believed me after I told him it wasn't true, and from that day on, he took great pains to win Nicole over. Nicole became her father's favorite, if for no other reason than guilt.

~

When Nicole was two months old, Butch and I decided to take a second honeymoon, not that we had a first. It was evident our marriage needed it. Marie offered to come up again and stay with the kids. We decided to stay at a near-by ski resort for three days and I made the mistake of letting Butch make all the arrangements.

I had never skied, but my brother Billy, an avid skier, came over with his equipment and we practiced on the living room rug. Billy had married the year before and his wife Pat had just delivered their first baby on the twenty-sixth of January. Nicole and her cousin, Susan, a beautiful blond, blue-eyed cherub-like infant, were only two months apart.

Marie and her son, Carl, arrived the evening before we planned to leave. Carl was a little younger than three-year-old Noelle and they were great pals. I was packed and ready, and had given the kids the usual lecture on what not to do while I was gone, mainly in regard to terrorizing their aunt. I went into the baby's room to change her before bedtime. Butch and his sister followed me in, hoping that Nicole would be awake.

As I removed her one-piece sleeper, Butch noticed that two of her toes were red and swollen, although she wasn't complaining.

"Look at her foot, Mick. What's wrong with it?"

"My God," I said, after closer inspection. "I think she's wound strands of her hair around her toes. Quick! Get me the baby scissors. The flat ones."

Nicole had developed the unique talent of weaving things with her fingers--bits of lint, thread, hair--whatever she could glean from her mattress and clothing. This odd talent must have extended to her toes. She had wound hair that had collected in her sleeper, probably due to static from the dryer, around two of her toes.

"I've never seen anything like this," Marie said, watching me attempt to press Nicole's toes flat enough to snip the hairs. The fine baby hair was wound tight, like sharp wire and would soon cut off her circulation.

"We've got to take her to the hospital," I said. Marie and Butch agreed. Her father was starting to get a little green.

The hospital was only five minutes from our home. We were taken right into the emergency room. A small, chubby Asian doctor walked over to us and examined Nicole's foot.

"Oh dear," she said, "This is terrible. How could you let this happen?"

I was at a loss for words. When I tried to explain what I thought had happened, she brushed aside my explanations and accused me of neglecting my child. Butch turned pale and quickly left the room, leaving me to deal with the outraged doctor.

The doctor continued to voice her dismay, oohing and grimacing, until I was ready to shout, "Shut up and cut the damn hair!" Her unprofessional manner was ludicrous. She was acting the part of a near-hysterical mother, while I stayed calm and cool-headed.

Instead of using the more sophisticated surgical scissors to try and cut the hairs, she started to slowly and methodically unwind them, which caused the baby to cry out in pain. Nicole screamed and the doctor moaned and keened until I was ready to scream myself. It was good that Butch had left. He would have probably fainted--possibly the doctor with him. I was not queasy over what should have been a simple, relatively painless procedure. I was furious.

The last of the hair was removed and Nicole settled into steady sobbing. I held her in my arms to soothe her while the idiot intern put antibiotic salve on her toes and bandaged them.

"Watch her more carefully," she said, shaking her head in disapproval. "A little longer and she could have lost both her toes."

I could have cheerfully strangled the woman. Butch drove us home, and I could sense that he blamed me, too. It was a fine way to initiate a second honeymoon, and I intended to tell Marie that we couldn't go.

"Don't be silly, Mick," she said, when we returned home. "Go on and go. I can handle the baby. I've got the doctor's instructions and if anything should happen, you're only an hour and a half away. Go. Don't be a jerk."

Butch agreed with her, and between them, they browbeat me into submission, aided by the older kids who had their own reasons for wanting us to leave. My heart wasn't in it. I had never left an infant so young, and I was still angry over both the cowardly and accusing attitude that Butch now denied having displayed.

~

We left early the next morning. The ski lodge was in Milford, Pennsylvania, bordering upstate New York. Butch had directions from the customer who had recommended the place. Of course, he got lost. And of course, being a man, he refused to stop and ask for directions until nearly three hours had elapsed. We arrived at the lodge which was intended to rejuvenate our marriage.

It was the ski lodge from Hell. After walking into the lobby and looking around, I decided that "seedy" was too complimentary for its decor. Condemned was closer. There was a large fireplace dominating one wall, the stone front charred black from ill-tended fires. The walls were papered in either a very old or much abused print--peeling in strips and blowing about from drafts of wind of no particular origin. An ugly, ornate chandelier from the 1920's hung from the center of the room, half the bulbs either missing or burned out. I sat down in amazement on the one piece of furniture in the lobby; a dilapidated, spongy sofa, then leaped back up, poked unceremoniously in my posterior by one of its many broken springs.

"Let's check out the dining room," said Butch, in a tone meant to sound optimistic. He was pretending not to notice that this hovel was not quite what he had planned.

"All right," I answered in a dull monotone, still shocked by my surroundings. "I am starving."

The dining room was long and narrow, with card tables set up in rows. The seats were folding chairs. The room was packed with college students in various degrees of inebriation. The smell of the food set out buffet-style was familiar. I had suffered it all through high school. The heavy, choking aroma of incense permeated the room, covering up the obvious scent of marijuana.

"We don't have to eat here," Butch said, quickly sensing my mood. "Let's check into our room and look for a restaurant."

Our room was in a motel adjoining the lodge and it was uninhabitable. Two single beds (perfect for a honeymoon) were covered in torn, dirty white chenille bedspreads. The mud-colored rug was worn, bare in spots and filthy. I looked around for a clean place to set my suitcase down, but couldn't find one.

"I don't think this is going to work," I said to Butch, in a flat, overcome voice. I didn't know whether to laugh or cry.

Butch nodded in agreement and then I saw the flicker of an idea cross his face.

"Let's try another place," he said, as we piled our belongings back into the car. "We can even drive to Connecticut or further upstate."

"I don't think so," I said quietly. "Let's quit while we're ahead. You should have checked this hellhole out, not taken the word of a stranger. You always do this. It's a nightmare that's just going to get worse. Take me home."

He tried all the way home to get me to change my mind, but I knew disaster when I saw it and couldn't be swayed. He ended up becoming angry, I remained self-righteous, and the ride home was silent, heavy with emotions, none of them pleasant.

~ *Nineteen* ~

June, 1973

The next six years on Knickerbocker Road passed quickly. The kids grew so fast that I could barely keep them in clothing, and often worked into the night sewing clothes for them. Like seedlings, babies grow steadily, but suddenly, by the ages of six or seven, they begin to shoot up like tulips in the spring. The only baby I had left was Nicole, who was almost three years old.

She was a beautiful child, with wide brown eyes nearly as startlingly large as her brother Michael's, but tinted with a reddish hue, which added sparkle. Her dark brown hair fell in waves down the middle of her back and her slim little body, devoid of baby fat, made her resemble a miniature woman. She was spoiled rotten, but not of her own doing.

"You're creating a monster," I told the rest of the family repeatedly, as they continued treating Nicole like the little princess she most certainly was not. "And when it gets to the point where you can't stand her, don't hand her back to me to fix!"

They refused to heed my warnings. Kim treated Nicole as if she were her own daughter. I rarely fed her, dressed her or bathed her. It was nice for me, no doubt about it. I was able to enjoy a child without doing any of the nasty, boring or mundane parts of childrearing. Kelly and Noelle were crazy about her, to the point where they even let her toddle around with their friends without objection. The boys, smaller duplicates of their father in looks, temperament and chauvinism, protected their baby sister and treated her as if she was a fragile little doll, instead of the manipulative tyrant she was fast becoming. I could hardly blame them. She was so incredibly cute and lovable--when she wasn't throwing temper tantrums in the middle of the stairs. At that age Kelly and Mike had directed their temper toward other people, but Nicole's rages were internal. I often had to splash water in her face to shock her, because she was so out of control that I feared she would throw herself down the stairs. Fortunately, her tantrums were rare and rightly so, since she usually got what she wanted. Although extremely bright, she refused to talk until she was well past two years old, because she could point to whatever she wanted and have a willing sibling jump to get it for her. Her father, of course, spoiled her even more.

As the children grew taller and older, I expanded socially, gained self-esteem and my previous narrow lifestyle became enriched. Loneliness became a thing of the past through daily interaction with other people. My day to day existence still centered on raising half a dozen kids, being the "Kool-Aid Mom" for another dozen neighborhood children, and assistant den mother for Dante's Cub Scout Troop; but I was no longer trapped in solitude. My sole discontent was that Butch still placed his priorities in his job, instead of his family. My circle of friends and neighbors was broadening at such a rapid pace that it took away some of the sting of what I felt was rejection by my husband.

In the beginning of our third summer in Island Park, Butch and I had a major battle that seemed to blow up out of proportion. Consequently, I left him. Actually, I went to his parent's, which our friends found hilarious, and no one took seriously except for Butch and myself.

The fight was the same as all our fights, only much more intense. I complained that the small bungalow was suffocating me, he was never home, leaving me the sole responsibility of raising the kids, and that working at Benny's was an obsession, rather than a job. I resented going to school functions, church and social affairs alone, as if I were widowed. He countered that I never appreciated how hard he worked to take care of all of us. We were lovers and best friends most of the time, able to discuss anything that didn't involve his own emotions. I opened myself to him completely and needed for him to share his innermost thoughts and feelings with me. He thought that I wanted to expose his soul, examine it for the flaws he was sure existed, and then maybe stomp on it. Exposing himself was, to him, a sign of weakness and must never be shown. Strength had to be manifested at all times, or he felt he would somehow be emasculated or destroyed. What kind of person did he think I was that I could or would ever hurt him? In his way he was as much an enigma as our son, Michael, and I sensed that I would probably never understand either of them.

"Take me as I am," was his constant answer to my pleas.

But I had grown up and was no longer willing to do that.

"Then leave," he said, in a tone that was both sad and resolute. And I did.

The station wagon was overloaded with kids, clothing, favorite toys and books, and the huge ninety-pound Saint Bernard. I sat in the front seat, stone-faced and silent, wondering if I knew what I was doing and if it was right. Frustration and helplessness settled over me like a gray cloud. I was leaving my husband, going home to his parents, and he had to drive me there. He sat in the driver's seat, darkly angry and resigned, and turned on the ignition; the first step in separating himself from the family that he loved fiercely, but didn't know how to display that love.

About halfway through the two hour trip to Easton, the dog threw up. That action set the kids, who were still prone to carsickness, off on a retching, heaving and vomiting spree that didn't end until we pulled up in front of Grandma's house. Dante, the only one with a strong constitution, had turned a pasty shade of yellow, but he made the trip intact, except for the spray from his dog and siblings. Butch, who could never stomach bodily excretions of any kind, was furious and disgusted--glowering at me, as if somehow I had deliberately caused this catastrophe. I almost laughed, but restrained myself with great difficulty. I always carried plastic bags and paper towels for such occasions, but I had never thought to train Luna, who rarely traveled by car, to use one.

Grandma rushed out of her house and ran up to the car, consoled the kids, scolded Butch for being angry with them, and took them inside to refill their empty stomachs. Butch stayed only long enough to unload the car and have a cup of coffee while I cleaned up the mess.

We stayed in Easton nearly two months. Butch came down once a week to see the kids, but we rarely spoke unless it was necessary. He didn't leave me any money, but I was sure that he gave money to his father, who didn't pass it on to me. He gave five dollars allowance a week, an exorbitant amount, to each child, which thrilled them, but infuriated me, since my children were now richer by far than their mother.

The kids had a great summer. Over the years, we had often spent weeks during the summer at Grandma's, since Butch worked at both Benny's and the Atlantic Beach Hotel during the tourist season and was hardly ever home, except to sleep. They had a whole different set of friends there, as well as their cousins. I went out a few nights each week with Marie, who had divorced her husband shortly after the birth of her second son, Christopher. My sister-in-law, Lynn, had one son, Mark, who was five months older than Nicole, and was pregnant with her second child.

Gerry, Butch's older sister, was living at home. She'd left college permanently after being diagnosed with schizophrenia. Gerry had become delusional, but was so convincing that at first her hallucinations were believable. To her they were--it was her reality. She was stabilized on medications, but with terrible side effects, which made her lethargic and drowsy; sleeping her days away and roaming the house at night. It was sad to see a beautiful young woman with her life ahead of her, become stricken by such a physically wasting, chemical disease that affected her bright mind. Gerry had been in and out of hospitals over the past few years, but that summer, she was the best she'd been in years. She drove, she worked, and she fell in love--leading a normal life for a change. She met Oliver at the bowling lanes a few blocks from her home. By the end of the summer, she left with him and flew to Los Angeles, California, where they were married in a Catholic church. My mother-in-law was beside herself. One never knew when Gerry would have a schizophrenic episode. Being so far from home was torturous to her mother. The rest of us were ambivalent--wishing for Gerry to have a wonderful, deserved life, but also leery of how long she would remain healthy.

My old friend, Shirley, who still lived in Easton and had married one of our classmates, came to visit; picking up me and the kids and taking us to her home way out in the country. She had two children, whom I knew only from the pictures she faithfully mailed.

Mostly, I passed the time looking for work and contemplating my options, soon finding that there were none. The day I walked the twelve blocks back to my in-laws after applying for a job at a Dunkin' Donuts shop, I climbed the long cement steps to the back porch and threw myself down on the lawn chair. It was clearly evident that I would have to go home. Minimum wage was under two dollars an hour and I had no marketable job skills. Once my mother-in-law realized that Butch was not going to move back down to Easton with us, her attitude changed and I realized that she wanted me to go home and make my marriage work. She was upset enough over Marie's divorce.

Butch spent that summer working and sulking. I kept tabs on him through mutual friends, who insisted that he was lost, miserable and lonely; but I knew he was still not amenable to personal change. Towards the end of the summer, he came down on his weekly visit and asked me to go for a drive. We rode for about fifteen minutes, through the towering, lush mountains of neighboring New Jersey and up towards the Ingersoll-Rand Reservoir before he finally spoke.

"If you come back," he said, "I'll jack up the house and build bedrooms downstairs for the kids."

"What about us?" I asked.

"That's up to you. You know that I love you more than anything in the world. But I don't want you back unless you want to come home. You decide what you want to do."

"You know what I want."

He didn't answer and as we started back down the mountains, I realized that he was not capable of giving me what I wanted. I would have to learn to want less, or leave him permanently and reduce the quality of our children's lives. I knew I couldn't do that. They didn't deserve to suffer for my problems. We rode in silence for a long time, lost in our own thoughts, oblivious to the beauty around us, which only served as a backdrop for our misery.

"Well, what do you want to do?" he asked as we neared his parents' house.

"I'll come home," I said. "Do I really have a choice?"

"Yes," he said.

But we both knew that I didn't.

The kids and I remained in Easton until the house was jacked up and it was safe to return. Butch's brother Don went back with him to help, and Danny, who was a year or two older than Don, helped when he wasn't working at Benny's. Building contractors shoved metal poles through the length of the house, directly above the foundation, and lifted the house five feet. Then they filled in the open space with cement blocks. Amazingly, not a glass or dish or knickknack broke in the process; nor was there a crack in any interior wall.

Raising the house made an incredible difference. The two bedrooms on the first floor were combined into one twenty-five-foot long master bedroom, with a door at each end. Now when Butch felt the need to pace, as he often did, he could do so in a complete circle, through the bedroom into the living room and back. It also gave Noelle and Nicole and sometimes Kelly, two doors to try and beat down in the middle of the night, until we relented and let them into our bed.

The wall between Nicole's bedroom and the kitchen was broken through, which enlarged the kitchen to almost twenty-four feet long, twice its original size. Nicole's former room had been papered in a wild, screaming print of large black and red flowers on a white background, which was an interesting, if unusual motif for a kitchen. Butch built a staircase to the lower level along the outer wall of the kitchen, which took up space, but still gave the illusion of a very large kitchen. He found an old baker's counter in the storeroom of the Atlantic Beach Hotel, converted it into an L-shaped counter and covered the top in laminated garden slate; making a very impressive, unusual and workable kitchen.

There was enough room downstairs for three large bedrooms, side by side for the kids, plus a good-sized playroom right outside their doors. Behind the bottom of the staircase, he built a combination bathroom and laundry room. We worked together every minute that he could spare from work and were finished completely in about four months. Butch laid chipboard down for flooring and I used his router to carve lines in it, making it look like planked flooring, which was then stained and varnished. The router was heavy and vibrated so much that I added a few inches to my bust line along with the constant fatigue from the hard work.

Butch came up to me one afternoon, his day off, covered in sawdust and holding his bruised hand.

"Mick?" he asked. "Seriously, would you really mind if I didn't wear my wedding band for a while? I'm afraid I'm going to snag it on one of my tools and lose my finger."

"Go right ahead," I said with a perfectly straight face. "I can always have it made into a bullet."

He gave me an odd look, started to laugh, changed his mind, and turned and walked away. His wedding band remained on his finger.

Soon the walls were up, papered and painted and all the kids, who had been camping out on the living room rug at night, moved down into what was like their own apartment. What we hadn't figured on was that they also had their own outside door to come and go as they pleased. We decided to worry about that when the time came. Since they were beneath the main floor, they could make noise but we couldn't hear it. The upper level stayed clean, and orderly since everything the children needed was on their own level, with the exception of the kitchen. The little bungalow was now a tremendous home and we were proud of the changes, which also doubled the value of the house.

Ann Eunice brought John Andrew over to the house as often as she could and he usually stayed for several days. He was as close to my children as if he was related. In fact, he considered them his cousins. He was a year younger than Noelle, who was nearly six, and was still a remarkably handsome little boy, with sun-blond hair and opaque blue eyes, plus an intelligence level high in the genius range. He was also a little devil, but there was never a child that I couldn't handle.

Besides Jo Romano, I had met Carol McNeil, a woman my age, who lived three doors down from me. She was a little over five feet tall, with great-looking long, chestnut hair and lovely brown eyes, set off by a wide, generous smile. Carol had a daughter Nicole's age, Theresa, and a son, Danny, who was a year younger.

Rosie Miranda was a few years older than me, had six kids all about the same ages as mine and was Dante's den mother. She was even shorter than Carol and always wore those horrendous platform shoes and hot pants that had the good grace to go out of style quickly. Her hair swung below her shoulders, almost black and worn in a kind of curly disarray that matched her life. She was slim and tiny, cute in a precocious, sexy way and had a lifestyle similar to my mother's. Things happened to Rosie that just didn't happen to ordinary people. She was a flower child that never grew up. She lived a few blocks away in a huge, disorganized house right on the canal with a small private beach and a dock leading to the water.

Kathy and Scotty Scot moved into the house behind us a few years after we moved in. They had a ten-year-old boy named Chris and eight-year-old twins, Laura and Lynn, who became fast friends with Kelly and Noelle. Kathy was tall, attractive, with short, light brown hair, fine features, and sky-blue eyes. She had an ironic sense of humor which she drawled in a husky, whiskey voice. Scotty was, in contrast, a quiet, pleasant-looking man, who was difficult to get to know really well. Kathy would later admit that they fought constantly and their marriage was in serious trouble.

Pat, my brother Billy's wife, often dropped by with three-year-old Susan, who was still breathtakingly beautiful and lovable as well. My home was beginning to resemble a day care center and my social life reminded me of that old saying: "Be careful of what you wish for. You just might get it."

Those were also the "broken bone years." There was rarely a time when one or more of the kids wasn't in a cast. I was surprised that I wasn't arrested for child neglect. Their friends didn't break their body parts, just my kids; except for John Andrew, who was possibly the most accident-prone child that I had ever known. But he was more into cuts, scrapes and bruises. Dante, ten years old at the time, started the trend by breaking his hand while punching his friend, also named Dante, in the face.

"This wouldn't have happened if you didn't constantly get into fights," I said to Dante, who was quite pleased with his cast and the homework it kept him from completing.

"But Ma," he said. "He hit me first!"

"I don't care," I answered, glaring at him. "He's not the one in a cast. And his mother isn't stuck with a doctor bill of over $200.00. Get in one more fight young man, and you're grounded for the next six months."

He wasn't listening. He was seeing if he could dent the kitchen counter by banging it with his cast.

"Dante! Knock it off!" Butch said as he walked into the kitchen. It was a Monday, his one day off. "How many times have I told you not to make a fist with your thumb inside?"

"I didn't, Dad."

"Yes you did, or you wouldn't have broken your hand."

"Look," I said. "The two of you can argue over the finer points of fist-fighting. I've got better things to do. But I'm telling you both. The next time this happens," (and it would), "the two of you can sit in the emergency room for three hours. Not me!" *If the male race ever learned to use their brains as often as their fists, it would be a far better world*, I thought to myself as I left them to their discourse.

Michael was no better. He never completely shed the clumsiness of childhood, plus he was a daydreamer who could walk right into a wall with his mind on whatever it was that Michael thought about. He managed, on a school trip to a large park in Hempstead, Long Island, to jump off a swing in mid-air, breaking both his arms and nearly damaging the growth plate in his wrist.

"What made you do such a dangerous thing, Mike?" I asked, trying to determine if his wrist was really broken or merely sprained. He looked at me, his large brown eyes tearing from the pain and shrugged.

Even the delicate, lady-like Noelle somehow broke her collarbone while swinging from the extra length of rope hanging from the backyard clothesline. Her fall couldn't have been from higher than two feet off the ground. I started to wonder if the kids were getting enough milk, although the two gallons delivered every day by our local milkman seemed adequate.

Kelly never broke any bones, but her appendectomy well made up for it, and she still had not forgiven Dante for stomping on her "yiddle baby finger," a clean break, when she was four.

Kim was in a cast from her hip to her ankle one entire summer. Nothing was broken. She had grown so tall so quickly, over a foot during the course of a year that the cartilage in her left knee couldn't keep up with her bone growth. At thirteen, she was already two inches taller than I was. Puberty had kicked in early and she was slim, but shapely, with the longest legs I had ever seen, reminding me of a young foal, ready to bolt and run at any moment. Her unusual height was hard to bear, her peers being no less cruel than mine had been at that age, causing her to become moody, sullen and mouthy. When I found a pack of cigarettes in her room, I knew she was getting out of control.

Her father called her into the living room and showed her the pack.

"Where did you get these?" he asked. The look on his face was deadly.

She gave him the typical answer.

"They're not mine, Dad. I was keeping them for a friend."

"Don't make it worse for yourself by lying, Kim."

She was as stubborn as he was and stuck to her story.

"You like cigarettes so much? Start smoking!"

"No Daddy, please! I swear they're not mine."

Butch was firm, and made her chain-smoke what was left of the pack, until she ran into the bathroom to throw up. When she came out, white-faced and crying he took her in his arms and held her tightly, positive that he had made his point and that she would never smoke again. In one of his few attempts at dabbling in child psychology, he apparently forgot the episode when he paraded her around Nebraska Street to show off her hated hair cut. Now she was both humiliated and outraged again and would continue to smoke if for no other reason than to spite him.

Anyway, when Kim dislocated her bad knee during her favorite activity, roller skating, she was forced to wear the cast for six months. At the time aspirin every day was supposed to help, but all it did was aggravate her stomach. She hated the cast, which curtailed her frenetic energy and forced her to spend her days reading or playing her guitar.

Strangely, the cast also caused Kim to begin sleepwalking. Sleepwalking can be dangerous in itself, but Kim was unlocking the back door and leaving, making loud, banging noises as she dragged the cumbersome, heavy cast across the floor of the den. The noise was so loud that it always woke us up and we caught her before she wandered the neighborhood. We finally placed another lock on the door, where it was awkward for her to reach, and if she did, it was too difficult for a sleepwalker to unlock. Wearing the cast for months accomplished nothing, except to dislocate her hip from swinging her leg so much, and that fall she had to undergo knee surgery. Nicole was so upset about her "Muuny", which is what she called Kim, going into the hospital that Kim gave her a huge, hardcover book to take care of while she was away. When Kim came home, Nicole dragged that book, heavier than she was, across the living room and dropped it at her sister's feet. Nicole threw herself into Kim's arms and cried over and over "my Muuny!" The surgery accomplished nothing except to leave a gaping, disfiguring scar, shaped like a wide smile, which enlarged to two inches wide as she continued to grow.

Besides broken bones, the kids had an affinity for stitches, mostly the boys, and always on their faces where it showed. Nicole's bones were intact so far, but she tipped forward on her rolling toy pony and hit the floor hard, splitting her chin wide open. By sheer luck and in spite of her screaming and thrashing, I managed to butterfly the flap of skin that was hanging down, back to her chin, fitting it perfectly. I called Butch at work and told him that we had to get to the hospital again.

In the emergency room, the first thing they did was rip off my perfect butterfly bandage and then leave us sitting for hours. As a result, not only was Nicole left with an unsightly scar from the stitches, but the gash, exposed so long to the myriad of germs always present in hospitals, became infected. Her later pediatrician remarked that I should have trusted my own judgment and gone with the butterfly. But when your child's chin is gaping open and bleeding profusely, a mother realizes quickly that she is neither God nor a doctor. Nevertheless, I had learned a lesson. On other less serious calamities, I usually patched the kids (and their friends) up by myself.

~

Anita King started dropping over for coffee and/or lunch, as well as attending the parties we held after work for the crew at Benny's. It was a younger group now, since the old German waiter, Gene, and his wife Olga, whose health was failing, didn't go out much anymore. Russ and Gloria had realized their dream and owned their own restaurant in Reading, Pennsylvania, and since Jim died, his wife Sally made fewer trips up north from her home in Florida, finally stopping them completely. We also slowly eliminated the waitresses and waiters that we didn't particularly like, including the wicked witch, Hannah.

Anita had left her home in Sweden at the age of eighteen, and with her friend Liz, a Nordic blond bombshell, sailed on an ocean liner to California. Both found jobs as governesses and finally migrated east to New York; ending up as waitresses at Benny's. Originally they were both, particularly Liz, an annoyance to me, and I didn't like or trust them. They, along with other members of Benny's work crew, mostly waitresses and mostly young and attractive, would often drop by to see Butch when I was away in Easton, making me livid with jealousy.

Liz eventually returned to Sweden, but Anita stayed and married George King, a lighting and props technician for Broadway plays and television shows. They had a son, Steven, who was two years older than Nicole. After meeting me several times, Anita pursued a friendship, in spite of my reservations, until I finally realized that while she was an outrageous flirt, she was not a threat to me or my marriage. She was, however, a certifiable nut. Anita had no inhibitions whatsoever, and spoke her mind to anyone, friends and foes alike--even standing up to and berating Benny, who oddly enough, not only took it, but seemed to enjoy it.

She was particularly fond of one English word, which she pronounced "fock." There was no equivalent for that word in Swedish, only words for making love in a more loving manner, and she became obsessively attached to it. Usually that one obscenity, more than any other, grated on my sensitivities, but somehow hearing it with a Swedish accent and without malice, made it less offensive.

Anita was in her early thirties, stood five feet eleven-inches tall, was built boyishly slim, and wore wild, long curly wigs at work; keeping her own dark, straight, waist-length hair in an upswept bun on everyday occasions. She had large, pale blue eyes, which sometimes took on a greenish hue, always opened wide like question marks, a long turned-up nose and a wide toothsome smile. While not beautiful in the conventional sense, she was striking and turned heads wherever she went.

Anita was probably the first truly liberated woman I had ever met and she, more than anyone, contributed to the gradual loss of Butch's chauvinism. She laughed at him, mocked him and made him see the absurdity of his insecurities where I was concerned. Because of her, I soon realized that I did not have to live in a box marked wife/mother, but had the right, even the obligation to pursue my own interests. Soon, much to Butch's consternation, we became fast, close friends and were nearly inseparable.

Her husband, George, was a rogue. He was about twelve years older than Anita, Jewish, with a worse mouth than hers, but not as endearing, and a mind that was always on sex and off-color jokes. George was equally certifiably crazy. Butch and George soon became good friends, and I could only hope that George's influence on Butch would be purely superficial. Had it been the 60's and had they been younger, the Kings would probably have been underground radicals, rebelling against societal laws and regulations and fighting for individual freedom, mainly their own.

Danny, Benny's nephew and Butch's best friend, in spite of the ten year difference in their ages, brought his new girlfriend, Pamela Atkinson, over to meet us one evening. When we first met her, Pamela was an opinionated Irish girl of nineteen, whom Danny had met while they both worked summers at the Atlantic Beach Hotel. She had beautiful, thick, long hair, the color of gingerbread glazed by the sun, laughing blue-gray eyes, and the "Atkinson smile" which entailed a lot of white, even, perfect teeth; a trait shared by her large family of nine. In her own way, Pam was as liberated as Anita and between the two of them, Butch's days of Italian macho chauvinism was drawing to a close.

On Mondays, Long Beach and Island Park became ghost towns. Benny's and other restaurants were closed, as well as various other stores and facilities, while the active beach community took a day off to recuperate. Entertainment usually entailed traveling to other Long Island towns for dinner, or gathering in my home, which was the norm. Sunday nights Benny's closed early, and that was "Italian night" at the Peluso residence. There were always huge trays of eggplant parmesan, stuffed shells, sausage and peppers or lasagna, and always over a half-dozen mouths to feed. At that time, Italian food was still inexpensive to make, filling, and, of course, delicious. Being the only non-Italian woman in Butch's family challenged me to learn to create exceptional Italian food. It was no hard task, since most Italian food, except for Northern Italian delicacies, consisted of three ingredients, sauce, pasta and cheese in various shapes and combinations.

Even on ordinary days, it was rare not to have company for dinner. Anita only had Steven and thought it was wonderful to eat with a large family. Carol, with Theresa and Danny, felt the same way, and my sister-in-law Pat, was no exception. I was frenzied just feeding my own brood, and longed for a quiet dinner, completely alone. All of our husbands worked past dinnertime, so my house became a diner of sorts. It was an exhausting, exhilarating time, yet I sometimes yearned for the relative peace and quiet that I had once despised. But my life was always "feast or famine," too little or too much.

~

When our Saint Bernard, Luna, was about four years old, she had to be taken to the Bide-a-Wee Home on Long Island, where there was a guarantee that she would be adopted. The allergies that Luna had been born with now affected her skin, aggravated by being around grass and hot temperatures in the summer. She had painful, bleeding sores over most of her body which itched constantly. Luna bore her pain stoically, but it broke my heart to see her suffer. The alternative was fifty dollars every few weeks for allergy shots, which we couldn't afford. I made Butch take her himself, because I couldn't bear it.

"This is the last animal in this family," he said, trying to sound angry when he really was as upset as I was over losing Luna. "I'm always the one who has to get rid of them."

He took her while the kids were in school and I cried as they drove down the block, remembering that a great, loyal and companionable dog had shared our lives and I would miss her. I smiled, recalling the time she chased the bible salesman up the tall elm tree in the front of the house. Another time she nearly pulled the patio roof down and dragged it, along with the twelve foot picnic table, into the side of the yard because she saw me pick up the hose and she was terrified of water. She loved to play touch football, except that her touches bruised us for weeks and she often flipped the smaller children up into the air, as she plummeted through everyone playing, to catch the ball--and then wouldn't give it back. As dogs go, Luna was a special one. My rotten, coldhearted kids hardly seemed to notice or care that Luna was gone, except for Nicole, who had grown up with the dog. The rest of the kids were too involved with their friends and school activities.

~ *Twenty* ~

On February 11, 1974, Butch and I celebrated our fifteenth wedding anniversary at a surprise party held at Pamela's parents' house in Little Neck, New York. The dinner party was also in celebration of Pamela's twenty-second birthday. She had married Danny Testerman two years earlier and was the mother of a gorgeous little boy named Brian.

Olga and Gene were there, Danny's mother Fran, who still worked as a short-order cook at Benny's, all our close friends and Pam's large Irish family, which constituted a party in itself. The dinner was outstanding, embellished by fine champagne and a huge decorated cake. We received wonderful, thoughtful presents, mostly appliances to replace the ones that had broken down or were just plain old and outdated. It felt like the bridal shower I'd never had. After the party ended, Pam, Dan and Anita (George was in Las Vegas) came back to our house and we talked so late into the night that they all slept over.

The next morning as I was scrambling eggs for breakfast, I casually remarked to Butch who was complaining that the eggs were too dry as usual, that, "The last fifteen years were yours, but the next fifteen are mine." There was a stunned silence in the room as Danny, Pamela and Anita all looked over at me. Finally laughter broke out, softly at first, but it soon resonated into a roar.

"Good for you, Mick," Pam sputtered, trying to regain control of herself. "It's about time."

"Ya, Micki," said Anita. "And you better stick to it."

"Well, Butch old boy," Danny said, chuckling. "It looks like you're in for some rough times."

Butch, who hadn't laughed, said, "That's fine with me, Micki. I have no problems with that."

"Yep," Dan said. "Looks like there'll be no more watch-winding in this house."

He was referring to a dinner party the four of us had a few weeks before, when Butch reached across the table with his watch and handed it to me. I took it and started winding it.

"Sweet Screamin' Jesus!" Dan yelled, slamming his open palm down on the table, nearly overturning the gravy boat. "We all know you to be a tad chauvinistic, Butch, but you're making her wind your watch? Now I've seen it all!"

"No, no, Danny," I said. "You don't understand. His fingers are raw from cutting lemons at the bar and he can't wind his watch. Really!"

"Don't hand me that crap, Mick. You still bring the man coffee in bed every morning and wait on him hand and foot. Now you're winding his watch. Do you brush his teeth for him, too?"

He turned to Butch, who was laughing so hard that he couldn't talk and said, "You sure got it made, man. If I ever asked Pamela to wind my watch, she'd wind it around my neck."

"You got that right, Danny boy," said Pam.

"Listen Dan," I said, getting annoyed because he refused to believe me. "I only serve him coffee in bed to appease him."

"Appease me?" Butch asked, his laughter quickly stifled.

"Well of course. If I give you coffee in bed you get up in a pleasant mood and it makes my life easier. If I don't, you get up like a bear."

"Appease me," Butch repeated, in a voice that was both hurt and surprised.

"Good word, appease. I like it," Danny remarked. "Maybe his fingers really are sore and there's hope for you yet, Mick. What we have here might be the dawning of a new era."

"Look Dan," Butch said, "I can't respect the opinions of a man who voted for Jimmy Carter."

"Yeah, well if the rest of you had any sense we wouldn't have had Watergate," Dan answered, getting ready for a political debate, as usual.

"Nothing wrong with Nixon. His only mistake was getting caught. He was a good president and history will prove me right."

"I don't know," I said. "I watched him throw a temper tantrum on TV when he lost the California primary for governor. I don't want a president who can't control his emotions. Makes me nervous. Especially if he happens to be in the room with the D-Day button."

"You don't know what you're talking about, Micki," Butch said in disgust.

"No, I agree with her," Pam said. "No matter how much good he may have done, we don't know how much more he got away with. Besides, he looks sneaky and has a rotten personality."

"Countries aren't run on personality," Butch said.

"Let's get back to the politics in the Peluso house," Dan said. "I sense a definite shift in power."

"Astute observation, Dan," I said. "And it's only the beginning."

Butch tossed a throw pillow at me and I ducked a little too late. From that day on he never allowed me to serve him coffee in bed, although he occasionally served me.

That year, Butch made a great effort to fulfill my "the next fifteen years are mine," prophesy. He did, however, suffer a few relapses. Anita, Kathy, Carol, Rosie and I often went out to local restaurants, pubs and bars where we all knew everyone. Butch worked late and sometimes joined us later, but more often went home to bed. Our favorite hangout was Mariner's Haven, a restaurant overlooking the canal. They served succulent fresh lobsters and featured a piano bar. Nick was a local singer a few years older than us, and he would probably never rise above his present position. But he catered to us, playing piano and singing songs that he thought fit us. He sang, "The Most Beautiful Girl in the World" to Anita and "Malla Femina" to me, and Bobby Vinton's "Melody of Love" for Kathy. One night, time got away from us, because we were having deep conversations on the pros and cons of men, particularly husbands. Suddenly the bar door was flung open, like yet another scene in a Clint Eastwood movie, and Butch strode, as only he could, into the room and up to the bar stool where I was perched.

"Do you have any idea of the time?" he snarled. "Get home now!"

I was mortified, but determined not to show it. I acted as if his behavior was perfectly normal, rather than that of a raving lunatic, and said, quite calmly, "I will be home as soon as I finish my drink."

"Make it fast," he snapped. "I'll be waiting in the car!"

With that, he turned and stomped out of the bar, which had become so quiet that I thought for a minute I'd lost my hearing.

"God," Anita whispered. "I don't believe him. What's his problem?"

"I don't know, but he's going to be one sorry man when I get him home," I answered, trying to make it look like I was sipping my drink, when in fact, I was chugging it in fear that he would come in and make another scene.

I made a slow but steady exit from the lounge, as if I had all the time in the world, went out the door and ran to the parked car. I screamed at him all the way home and didn't stop until an hour later when my voice gave out. He had never seen me so furious and backed down with a few "I'm sorry's" and "I was worried about you," which I ignored. I slept on the couch.

Anita slipped in through the downstairs door around four in the morning and slept with the kids. That always spooked her, because she claimed that they all talked to each other in their sleep, asking questions and answering them as if they were awake. The next morning she told me it must have been a full moon, because right after I left, Carol's husband came in and dragged her home, followed by Rosie's husband, who did the same thing.

"Really weird," Anita said. "It was like it was contagious or something. George would never do that to me or I would cut his little Jewish heart out!"

"Well, I think it'll be a long time before Butch ever tries that again," I said, my throat still raw from yelling.

Every few months, Butch would take three consecutive days off from work and send me on mini-vacations with Anita, Carol, Kathy and sometimes Rosie. We would drive up to Vermont where one of Anita's friends lived and go out on the town, narrowly missing getting ourselves into trouble--like a bunch of teenagers. I had missed a normal teenage social life so I loved it. There were mild, innocent flirtations in some of the night spots we hit, which boosted my self-confidence and made me feel desirable. Butch rarely complimented my looks, unless we were in bed and it was his hormones talking.

The kids were not so pleased when I took my small vacations with the girls.

"Daddy makes us yucky, soft-boiled eggs and sits them in little tiny glasses," Kelly complained.

"Yeah," Noelle said. "And we don't know how to eat them. Besides, I like my eggs fried."

"And I hate eggs," Dante stated. "I want my cereal."

"I think it's neat," Mike said, grinning.

"Yeah, you would, Mike," said Kim. "You're not the one who has to scrub the egg gook out of those shot glasses."

"Don't go away no more, Mommy," Nicole said, crawling on to my lap. "I get scared when you're not here."

"Look kids, I'm only attempting to teach you to eat like civilized people," Butch said in self-defense.

On my next birthday, Butch gave me a crisp, new fifty dollar bill and sent Anita, Carol and me off to New York City on the train and subway. We left after lunch and George and Butch took Steven and our kids for a trip to Bear Mountain in Upstate New York. Carol dropped her children off at her mother's house.

For hours, the three of us strolled all through Bloomingdales looking for a present to buy with my birthday money. There were so many beautiful things to choose from that I couldn't make a decision and somehow hated to break that fifty dollar bill. As a result, we returned home empty-handed around eight o'clock in the evening, exhausted from so much walking.

The house was quiet. The kids were all in bed, including Steven, who was sleeping over. A delicious aroma wafted from the kitchen filling the entire house. It turned out to be shrimp scampi. The house was spotlessly clean and uncluttered.

"I don't think we're in the right house," I said to Carol and Anita.

The table was beautifully set, complete with candles and the stereo playing softly in the background. Carol was envious, but needlessly so, because when she walked home, her husband, Danny, had done the same for her. The entire day was almost too good to be true and I was genuinely impressed.

"How did the kids like Bear Mountain?" I asked Butch, as I reached gluttonously for more shrimp.

"They had a great time," he answered, refilling my wine glass with a vintage that was almost a very good year. "But that Noelle is really some kid."

"That's for sure," George snickered. "One in a million."

"Why? What happened?"

"Well, a little after we got up there she fell and cut her thumb on a rock and started crying. I washed it off and told her to press her finger tight against her thumb to stop the bleeding."

George and Butch started to laugh again.

"And?"

"We stayed up in the mountains for another two hours, drove all the way home, fed them supper, bathed them, and just as I was tucking her into bed, she said, 'Daddy, can I take my finger off my thumb now?' The poor kid stayed like that for over five hours."

"That's Noelle all over," I said, adding my laughter to the rest. "The only child we have who obeys orders unquestionably."

Noelle had always been a quiet child, albeit a little whiny, and her rambunctious brothers and sisters kept me so busy that I often literally forgot Noelle.

"Remember all the times we've forgotten that poor child," I asked Butch.

He nodded, laughing. "It's a wonder we haven't given her a nervous breakdown by now."

"One time in Long Beach, when she was still an infant," I said, turning to Anita and George, "we all piled into the station wagon to go grocery shopping and were halfway down the block."

"Hey Ma!" Dante yells at the top of his lungs from the back seat.

"Dante! stop that yelling," I say.

"But Ma!" he says, "Where's the baby?"

"Oh my God!" I say to Butch. "We forgot Noelle."

The kids started laughing, except for Kelly, whose three-year-old face was both stern and horrified at the same time.

"There goes your 'Mother of the Year' award again," Butch says as he backs the car down the block.

I rush back into the house and pick Noelle up out of the playpen. I had at least remembered to dress her in her snowsuit. She gazed at me blandly, as if to say, "I knew you'd be back for me eventually."

"How about the time we drove down to Mom's," Butch said. "Remember that?"

"God, yes. That was awful."

"What happened?" Anita asked, reaching for more wine. "With so many kids I'm surprised you didn't forget them more often. I can hardly keep track of Steven."

"For once we got down to Easton without any of the kids throwing up. We pile out of the car and head up the sidewalk to his Mom's house. Mom lets us in, smothering everyone with hugs and rushes us into the kitchen where she's prepared a gigantic lunch. We spend about fifteen minutes eating when Mom asks where Noelle is. We all look at each other in shock and rush back out to the car.

"Oh no," Anita says, giggling.

"It wasn't even funny. There she was, her little waif-like face pressed against the car window with tears streaming down her cheeks."

"Some parents," George remarked dryly.

"Apparently she had fallen asleep and didn't hear or feel the rest of the kids trampling over her to get out of the car," Butch added.

"When I asked her why she didn't just open the car door and come out, she sniffled and said that she couldn't get it open."

"That poor baby," Anita said. "How could you be so cruel to such a sweetie?"

"How about the time you drove all the kids to school in the rain, Butch? Remember that?"

"Oh, geez," he said. "That was terrible. It was pouring buckets and I drive up to the school, only half awake and tell the kids and their friends to hurry and get out. They all do and run for the school building. I'm about to pull away when I see Noelle standing in a puddle next to the passenger side of the car. She's rubbing her eyes and sobbing."

"So I roll down the window and yell, 'Noelle what are you crying about now? Get to school!'"

"'But Daddy,' she wails, looking at me with those big sad eyes of hers, 'It's not my school.'"

Anita and George roared.

"We're laughing now," I said, "but it wasn't funny then. We've probably traumatized that child for life."

"Well I think we should take Noelle away from you. I can't have any more children and Steven could use a sister."

"But she's changing" I said, ignoring Anita's comment. "She doesn't take any nonsense from anyone lately."

"Maybe we've strengthened her character," Butch noted.

It was true. Since entering first grade Noelle was becoming the "little mouse that roared." She stood up to Kim, unheard of in the family, put the irascible Dante in his place, refused to kowtow to Kelly, stopped spoiling Nicole and even learned how to manipulate her brother Michael--not an easy task. She was developing a whacky, sarcastic sense of humor which somehow took the edge off her new-found fierceness. I attributed much of her new personality to her teacher, who, like Ann Eunice and Johnny, instilled self-confidence and security within her. But whatever the reason, Noelle was fast becoming a force to be reckoned with among her siblings.

After Anita and George went home, carrying a sleeping Steven, I went up to Butch and hugged him.

"Thank you," I said. "That was the loveliest birthday I ever had."

"Good," he said, with a wicked grin. "You can thank me properly later tonight."

~

Just when you think you have your life the way you want it, a time when things seem to be working out perfectly, change comes along uninvited and nothing is the same. It is as if fate holds some objection to continuity. Almost at once, everything on Knickerbocker Road began changing rapidly.

It began with Anita and George. While George was on a job in Las Vegas, causing him to miss the anniversary party, he fell in love with the gambling desert town. Anita flew out with him on his next trip and was equally smitten. Soon all any of us could talk about was the West and how great it would be if we could all get out of New York.

I was certainly all for that. My dislike for Long Island had never lessened, in spite of having met wonderful friends. If I couldn't have the mountains of Pennsylvania, the deserts of Nevada seemed like a good second choice. Besides, I had more serious motives for wanting to leave than the scenery. Kim had just started high school in the neighboring town of Hempstead (Island Park was too small to have its own high school) and I had reason to worry.

Her grades, always high, began dropping, and we received notices that she was skipping classes. After a meeting with the principal, we discovered that she had not attended some of her classes for over a month. The school was overcrowded and understaffed and it was simple for kids to get lost in the paperwork. Drugs and alcohol were rampant in the school.

Kim was still smoking cigarettes, although she did her best to hide it from me, and now I worried about drugs. She never displayed the telltale signs I knew to watch for, but that was not enough of a guarantee. Upon reaching her full and remarkable height of six foot one, she was a misfit among her peers, a beautiful misfit, but a misfit all the same. Remembering the cruelty of my own school years, my heart broke for her and there was nothing I could do except try and reinforce her confidence at home. Peer pressure among teenagers is far stronger than any parental bond and I knew I was fighting a lost cause. When she was home, after her chores, she stayed in her room playing her guitar, and writing songs and poems. When not home, she was usually across the train tracks on the other side of Island Park, with her one friend; a short, really short, fat, almost square-shaped girl who was as homely as Kim was beautiful. The girl's home life was as unsavory as her neighborhood.

In spite of threats and punishments, Kim cultivated this unlikely friendship as if to spite the world for rejecting her. She elected to become as unique and different as possible. Her thick, straight dark hair hung down to her waist secured by an Indian headband around her forehead. She dressed like a hippy from the sixties and carried her perfect posture proudly with her head held high. What went on inside her I had no idea, because she wouldn't let me into the retreat that she had chosen. Getting Kim and the rest of the kids out of New York was becoming more than just a dream. It was crucial and I used it as the main argument when trying to convince Butch. The idea of moving west appealed to him, but he was still bound by a strange umbilical cord to Benny and it wouldn't be easy severing it.

Anita and George made their decision. George moved out to Vegas immediately and Anita stayed until he could find housing for them. The biggest shock came when Kathy and Scotty, whose job was such that he could work anywhere, announced that they had a buyer for their house and were moving to Vegas in a few months. Carol and Danny couldn't move west, but Danny's insurance company had an opening in upstate New York, near Rochester. Within six months, they were gone. The year before, Jo Romano, the first friend I had met in Island Park, had, of all things, joined the Air Force, and put in her training while her husband watched the kids. She was permanently stationed in Florida, right near the Everglades. Of a closely knit group, our numbers had dwindled greatly. My world was emptying fast and I was feeling both lost and left behind.

~ *Twenty One* ~

August 25, 1981

"Why don't you go home and get some sleep?" Butch asks, shifting a little from the weight of my head on his shoulder. "I'll stay here for the rest of the night."

"So will I," echoes my mother-in-law. "They can't make me leave. I intend to say the rosary outside the door all night."

Those are the first words Mom has spoken since arriving at the hospital, too overwhelmed by pain and tears to do anything more than embrace me.

"I can't go home yet. Maybe in a little while. I need to be here when the kids get here."

"How do you know they'll come here?" Butch asks. He paces across the small room, full of nervous energy that has no outlet.

"Because I left messages everywhere. Dad and your sister, Gerry, are at the house if they go there first," I add, trying to stifle an unwelcome yawn. "Nicole is with the Steigers, but I need to have the rest of the kids with me now."

"You're exhausted, Mick. Go home now. I mean it."

"No! Leave me alone. I'm just going to rest my eyes for a little while. And please sit down. Your pacing makes me nervous."

He reluctantly sits back down and I nestle my head back into his shoulder, but my eyes, raw and blurry, refuse to close. The room is dark and quiet, the silence broken only by an occasional nurse bustling through the doors of the ICU and the soft, barely audible sound of Mom repeating the rosary. Friends and neighbors, feeling helpless and inadequate, have all left. The two children with us are still sleeping across the lounge chairs.

The soft red glow from the soda machine mesmerizes me until I slip, at last, into something similar to sleep, but neither soothing nor restful.

Suddenly I am six years old again, and in my bed at my great-grandparents' home. They are Hungarian immigrants and speak broken English. They have allowed us to live in the downstairs apartment of their house.

It is hard to sleep with so much fire around me. I am certain that it will surely consume me if I dare to look away from it. There is only the heavy blackness of the room and the constant flames shooting ever upward. To a small child raised on the fire and brimstone Christianity of the Baptist Church--complete with traveling evangelists toting their vivid flannel boards depicting the damnation of a vengeful God--I am certain that I sleep upon the borders of Hell.

My bedroom is at the front of the house in what should have been a living room. The two large windows in the always chilly room look out through the porch and into the back of the Bethlehem Steel Plant where my stepfather works.

The unceasing fire snarls grotesquely from tall, cylindrical smokestacks, spouting vivid colors of red, purple and blue. The black chimneys blend in with the darkness of the night, so that only the flames are visible, floating like patches of fire in the sky. Fingers of flame seem to reach for me, beckoning me to come closer, to join the fire. I am afraid to close my eyes for fear that the hellish tendrils will descend upon me as I sleep.

Strangely, in daylight the fire emanates only as a fine iridescent haze, barely discernable. The devil, I remember being told, only comes out at night.

The year before, my mother, new stepfather and me, had ridden a train from Texas to Bethlehem, Pennsylvania where my stepfather's family lived. The contrast between the open ambiance of San Antonio, with streets so wide the clanging trolley cars seemed lost in them--and this stark and dingy steel town made me feel as alien as if I had moved to another planet. There was no fire in San Antonio, no darkness like the darkness here. And I felt safe.

Why am I thinking of this now, I wonder, having come back into a hazy wakefulness. *I haven't recalled those childhood terrors in years. Maybe I really am losing my mind.* As a child I felt that I was being consumed by frightening things beyond my control or comprehension. Now I feel I am being consumed again. But it isn't flames this time that threaten to destroy me. It is the bottomless pit of grief.

There will be no more sleep for me this night, so I rise unsteadily, walk over to the soda machine, put in the last of my change and wait for the clunk of the can dropping within my reach. I light up a cigarette, sip the cold, sweet cola, and continue the long vigil. I know in my heart that the wait is all I have. The end of the vigil will result in the loss of my child; even as my soul cries no, my maternal instincts know better. It is not something that I can accept now. Like Scarlett in "Gone with the Wind," I'll think about that tomorrow and whatever tomorrows are left.

~ Twenty Two ~

April, 1974

It was a wild idea--downright crazy. I was beginning to believe that Butch had either completely lost his mind or was plotting to get rid of me; possibly both.

Anita King was ready to join George in Las Vegas. The three of us and George, through long distance phone calls, were trying to come up with an inexpensive, speedy way to move Anita, Steven and all their belongings out west.

One evening Anita and I were having coffee and moping over the impact her moving would have on our close friendship, when the phone rang.

"Do you think Anita could learn to drive and handle a moving truck?" Butch asked.

"Why?" I asked, leery of strange questions.

"Because, if she can drive a U-Haul truck and if you can get someone to come and stay with the kids, then the two of you and Steven can drive out to Vegas and you can fly back alone."

"You really mean it?" I yelled into the phone. "Of course she can handle a truck. Anita can do anything she sets her mind to."

By now Anita was looking at me with raised eyebrows. I handed the phone to her. As Butch unfolded his plan, she became so excited that she burst into a stream of Swedish expletives. But the grin on her face, growing wider every second, assured me that she was wild about the idea. The rest of the evening was spent planning our adventure. Having temporarily forgotten about Murphy's Law, we'd no concept of just what an adventure it was going to be.

When Butch came home from work, the three of us sat up into the middle of the night, trying to formulate a workable plan. The main problem was George's Volkswagen. He was quite fond of that old car, overly so in my opinion, so selling it was not an option.

"Maybe we could put the car up inside the truck and pack the furniture around it," Butch suggested.

I commented that maybe he'd been working too hard lately. Anita pointed out pragmatically that any truck large enough to carry the car and all her belongings was far too large for her to handle.

"I will not drive an eighteen-wheeler with fifty different gears across country," she added firmly. "I don't even know how to drive a stick shift and I'm not about to learn now."

"Well," Butch said, "Then the Volkswagen will have to be towed behind the truck. Do you think you can handle that?"

"Sure," she said. "How hard can it be? The car will follow behind us, that's all."

Since Las Vegas' time zone was three hours earlier than ours, and George was working late shows, we called him and related our plans. He thought it was a great idea, but warned Anita that nothing had better happen to his car. The following morning I called my mother-in-law, the only person in the world who would watch my six children and feel genuinely honored to be chosen. She promised to drive up to Long Island the day before we planned to leave. I didn't mention that we would be driving a large truck and towing a Volkswagen. She had more than enough people on her prayer list.

The following two weeks were both exhilarating and hectic. Anita started to pack up her entire apartment and held a garage sale. She made me promise not to tell George, something of a sentimental pack rat, what all she sold. I had to organize my household so that Mom wouldn't walk into total chaos. That would follow soon enough. The kids were on their best behavior, wondering, since I seemed so ecstatic about leaving them, if I planned on returning.

We had planned to leave on April first, April Fool's Day, an apt choice as the day proved. I had forgotten that Anita was not endowed with any household organizational skills. A few hours from our planned departure, her garage sale was still going on, her closets were filled with clothing, the apartment was trashed and food was in her refrigerator.

"Don't worry," she kept repeating, to those of us snapping at her. "I know just where everything is."

Friends helping her pack did not. Butch was about to cheerfully strangle her as she left to close out her bank accounts, something she could have done days before. I glanced around the apartment, which was in total disarray and realized that we would not be leaving that day. Butch and the guys loading the truck left nasty notes to George taped onto the packing boxes.

Around six in the evening, Anita and I finally swept our way out of the apartment and threw away our brooms. Exhausted and hungry, we drove back to my house, where Butch had gone earlier to hook up the Volkswagen to the truck. The U-Haul company rented tow-bars, but would not install them, unwilling to ensure their safety. I wished Butch had kept that information to himself. Anita and I were in bed before midnight, the fatigue of the day sufficient to make us sleepy, even through our excitement. Four-year-old Nicole slept in my bed for a change, in a last ditch effort to try and convince me not to leave her. After feigning several life-threatening diseases, she finally fell into a fitful sleep. Due to unforeseen difficulties with the tow-bar hook-up, we were not to have an early start at all.

Around two in the afternoon, we were finally on our way. The kids kissed and hugged me solemnly, never having been parted from me for so long in their entire lives, except when I was in the hospital birthing their siblings. It was pouring rain as I kissed Butch's worried face. The trip, initially so exciting, was bordering on ominous.

During the downpour which followed us out of New York, I discovered that the truck leaked, but only on my side. The headlights started to flash off and on. Anita and I began voicing unkind comments about my overconfident husband, who had hooked up the wiring from the truck to the car.

I was the navigator of this trip, because I could read maps. I had no idea how to relate the map to where we were at any given point, but saw no reason to mention this, since Anita couldn't read maps at all. I had trouble getting us out of New Jersey, immediately losing #287. Frantically roaming in and out of industrial Newark, we often spotted #287, but always teasing us from the other side of the highway. We pulled into a dump truck depot and made a huge u-turn, much to the dismay of the management. Nevertheless, we ended up on #287 and Anita breathed a sigh of relief. I didn't, because I couldn't remember if we were supposed to be going north or south. I decided not to mention this either.

We seemed to be heading in the right direction, at least for the moment and everything was going well, except that the plastic bag with our napkins in it began to melt. I checked to see if we were on fire, but it was just the overly efficient heating system, which started scorching my feet. The rain stopped and the sky was brightening, so we decided not to have the headlights checked, since we no longer needed them.

By late afternoon we were all starving, but discovered that we couldn't stop at any fast food places because the truck was over twenty-four feet long. Butch had sternly ordered us not to attempt to back up the truck. We consoled ourselves with a three pound box of chocolates rescued from the truck heater in the nick of time.

By six in the evening we were in the middle of a long, steep hill outside of Allentown, Pennsylvania--and out of gas. I had mentioned to Anita about an hour before that the gas gauge was getting low, but in her optimistic, nonchalant way, she brushed me off--claiming there's always more gas in the tank than the gauge indicates.

"Well, Anita," I said, "now what?"

"Don't get worried," she answered in a voice that told me she was worried enough for both of us. Butch had told me the emergency flags were behind the front seat of the truck, but I couldn't find them. After what seemed forever, ignored by the few vehicles that passed us, two trucks came to our aid. One was a tractor-trailer whose driver asked if we had any chain so that he could pull us off the road. We didn't, to our knowledge, so he pulled us over to the shoulder with an ordinary rope, giving me my first real case of heart palpitations.

The second truck was a pick-up, and the driver, who introduced himself as "Russ, the soda-pusher," offered to drive me to a gas station. If Butch knew that I was getting into a truck with a strange man and leaving Anita and Steven alone on a deserted road with another stranger, he would kill me. There was no other choice. We drove to a small country gas station overrun with German shepherd dogs and small children. The proprietor gave me three gallons, demanding that we return the container. After returning to Anita, who seemed unharmed, and pouring the three gallons into the thirsty truck, nothing happened.

"So much for inaccurate gas gauges," I smugly noted to Anita. Russ drove me back to the station for three more gallons. Still nothing happened until the ingenious man poured some of the remaining drops over the carburetor. This time "Old Bertha" coughed, sputtered and sprang to life.

The late afternoon slipped into dusk as we missed the next truck stop, in spite of precise directions from Russ. Much later, fed, showered and snug in another clean, but expensive truck stop, I asked myself if the day had really been as bad as it seemed. Myself said unequivocally, *yes!*

The next day Anita, Steven and I rolled out of our warm beds a little after nine o'clock. Steven, normally a lively, rambunctious child, was becoming increasingly quiet. Butch had given us a long list of instructions for the trip. Number one stated emphatically: always start out early so you don't ever have to drive at night. Neither of us were morning people so naturally we ignored that rule. Rule number two read: check the water level each morning. Anita took that job, which entailed looking at the place where the water container was, noting that it was still there.

The biggest problem we faced each day was finding food. Shopping centers became our best bet, but they were hard to find. We stopped for an early supper at one near Wheeling, West Virginia on our second day of the trip. There was a restaurant of sorts and we were too hungry to be selective. Anita, feeling more confident with the truck by now, whipped into the parking lot as if she were driving a sports car and narrowly missed the large ditch by the side of the road.

"It was a piece of cake!" she said, proudly.

Again, my adrenalin soared.

We decided to have the "all you can eat" special for $1.69 and we all had seconds. This time we remembered to pick up fruit and snacks so we wouldn't starve the next day. As we headed back into the truck, Anita marveled on how well she'd manipulated the truck. Steven and I just looked at each other and grinned.

With the skies quickly darkening, we hoped to make Wheeling by nightfall, remembering Butch's warning not ever to drive at night. Our search for sleeping quarters was officially on and as usual we were foolishly optimistic--at least one of us.

The wind picked up, rocking the truck, as clouds swirled with sudden intensity and warnings of tornado watches across Ohio came over the radio. We took a quick exit to a small, but enticing motel, but couldn't fit the truck into the parking lot. Butch's warning, "DO NOT EVER BACK

UP" flashed through my mind as she quickly swerved into the lumber yard next to the motel, leaving the night watchman gaping.

The sky was terrifying, with fast-moving dark clouds interspersed with patches of unnatural gray, yet we had no choice except to get back onto #70 and keep going.

Passing trucks kept signaling from the opposite side of the road, because our headlights were flashing again. It was pitch black and pouring rain. We stopped for gas, something Anita now did regularly whenever the gauge read half full. The pelting rain again deterred us from getting the headlights fixed. With directions from the gas attendant for the next truck stop, only three exits down the road, we carried on--with caution and a great deal of fear on the part of Steven and myself.

Later we heard of the death and destruction from a deadly tornado that hit Exenia, Ohio. Had we been early risers, we would have driven right into it.

At last we pulled into the Shenandoah Motel and Truck Stop. It was storming heavily and we had to park at least a long block from the entrance. We were too hungry to bother with the luggage and ran for the restaurant. The coffee was fantastic--a must for truckers. We found ourselves getting silly from relief and fatigue; except for Steven who kept saying that he wanted to go home. This truck stop was huge, complete with pool tables and pin ball machines, which slightly cheered Steven; as well as laundromats, clothing stores and everything a traveler could possibly need.

The large complex was circular. We walked halfway around it to get back to the entrance and retrieve our luggage. That explained how we lost the truck. We laughed at first, but after searching for it amidst countless mammoth trucks, slipping through oil slicks in a downpour that had no intention of abating, panic set in. What were we to tell Butch and George?

The truckers chuckled at the sight of two soaked women and a small boy, cringing from fierce lightning flashes as we wove in and out among them.

"Lost your truck, did you?" more than one of them remarked. "What are you doing with a truck in the first place?"

We were beginning to wonder the same thing. After retracing our steps for the third time, we found the truck right where we had left it, breathed a sigh of relief and dragged our luggage back to our rooms. Anita and Steven were exhausted and fell asleep watching television. I filled in the expense logs and checked the maps for the next day. The management was nice enough to give us an extra folding cot and since I was the last to go to bed, I got it. It collapsed every time I tried to lie down and after several futile attempts at fixing it, I figured sleeping in a V-shape would only be a problem if I turned over.

~

The next morning we started out a little earlier than usual and left #70 to go into Exenia and check out the damage done by the tornado. We left the truck in a residential area, untouched by the storm, and walked toward the center of the town. Everything was so peaceful and undisturbed that we were unprepared for what awaited us.

It was a sight we would never forget. National Guardsmen were everywhere, trying to restore some semblance of order in a town that had literally been turned upside down. At first, it was an occasional tree uprooted or a squashed car, but the horror grew as we continued to walk.

The people wore lost, vacant looks in their eyes, not seeming to notice us. Roofs were caved in, house siding ripped off and flung at random, or wrapped around telephone poles and trees; sidewalks were caved in or simply missing. Street signs, if standing at all, were bent into grotesque shapes and wires hung everywhere. Sometimes a house stood intact, the garage behind it, collapsed, as if something drew in a huge breath. Other times the garage was there, but the house was demolished. More times than not, it was both.

We walked on, into the heart of the town. We were touched by the irony of one house, completely in ruins, except for a mahogany upright piano that was unharmed--all that was left of a home. Another house was intact, except for one room that had no walls around it, as if a giant had removed the walls to look inside; yet the furniture inside had remained in place. Several cars were upside down and a large camper had been sliced in two. Ducks were swimming in a large pond, in what had once been a lovely park, surrounded by trees now bent, cracked or ripped apart-- flanked by a high school severely damaged. People told us that students had been practicing in the auditorium when a school bus was lifted by the tornado and dropped down on the stage in front of them. Mother Nature has a bizarre sense of irony.

Walking on to the main shopping area, we found more destruction. The streets were busy with men and trucks of all kinds. Now and then someone paused to smile and say hello. A large bank had its windows blown out and draperies blew in the wind. Next to it a gas station attendant was busily sweeping around his pumps, although they were no longer standing; his roof was off, his sign had blown away and cars were tossed about his station as if by a small boy tired of his toys.

Next to what might have been a MacDonald's, we stopped to talk to a middle-aged woman who didn't seem to resent our presence. She told us how she heard the warning, but the tornado was traveling at sixty miles an hour and struck fifteen minutes sooner than expected. She and her family made it, barely, to their basement, but her friends are missing and her neighbor's house completely disappeared. She told us of a young mother who held her baby in her arms, until the storm whisked the infant away from her, never to be found. The woman couldn't seem to stop talking, as if relating these horrors would make them go away. We said goodbye, wished her well and walked on.

We were turned back by policemen. The destruction ahead of us was so horrendous that they were still finding bodies flung about like broken dolls. This section contained low- to middle-income housing and while most of the homes were new, they were built on slabs with no basement for shelter. The people could not take cover and were left to the discretion of the beast that struck in the night. The area was also widely used as daycare centers for working mothers, who walked around begging, "Have you seen my children?"

We retraced our steps through the town, seeing wreckage that we had missed before. In front of City Hall, which was spared by the tornado, lay three telephone booths, side by side, and unharmed, as if carefully placed there. Weariness and a sad, hollow feeling settled over me, and we barely spoke. A sidewalk along our way lead to nowhere; only a wash basket and large mud hole gave proof of the home that once stood there. Walking out of Exenia, where all was in order, made the horror we had witnessed seem unreal. Climbing back into the truck, tired and grateful to be alive, we rode to #70 in silence. Contemplating all we'd seen, we voiced aloud how unimportant possessions really are. *How quickly and brutally we can be rendered helpless or worse*, I thought.

~ *Twenty Three* ~

At six o'clock the next morning I woke up cold and uncomfortable in a truck stop not nearly as nice as the last. A knock on the door was our wake-up call, but when I looked out the window to see large snowflakes drifting steadily to the ground, I turned over and went back to sleep. An hour later when we all woke up, it was snowing even harder. We started off, in spite of the inclement weather; Butch had us on a strict timetable and George didn't want us to waste time or money. A few hours later, still driving in whipping wind and snow, a car passed us. The driver yelled out that our tow bar was slipping. Taking the next exit, we pulled into a Texaco Station, where the attendant confirmed that one side of the tow-bar was off and the other close behind. He somehow wired it back together with two coat hangers, which did little for our peace of mind. Even the eternally optimistic Anita looked worried.

"Anita, I say we back up to a cliff and let the damned VW drop off!"

"Jah, Micki, good idea, except that George would kill us, and Steven would tell on us."

"Would you really, Steven?" I asked.

"Yep, Aunt Micki. There's a lot of stuff I'm gonna hafta tell my dad."

Reaching St. Louis, Missouri around six o'clock in the evening, we were happy at last to see some gorgeous weather. The sun was all smiles, raining beams of golden rays over the great arch that welcomes visitors to St. Louis.

We stopped a few miles outside of St. Louis at the Diamond Restaurant for dinner. The radio broadcast a measles outbreak, which might explain the spots all over George's rubber tree. There was a motel right next to the restaurant.

"Let's stop here for the night," I suggested to Anita.

"No, this is a tourist trap. It'll be way too expensive. We have daylight, so we can go a little farther."

"Okay, but it will be dark soon and you know bad things happen when we drive at night."

"You worry too much. We'll go a few miles, find a cheap motel, and call it a day."

These were the proverbial "famous last words." Steven was twitching again--not a good sign. I squeezed his hand in reassurance. Twenty minutes later, we pulled into a weigh station for trucks. I ran into the office, avoiding anything resembling a scale. A lanky, white-haired man with smiling eyes assured me there was a truck stop down the road on Route 44. We missed it, of course.

All signs of life disappeared on the narrow, winding dark road. Steven snuggled against me fighting a losing battle to stay awake. Fog rolled in. Signs of civilization appeared as we drove through a small town called Cuba, Missouri. A policeman directed us to the Broken Wheel Motel, an apt name, we later discovered.

The place cost ten dollars for the night, proving the adage, "you get what you pay for." The room was old, dirty and damp. It offered a small black and white television set with bad reception--not a problem since all programming ended before midnight. The bathroom faucets stayed on if you held them, and the toilet ran constantly. The only outlet for our coffee pot was a foot from the ceiling.

"Oh no," Anita said, doubling over with laughter. "I can just see you making coffee holding the pot up in the air."

There was no phone in the room which made Anita uneasy. I no longer cared. Steven fell asleep in his clothes, and we left him that way.

"I'm propping a chair against the door," Anita said.

"Go right ahead. Anyone can come in through this open window that won't close."

We fell asleep to the ticking of a little alarm clock, handed to us by the clerk at the front desk when we requested a wake-up call. It was accompanied by strange creaking noises and buzzing insects.

Steven and I awoke to use the bathroom. He tripped over the electric cord to the coffee pot and I was pretty sure water spilled into Anita's opened suitcase. We made a secret pact not to tell her, and crawled back into bed for a few more hours sleep.

The trusty little alarm clock never went off, so we got a late start--for a change.

We stopped at a gas station for fuel and a check-up for Old Bertha. The mechanic said, "No way can I fix the short in the headlights. It'll take all day." He agreed to check the tow-bar pulling the

Volkswagen. "Who the heck hooked up this mess? It's a wonder you weren't killed!" He spent a few hours trying to fix it and told us not tell anyone, because mechanics weren't allowed to work on tow-bar hitches. He refused to guarantee his work or our safety, but wished us well.

"We'll be fine," said my optimistic, albeit unrealistic friend.

Traveling across Oklahoma opened up a vista of rolling hills; green mixed with amber and wheat-colored grasses. Black Angus cattle grazed as we passed. We witnessed early signs of spring--trees budding, flowers popping up after a long winter's sleep. The most amazing sight was the miles of oil pumps, continually pumping up and down, set on top of the rolling hills.

Entering Texas, we noticed its contradictions. Parts were dirty, barren, lonely, but beautiful. Sand-blown deserts stretched for miles, broken by breath-taking gullies and buttes. Most of it was bare except for Amarillo, teaming with all sorts of life. We crossed the Texas panhandle, a poor example of the overall state. The sunsets were stunning. I did notice one thing--many cowboys without their boots and ten-gallon hats stood only a little over five feet tall.

Driving on towards Albuquerque, New Mexico opened up a panoramic beauty. The weather was crisp and cool, the skies clear. The time change at the Texas-New Mexico state line put us back an hour, which made me happy. I considered daylight savings time a curse; suffering when springing forward, losing an hour. Anita looked at me quizzically when I tried to explain this to her.

The difference between Texas and New Mexico was like leaving Kansas for the Land of Oz. The sky was a true turquoise; the hues of the mountains, a mixture of gold, brown and pale green. Aside from its natural beauty, New Mexico was dirty, the restrooms beyond description. We picked up the bare necessities, hoping to log many miles before dark-- driving through areas of trees and shrubs, with snow-capped mountains flanking us. My camera kept me busy trying to focus through the truck window at 55 mph. Climbing steadily up long mountain elevations, we reached 7,000 feet above sea level. The three of us barely noticed the height, but Old Bertha coughed and sputtered as if gasping for oxygen.

We pulled up to a truck stop for lunch, surprised to find the food was awful. We ordered finger steaks, which were strips of tough steak breaded like chicken.

"I can't eat this stuff, Mom," Steven complained. He nearly gagged.

"I can't either, Steven," I said, "We'll find something better later--let's get out of here."

We hoped to log another hundred miles before stopping for the night. Driving down the right road, but in the wrong direction, allowed Anita to do some of her now famous stunt driving. Steven clung to me as I said a quick prayer.

"Gallop, New Mexico is next," I mentioned to Anita.

"Jah, well you're the map reader, so just point the way."

It wasn't that simple, but I let it go. We drove into a glorious sunset resembling the gemstones sold by the local Indians. Clouds were visible for the first time in two days. I never tired of those majestic mountains.

As twilight crept upon us, the anticipation of finding sleeping quarters sent chills along my spine. We drove right past Grant, a small town teaming with lodging. *Did my maniacal friend stop? No!*

"Just a few more miles while we have some light left," she said.

Steven and I looked at each other and sighed.

Bertha started flashing her lights as the countryside turned pitch black. The abundance of stars in the western sky was not bright enough to offset the darkness.

A police car pulled alongside. We pulled over and the officer asked us to step out of the truck. I explained our dilemma to him, but he had trouble keeping his eyes off Anita's snug jeans. He agreed to lead us to the city line of Milan. I suspected he would have agreed to just about anything we asked. Once there, he radioed for another policeman to lead us to the Holiday Inn in the town of Grant. "A name brand motel," I whispered to a drowsy Steven. "Imagine that."

The motel was an oasis after a long desert trek. Steven fell asleep at once; too tired to watch the color television set or have a snack. The lounge bar was a few doors from our room, and we really wanted a relaxing drink. Anita insisted that Steven would not wake up. The lounge was only a few feet from the door of our room. Still, we took turns checking on him at fifteen minute intervals. The lounge was full of local color and some transients like us. We discussed our routes, maps and travel time, although a few eyebrows were raised at our escapades. Apparently it was possible to cross country without harrowing adventures. Saying goodnight to our new-found friends, we walked back to our room, unaware that one of the men from the bar was watching us.

Just as we climbed between fresh, clean sheets, we heard pounding at the door. Anita looked out through the peephole, frightened. The man at the door was drunk beyond reason, begging us to open the door. I started to laugh. Then it became more hysteria than funny when the man refused to leave.

"I bought you all those nice drinks," he said, over and over.

Actually, he bought one round of drinks for the whole lounge and we were included, but his brain was too fogged by liquor to be coherent. I saw another man walk up and thought he would get rid of this obnoxious drunk, who whined at our door like a male dog after a female in heat. But no, this man wanted in now, too. Anita turned ashen as she began stacking all movable furniture in front of the door. We could hear them trying to pick the lock.

"Anita, don't get so upset," I said. "I'm calling the front desk. They'll get rid of these two in a second."

Motel security quickly arrived and removed the two rowdy men, but neither of us could sleep. We crawled back into bed, leaving the furniture against the door and held cans of deodorant spray firmly in our hands until sleep took us to a realm of safety.

We all slept late, had a warm and delicious breakfast and headed for the truck. During the night two of our tires were flattened, and we had a good idea who might have done this. It was unlikely we would reach Las Vegas this day. Anita's tooth was throbbing again, and I was fairly sure clenching her jaw in fear the previous night hadn't helped. The truck was climbing to higher elevations as we crossed the Continental Divide. I felt like I was the only one worried as the winds picked up, howling and blinding us with sand. Soon the inside of the truck was filled with fine red sand.

"Yuck!" Steven said. "I need a soda."

"Not now, Steven," Anita said. "Be quiet so I can see where I'm driving."

The sandstorm billowed around us like brown pea soup. Sagebrush tumbled across the highway, sometimes flinging itself against our windshield. Both The Painted Desert and Petrified Forests were hidden by the vicious sandstorm. The weatherman on the truck radio forecast "a little wind in Arizona today".

As we climbed upward toward Flagstaff, the temperature dropped, winds died. We drove into a virtual paradise; so unlike the dry barren desert. The mountains were glorious, hidden demurely by a mist of snow-capped peaks.

Anita's tooth ached, pulsing pain which she bore stoically. We gained another hour due to the time change. I thought we might make our deadline after all. The sands pummeling the truck, finding its way inside, made us thirsty. We carried no water, no snacks. Steven was beyond bored. Anita and I took turns singing him songs. I told him the story about "The Boy who Cried Wolf" over and over again.

We crossed into the Arizona State Inspection Station--required to stop even though the storm blasted us with a thick grit that got between our teeth, in our hair, clothes--everywhere. Sagebrush tumbled across the desert onto the highways. The truck shook. Steven shook. I shook a little myself. Anita drove on, like a woman possessed.

The air was crisp; it felt like autumn. Beautiful pine and spruce trees surrounded us. Flagstaff sat at the bottom of all this beauty, flanked by the snow-capped mountains. I could live here forever. Now that our trip neared its end, we fared better. We found a motel before dark--a first--and had dinner at a great steak house. We split a bottle of champagne to celebrate our last dinner on the road. It was cold, no more than thirty degrees, a shock after the desert heat. The sounds of rushing trains rumbled past our windows, lulling me into a deep, contented sleep.

I awoke on my own, refreshed and cozy. Anita felt fine, too. Her tooth had calmed down, no longer paining her. Old Bertha staged a protest. She was way too cold to start up without some coddling and soothing pats.

"Have we checked the water lately?" I asked Anita. Reminding her.

"Who cares? We're nearly in Las Vegas. We'll make it."

I wondered whether she had a crystal ball or high expectations. Steven yawned, stretched and the light in his sky-blue eyes sparkled. This crazy trip neared its end, none too soon for him. I wondered how much he would remember, when he told on us.

It was eighty-five miles to Kingman, Arizona; a hundred miles to Las Vegas. Almost there.

Descending from the high elevations made our ears pop. The desert once more stretched before us. We felt the heat return. Forty miles before Kingman, we stopped for gas and learned from the sharp-eyed attendant that Old Bertha's tank was leaking gas. That was the bad news. The worst was he refused to repair it.

"What now, Anita?"

"We got this far on guts, and God willing, we'll drive the last hundred miles safely," she said with a bravado that fooled neither of us. We pushed on until the city line of Las Vegas appeared before us. We made it.

~ Twenty Four ~

We limped into Las Vegas in late afternoon, gas leaking from the tank, blissfully unaware we could blow up at any moment. There was an angel on watch that day, perhaps the entire trip. Steven could hardly wait to get out of the truck and into his dad's arms.

Pulling into Anita's apartment complex, with the truck and towing the Volkswagen, required more of Anita's most excellent skills. The array of run-over garbage cans, squashed shrubs and a few kid-toys wouldn't endear her to her new neighbors.

"What took you so long?" George asked, grabbing Steven in a bear hug and winking at Anita over his son's shoulder. "Lewis and Clark made better time."

Anita let out a stream of Swedish words which needed no translation. George just laughed and kissed her hard.

"Stay back," I warned, hands held out in front of me.

I was safe. George headed straight for his precious car. He caressed it like a lover. The poor rubber tree plant succumbed to an untimely death back in Missouri, but the car showed little visible signs of the abuse it took. Unlike Steven, it couldn't talk. If George noticed the jerry-rigged tow-bar, he said nothing.

We didn't care. We wanted food and sleep. George offered us freshly delivered Chinese food, and we ate; then collapsed into a deep and restful sleep. I had a feeling that Steven, who'd slept in the truck on the way to his new home, was avidly filling his dad in on our adventures and misfortunes. I didn't care. Sleep swept over me like a fog of sweet bliss.

The next morning, after a brunch of bagels, cream cheese and lox, we began the arduous unloading of the truck. It was not a pretty scene. George had comments--negative--on how things were packed, ad nauseam. The notes from Butch and Danny did not bolster his blackening mood. I helped as much as possible, but stayed out of sight as sparks flew between my two friends. Steven and I busied ourselves washing and putting away dishes.

After a long trip filled with fun, danger, intrigue and adventure, Las Vegas seemed tame. That was before we hit the casinos. Casinos in Las

Vegas in 1973 were an experience second to none. Ostentatious, glittering--a make believe world, where waitresses dressed like Playboy Bunnies offered free drinks on a continual basis. The call of the slot machines was seductive. Anita played "21" at dealers' tables, but I refused to lose more than a quarter at a time. I won forty dollars and lost it just as fast, which is how the system works. To soothe losses, incredibly delicious late night dinners were offered for just $1.95--steak, shrimp cocktail, the whole works. You rarely leave a casino with more money than you came with, but you will never leave hungry--or completely sober.

~

August 24, 1981

I can't stand it! *My God, why do you not hear my prayers? How can you take my child?* God chose not to answer that night.

The room, dim as always in the hours after midnight, keeps closing in on me. I will not survive this; I don't want to survive it. I just left my beloved child, seeing that flicker of fear in large, brown eyes that dart about following my voice. There is life here, faraway in a place between Heaven and Earth; but still linked to me, as if seeking me out to hold onto. Another realm reaches out in a slow, insidious attempt to steal away the love of my life, the child I brought into this world. Why?

A kaleidoscope of emotion twists through my mind, body and soul--rage at my Creator for allowing this, anger at His ignoring my pleas, not even comforting me in my darkest hour; terror that I am facing this alone, and heartache that my God, loved above all else, has forsaken me. These emotions swirl through me like a potion in a witch's caldron, brewing horrible things. Finally spent, hopelessness and deep sorrow set in, along with the knowledge--whispering in an inner core of my psyche--that the worst is yet to come.

No answers, no soothing words are forthcoming from God. I sink into the worn cushions of the ICU chairs and let the tears flow, unbidden.

~

April, 1973

By the third day at Anita's new apartment, it was time for my flight home. I felt uneasy, not having flown before--adhering to the belief that if we were meant to be airborne, we'd have been equipped with wings.

"Micki," Anita chided. "I fly all the time. Safer than cars. You know that. You'll love it. Trust me."

The only positive thought I had about flying was that Anita would not be the pilot.

"Gonna miss you, Aunt Micki," Steven said, throwing himself into my arms.

"Me too, baby. I'll try to get the whole family out here soon. I promise." I swept my fingers through his white-blonde hair, looked into those mischievous, deep eyes, the color of a summer sky, and felt like I was leaving one of my own kids.

Anita, George and Steven drove me to the airport, surprisingly small for such a busy tourist city like Las Vegas. I hugged them all, took a deep breath and climbed the ramp into the airplane from hell.

My first mistake was passing on the complimentary drink offered at the beginning of the flight. It was never offered again. Things went well for awhile, lulling me into a false sense of security. I had a window seat-- until a whiny young pregnant woman plopped down next to me and asked to switch seats.

"I hate to ask you," she said, throwing in a mild retching for effect, ". . . but I feel like I'll throw up if I don't sit by the window."

Given those odds, I agreed. This plane was not the luxurious one Butch had taken, with lounges and room to walk around, or spread out. It was a Greyhound bus with wings.

I managed to peek over my nauseous seat mate to glimpse out the window. Soaring through billowy powder-puff clouds was an amazing experience. Flying over the Grand Canyon was magnificent--the last of the good things on this flight, which consisted of hung-over gamblers who bitterly complained over their losses. These were tourists, not professional gamblers; not a happy group as they chain-smoked and complained.

Then the storms hit. The plane rocked from side to side, and turbulence caused sudden ascents or descents, both equally terrifying. The pilot spoke over the PA system, relating that a fierce tornado was nearby, as lightning sparked inside the plane leaving zigzag lines of bright light.

Scared? Oh, yes! My stomach sank somewhere near my feet and my heart slammed against the walls of my chest as if attempting to "jump ship." I was certain my children would be motherless.

Kennedy Airport loomed ahead and my heart stopped racing. Not for long though, as dense fog covered the New York area, preventing the pilot from landing. I thought, *I hope my husband takes another wife, for the kids' sake*. We hovered over the airport for four hair-raising hours. The pilot announced over the intercom that fuel was low. My heart leaped. He said we might have to detour to Boston, Massachusetts. *Boston? Boston was over four hours by car from Long Island*. I felt trapped. Alone. One thing was certain--I would never set foot aboard a plane again.

~ Twenty Five ~

After the harrowing flight, I looked forward to home. To my surprise, my house looked garish, with its bright colors of royal blue, red and lime green. I expected to feel warmth and comfort in my own home. Instead I felt as if I'd flown from the openness of the west into a bleak and crowded east. It was foggy, damp, rainy, and devoid of the constant sunlight of Nevada.

The interior of homes in the west blended with the landscape. Houses were light and airy; colors used in the decor matched the environment-- subtle, adapting to the surroundings, but never dominating it. I could barely wait to convince Butch that moving west was the answer to our dreams--the solution to all our problems.

The kids couldn't contain their exuberance at my safe return. Some, I felt, and they knew who they were, feared their behavior might have kept me away forever. Still, I was hugged and kissed as the girls all tried to speak to me at once. Nicole tried hard to remain aloof and uncaring, upset that I had dared to leave her. That lasted about five minutes before she was glued to my chest; arms locked tightly around my neck, as silent tears streamed down her face.

"Why did you go away so long, Mommy? I thought you were gone forever." Tears turned into sobs, wracking her small body, as she sniffled and shook.

"I don't know what's gotten into her. She was fine the whole time you were gone," my mother-in-law said, a frown rippling across her brows.

"It's okay, Mom," I said, smiling through my tears. "She just missed me. I've never left her so long before."

"You never left any of us before," Noelle added, wiping away tears that rolled down her face with annoyance. "Mom, it wasn't the same with you gone. I'm glad you're back." She fell into my open arms. I smiled at her ensemble of plaids and stripes; just like her Aunt Lynn at that age.

Kelly looked too distraught to speak, but managed to say, "Mom, I prayed God would get you down safely from that plane." Her large, round eyes welled with tears.

"Well, sweetie, he heard your prayers because I'm home safe and sound." By now I had my three girls hugging me at once. I could barely breathe, but it was heaven to feel their sweet touch.

"Dante, did you and Mike miss me too?"

"Nah, too busy," Dante answered. Mike just grinned and shrugged nonchalantly, but his eyes were teary. Hmm, I thought . . . a busy Dante meant trouble. I hugged them both.

"Actually, Mom," Kimber spoke up, "Grandma and I had everything under control. We had no trouble at all, and I wrote some new songs." She hugged me too, hard and long. I wondered who was in control while I was gone--Kim or Grandma? Both bore strong personalities and I could only imagine the power struggles in my absence.

"Kids, let your mom get some rest now," Butch ordered. "She's had a long, tiring trip. Get into your pajamas and you can ask her all about her trip tomorrow. And I do not expect any visitors in our bed tonight, is that clear?"

"Yes, Daddy," the three younger ones answered. The older three shrugged in disgust.

The kids dutifully left, but I knew at least Nicole would soon be in our bed. While Mom got the kids settled, praying the rosary with them, Butch poured me a scotch and water. I changed into a comfortable night shirt, stretched out across the corner of the curved couch, and relaxed fully for the first time since flying out of Vegas. Butch snuggled next to me on the long end of the red sectional sofa.

"I've missed you," Butch said, softly. "Never leave me so long again. The reports of your escapades worried me, and I'm sure you omitted the worst." I smiled, and sipped my drink. *Oh, yes, there were many parts of that trip I would never tell him.*

"Honey, we have to move out west. It's gorgeous, so open, wild, free . . . nothing like here. We owe it to the kids to get them out of New York while we still can. You have no idea what it's like out there. You'll love it."

"We'll see." His signature comment.

I had forgotten how sensual he was, but I would be reminded before the night was over. I was proven right. Soon after, the padding of little feet sounded as Nicole climbed in between us.

"Why do there always have to be three people in this bed?" Butch asked.

"Because I love you both," came a muffled voice from under the sheets.

~

I resolved that "we'll see" would not work this time. We were moving west if I had to lasso him to the station wagon and drag him there. I knew in my heart the time was right for a change. Not soon, but now. I glimpsed our future and intended to claim it.

"Now" didn't happen. It was two years before we made actual plans to move west. During that first year our friends had caught the fever as well. Kathy and Scott moved out to Las Vegas, not far from Anita and George. Carol and Danny didn't go west, but abruptly sold their home and moved upstate to Rochester, New York, home of the Kodak film company. Most amazing, Jo Romano finished her army training and intended to make a career of it. I never saw that coming.

"I am so proud of you, Jo," I said, recovering from this new development.

"Hey, Mick, Paulie's always gonna be Paulie, ya know? I gotta make a life for my kids while I have the chance."

When boot camp was over, her family moved to her army base in Florida. I marveled at her guts. Rosie and her brood decided to stay in Island Park. But aside from them, almost all of our closest friends left, pursuing a dream that we women instigated. It was the early 70's and more and more women took the helm and steered in the direction of their dreams and choices. Their men were not quite sure what had happened to them. While our friends accepted the gauntlet of change, we procrastinated. By we, I mean Butch.

~

Things were not getting better at Benny's. Tension sparked like lightning hitting a live wire. Benny cracked the whip and Butch and Danny, although hating the bondage, could not break away from his pull on them--almost like captives forming a bond with their captors. My disgust for the fat despot grew. Butch was unhappy, stressed out, overworked, which, as always, set the tone for the whole family. Except this time, I had seen what could be and intended to claim it. Tension grew between us and it was coming to a head.

~

I was constantly either nagging or beguiling Butch to make the decision to move out west. Kim and Mike were in high school now, with a high rate of absenteeism and poor grades. Drugs were rampant and I suspected Kim was getting into pot. She slept a lot and lost weight. Their school was not one to make parents aware of skipped classes or missed days until they compiled into months. We needed to get our kids somewhere safe. Long Island was no longer a safe place. Mostly Butch "yessed" me to death or ignored me, beset as always with ungodly work hours and few days off. Summer was the worst--he rarely took a day off, working both the Steakhouse and the Atlantic Beach Club. I was building up an anger that would not be squelched with "we'll sees."

It came to a head one night in midsummer. We held our usual barbeque. Butch avoided inviting our older friends like Olga and Gene, the elderly German couple, and Ann Eunice and Johnny. Instead, he invited all the younger, new help at Benny's, especially one young waitress, Annmarie, who fawned over him and Danny at work. I was furious. My anger was, typically, ignored. I simmered in silence, as always, and Butch either sensed my mood, or knew enough to not ask questions.

Pamela was equally upset with Danny, but far more proficient than me at showing it. Yet even Pam could not make Danny budge. The party was ostentatious as always. Huge half barrels served as grills for fresh lobster caught by friends off Long Island waters; plus a large sea bass, tender steaks, baked potatoes, corn on the cob, homemade salads, and all the usual chips and dips. We served beer, wine, and mixed drinks, not to mention delectable desserts, thanks to Pamela, who had an insatiable sweet tooth. It was a feast!

The young waitress flirted openly with Butch and Danny, as if we, their wives, were non-entities. Pam and I seethed, too sophisticated to make a scene, or sink to her level. Annmarie called Danny her "teddy bear" after the popular song--and even sat on his lap. I thought Pamela was going to explode. There would be hell to pay the next day.

Both of us looked outrageous that summer night. Pamela wore a sarong-type mini skirt over her bathing suit, revealing her best attributes, and I wore an animal print sarong, similar, but longer in length. I had sewed the outfits. We both looked great and we knew it. Our husbands didn't notice--big mistake on their part.

I had a nasty hangover the following day, which didn't improve my mood. The kids were off with their friends so I had the entire day to fuel my anger. Butch walked past my silent rage, unaware of the brewing storm.

"Leave Benny's, sell this house, and move somewhere safe or I'm leaving you."

"Mick, I'm not in the mood for more of your nonsense. You do what you have to do."

He pulled off his black tie, slipped out of his shoes, and leaned back into the recliner, lighting a cigarette.

"Oh, I intend to. You can bet on it. I've left you before, but this time it's different. It is Benny or me. Choose now. Be very careful. There won't be a second chance. Not this time."

Something in my voice made him hesitate, his usual confidence lost for a moment. Perhaps my steely tone, or lack of light in my eyes, more likely the note of finality. Or maybe he wanted me to make the decision for him. Second-guessing Butch was always a toss-up. I knew him no better than when we'd eloped. He took deep and mysterious to a whole new level. I knew where Michael got it.

He left the living room and went upstairs for a half hour or so, as I sulked, feeling once more a failure in establishing any real communication with him. *What if he called my bluff?* He walked back into the room and sat on the edge of the sofa.

"Go get dressed. We'll go out and discuss this over dinner. Find Kim and tell her to order a pizza and watch the kids." He had changed into a black turtleneck jersey and blue jeans. I refused to think about how good he looked.

"I don't want to go out."

"Well, I do. We need to talk in a neutral area, with no distractions."

"Fine." I walked into the bedroom, changed clothes, put on some make-up, and made an entrance that caught his attention for a change.

"You look nice," he said.

Nice? I thought, "Yeah, so do you. Let's go."

I gave instructions to Kim, kissed them all good-bye and slid into the station wagon. We rode in silence. Our lives, I thought, were an abyss of quiet--devoid of shared emotions. The silence had overshadowed our marriage for more than fifteen years. Tonight was the end of the road. Things would change between us--or not--but before this night ended, either our lives moved forward or our marriage dissolved. There was no turning back.

The waitress led us to a table for two at The Twilight Lounge, a favorite hangout full of good memories. The ambience was a perfect backdrop for either a reconciliation or breakup. Soft lights, juke box music, low ceilings spackled with thick swirling white paint, and dimly lighted lamps, created a lovely setting for romance. We placed our drink order first and when the scantily clad young waitress brought them, we ordered a light meal we barely touched.

"What do you want from me?" Butch asked. His face was framed by candlelight, his green-flecked brown eyes cold, his mood deadly.

"Apparently more than you can or care to give," I answered. "But let's not go down that road again. It's a dead end. What I want is your emancipation from Benny and a new life for us and the kids. I don't just want it, I demand it."

"What right do you have to demand anything? I work hard to provide for you and the kids."

"Stop right there! It's old news. I won't argue with you about all you do for us. I've heard it for years. You kill yourself for us and we just sit back and wallow in ingratitude, while spending your hard earned money lavishly on ourselves. There is no debate. Me or Benny. Make your choice and make it now." My voice was as steely as his eyes. "I am tired of being second in your life to your 'mistress'--your work--that seductively lures you into the illusion that hard work and long hours will excuse you from being a husband and a father."

Silence hung between us, surrounded by gentle murmurings of other patrons at the surrounding tables.

"That's not a choice. You know you are first in my life."

"No, I don't!" My laugh held rancor and bitterness. "I have never seen any sign of it."

The waitress brought another round of drinks and sensing our mood, quickly left us alone.

"There's nothing left to say. We've been there. A simple choice. Me or Benny. Choose wisely because this is your last chance."

"Okay, if I leave Benny, what are we going to do? Drop everything and go west?"

"That's what I want. A clean break. A new beginning. And yes, let's go west."

"All right."

"What did you say? Don't build up my hopes and dash them again."

"I said we'll do it. I'll give Benny notice tomorrow."

For once, I was speechless.

"Well, isn't this what you wanted?"

"Yes." I gulped, taking a long swallow of the mellow Johnny Walker Red scotch and water, nearly draining it. The flickering neon lights from the dimly lit bar suddenly made me dizzy. I felt out of touch with reality. "Yes," I whispered, "but it is more about what we need to make our marriage work. Don't do this as a sacrifice for me. Do it because you feel it is right." I felt so drained.

"You get what you want. I won't lose you or the kids, ever. So if this is the only way I can keep you, then I'll do what I have to do." He signaled the waitress for the check. "Let's go. I have an early day tomorrow."

I followed behind his quick pace to the car. We rode home in silence, each caught up in our own thoughts. It was quite an evening. We fell into bed, not too tired for lovemaking. Passion and emotional trauma oddly made for great sex. We made love, tender at first, but reaching a crescendo that burst into flames as we joined as one. We fell asleep, still connected by a bond that had held us together in the past, and would perhaps, in the future.

~ *Twenty Six* ~

Butch was true to his word. Benny was furious. He gave him the "after all I've done for you," speech, even offered him a raise in pay. Butch stood firm.

"I'll stay two months and train my replacement, but that's it."

Benny stormed into his office and slammed the door. Poor Danny. Being Butch's friend, he took the brunt of his uncle's wrath. His days were numbered now and Pamela and Dan made plans to move as far away from Benny as possible. Pam's brother got Dan a job in Washington, D.C. working for a well-known hotel chain.

Our house sold quickly. In two months we had a buyer and a closing date for late September. We'd bought a white pick-up truck with a camper on the back. It wasn't much of a camper, but had all the amenities we needed, and it would fit us all--if a little cramped.

My mother had agreed to let us store all our furniture in her basement. She drove out early one morning to see the kids and discuss the moving plans. She was working in an airplane factory now and living in Shirley, Long Island; close to Fire Island, a tiny strip of land off the main island where tourists spent the sultry New York summers.

For the first time in years, she was an early riser and got to my house, a two hour drive, at around seven o'clock in the morning. Butch and I were asleep. So were the kids. Mom banged on the back door, with bags of goodies for the kids and her snooty little poodle, Sherri, in her arms.

Kelly was also an early riser and a light sleeper. Her room was closest to the back door. She ran to unlock the door for her Grammy. My mother charged forward as the door swung open, pinning Kelly between the wall and the door. Only Kelly's face showed through the diamond-shaped glass window pane--eyes wide in horror. Mom pitched flat on her face, on top of her packages and her irate poodle. Kelly was wedged by shock and Mom's body against the door.

Butch and I awoke to screams, some human, some canine. We helped Mom up, checked both her and her little dog for injuries and pried Kelly off the wall, her face still horrified. Kelly was crying and shivering, my mother was groaning, and the damn poodle was snarling. Butch was stifling laughter that would soon be out of control. He quickly left to make fresh coffee. Mom hobbled upstairs, still groaning. Sherri refused to be carried--she wasn't a stupid animal--and by then the rest of the kids were up and asking what happened.

Grammy unloaded her bag of treasures for the kids, including the dreaded candied popcorn, which she knew I forbid in my house. Within an hour she had created enough chaos to last a month. It wasn't even time for breakfast. The kids ate her snacks instead. Sticky popcorn was soon strewn all over the place. My mother's whole body ached and the poodle's mood did not improve either. Butch stayed in the bedroom. Loud bursts of laughter came from the room, but I convinced Mom he was watching a funny show on television. Any kid who even snickered got a black look from me that meant trouble later.

"Micki, Ah'm gonna have to leave y'all and drive home before I start to get stiffer from that fall."

Uh oh, the southern accent was in full swing. "Sure, Mom, are you okay to drive?" *Please God, let her be okay to drive.*

"Ah'll be okay if ah leave right now...." heavy sigh for effect.

"Have some breakfast first," I offered.

"No, no, mah body's gettin' stiff. Better to hurry and get home." Sherri yapped as if agreeing. Miserable little cur had her own room, complete with a single bed and a television set. Kelly looked stricken as they drove off. All plans for moving furniture were put on hold.

"Honey, what's wrong?"

"I almost killed Grammy."

"No, no, she just fell in the door. It's lucky you weren't hurt, squashed by the back door." I hugged her as large tears rolled down her face. Apparently her father heard this exchange as he was now bent double with laughter, nearly choking.

"It's not that funny," I said under my breath.

"Yes it is!" He sputtered, turned red and if any mention of that morning came up, he broke into hysterical laughter. This went on for weeks. His children were shocked--actually, just Kelly, Noelle and Nicole. The other three were nearly as bad as their father.

~

The closing for the house drew near. Most of our furniture had been trucked out to my mother's house; some special pieces I couldn't take, given to friends. The die was really cast. It was going to happen.

Butch was in his "marine drill instructor" stage, making lists, campsite rules, checking maps and compiling rules for trip procedure. I laughed behind his back. I'd traveled west and knew all about "the best laid plans of mice and men." Why should I tell him? He wouldn't believe me anyway.

Butch's mom was devastated by our move, but we were too caught up in it to realize or feel her pain. The kids weren't too thrilled either. Especially Kim, who had shaped up a little and was dating a boy taller than she, who could pass for her brother--as sweet a boy as any mother could hope for. *I am doing to my children what my mother did to me*, I thought, stricken. I remembered the reason for the move--to give the kids a new and better life. Kim would get over it. The end justified the means, I told myself, wondering if my own mother, shallow as she was, had thought the same thing. No, not my mother. She structured our family life to fulfill her own needs. Kimber barricaded herself in her room, and the rest of the kids alternated between excitement for a new adventure and fear of losing a familiar past.

~

August 26, 1981

The vigil continues. Endless days merge into endless nights. My heart is an empty well, filling with so much hurt, and blending with the deep cold water of my soul. My mind sends out endless buckets to pull me out of the blackness, but even as the buckets fill, again and again, the well remains ever empty. Like a drowning swimmer, my mind struggles to surface, to breathe in the fresh air of hope. The struggle is ongoing, relief beyond my mind's grasp. I am sinking, sending out a cry for help that goes unheard. I sense, for the first time in my life, that God may not answer my prayers. The thought terrifies me.

The doctors give us no reason to hope. They insist our child is no more than a vegetable. A severed spinal cord cannot be fixed. They apply constant pressure on us to disconnect the life support and put an end to all the suffering. Neither Butch nor I will even entertain that option.

Two of my children are still missing. Michael is on an Army Reserves training expedition in South Carolina and can't be located. Kimber is at a weekend party with friends, for the annual "Put Your Fanny in the Suquehanny" festival; with hundreds of people riding the rough river on rubber rafts and inner tubes. There is no way to reach her and at the age of twenty, Kim resents having to relate her whereabouts to her parents. She is living on her own now, no longer at my beck and call. I need her.

Dante's friends, the Engler twins, Mick and Mark, are always with us, telling awful jokes to keep our spirits up. It helps. But Dante cannot be cheered by even his best friends. Jimmy-Joe and Brian and a few others of his friends drop in and out each day and night. It gets so loud sometimes that the nurse comes out to reprimand us. We need the relief of laughter now and then to break the hold of fear and terror gripping us. Sometimes strangers with loved ones of their own in the ICU sit in the large waiting room with us, and we share our stories and our hopes. Most times, because of the limited visiting hours, we have the room to ourselves, day and night. Due to the supposed hopelessness of the situation we can visit anytime, unless the nurses are adjusting the various tubes and life support mechanisms.

It is late this evening, how late I cannot say, for there are no clocks in the room and time has stopped for us. The room is dark. Butch, Kelly, Dante, and my mother-in-law are with me.

The door to the waiting room swings open and Kim bursts through, falling into my arms.

"What happened, Mom?"

I gently tell her.

"No!" she sobs. "No, not Noelle! Not my sister."

She slumps into a chair, overwrought. I hold her in my arms as her body heaves with grief and tears, until she calms down a little. Later, we fill her in on the details. Kim had called home to relate her weekend fun and my father-in-law, who stays at my house to take calls, only told her we were at the hospital. Dad won't speak of the accident, nor come to the hospital. From that night on, Kim stays at the hospital. She cannot be consoled.

~ *Twenty Seven* ~

September, 1975

It was happening. The house was sold. We were packed up and ready to go. We had said our goodbyes, excited at beginning the greatest adventure of our lives--well, their lives. I had done this two years ago and knew some of what was ahead.

I walked through the house on Knickerbocker Road, alone. I spoke to the house as to an old friend. *I'll miss you*, I mused, savoring each room that Butch and I had transformed into its present state of beauty. The house was silent. Perhaps imprints of my family remained upon it. Maybe, it was simply a house.

I was so sure my decision to move was the right one. Now that it was a reality, I wondered if I'd made the right decision. Too late to look back. The only direction left was forward.

The closing on the house was at ten in the morning and over within an hour. We drove to Ann Eunice's house for lunch and a sad goodbye. If tears shed by friends and relatives were measured, we would have floated cross country. I don't think any of us grasped the depth of the love felt for us until we were leaving it behind.

"Goodbye, New York," I whispered. "You gave us rough times and great times, but now it's time to move on."

"What did you say?" Butch asked, as we drove away from Nebraska Street. It began to rain hard, but the Flanagans stood outside, waving until we were out of sight.

"Nothing, I was just thinking out loud."

"Having second thoughts?" Butch asked.

"No, no way. We are doing the right thing. I just didn't realize it would be so hard to leave a place I thought I hated. And our friends, the ones still here."

"You hated the place, never the people."

"Exactly. I wonder if we will ever see them again."

Butch offered no answer, concentrating on handling the camper as the rain came down in torrents. Hurricane Eloise escorted us out of New York.

It seemed right and fitting that the east coast should rage over our departure. It was quiet in the back of the camper. Some of the kids were deep in thought, some crying faintly.

Kim's boyfriend, Richie, gave us a motorcycle escort. His face was stricken beneath his helmet. Kim's matched his as she watched and waved from the camper window.

We rode through high winds and torrential rains during the three hour trip to Grandma's house; usually a two hour trip. It was freezing in the front of the camper, because we needed the air conditioner on to keep the windows from fogging. I regretted wearing sandals. There was flooding on the Sunrise Highway as we approached the Verrazano Bridge, leaving New York for New Jersey. About that time we realized that the camper leaked. Shades of my trip west came flooding back to me.

After reaching Easton, Pennsylvania, we had a hot meal, warmed up and changed into dry clothes and mopped out the camper, which was under two inches of water. Mom was still pleading for us to reconsider moving back to Easton, instead. Fed and warm, we shared hugs and teary goodbyes, hoping to make it across Pennsylvania to Pittsburgh, where Butch's brother, Donald lived. We would spend the night there. It was a bad decision because Eloise was outrunning us and pelting all her fury on the entire northeast. After eight hours of 50 mile an hour gusts, floods and freezing rain, we pulled up to Don's at four in the morning. Our first day of the trip we'd logged twelve exhausting hours. The kids were all queasy as we hurried them into makeshift beds. We fell into a deep sleep 'til noon the following day. Don gave us a hurried brunch and we were off again, hoping to reach Springfield, Ohio, by nightfall. It would be our first campsite. Eloise had blown herself out and the day was sunny and mild. The camper was slowly drying out on the inside.

~

We reached the Ohio campsite by six o'clock in the evening. A huge bumblebee flew into the camper. Screaming and trampling over each other, the girls evacuated. The boys had been riding up in the front of the pick-up truck. Butch heard the noise on the intercom and came charging back as his daughters tumbled over him in their panic to escape. I killed the innocent intruder and heated up the meatloaf Mom sent with us, along with instant mashed potatoes and corn. The girls warily climbed back into the camper, which was now dubbed, "Pandemonium."

"Ugh. I can't eat this," Dante said. His siblings agreed.

I hardly blamed them--it was awful; tasted like hospital food.

"Well, this is supper. Eat it or starve." They chose to starve. The white ducks swimming in the pond by the campsite eagerly accepted the meatloaf, although the kids insisted a few sunk and never resurfaced.

Mike and Dante set up the tent while the girls and I did the dishes. With sleeping bags, a lantern and a deck of cards, they had better sleeping arrangements than the rest of us; until the tent fell in on them--again and again.

Breakfast was cream of wheat with honey and reconstituted skim milk, not yummy, but far better than last night's supper.

"Let's get rolling!" Butch ordered through the intercom connecting the truck to the camper.

"In a few minutes," I answered back.

"No! Now!"

I was brushing my teeth at the same time Butch was emptying the toilet holding tank, splashing him with toothpaste. To my mind, it could have been far worse, but he was annoyed now and left me in the back of the camper with all the kids. He revved the engine and took off toward St. Louis, Missouri. Hours later, he asked me if we should pull over to a rest stop and eat. The intercom garbled his words and I misunderstood him. So the bastion of patience continued on while I balanced precariously, making bologna and tuna fish sandwiches for dinner. No easy feat going 65 miles an hours in the camper from Hell. Nicole began whimpering to go home. Kim was sulking over the loss of Richie. Noelle and the boys played cards, oblivious to the somber beginning of our new adventure.

"Are we still in America, Mom?" Kelly asked, gazing out the window at unfamiliar sights.

"Kelly, what exactly do you learn in geography class? Of course we're still in our country. We're crossing it not deserting it." I doubted she believed me, her brows drew together as she sighed and continued to stare outside.

~

The fourth day of the trip, we pulled into a Ramada campsite. It was a large site, heavily wooded with a lake in the middle. It was difficult to find a spot where trees would not attack the roof of the camper. The only suitable site was set on a hill. The boys had to clear away rocks to put up the tent. Kelly, Noelle and Nicole swung on the park swings, then as the temperature dropped, joined Kim, Mike and Dante at the recreational center. The kids loved this place. Pool tables, pinball machines, paddle boats to rent, made it a paradise for tired campers with cranky kids. Typically, we arrived late, so their pleasure was short-lived. Kim and Noelle slept in the tent and kept rolling downhill. I slept on the downside of the double bed that lay across the upper part of the camper, over the roof of the truck. Nicole was in between Butch and I, as usual, and stayed warm, even when the camper door swung open during the night, letting in 50 degree temperatures.

The next morning I was returning from the rest rooms when the fire in the camper ignited. The pump transformer for the water started burning through its insulation and was about to consume the paper plates. I didn't know what to do and screamed for Butch.

"Get out of my way," Butch yelled, pushing me back out of the camper. "Well, that's all I can do for now," he said, after making sure the fire was completely out. "We'll need to stop at the nearest town for some new parts."

The camper stunk from the three pound loaf of Lebanon bologna his mom had sent to accompany the meatloaf. We no longer had water for the toilet or water faucets. The kids were gagging over the odious aroma of charred bologna. Butch missed the holding tank when emptying our waste, leaving a mess behind us. By now I had a twitch in my left eye.

"Throw that damn bologna out," Butch muttered as he checked the water level under the hood of the truck. As I watched him, I realized what Anita and I were supposed to have been doing each morning on our trek west. So far, this trip was surpassing the other, in spite of Mr. Drill Instructor's rules and we had a thousand miles to go. In spite of my misery, I smirked.

The fifth day of our journey took us to the outskirts of Miami, Oklahoma, on the Will Rodger's Turnpike, heading for Oklahoma City. Around noon, we stopped in Kansas City, Kansas. One of the waitresses from Benny's, Eileen, had driven our station wagon to her hometown, where we planned to meet up and drive to Vegas together. We met her grandmother, had tea and cookies and headed off again, with Eileen taking whatever kid wanted to ride with her in the station wagon.

With shades of Anita's logic, we passed a few nice KOA campsites because they were expensive. I was reminded of the old adage, "Penny wise, pound foolish." The kids hadn't eaten since the cookie break at noon, and were tired and carsick. I had tossed the bologna, but the odor permeated the camper, setting Kelly off into spasms of retching.

"Are we almost at Lost Vegas?" Nicole asked.

"Nope," I said. "We have a long way to go but it will be fun."

"I wanna go home. Now!" She was building up to a temper tantrum.

"Come sit by me and I'll read you a story about a little girl who went on an adventure just like you're doing."

She sniffled and climbed on my lap. I guess "Alice in Wonderland" was not a good choice. Nicole grabbed her doll and crawled into the top bed and softly cried herself to sleep.

"Nice try, Mom," Noelle noted, looking up from her card game with Kelly. "Maybe she would have liked "The Wizard of Oz" better."

"Very funny, Noelle. Next time she gets wigged out, she's all yours."

Noelle just grinned. "Well I couldn't do any worse."

"Are you sure we're still in America, Mom?" Kelly asked, yet again.

In spite of a starlit sky, it was very dark as we drove down the ten curvy miles leading to the Grand Lakes State Park. Again, all the best spots were taken. Butch had to wander through the park with a flashlight, looking for a site with electric hookups. Mike and Dante went with him. We missed supper again. I cooked up some hamburgers made from four day old chopped meat, hoping not to kill any of us.

The ground was so dry from a long drought that the boys couldn't get the tent spikes into the soil. Little matter. Later, a violent storm broke the dry spell and the tent collapsed in on Eileen, Kim and Noelle. They scrambled for the camper. Thunder bellowed, flashing laser beam lightning and pelting rain, so loud that we didn't hear them banging on the door to get in. Around eight o'clock in the morning, I opened the door to which they had tied the tent--in order not to be blown away. As the door swung open the tent flew off them and there were shrieks of fury coming at me. Apparently, they had spent the stormy, rainy night huddled under the collapsed tent. Noelle in a frenzy of panic--her claustrophobia kicking up in a big way. Kim tried to shield her from the wet orange tent that was laying over all of them with her body, but it wasn't much help. The girls and Eileen were rather grumpy. I realized it was still raining and finally let them inside, trying not to laugh out loud.

We moved our vehicles to the pavilion so the kids could stretch a little and sit at tables without fear of getting drenched again. I managed to whip up French toast, sausages and pineapple juice for breakfast, along with hot steamy coffee. Everyone gobbled it up, either because it was good, or because they were starved. I chuckled at Butch's frustration. I did try to warn him. He gave his daily lecture on organization and camping protocol over the intercom as we pulled away from the campsite. He drove around a curve a little too fast, turning the five gallon water container and the large bag of charcoal into flying missiles. Ahhh . . . organization.

On our sixth day we headed toward Amarillo, Texas, to a state park named, The Little Grand Canyon, or Palo Duro as it was called, literally meaning "hard wood", named for the juniper and mesquite native to the canyon. After reading a warning along the road--"deep descent"--I battened down the camper. The girls were no longer bored--they were frightened. The road was narrow with no fences and deep drops.

"Lean to the right, everyone," Butch called over the intercom. A few minutes later, as supplies flew everywhere, "Lean to the left!" It was a hairy ride and the kids and I weren't sure we were going to survive it. We finally reached the bottom of the canyon shaken, but safe.

Palo Duro Canyon was stunning. There is no way to adequately describe such beauty. We left the Texas plains at 4,000 foot elevations and drove down into the deep canyon. It was both breathtaking and terrifying. The Red River crossed the canyon at will and we rode through it. Had it rained, the river would have inundated us, but a dry spell kept the water at about a foot deep and passable. I hoped we wouldn't be breaking yet another drought.

Butch barked orders to set up camp before we could relax and take in the magnificent panorama.

"Honey," I said, pulling him aside. "Can't you just slow down and enjoy this as a long-needed vacation?"

"I am relaxed. But there are right ways and wrong ways to do things."

I sighed and walked away to join the kids. The area was an interesting mixture of red clay, white salt-like rocks and small cacti. The kids were cautious.

"It feels like we're in a prehistoric era," Kim said. She looked around, seeming both in awe and fascinated.

"Yeah," Noelle said. "I expect to see dinosaurs stomp out from the caves."

"You girls are so silly," Michael said, sneering with disgust. "It's only a canyon. Nothing here but snakes and lizards."

"Snakes and lizards!" Kelly and Noelle screamed in unison as Nicole raced to my side.

I was laughing too hard to offer them any comfort. Eileen grinned, raising her eyebrows as if questioning the sanity of our family. She had bright red hair that refused to behave in any reasonable fashion and blue/green eyes sparkling through a slightly freckled face. Luckily for us, her most redeeming qualities were patience and a highly developed sense of humor. I was not too happy about snakes and lizards either, but I kept that to myself, hoping that Butch in his "Great White Hunter" role would protect us.

We feasted on barbequed chicken, roasted potatoes, corn on the cob and applesauce--our first good meal in days. Bugs bit occasionally, but not too bad. As the sun abruptly descended, we were awestruck by the huge velvet dome of diamonds sparkling above us. We spotted the Big and Little Dippers, Venus, Mars, and the Milky Way, which spread its filmy white aura across the dark western sky. It was mesmerizing.

The next morning we set off to explore. All paths led straight up. Nicole scampered up and over the rocks like a little monkey. Kelly got herself lost in a ravine and had to be rescued by her brothers who tortured her by threatening to lose her on the way back. We hated to leave this special place, but made our way back to the canyon floor, ate fresh pancakes, showered and changed.

On the way back up, the truck spilled over with water. We stopped in Amarillo for some needed truck parts. I loved revisiting that town. A cold front moved in and the winds nearly ran us off the road. We all shared the suspicion that Butch really did carry a black cloud over his head. Anita and Butch should have taken the trip west together. I would have paid to observe that scenario.

Next stop was Tucumcari, New Mexico. We pulled into the Red Arrow campground around sunset. The winds blew fierce and we were in the open, at its mercy. Supper was a quick affair of hot dogs and beans. There was a free laundry room off the campground office. A joke. The owner, speaking in a fake western accent, turned out to be from Long Island. He altered the washing machines so that they would only fill halfway. Eileen and I cleverly filled the machines with an empty waste can full of water, but the dryers were gas and the pilot light was permanently turned off. We ended up toting clean, but wet clothes with us.

Cold winds drove us inside the camper and car. The kids were allowed by the management to sit inside the office and watch television until ten o'clock at night. Kim called Richie on the pay phone, then sulked all night. I cut Eileen's unruly hair and trimmed Kelly and Noelle's bangs. The wind was too wild to even try to set up the tent, so Butch and Michael slept in the front of the truck and Eileen and the girls and I slept in the camper. Dante got the floor.

"But Ma," he said, launching a list of complaints.

"The floor or outside the camper in a sleeping bag, Dante."

"It's not fair."

"Nope, just live with it. Life's not always fair," I said.

~

While in New Mexico we were careful not to drink the water. We had heard stories of the water in this state causing illness--plus it tasted bad. We were not smart enough to avoid using bags of ice. We had brunch at a diner with greasy burgers and fries. We drank coffee and sodas, again forgetting they were both made with water.

We camped out at Blue Water Lake State Park. It was out of this world, as panoramic as Palo Duro, but in different ways. Earlier we had stopped in Albuquerque for groceries. This park had no hook-ups for the camper so we would be really camping out. There were a few water pumps around and some shabby outhouses only the brave or desperate dared try. We found a flat spot to park, above the lake, and quickly started a fire before darkness fell. The air was crisp, but not cold, the dinner scrumptious. Fresh hamburgers, sweet melon, and green salad. One small error would mar this night. The ice cubes were made from New Mexico water.

After dinner we sat around the fire watching it burn down to glowing embers, and once more we were awestruck by the southern skies. Due to the elevation, it outdid the Palo Duro Texas skies in beauty and brightness.

In the middle of the night Nicole became violently ill; headache, stomach pains and throwing up all night long. She fell asleep near dawn, but slept fitfully, crying out in her sleep. No one else got sick, but I still blamed the ice cubes in her soda. The temperature dropped so low during the night that the ice from dinner never melted. Butch rose early and boiled water while Nicole and I tried to catch up on some sleep. Eileen and the girls laid out the still-wet clothes from the last campsite on bushes and rocks to thoroughly dry. The warm sun replaced the chill of the night and a lovely day lay before us. We spent the early part of it going down into the lush green canyon and exploring. Once acclimated to the air at that elevation, we felt exhilarated and Nicole showed no signs of sickness. We hated to drive away from such beauty, but Butch was anxious to get to Flagstaff, Arizona by nightfall. First vacation in our married life and he managed to rush through it, expecting to reach Vegas in ten days.

Flagstaff was as lovely as I remembered, pine trees dominating the air with their strong scent, while blue jays sang from treetops. We stayed at another KOA campsite, a real treat--pulling in late at night. Eileen and I drove the station wagon into town to pick up McDonald's for supper, while the boys attempted another try at setting up the tent in the dark. I held hopes they might get it right before we reached Las Vegas.

Butch awoke with a headache. Eileen and I went to the campground laundry room, leaving the kids to clean up and then explore a bit. Noelle came running to get us.

"Mom, the camper's on fire! Come quick!"

"Again? Okay, I'm right behind you. Don't let anyone go inside."

By the time I got back to the camper, Butch had put out the small fire, started again by the refrigerator, now useless for the rest of the trip. This was another campground with lots of fun things to do, but the drill instructor insisted we get on our way. I did have time for an early birthday present from the gift shop--a gorgeous bracelet with three large Persian turquoise stones that matched my favorite turquoise ring. Maybe it would bring us luck.

We were heading for the best part of the trip--the Grand Canyon. On our way we stopped at the Petrified Forest, where the older kids were vastly disappointed--expecting a tall forest of stone trees. Instead, there were hundreds of chunks of petrified wood spread across the desert. It was well-marked with ominous signs stating terrible ramifications for those who took even a small piece of these precious relics of the past. Everyone piled back into the camper, and I got in the station wagon with Eileen, Nicole and Kelly. Nicole was playing with something that seemed to fascinate her.

"Mom! You're not gonna believe what Coly's playing with!" Kelly said in her "horrified" voice.

"What?" I asked. "What do you have now, Cole?"

"It's a bootiful rock, Mommy! I found it in the sand."

"You found it in the sand with the stone trees?"

"Yup."

Oh no, I thought, *What has she done?*

I flagged Butch down just as he started to move back onto the highway. He backed up and climbed out of the camper, with that "what is the problem now" look on his face.

He leaned into the station wagon and asked what was wrong.

"Well," I said. "It seems our daughter has lifted a National Treasure."

"What?" Butch exploded.

At that point Nicole started crying.

"What's she crying about now?"

"Cole, show Daddy what you found."

"That's just great!" he said, fuming. "Nicole, there were signs everywhere saying its illegal to take anything from that place."

"But Daddy, I can't read yet." She started sobbing in earnest now and handed over her bootiful bounty, which her father took from her little hand and marched her back to the desert and made her put the National Treasure back in its place.

Nicole didn't pick up any more rocks anywhere without asking first.

The 125 mile trip to the Grand Canyon took us through Navajo country, where we stopped to admire and purchase some native jewelry.

The Indians thought Kimber was a Native American, in spite of her height, which towered over this rather short tribe.

One of the Navajos said to Kim, trying to sell her a turquoise trinket, "You some tall Indian."

"I'm not an Indian though," she replied.

"Well, you look Indian to me--but some tall Indian."

~

We arrived at the Grand Canyon at four-thirty in the afternoon. There were wonderful campsites, wooded and private with plenty of room for the tent and safe places for the kids to explore. Two large black birds shared our site; the size of large turkeys with three-foot wing spans. I guessed they were either ravens or the largest crows in the world.

The weather was pleasantly warm and after an especially creative cookout, Kim, Eileen and I walked to the canyon's edge to watch the sun setting. At that elevation it came almost without warning and we missed it. The sun set at six p.m. and we were a only few minutes late. We walked the three mile trek back to the campsite in the dark.

"Where were you?" Butch asked, anger etched across his face. "How many times do I have to say it? Clean up the campsite before leaving it."

"We wanted to catch the canyon at sunset," I snapped. "Dishes can be done anytime."

"No, camp protocol is what it is. No exceptions."

"Nazi," I muttered under my breath as I walked past him.

Butch strode off in a different direction--with me hoping he'd get lost or carried off by one of those huge birds. Or maybe walk into a tree and knock some sense into his stubborn head. He didn't.

We spent four whole days at the Grand Canyon. We could easily have spent a month there and not see all its glory. The area supported a myriad of wildlife, but all we spotted were chipmunks, squirrels, mule deer and those big birds. Kim posed on a precipice, hanging over the canyon with more miles below her than I cared to know, scaring me half to death. I yelled for Butch to do something--so he took his camera out and snapped her picture. He asked her to back up a bit, so she sat down, dangling her legs over the canyon and he snapped yet another picture.

How we hated to leave. The desert between Las Vegas and Arizona was as ugly as the canyon was beautiful. We left the pines we loved and descended into a scrubby expanse of sand and heat. The temperature rose above 95 degrees inside the camper. There was no place to stop until Kingman, Arizona, one hundred miles from Las Vegas. The fast food place at Kingman was a horror, but we were too hungry and thirsty to be picky. The kids were about to mutiny again and Nicole was whining her litany to take her back home.

The very last stop we made for gas and some sodas was at a lone gas station out in the middle of nowhere. It was surrounded by huge spiky joshua trees that looked like tall scarecrows dotting the barren desert. Butch let the kids stretch their legs awhile, while he filled the truck with enough gas to get us to Las Vegas. For a change, I decided to ride the last leg of the trip up front in the truck with Butch. We drove about ten miles down the deserted highway, when Butch called to the back on the intercom. "Everybody okay back there?"

No answer. Butch repeated the question. Then added, "Is everyone back there?"

We heard a low, "Huh, huh, huh," from Michael.

"Michael, answer me. Is everyone back there?"

"Well, I don't see Kim," he said, chuckling again.

We glanced into the station wagon driven by Eileen, but there were no passengers with her.

"Damn!" Butch said, screeching the camper to a halt and doing a fast u-turn. He drove back the ten miles to the gas station at over 80 miles an hour. There she was, hand on her hip, leaning against a gnarled dead tree. Kimber was not smiling.

"Why the heck can't you stay with the rest of the kids?" Butch yelled as she climbed into the back of the camper.

"Dad, I told Mom I was going to the rest room and when I came out, you were driving away! I knew you'd miss me and come back for me," she said, obviously furious with her father.

"Just get in the back and stay put," her father ordered, pretty much shaken himself.

"I knew I should have ridden in the back," I murmured under my breath.

Butch gave me a black look and started off again--this time with all the kids.

~

Hoover Dam was like a rollercoaster ride. It spiraled around and around overlooking the Colorado River, with narrow, winding roads. Not for the faint of heart--that would be me and most of the kids, who refused to look out the window. Aside from that, it was a remarkable man-made phenomenon.

We pulled into "Lost Vegas" as Nicole called it, at five in the afternoon. The kids were not impressed. The heat was stifling. We phoned Anita, and George drove out to meet us and lead us to their apartment. We had arrived at our new destination and whatever it held for us.

~

August, 25, 1981

I drift in limbo. Time stands still. I am wrapped in a sense of nothingness. I wait for something to propel me into the future, but I am locked in this room, in this moment. As is Noelle. She cannot move physically, or breathe or speak, but it is more than that. Noelle cannot bring herself into this world fully. She lingers, trapped between her love for us and the Heaven that tugs at her soul. It breaks me, it really breaks me. I know I need to let her go. Butch knows this too. I read it in the depth of the grief in his eyes. How awful are we that we put our needs ahead of hers, have not the courage or strength to let her go? I can't, Lord God, I just can't.

I remembered how claustrophobic Noelle was--she couldn't stand to have both her hands held--something her brothers tortured her with, by grabbing them and holding tight. *Is she awa*re *that she can't move?* I thought. I recalled the time, just a few months ago, when Noelle, Kim, Kelly and I watched "The Other Side of the Mountain," a television movie based on the biography of Jill Kinmont, an eighteen-year-old Olympic hopeful who fell down the slopes in a bad accident and became a paraplegic. We were all sobbing through the movie. I told the girls how brave the girl was to overcome her paralysis and learn to teach, making a success of her life, despite her disability. "Well if that ever happened to me, I wouldn't want to live," Noelle had firmly stated. *Was that an omen of what was to come?* I asked myself. *Do I have the right to force her to* *live in such a condition*? I have no answers. I just know that for the moment, I cannot do it. Not now. Surely, a miracle will come.

The waiting room is full tonight. The twins, a few others of the kid's friends, Dante, Kim, Kelly, Butch and of course, Mom. There are more, but the dim room shadows their faces. I start to doze off, too exhausted to consider this dilemma. Better to escape into restless sleep and better memories.

"Mom!"

I jump and sit up, rubbing my eyes.

"Go to her. She's calling for you."

"Dante, what are you talking about?"

"Mom, Noelle is talking to me in my head. She keeps saying, 'Where's Mom?'"

I run into the ICU to Noelle's bedside, as machines whirr and hiss, keeping her alive. I kiss her forehead, remembering she can only feel sensation there, and as I speak soothingly to her, she opens her eyes. As always, I gently tell her that she has been in an accident but that she will be all right.

"Are you in pain, sweetie? Blink once for yes and twice for no." Noelle blinks twice, but her eyes are still darting around, searching, always searching. *Can she see me? God, I hope so.* I see confusion in her eyes as if she doesn't know where she is. And I see fear. My soul crumbles.

"Baby, hang on. You will get through this. Don't give up. Okay?"

Her glazed eyes blink twice. Noelle will not give up. Not yet.

~ *Twenty Eight* ~

Anita's small apartment seemed to burst apart from the eight of us and Eileen. Like relatives and fish--which go bad in three days--our welcome soon wore thin. Butch checked out jobs while Anita, Eileen, and I looked for a house to rent. None of us were successful. One little detail everyone forgot to mention was that Butch needed to have a health card for a full year before he could work in Vegas, per Union rules. Not having that card meant he couldn't work in the capacity of manager, bartender or even waiter. The best he could find was barboy at one of the casinos; a humiliating defeat. The money, while not good, could keep us going--but not his spirits.

By the end of the first week, we found a home in the east end of Vegas, sitting at the end of a street right next to the desert. It was an adobe house, shaded by trees and a large backyard. We had no furniture, but took what meager possessions we'd brought with us, and moved in. The large living room had a wall to wall stone fireplace with a ledge to sit on. The kitchen, antiquated, was good enough for the present. The rest of the house was nondescript; three carpeted bedrooms and a medium-sized bathroom.

The kids were excited to finally have a real home again. Steven missed them, but he was close enough to visit often. In 1975, Las Vegas was not a large city; it was flanked on two sides by rolling hills that resembled gray elephant hide, all wrinkly lined stone with no trees. On the other end of Vegas loomed the Red Rock Mountains; also with little sign of vegetation except for cacti, but much more colorful.

There was one problem. The landlord neglected to turn on the utilities included in the rent. After nightfall we were without electricity or heat. Even in mid-October, the desert temperature fell each night. It was cold. George and Butch ingeniously figured a way to bypass wires and by some miracle we got both heat and electricity. Our calls to the landlord went unheeded. We decided this would be a temporary home until we figured out what to do. Butch took the five hour drive across the desert to Los Angeles to see it he could find work there. He returned exhausted and despondent.

He swallowed his pride and took a job as barboy in a casino where Robert Goulet sang each night. His mood was dark, but he didn't complain.

I drove the camper and enrolled the younger girls in school. Kim, Mike and Dante enrolled themselves in Las Vegas High School. I got the girls off to kindergarten and grade school. I left them at the door to their rooms and drove off, only to later learn they were locked out. They were wrecks; all three hated "Lost Vegas." Nicole, at four, was enrolled in New York schools before we left, but Las Vegas refused to accept her unless she took extensive entrance tests. She would have been the youngest child to enter a Las Vegas school in its entire history. I couldn't put Nicole through tests in her state of anxiety. I kept her out of school for the rest of the year. Kelly and Noelle's school looked like long trailers in the middle of the desert. They were miserable every day. Meanwhile, Kim and the boys loved their school, which was huge and included an outdoor picnic area for lunches. All three loved the environment. I spoke to the principal regarding Dante and his dyslexia and the man asked me how to spell it; not a good sign.

~

We were able to find a brand new ranch home to rent in the same development where Anita and George were buying a similar home. Butch and Eileen drove back east to retrieve our belongings, one driving while the other slept. They returned in less than a week with our furniture. At long last we had a real home.

It was a large four bedroom ranch with a huge eat-in kitchen, small dinette and long living room. Sliding glass doors opened out to a big back yard. A double bathroom connected the two bedrooms on each side of the house. It was the first new home we had ever lived in. We didn't bring our washing machine or dryer, so each week, the kids and I drove to the laundromat in a nearby mini-shopping mall. I tried not to go far unless it was important since I still didn't have my driver's license. Butch had reminded me not to ever put the station wagon in park, because there was a problem with it. I forgot.

I was folding the clothes for a family of eight, plus Eileen, when Kim said, "Mom, look out the window, I think the car's leaving."

I glanced out the window of the laundromat. My Vista Cruiser was, sure enough, leaving the parking lot on its own. We dashed out the door, ran after the car, which was moving slowly through the parking lot, miraculously avoiding hitting other parked cars or people. The car moved at a deliberate pace, as if it had definite plans on where it was going. We raced after it. I opened the door and jumped in to step on the brake. My heart pounded, but I saved the day. The station wagon did not escape that day.

Butch was not happy with his job, even though tips were good. He grew morose and often took the camper out on his days off and drove to the mountains to "talk to God." He took the shotgun with him. He was clearly depressed and I worried he might do something foolish. He refused to talk about it. I had no recourse except to worry and pray.

It was nearly Christmas and I hoped that would cheer him up a bit. The kids and I put up the lovely six foot fresh-cut tree Butch brought home. We decorated it with familiar decorations, including the popcorn chains made so many years before. I decided to mix up a batch of cookie dough for ornaments; stars, trees, reindeer, horses and doves--all came out perfect. The kids painted them. Somehow Dante created a gingerbread man that looked exactly like "Mr. Bill" from the Saturday Night Live television show. Mr. Bill had a red shirt and blue pants and was given a prominent place on the tree.

I tried to give the kids a familiar Christmas, but it wasn't easy. Las Vegas didn't carry the typical Italian food supplies I needed, yet somehow I managed to recreate a New York Christmas in Nevada.

Mike and Kim did well in Clark High School, in this new school district. The school had a very strict curriculum, allowing little time for either one of them to get in trouble. Dante just crept through in junior high. The older three loved Las Vegas, but Kelly, Noelle and Nicole still wanted to go home. I was reminded of the book title, "You can't go Home," by Thomas Moore, and knew it was true. Our old life was gone from us for good. Butch grew more depressed.

Anita often took me to the old "Strip," the original Las Vegas before the big new casinos were built. It was so much more fun. We visited country-western saloons, where pseudo-cowboys hit on us and the juke box played country-western music, which always struck a yearning for something in my soul. Something I could not name. Anita and I did nothing more than talk to the local patrons that surrounded us. It was innocent fun--an escape from ever-present problems.

By February Butch could no longer tolerate his job. Subsequent trips to Los Angeles proved fruitless. We looked at a large, newly built colonial house in the neighborhood, empty and ready to move into. If we stayed, we had just enough money to put a down payment on it. By now I loved Las Vegas and even the younger kids were adjusting a little better. I wanted that two-story house badly. The only thing I disliked about Las Vegas was the heat, which was brutally hot in the daytime, even in winter. Dry heat or not--hot was hot. Butch was contemplating calling it quits and either going back to Easton to his family's house or taking a chance on Los Angeles.

~

On one trip he took Nicole and me with him to stop in and visit Gerry and Oliver, who had an apartment in Los Angeles--keeping a promise to his mother to check up on her. Gerry was doing great. She'd decorated her chic apartment with taste. She had a natural knack for style and it showed in her wardrobe. Gerry had a natural sense of style and could throw on a skirt, sweater and jacket and look like a fashion model. It was an art I sure never managed. We dined that night on a gourmet meal that she'd prepared and it was wonderful to see her doing so well. Then Nicole started to get severe stomach pains and ran a high fever--off to the emergency room in nearby Burbank. We were frightened that it was the same appendicitis that nearly killed her sister Kelly at Nicole's age. The doctor said it was tonsillitis, even though her throat wasn't sore. He gave us antibiotics and we left early the next morning to get Nicole home to recover. Gerry promised to come for a visit to our house soon. Later that month, she visited and stayed the week.

"Gerry," I said, as we shared some wine after dinner. "It's so wonderful to see you so happy."

"I know," she said. "I love Oliver so much and I never expected to have such happiness in my life."

"Remember, Gerry, to be watchful for any signs of the disease returning. You know how easily it slips up on you and gets out of control before you notice it."

"I know," she said. "I don't ever want to get sick again."

"You won't," I said, hugging her, "if you're vigilant about taking the meds and watching for any signs of delusions. If something seems odd, ask yourself if it's realistic or a delusion, before it overtakes you."

Gerry promised she would and returned to Los Angeles a few days later. I prayed she'd have happiness and sanity for the rest of her life.

~

Dante loved the desert. He and Michael would disappear for hours and bring home cacti, odd rocks or wood they found. The girls stayed close to home and stuck together. Except for Kim. She had a wild assortment of friends already, some as unstable as the ones we'd left behind in New York. Trouble always follows and can't seem to be outrun.

One happy exception was a trip to the mountains. We took the kids beyond the Elephant Mountains to a place where prehistoric Native Americans had lived. There were Indian drawings on cave walls and mountainside Native artwork from thousands of years before.

Their favorite place was The Red Rock Mountains, just a few miles from our house. Nicole climbed so high I was certain she would tumble down. I went up after her, but she was more surefooted than me. The rest of the kids roamed the sharp, rocky hills, devoid of vegetation, except for cactus and scrub brush. We never tired of exploring.

One weekend we camped out overnight there. The sky was not so clear due to the neon lights of the city, but lovely nonetheless. George, Anita and Steven joined us. We sat around the warm fire as the desert chill struck after sunset and had a wonderful time. Like the mountains and beaches, deserts have a calming aura about them. For this night at least, our troubles were soothed by the quiet serenity of nature.

Our homecoming changed that. The house was broken into while we were gone. They broke into the kitchen window, and smashed all the Hummel figurines I'd placed on the windowsill. The old German waiter, Gene, and his wife, Olga, had given them to me and I treasured them. I didn't even realize their worth. The thieves, probably teenagers, stole my new turquoise bracelet from Flagstaff and some other jewelry--so much for it bringing good luck. They may have taken other things, but I couldn't remember what I had or what was missing. Mostly, they trashed the house, raided the refrigerator and had one heck of a party.

I think that was the turning point. More and more Butch spoke of returning home.

~ *Twenty Nine* ~

It was late March. We'd spent nine months in Vegas, the time it takes to create a new life. It didn't look like we'd accomplish a new life here.

"What should we do, Mick?" Butch asked after another trek in the mountains.

If God did not have his answers, why did he presume I did? I thought.

"Do what you need to do," I said, echoes of similar words said in the past. Eileen, too, was disgusted with Las Vegas, couldn't find work and decided to return to Kansas. It took more than the click of shiny red shoes and a hot air balloon. She flew home.

I spoke to the kids, not that their opinions would impact the decision, but they had the privilege to give them.

"Mom, I love it here," Kim said. "It's the best school I've ever had." She was not as happy as she projected. One of her friends, Billy, had been arrested for possession of marijuana, a joint, no more. He hung himself with his own blue jeans after being told that his parents refused to come and get him out. She was upset and deeply affected by his death. She went to his funeral with the rest of her entire high school, hundreds of kids and teachers and neighbors were there to say goodbye. Kim was his girlfriend and she was allowed to touch his closed casket in farewell.

"What about you, Mike?"

He shrugged. "It's nice here. I like it."

"Dante?"

"Mom, it's neat out here. Lots of stuff to do. Let's stay."

"Dante!" Kelly stamped her feet. "It's not nice here. My school's terrible."

"But Kel, you're in a real school building now. Don't you like it?" I asked.

"No, the teachers here are mean."

"They really are, Mom," Noelle said. "And we have no friends."

"Glad I don't hafta go," said Nicole. "I just wanna go home."

"Kids, I'm kind of liking it for now, which I didn't at first. But it's your dad's decision. He's the one who has to work to support us and if he's not happy, none of us will be."

"That's for sure," Kim said, sulking. She tossed her long dark hair back to stress her point.

"Okay then," I said. "Whichever decision your dad makes, we agree to. You guys okay with that?"

"Whatever," Kim said.

"Yeah," Mike and Dante both said. They walked out of the room and off into the desert.

"Yea! We're leaving Lost Vegas," Nicole said and ran to hug Kelly and Noelle.

"Nicole, you don't know that Daddy will want to go home," Noelle said.

"Yeah, I do too know. Daddy hates it here, just like me."

Nicole's predictions were right. The outcome was quick. Within two weeks Butch took the camper along with Noelle and Michael and drove back to Easton. They would stay at Grandma's house and enroll in the school there, until we joined them. He planned to fly back alone, rent a truck for our furniture--barely unpacked--and then drive the truck back to Easton. I'd follow him with the rest of the kids in the station wagon.

I'd recently acquired my driver's license in Vegas. It was simple, not like in New York. I had driven the station wagon around the building and back.

"Ok," my instructor said. "You pass."

"Don't you want to see if I can parallel park or at least back up?" I had asked him.

"Lady, if I can't tell how you drive by going around the block, I don't know my job."

You got that right, I thought, but I had my license and drove proudly home taking a shortcut across the desert. A clever idea, I thought at the time.

"What did you do?" Butch said, loud enough to catch the attention of the neighbors as I walked back to the driveway, where the station wagon was perfectly parked. He was holding some car part in his hands and the look on his face wasn't pretty.

"Nothing."

"Don't say 'nothing.' You had to hit something to rip this tailpipe half off."

"Well, maybe a small rock or two in the desert."

"The desert? What the hell were you doing driving in the desert?"

I was beginning to break a sweat. "I cut fifteen minutes off the trip home and missed the rush hour traffic," I said, attempting to look proud.

"Stay on the road from now on. It took more than the desert sand to do this." He walked over to the car, shaking his head and started to try and fix the car.

To my mind, the rusty old tailpipe was due to drop off anyway. And there was no concrete proof that it was my fault. After all, they were small rocks, except for that one ...

~

The problem gnawing at me was that I disliked driving; and the thought of driving cross country after having my license less than a month, terrified me. Flashbacks of going around the Hoover Dam added to my fears.

Butch left for Easton with Mike and Noelle and as I kissed them goodbye, I whispered to Noelle, "Stay in the car at all times, honey."

"Don't worry, Mom. I'm not gonna get left behind anywhere."

I heard Michael let out one of his low, devious little chuckles.

"Take care of your sister, Mike. And sit up front with your dad to help keep him awake."

They pulled away, promising to call me along the way. I felt an empty feeling in my stomach. Almost half my family was gone and I was now responsible for the rest of us. I managed to get over that rather quickly. Anita and I had a ball while Butch was gone. I had a built-in baby sitter and no husband to answer to--the possibilities were endless. We got in as much casino time and country-western saloons as we could, getting home sometimes near dawn. This was Las Vegas, after all. I reveled in the knowledge of no spaghetti western scenes--Butch dragging me home with a lecture thrown in for good measure. He was thousands of miles away and I answered to no one but myself. During the day, I packed up the house; nights, I enjoyed my short freedom.

Butch flew back the week after he arrived in Easton. I missed Noelle and Michael terribly. Butch had enrolled them both in school before he left. Noelle went to an elementary school a few blocks from Grandma's house, and Michael entered Wilson High School, my old alma mater. As soon as the rest of us drove east, Kim and Dante would be joining him there. What a coincidence to have three of my kids going to my old school.

The kids and I packed up the rest of the house. We had a final dinner with a teary King family and planned to leave in a few days.

"Mick, are we doing the right thing?" Butch asked, lying in bed, unable to sleep.

What do you mean, we? I wanted to say.

"I don't know, Butch, I really don't. Three more months and your health card will be activated. You could make a lot of money here in management."

"I can't take three more months."

"Then it's a done deal. Why are we even discussing it?" Butch looked like a man tortured with indecision, but I knew he couldn't take any more groveling as a barboy.

"We could go to Los Angeles, or some other part of California. What do you think?"

"Mike and Noelle are already settled back in Easton."

"I can go get them," he said, looking torn with guilt and frustration.

"I don't know Butch, I just don't know."

~

We drove past Anita's house on our way to wherever, said final goodbyes and pulled out onto the main road. Butch had Kim in the rental truck with him and I had Dante up front with me, with Kelly and Nicole wedged between boxes and bags of our possessions in the back of the station wagon. Butch bought CB radios for him and me. Oh, did he regret that!

"Well," he said over the CB, "Do we go east or west?"

"Your choice," I said back. "Pick one and I'll follow."

We went east. The first disaster happened on the two lane highway heading out of Vegas. Butch said to stay close behind him. I took that literally. He passed a car on the highway and I got right behind him. He tried to tell me to get back in the right lane, but the CB was full of static.

Meanwhile, an eighteen-wheeler was heading right at him. He wouldn't move over until I did, trying to protect me, but finally he had to get over or hit the big rig head on. In the nick of time he pulled over to the right and I saw the huge truck bearing down on me. I dutifully followed him, faster than I normally did once I saw the trucker's eye color. Butch nearly wet his pants. I wasn't far from it myself. He had quite a bit to say, a tad loudly, but static wiped out most of it.

Next came the perilous ride down Hoover Dam--much worse than driving up. I think Angels drove the station wagon that day, as it couldn't have been me. I had to, as a new driver, keep both hands on the steering wheel at all times. Kim, back in the station wagon with me now, handed me a soda to drink or held a cigarette to my lips for a quick drag.

After the dam, it was boring desert for hours. With the CB, we all had "handles" or names. I was "Goldilocks," Kim was "Snow White" and Butch was "The Italian Stallion." The man had no shame.

Kim and I were having a great time talking to other CB'ers, especially truckers. When one of the truckers pulled alongside us on the shoulder of the road to get a look at "Goldilocks" and "Snow White," Butch had had enough.

"Put the radio down, Snow White!" His voice boomed through channel 19 and spoiled all our fun. The approaching eighteen-wheeler dropped back behind us and after that, we had to behave ourselves.

The radio did have important uses, though. For one thing, we were able to get weather updates and find out if there were any State Troopers, or "Smokys" ahead of us. I got very good at warning others of "Bears in plain brown wrappers at the 166 mile marker--east-bound." One afternoon I spotted a "bear" and got right on the radio to warn the CB world.

"There's a Smoky at the 137 mile marker--east-bound." I repeated the warning when I got no answer. Then a very clear, angry male voice came on the radio and said, "Lady, we are on a manhunt. We're not looking for moving violations or speeding vehicles. Please do not broadcast our location."

Kim says he repeated this twice. I swear I never heard it--damn static.

So, ten miles later, when I saw another State Trooper hiding along the west-bound side of the highway, I got on the CB and sent out my warning.

This time it was Butch who answered.

"Mick, put the radio down! Didn't you hear that there's a manhunt on? Go back to channel 3--now!"

Channel 3 was the boring channel that only Butch and I used. I sighed. Kim grinned. We switched to channel 3 for an hour or so and then switched back to channel 19. The truckers kept me wide awake, that's all. They kept me alert. That's my story and I'm sticking to it.

We drove straight across country--non-stop. We would drive eight to ten hours--or more--until my eyes began closing, then stop, sleep two or three hours, eat caffeine candy to wake up, and get right back on the road. It was a grueling trip.

I stayed right behind Butch to such a degree that when he tried to do a u-turn over a grass divider--which was clearly marked "NO U-TURN"-- the truck ended up in a ditch. It was a dark night and we'd (he'd) missed his exit and didn't want to drive all the way back. So he tried to make the u-turn with me snuggled up to his rear bumper. He couldn't maneuver the truck and kept shouting at me.

"Back up!" he kept screaming over the CB. All I heard was static. The truckers came in so much clearer. Butch was able to get out of the ditch after some tricky moves. He walked back to the station wagon to say a few words in person. It wasn't pretty.

Ten more hours of driving, three hours sleep, caffeine candy, and off again.

He pulled into a gas station, me right behind him. He didn't give me enough room to get off the road and a car was coming right at me. I pulled in closer and hit Butch's truck. He jumped out and ran back to me.

"Are you all right?" he asked, his face pale.

"Yes, why did you back up and hit me?"

It almost worked, but "almost" only works with "horseshoes and hand grenades." Once again, Butch had a few words for me. Again, not pretty.

We were averaging a thousand miles a day. How we managed this, I'll never know. The last leg of the trip was even more terrifying than Hoover Dam. We were on a six lane highway in Memphis, Tennessee, right in the morning rush-hour commute. Traffic was bumper to bumper and everyone was going 65 miles an hour. I stayed right behind him, my fear of getting lost deeply embedded in a host of other fears, death being the most imminent.

Butch kept zigzagging across six lanes full of fast-moving traffic--me right on his tail. I figured we'd never get through this alive. He radioed back as we got to the off ramp.

"Everybody ok?"

"Yeah, but I'm going to need a change of underwear."

It seemed a dozen truckers burst through the CB with hoots of laughter. I was mortified. We pulled in to his mom and dad's house three days after leaving Las Vegas.

I thought I would collapse and sleep, but found I was too wired up. Mom laid a huge spread of food, real food, the first in days and we ate and ate. Then we slept.

~ Thirty ~

It was late March. We'd spent nine months in Vegas, the time it takes to create a new life. It didn't look like we'd accomplish a new life here.

"What should we do, Mick?" Butch asked after another trek in the mountains.

If God did not have his answers, why did he presume I did? I thought.

"Do what you need to do," I said, echoes of similar words said in the past. Eileen, too, was disgusted with Las Vegas, couldn't find work and decided to return to Kansas. It took more than the click of shiny red shoes and a hot air balloon. She flew home.

I spoke to the kids, not that their opinions would impact the decision, but they had the privilege to give them.

"Mom, I love it here," Kim said. "It's the best school I've ever had." She was not as happy as she projected. One of her friends, Billy, had been arrested for possession of marijuana, a joint, no more. He hung himself with his own blue jeans after being told that his parents refused to come and get him out. She was upset and deeply affected by his death. She went to his funeral with the rest of her entire high school, hundreds of kids and teachers and neighbors were there to say goodbye. Kim was his girlfriend and she was allowed to touch his closed casket in farewell.

"What about you, Mike?"

He shrugged. "It's nice here. I like it."

"Dante?"

"Mom, it's neat out here. Lots of stuff to do. Let's stay."

"Dante!" Kelly stamped her feet. "It's not nice here. My school's terrible."

"But Kel, you're in a real school building now. Don't you like it?" I asked.

"No, the teachers here are mean."

"They really are, Mom," Noelle said. "And we have no friends."

"Glad I don't hafta go," said Nicole. "I just wanna go home."

"Kids, I'm kind of liking it for now, which I didn't at first. But it's your dad's decision. He's the one who has to work to support us and if he's not happy, none of us will be."

"That's for sure," Kim said, sulking. She tossed her long dark hair back to stress her point.

"Okay then," I said. "Whichever decision your dad makes, we agree to. You guys okay with that?"

"Whatever," Kim said.

"Yeah," Mike and Dante both said. They walked out of the room and off into the desert.

"Yea! We're leaving Lost Vegas," Nicole said and ran to hug Kelly and Noelle.

"Nicole, you don't know that Daddy will want to go home," Noelle said.

"Yeah, I do too know. Daddy hates it here, just like me."

Nicole's predictions were right. The outcome was quick. Within two weeks Butch took the camper along with Noelle and Michael and drove back to Easton. They would stay at Grandma's house and enroll in the school there, until we joined them. He planned to fly back alone, rent a truck for our furniture--barely unpacked--and then drive the truck back to Easton. I'd follow him with the rest of the kids in the station wagon.

I'd recently acquired my driver's license in Vegas. It was simple, not like in New York. I had driven the station wagon around the building and back.

"Ok," my instructor said. "You pass."

"Don't you want to see if I can parallel park or at least back up?" I had asked him.

"Lady, if I can't tell how you drive by going around the block, I don't know my job."

You got that right, I thought, but I had my license and drove proudly home taking a shortcut across the desert. A clever idea, I thought at the time.

"What did you do?" Butch said, loud enough to catch the attention of the neighbors as I walked back to the driveway, where the station wagon was perfectly parked. He was holding some car part in his hands and the look on his face wasn't pretty.

"Nothing."

"Don't say 'nothing.' You had to hit something to rip this tailpipe half off."

"Well, maybe a small rock or two in the desert."

"The desert? What the hell were you doing driving in the desert?"

I was beginning to break a sweat. "I cut fifteen minutes off the trip home and missed the rush hour traffic," I said, attempting to look proud.

"Stay on the road from now on. It took more than the desert sand to do this." He walked over to the car, shaking his head and started to try and fix the car.

To my mind, the rusty old tailpipe was due to drop off anyway. And there was no concrete proof that it was my fault. After all, they were small rocks, except for that one .....

~

The problem gnawing at me was that I disliked driving; and the thought of driving cross country after having my license less than a month, terrified me. Flashbacks of going around the Hoover Dam added to my fears.

Butch left for Easton with Mike and Noelle and as I kissed them goodbye, I whispered to Noelle, "Stay in the car at all times, honey."

"Don't worry, Mom. I'm not gonna get left behind anywhere."

I heard Michael let out one of his low, devious little chuckles.

"Take care of your sister, Mike. And sit up front with your dad to help keep him awake."

They pulled away, promising to call me along the way. I felt an empty feeling in my stomach. Almost half my family was gone and I was now responsible for the rest of us. I managed to get over that rather quickly. Anita and I had a ball while Butch was gone. I had a built-in baby sitter and no husband to answer to--the possibilities were endless. We got in as much casino time and country-western saloons as we could, getting home sometimes near dawn. This was Las Vegas, after all. I reveled in the knowledge of no spaghetti western scenes--Butch dragging me home with a lecture thrown in for good measure. He was thousands of miles away and I answered to no one but myself. During the day, I packed up the house; nights, I enjoyed my short freedom.

Butch flew back the week after he arrived in Easton. I missed Noelle and Michael terribly. Butch had enrolled them both in school before he left. Noelle went to an elementary school a few blocks from Grandma's house, and Michael entered Wilson High School, my old alma mater. As soon as the rest of us drove east, Kim and Dante would be joining him there. What a coincidence to have three of my kids going to my old school.

The kids and I packed up the rest of the house. We had a final dinner with a teary King family and planned to leave in a few days.

"Mick, are we doing the right thing?" Butch asked, lying in bed, unable to sleep.

What do you mean, we? I wanted to say.

"I don't know, Butch, I really don't. Three more months and your health card will be activated. You could make a lot of money here in management."

"I can't take three more months."

"Then it's a done deal. Why are we even discussing it?" Butch looked like a man tortured with indecision, but I knew he couldn't take any more groveling as a barboy.

"We could go to Los Angeles, or some other part of California. What do you think?"

"Mike and Noelle are already settled back in Easton."

"I can go get them," he said, looking torn with guilt and frustration.

"I don't know Butch, I just don't know."

~

We drove past Anita's house on our way to wherever, said final goodbyes and pulled out onto the main road. Butch had Kim in the rental truck with him and I had Dante up front with me, with Kelly and Nicole wedged between boxes and bags of our possessions in the back of the station wagon. Butch bought CB radios for him and me. Oh, did he regret that!

"Well," he said over the CB, "Do we go east or west?"

"Your choice," I said back. "Pick one and I'll follow."

We went east. The first disaster happened on the two lane highway heading out of Vegas. Butch said to stay close behind him. I took that literally. He passed a car on the highway and I got right behind him. He tried to tell me to get back in the right lane, but the CB was full of static.

Meanwhile, an eighteen-wheeler was heading right at him. He wouldn't move over until I did, trying to protect me, but finally he had to get over or hit the big rig head on. In the nick of time he pulled over to the right and I saw the huge truck bearing down on me. I dutifully followed him, faster than I normally did once I saw the trucker's eye color. Butch nearly wet his pants. I wasn't far from it myself. He had quite a bit to say, a tad loudly, but static wiped out most of it.

Next came the perilous ride down Hoover Dam--much worse than driving up. I think Angels drove the station wagon that day, as it couldn't have been me. I had to, as a new driver, keep both hands on the steering wheel at all times. Kim, back in the station wagon with me now, handed me a soda to drink or held a cigarette to my lips for a quick drag.

After the dam, it was boring desert for hours. With the CB, we all had "handles" or names. I was "Goldilocks," Kim was "Snow White" and Butch was "The Italian Stallion." The man had no shame.

Kim and I were having a great time talking to other CB'ers, especially truckers. When one of the truckers pulled alongside us on the shoulder of the road to get a look at "Goldilocks" and "Snow White," Butch had had enough.

"Put the radio down, Snow White!" His voice boomed through channel 19 and spoiled all our fun. The approaching eighteen-wheeler dropped back behind us and after that, we had to behave ourselves.

The radio did have important uses, though. For one thing, we were able to get weather updates and find out if there were any State Troopers, or "Smokys" ahead of us. I got very good at warning others of "Bears in plain brown wrappers at the 166 mile marker--east-bound." One afternoon I spotted a "bear" and got right on the radio to warn the CB world.

"There's a Smoky at the 137 mile marker--east-bound." I repeated the warning when I got no answer. Then a very clear, angry male voice came on the radio and said, "Lady, we are on a manhunt. We're not looking for moving violations or speeding vehicles. Please do not broadcast our location."

Kim says he repeated this twice. I swear I never heard it--damn static.

So, ten miles later, when I saw another State Trooper hiding along the west-bound side of the highway, I got on the CB and sent out my warning.

This time it was Butch who answered.

"Mick, put the radio down! Didn't you hear that there's a manhunt on? Go back to channel 3--now!"

Channel 3 was the boring channel that only Butch and I used. I sighed. Kim grinned. We switched to channel 3 for an hour or so and then switched back to channel 19. The truckers kept me wide awake, that's all. They kept me alert. That's my story and I'm sticking to it.

We drove straight across country--non-stop. We would drive eight to ten hours--or more--until my eyes began closing, then stop, sleep two or three hours, eat caffeine candy to wake up, and get right back on the road. It was a grueling trip.

I stayed right behind Butch to such a degree that when he tried to do a u-turn over a grass divider--which was clearly marked "NO U-TURN"-- the truck ended up in a ditch. It was a dark night and we'd (he'd) missed his exit and didn't want to drive all the way back. So he tried to make the u-turn with me snuggled up to his rear bumper. He couldn't maneuver the truck and kept shouting at me.

"Back up!" he kept screaming over the CB. All I heard was static. The truckers came in so much clearer. Butch was able to get out of the ditch after some tricky moves. He walked back to the station wagon to say a few words in person. It wasn't pretty.

Ten more hours of driving, three hours sleep, caffeine candy, and off again.

He pulled into a gas station, me right behind him. He didn't give me enough room to get off the road and a car was coming right at me. I pulled in closer and hit Butch's truck. He jumped out and ran back to me.

"Are you all right?" he asked, his face pale.

"Yes, why did you back up and hit me?"

It almost worked, but "almost" only works with "horseshoes and hand grenades." Once again, Butch had a few words for me. Again, not pretty.

We were averaging a thousand miles a day. How we managed this, I'll never know. The last leg of the trip was even more terrifying than Hoover Dam. We were on a six lane highway in Memphis, Tennessee, right in the morning rush-hour commute. Traffic was bumper to bumper and everyone was going 65 miles an hour. I stayed right behind him, my fear of getting lost deeply embedded in a host of other fears, death being the most imminent.

Butch kept zigzagging across six lanes full of fast-moving traffic--me right on his tail. I figured we'd never get through this alive. He radioed back as we got to the off ramp.

"Everybody ok?"

"Yeah, but I'm going to need a change of underwear."

It seemed a dozen truckers burst through the CB with hoots of laughter. I was mortified. We pulled in to his mom and dad's house three days after leaving Las Vegas.

I thought I would collapse and sleep, but found I was too wired up. Mom laid a huge spread of food, real food, the first in days and we ate and ate. Then we slept.

~ *Thirty One* ~

It took a few weeks to recover from our harrowing trip back east. We returned the rental truck and stored our possessions in Butch's parents' garage. All the kids were enrolled in school, making fairly good adjustments after all the changes made in their young lives in less than a year. Butch's mom took a job at a local sewing factory, since his dad was semi-retired due to his emphysema. I took care of the house and made supper for both families while Butch researched restaurant managerial positions throughout the Easton, Bethlehem and Allentown area. He wasn't having much success.

One weekend we took a ride back to Long Beach, Long Island, to visit Ann Eunice. She, Johnny and John Andrew were considering selling their home to her daughter and moving to Phoenix, Arizona. Ann Eunice was feeding a stray puppy that had showed up at her doorstep, but she couldn't keep it.

"No," Butch said, before I even brought it up. "No more pets. Don't even think about it." His arms were folded across his chest, his look forbidding.

"But she's so cute and think how much she'll cheer up Nicole, who's been moping around like a lost soul."

"Absolutely no more pets. How many times do I have to say this?"

"Okay, okay," I said. "Let it be on your conscience when this little pup is put down because no one wants her--except of course, for your own little girl."

After a late lunch, we said our goodbyes and headed back to Easton. Sheba, the newly-named black and white sheep dog nestled in my lap, sighing with content.

The kids were thrilled to have a new puppy. Sheba attached herself to Nicole--bonding at once. My father-in-law cringed. My precious mother-in-law accepted her without protest. She was so enthralled to have her son, grandkids and me under her roof again that she could barely contain herself. She took over the kids on the weekends, letting me sleep in and spoiled them--yet kept total control. *How does she manage that?* I wondered.

May was upon us and the weather warmed. Dad built a doghouse for Sheba, another of my animals who found the concept of housebreaking baffling. She stayed outside in the mild spring days. The kids made some friends in the neighborhood; many they knew from summer vacations at Grandma's house, and a few new ones from school. Our lives, still in limbo, were pleasant enough, even if our future was uncharted.

Mike caught poison ivy while walking Sheba out behind the house. His face swelled to grotesque proportions. I rushed him to the hospital, where he received a cortisone shot and medications for the terrible itching. He made "The Hunchback of Notre Dame" look presentable. Kim sold tickets to her neighborhood friends to come and view her "monster" brother and Dante followed suit. Both got grounded for three weeks, but I assumed whatever diabolical revenge Mike planned for them would be much worse.

~

By July, Butch had a lead on a job, but it was two and a half hours north of Easton, in Williamsport, Pennsylvania. He drove up to check out the position of General Manager for the Genetti Lycoming Hotel, a landmark of the historical city. It was the first one that held promise, but paid half of what he'd made in New York. He counted on the lower cost of living to make up the difference. Butch came back excited.

"It's a beautiful city, Mick." He sat at his mom's kitchen table, exhausted from the drive, drinking coffee and eating his favorite pie. No one made lemon meringue like Mom.

"Wait'll you see it. You're going to love it. I told Gus, the owner, that I'd take it, pending your approval. What d'you think?"

"Nothing else has panned out. The kids are out of school, driving your dad crazy. We've overstayed our welcome. Do we really have a choice?"

"Guess not," he said. The excitement faded from his face, replaced by disappointment.

I regretted causing that, but it was too late to take it back.

"Butch, let's just do it. We need to get back to being a separate family again. Mom would never admit it but we are exhausting her. I was just hoping it wouldn't be so far away from here."

I stepped outside on the back porch before I said something else to damage his pride. I wanted to stay closer to Easton, not travel to another strange place. I was acting like my kids.

"All right," he called out through the door. "I'll tell Gus I'm taking the position. He expects me to start right away."

The decision was made, right or wrong, causing our lives once more to veer off in a different direction. Butch started work the next week. I braced the kids for yet another move. I called them all together.

"I think we'll like where Daddy works. It sounds beautiful and until we find a home, we get to spend the rest of the summer in a hotel suite."

"Another school change, Ma?" Kim asked, as she walked in the door, suntanned from swimming in the Wilson Park pool. "Who cares?" She slumped into the sofa cushions with apparent boredom.

She cared, I knew, and I felt her pain. The boys didn't seem to mind so much, but the younger girls were attached to their grandma.

"Mom, why do we hafta keep moving?" Nicole asked, climbing up onto my lap.

"Yeah, Mom, how many more times are we going to move?" Noelle asked. "I like my school here and my new friends."

Kelly, looking distraught, quietly left the room. Sheba, allowed inside for limited periods, whined, but her opinion didn't count. It was done.

Within weeks we set off for our new home. Mike and Dante stayed to care for Sheba. Butch and I packed up our personal belongings, leaving the furniture in the garage until we found a house. We said tearful goodbyes to the family and climbed into the station wagon. Once again, I would be following Butch, who was driving the camper. We drove north on #33 through the Pocono Mountains where we would pick up #80, a major artery passing by Williamsport. After two hours of nerve-wracking driving amidst speeding eighteen-wheelers, we turned off onto #15 which would take us directly into Williamsport.

"Look girls," I said. "There's the Lewisburg Maximum Security Prison. It's where they send a lot of mafia convicts. Some of Daddy's customers from Benny's ended up there."

"Good," Noelle piped up. "Let's remember to tell Dante he might be heading there, if he doesn't shape up."

A few miles later we passed a building housing live snakes. "Wanna stop here?"

"Yes, lets," Kim said. "I love snakes."

"No!" came a trio of voices from the back seat.

We passed the Little league World Championship Baseball Center, but the girls were not impressed. We seemed to be steadily climbing a huge mountain. If driving up was traumatic, driving down that two-lane road was sheer terror.

"It feels like the top of the world, Mom," Noelle said in an awed tone.

"I'm scared," Nicole said, pressing next to Kelly, who was no less frightened.

"What a bunch of sissies," Kim said with disdain. "It's only a big old hill. You've been on roller coasters higher than this."

"No we haven't," all three cried out at once. I knew I sure hadn't. I tried to keep my eyes straight ahead, but it was impossible not to look down over the city of Williamsport from such a height. It was an exhilarating, if intimidating sight. We approached the Market Street Bridge which forged a pathway across the swirling blue-green Susquehanna River and dam. It was a fierce, stunning rush of river; brute power combined in a breathtaking panorama. The kids were impressed. Once over the bridge, I breathed a sigh of relief. I may have mentioned my dislike of driving over bridges.

~

"Look Ma," Kim said. "There's the Genetti Lycoming Hotel where Dad's working."

The old brick, ten-story hotel was the highest building in town, not beautiful, but lending a presence to the rest of the area. Within minutes, we were entering the turnstile gates in the parking lot of the hotel, ready to begin our new life. It was hot, and humidity embraced the Susquehanna Valley in a sweltering vise, unrelieved by the cool breezes of the mountains above it. Five-year-old Nicole clutched her teddy bear tightly. Kelly looked out the window cautiously, her large brown eyes widening as she took in her new surroundings.

"Well, it's not Las Vegas," Kim remarked, assuming her role as eldest child and authority on life.

It's not gonna be so bad," Noelle said, jumping up and down. "This hotel even has a big swimming pool."

It didn't take long to unload our few belongings and carry them up the service elevator to the apartment on the tenth floor of the hotel. We were exhausted and hungry. Butch went out looking for a fast food place and we all collapsed on the long living room couch. Noelle sprawled out on the antiquated oriental rug. The two bedrooms ran parallel to each other and were about twenty feet long by fourteen feet wide. The living room was just as large in area, but square. There was a narrow galley kitchen leading into a lovely dining room. The only closet, a walk-in, was the size of a small bedroom. The bathroom was twice the average size, perfect for four young girls. The furniture, mostly antiques, was simply gorgeous. We couldn't help but be happy with this place. We felt like we were on vacation--a real vacation with no tents and campsites; instead a plush apartment with an elevator leading to an in-ground swimming pool. And as Noelle pointed out, no nasty brothers to bug them.

We enjoyed the summer days. Beth, the lifeguard, often watched the kids for me while I ran to the nearby supermarket. Kim, being Kim, managed to find a biker gang--should I say biker group?--hanging out at the Arco gas station a few blocks from the hotel. When she brought Terry, a tall, hefty, bearded biker to the pool--gang or group--Butch squelched that by putting her to work in the kitchen of the Genetti restaurant-- "Rhonaby's." Her work hours were long, curtailing her free time. When Butch caught her kissing a red-headed waiter, her free time ceased completely.

~

It was 1976 and bicentennial celebrations were in full swing. We went to many of them, including a ride on an old train dubbed, "The Freedom Train." While the girls swam and Kim worked, I searched for housing for us. I had time to take in some of the sights of the city and it was fascinating. Williamsport was an architectural wonder, displaying nearly every type of building design, some beautiful, some rather oddly thrown together--but each coexisting in defiant individuality. Gothic churches with stone spires grasping at the heavens, dominated wide, tree-lined streets. Perhaps a single architect built the strange variety of churches, homes and buildings, unable to decide which he preferred.

The City Fathers, following the example of other cities feeling the financial crunch of the 70's recession, reconstructed the Center City shopping area in an attempt to lure residents from the sprawling Susquehanna Mall, twenty miles away. The historical splendor of the city was retained, instead of being replaced by prefabricated emotionless office buildings and stores--with no foreseeable past or future. Only the modern, newly erected courthouse stood out like an arrogant teenager amidst elder, sedate buildings of fieldstone; with tall, narrow windows, low stone fences and red tile roofs darting off in all directions.

The city sprawled leisurely into the rural farmlands of Loyalsock Township, where it was not unusual for traffic to come to a halt as a herd of cattle crossed the road to reach the grassy meadowlands. They would graze until sunset and cross back to the barns. An occasional horse clopped steadily down narrow country lanes, taking all the room it needed, often ridden bareback by several children, most no older than nine or ten. This was where I wanted to live and raise my children; safe from the drugs and crime of larger cites.

The Susquehanna River ran along the city, wide and purposeful, like a dog trotting obediently for home. The dam intersected the river, collecting the sapphire water and thrusting it forward in an attempt to hurry its steady course to the Chesapeake Bay. The Paddleboat, a new addition for the bicentennial celebration, and a replica of days past, splashed up and down the river, giving residents and tourists alike, a feel for the days when the city was a booming lumber town, inhabited by wealthy lumber barons. Two bridges spanned the river, one old and one new, taking travelers upward toward the misted mountains looming above the river. A train trestle running beside the water rattled with the weight of a daily cargo train whistling its arrival. What a delightful place to live. I owed Butch an apology for my rotten attitude.

~

We missed Dante and Michael, me more than their sisters, I feared. We even missed Sheba, whose presence at the hotel would have been trouble personified. The girls got to know other tenants, the cooks, who let them sneak into the kitchen for a snack, and the waiters and waitresses. Most of all they loved swimming each day in the pool. One steamy day we were all at the pool, except for Kim, who was doomed to kitchen duty.

"Mom," Kim said, furious. "It's not fair."

"Don't tell me," I said. "Tell your father. He's the one who caught you kissing that young waiter."

"Forget it, Ma," she said and stomped back to the hot kitchen.

My firstborn was wearing me down, but I knew she sneaked down to the pool whenever her dad was not in the hotel. Anyway, Nicole, Kelly, Noelle and I carted our towels, baby oil and sunglasses down the service elevator to the crystal clear blue pool. We swam, sunbathed, got burned, and were just heading upstairs to wait for the kitchen to deliver dinner. Noelle dashed ahead of us, getting on the elevator before us, hoping to get to the shower first. She stubbed her toe on the elevator ledge somehow and bled--all the way to the tenth floor. When we got off the elevator and followed the trail of bright red blood to the suite, we found her in the hallway, bleeding and crying. She was locked out of our rooms.

"Noelle, why did you run away?" I asked, digging out my keys.

"Don't know, Mom. Just wanted to get upstairs. I think I'm bleeding to death."

I quickly let us into the apartment and took Noelle into the kitchen making her hop to avoid bleeding on the rugs.

"Okay, baby, let me look." I quickly wiped away the blood and assessed the situation. "No, you're okay. A lot of blood, but you just sliced your toe."

She shivered in her wet bathing suit as I cleaned and disinfected her toe and bandaged it. Nicole, Kelly and I retraced her steps and cleaned up all the blood. It looked like a crime scene.

The following day I had an appointment with a realtor I had come to like and trust. By now, she knew I didn't want a city home, lovely as they were. She seemed smugly delighted as she drove me to the house on Bloomingrove Road.

~ *Thirty Two* ~

The doors to the ICU waiting room swing open and my six-foot-four son Michael, walks slowly into the room. He glances around, relief showing in his eyes as he spots his brothers and sisters. All except one. His eyes fix on Kim, who is closest to the door, and flood with relief. It is too dark in the room for him to make out the others. I rush over and hug him tightly as his tears mingle with mine.

"It's Noelle," I whisper.

He cannot speak.

Butch hugs him next and then Kim and the rest of the kids surround him with hugs as well. He sinks into the nearest chair and just sits there, exhausted from a long jeep ride from his Army Reserve training session in Fort Jackson, South Carolina. The Red Cross tracked him down, but it took them almost three days. They told him that one of his sisters was in an accident, leaving him with hours of worry, wondering which one was hurt. We let him rest. There is time to fill him in later.

We sit in silence. The nights are the worst, as we are alone with our thoughts; so much more frightening than in the light of day. Everything in the shadowy dim room seems bleak; devoid of conversation now. Some are napping while they can; all of us tired from another day of waiting for some good news, and torn apart by the bedside visits with Noelle.

Someone drives Michael and me home. As usual, Mom will stay through the night, kept company by Kim. Butch will stay a few more hours then come home, sleep a little and get ready to take us back to our hell on earth the next day.

I pour myself a glass of red wine. We sit at the kitchen table and I begin to tell Mike how it is with Noelle, lying paralyzed behind the closed doors of the ICU. Tears stream down his stricken face, listening to my account of the accident. The pain in his eyes is too hard to bear.

I tell him how Noelle was walking down the road, heading for the concert in Brandon Park, when a drunk driver in a pick-up truck slammed into her on the berm of the road. His over-sized mirror hit her in the back of the neck, severing her spinal chord. She was flipped up in the air and over the back of the truck, landing face down on the road. The driver kept going, then later stopped and tried to get his girlfriend to get into the driver's seat. I tell him how I found her face down and blue--how neighbors wouldn't allow me to turn her over, even though I knew she wasn't breathing. How Dante had walked up the road and found us there, horrified by what he'd witnessed. How I told Dante to not let his sister, Kelly walk up this road--to find her and meet me at the hospital. I recite this like a litany, written forever upon my soul. I see Michael's eyes smolder with rage through his steadily flowing tears.

When I can no longer speak, he holds me in his strong arms as I sob against his shoulder.

~

I crawl out of bed after a deep, dreamless sleep, induced by red wine and exhaustion. I am disoriented for a few minutes. Each morning reality jolts my senses as if it just happened. I want to sink back into bed and never get up, but I have little time to dwell on my thoughts. I function robotically, readying myself for the return to the ICU; my home now. Butch has let me sleep a little longer and is not home. Someone drives me to the hospital because I don't feel capable of driving safely. When I arrive, the waiting room is half full. Kim, Butch, Mom, friends of Noelle, the Engler twins, who are always with us, and other family friends wander in and out through the day. It is all a blur to me. I remember Jeanie comes and spends the day along with her son, Christian. All of Butch's relatives have driven in from New Jersey. They are always there for us; births, baptisms, and now impending death. Their love flows through us like an elixir, giving us strength to continue our waiting ritual.

My boss and friend, Carmella, comes in for a few minutes each day. Both Kelly and Noelle babysit her six kids while she runs The Villa, a family-run Italian restaurant where I work as a cook. Kim worked part-time for her as well. Carmella loves all my kids but Noelle is her favorite. Noelle should have been working for her the day she was brutally struck down, but she had a sore throat and Carmella gave her the day off, something that rarely happens.

I recall then the dreams Nicole related to us in the few weeks preceding the accident. Near-death experiences were just being written about and discussed; especially in a book by Raymond Moody. I believed in supernatural events and I knew a lot about the subject, or as much as was known at the time. Nicole came to me on several occasions, claiming she dreamt about a long tunnel with a bright light at the end of it. Someone was going through this tunnel, but she didn't know who. I had wondered about this, knowing Nicole had no concept of near-death experiences, even if she was as psychic as most of her siblings. Normally, I would have put everyone in lockdown until the dreams passed, but I did nothing but ponder it in my heart. Fate surely has a hand in this tragedy. How can I stop it?

~

The kids and their grandma are certain Noelle will recover. Only Butch and I know the probable truth and even he cannot accept it--will not.

I see Noelle's morning nurse, a pretty young woman who knows how to offer sympathy without judgment or comment concerning our decisions. I stay with her as she checks Noelle's life-support equipment; again rubbing legs that cannot feel my hands, stroking arms that do not sense my touch.

"How are you doing?" the nurse asks. She doesn't offer a smile, but a face clouded with concern.

"I'm bleeding from my stomach, I think. I haven't eaten since the accident. Caffeine and red wine are running through my veins."

"Be careful," she says, "You don't want an ulcer right now and you need to keep up your strength."

I nod, but her words ring hollow. I can only do what I can do. I stroke Noelle's forehead, and tell her again and again that she is fine and will be all right. *Please God, let my words be true.*

~

The story of the accident is in the Williamsport Sun-Gazette each night, but I don't read it. It is enough that I am living it. The man who destroyed our lives, the nameless man--I will not utter his name, nor look upon his face--is under arrest. He is charged with drunk driving, hit and run, leaving the scene of an accident, and driving without a license--while being on parole for a recent, previous hit and run. A repeat drunk-driving offender--and he is already out on bail.

The doctors and nurses continue to hound us to disconnect our daughter. One nurse, meaning well, tells me that Noelle will not feel it and it is the best thing for her. I look her in the eye, shake my head and walk away. At least the doctors now admit that Noelle is not brain-dead and is responding to me and to her siblings by blinking once for yes and twice for no. Somehow that makes disconnecting her seem murderous. I won't do it. Butch won't do it. And so we wait . . . and wait.

~ Thirty Three ~

The house on Bloomingrove Road sat back about thirty feet from the winding country lane. An acre of a land spread behind it with a small pond at the end of the property. Twenty-eight acres of woodland lay beyond, belonging to the large cemetery at the top of the mountain. On one side of the house there was a pasture filled with dairy cows and a barn across the road. On the other side stood another old farmhouse with a barn. The house, according to the realtor, was built over a hundred years before, by a famous local architect. He left the house to his two sisters, while he worked in India for twenty years. Upon his return, he moved them to an attic apartment.

The house was large with white wood siding, a large front porch with a slanted roof enhanced by gingerbread-style molding. The roof was gray slate. I knew before entering--the house was calling out to me. I was enthralled with it on sight. Walking through the wide front door into a foyer of high ceilings with intricately carved chestnut woodwork, I glanced around with pleasure. The house radiated beauty and charm. The realtor noted that the woodwork had been carved before a blight destroyed all the chestnut trees, so many years before.

It had a window seat in the dining room, again with ornate woodwork around the top of the window. The kitchen was modern, almost out of sync with the antiquity of the home. I walked up the wide wooden staircase into a pentagram-shaped hallway leading into the four bedrooms and small bathroom. One of the bedrooms had a narrow staircase leading to the attic apartment, containing two rooms, a small bath and a sink. The rest of the attic was used for storage. In one section, there was a ladder leading to the widow's walk on the roof. At one time, this walk was a railed pathway across the roof, where a woman could climb up and scan the Susquehanna River for signs of her husband's ship returning from carrying a cargo of lumber down the river. Ships were sometimes lost-- thus the term, "widow's walk."

This was the perfect home for me and my family. I told the realtor I would let her know--but I knew this house belonged to me. I could hardly wait to get back to tell Butch and the kids.

Butch was not overly impressed with the house, but agreed to buy it since nothing else seemed to fit our price range. I wondered why he didn't like it since it was structured much like his parents' home. Within a few weeks we had the closing and the house was all ours.

The kids loved it, especially the attic, which the three older girls claimed for themselves. Dante took a section of the attic meant for storage and created his own room, while Michael and Nicole took the two bedrooms off the center hall. Butch and I shared the largest of the rooms. The smallest one I planned on using as a craft/sewing room, unless one of the kids changed their minds about the attic.

Butch drove down to Easton to retrieve our possessions, taking Michael and Dante with him. The boys had arrived a few weeks before, just in time to enjoy the end of summer, the hotel and the pool. The infamous, still unhousebroken Sheba would be driving back with them as well. When he returned the next day with our possessions, we lugged it all into the house, carrying boxes and furniture to their various rooms, thoroughly exhausting ourselves. Butch still had to drive the rental truck back to Easton and drive the station wagon back to our new home. I sent Dante with him to keep him awake. We were all spent, but we had a new home and the future looked bright.

The house was vacated when I first saw it and fairly clean, but this did not stop me from scrubbing every inch of it, like a dog marking its territory. On that note, Sheba stayed mostly outside in a makeshift doghouse, since she'd also marked her territory the first time she entered the house.

The kids had my permission to redo the attic as they saw fit--within reason.

"Yuk, Mom," Noelle said, grumbling while coming down the two flights of stairs for more cleaning supplies. "There's red specks of something that looks like blood splattered all over the walls. I need plastic gloves, 'cuz Kim says I have to scrub it off."

"Sweetie, that can't be blood. The realtor said the last owners had lots of pets, including birds, which they kept in the attic." I took a cold washcloth and wiped her red, sweating face. "But you do need gloves and tell your sisters to put them on, too."

"No, Mom," Kim said, coming downstairs to get a cold drink. Her long, dark hair was bundled up in a red handkerchief to keep it off her face. "It's blood. Come up and see. It might be bug blood."

I sighed at the thought of climbing two flights of stairs yet again, and followed them upstairs. Their record player was blasting "Moon Shadow" by Cat Stevens.

"Hmm," I said, trying to be heard over the music. "It is red, that's for sure. Maybe the birds fought and splashed blood on the wall. It's only small dots of it, but birds will die losing even small amounts of blood."

"That's what we thought, too, Mom," Kelly said, her hair and handkerchief a replica of Kim's. "But it's so gross. I'm not touching it."

Michael walked into the room, covered in dust from cleaning and setting up a small den for himself at the back end of the attic, and observed the walls. "I think it would be easier just to paint over it," he commented.

"Good idea, Mike," I said. "It'll save time and disinfect the walls at the same time. Check and see if there's any paint in the basement and if not, we can drive to the store for some."

The walls were painted, painted and painted again. The red stains were barely visible by the third coat, but they never completely disappeared. I thought it was odd, since the walls were primed before painting them. This was just the beginning of odd things in my wonderful farmhouse.

"Oh well," Noelle noted with her usual irony. "Polka dot walls are pretty neat."

Kelly frowned at her, but Kim appeared happy with the effect. Noelle's attempt to arrange her hair like her sisters resulted in burnished brown strands popping out all over her head. They were finished with their cleaning and all set up in their new rooms.

"You know you guys don't have to sleep up here. We do have four bedrooms downstairs."

"No, Ma," Kim insisted. "We have some privacy at last and we can close our door to keep out the boys."

The attic floor was warped and it took a bit of effort to open or close it, but I left them to enjoy their newly found privacy. There was more than enough work awaiting me downstairs.

~

Our first few nights in our new home were strange. After we recovered from the fright of the bats screeching as they swooped down from the trees between the woods and our house at dusk, we heard an unusually loud whirring sound coming from the back of the house. It resounded all around us and grew even louder as the evening changed into nightfall. Why weren't others out wondering about this sound? Not being country people, the noise was alien to our ears, sounding much like movie spaceships as they hovered over land. The next door neighbor turned on a light, and walked over to the eight of us watching skyward while standing on our front lawn at nine o'clock in the evening. The rest of the neighborhood seemed to be sleeping. He patiently explained that the eerie noise was hundreds of bullfrogs croaking in the pond.

The next morning before dawn, the neighbor's rooster decided to alert his surroundings that night had passed. He was not happy with one alarm, but kept crowing for an hour which set off barking from all the neighborhood dogs, including Sheba. *What happened to the peace and quiet of the country?* I thought, piling pillows over my head to mute the sound.

The kids had some time to make new friends before school started. Across the rural road and high upon a hill lived Carole and her husband Gene, who owned the Steiger Milk Delivery. He obtained the milk from the family-owned dairy farm next door to them. Their three daughters were the ages of Kelly, Noelle and Nicole. Kelly decided to show off that she was a tough "New Yawka," and initially snubbed Betsy, who had walked down their drive with her sisters, all in overalls and long braids, to meet the girls. Kelly, at twelve, was entering puberty, a volatile time which reminded me of when she was a tyrannical four-year-old. Kathy was nine like Noelle and they even resembled each other. Nicole was still quiet and withdrawn, which worked out well because Gina was much the same--which made them a perfect pair. The barriers soon dropped and all six girls became the best of friends.

Dante met the Engler twins, Mick and Mark, who introduced him and Michael to their friends. The twins lived down the road from us, not more than half a mile away. I was glad they all found friends close by--thinking I could keep an eye on them more easily. I temporarily forgot how cleverly pre-teens and teenagers conceal their whereabouts.

~

It was late August when we moved into the house and I needed to enroll the kids in school before Labor Day. Nicole, ousted from "Lost Vegas" kindergarten, would go to the Four Mile Elementary school with Noelle and Kelly. Dante entered the middle school which was annexed to Loyalsock High School where Kim and Mike were entered, right across from the younger girls. They were nervous as the first day of school arrived--yet another change, but they went off with bravado, real or staged--except for Nicole. She clung to me, perhaps remembering the Las Vegas fiasco when she got locked out of the school and I drove away. I promised to drive her the first few days until she felt safe. I thought the last year was a grand adventure, but I knew, from my mother's disruptions of my own life, that it was hard on them--even if my intentions were for their welfare. Kids adapt, I told myself, too excited with my new home to burden myself with guilt trips.

~

After the kids left for school and Butch went off to the hotel for work, I relaxed in my new home. As the bus pulled away, taking all of them at once, I took my first cup of coffee into the living room, sat down on the corner of the red sectional couch and started my crossword puzzle. The new barn kitten, a housewarming gift from the next door neighbors, rubbed against my feet, hoping for more food. Cleo was a handsome orange tabby, originally dubbed Cleopatra until a closer look proved him to be male. Kim re-named him Cleopatrick.

Suddenly a flapping of wings made me jump. A speckled starling flew down the staircase and swooped around the room.

"Where the hell did you come from?" I said out loud, ducking as it flew past my head. Cleo was thrilled, and as the bird dove closer to the floor he grabbed it in his mouth. A starling is a rather plump bird, a little smaller than a crow, and Cleo was still a kitten. The outcome of this fiasco was anyone's guess. I ran to open the front door, hoping the bird would fly out. I ordered Cleo to drop the bird and oddly enough he did--just long enough for the bird to fly out the door. *And people say there's no excitement in the country*, I thought. I went back to the couch, wiped up the coffee I'd spilled, poured another cup and worked on my puzzle. The next day at the same time, down swooped the bird--up jumped the cat. I opened the door--out flew the bird. I wasn't used to quite so much early morning excitement. After a week of this activity, I realized it was probably the same starling. Butch secured the attic a little more, but this was just the beginning of our inside visits from the outside animal kingdom.

~ Thirty Four ~

Autumn, bursting with myriad shades of red, gold and orange, was a short season as the cold of winter enveloped us. The kids were settled into a school routine and while none of them were thrilled about it, they coped.

Kim worked from Friday through Sunday as a banquet waitress for her dad at the hotel. It gave her spending money and kept her out of trouble. She was allowed to date, but found little time for it.

As the days and nights grew downright freezing, Butch installed a Ben Franklin stove in the living room. It was black cast iron with glass doors, and radiated enough heat to keep the downstairs warm. Its warmth also drew outside attention and we were soon visited by more of the animal kingdom. I hate rats almost as much as I hate bats. Apparently, these were barn rats from the gentleman farm next door. I wasn't interested in their lineage. Rats are rats and I couldn't tolerate them in my home. Certain people have an affinity for attracting trouble. Nicole was one of them. The chance of stepping on a rat in one's lifetime is small, unless you happen to live in the ghettos of big cities; or next door to a barn. Nicole stepped on one twice in that many weeks. She wasn't bitten, since the rat was probably more surprised than Nicole, but she spent her nights sleeping on the floor at the foot of my bed. I refrained from mentioning that being on the floor wasn't the best option when hoping to avoid a rat.

One evening Noelle and I were home alone. Kelly was babysitting for a neighbor. Kim was working and Nicole was asleep. The boys were down the road at the twins' house, doing whatever fourteen- and sixteen-year-old boys do. I preferred not to know as long as they weren't arrested.

Noelle and I were just about to watch television when the little varmint stuck its feral head out from behind the Ben Franklin stove. Noelle screamed. Before the scream left her throat, I'd spotted the rat and was on top of the couch, my feet tucked beneath me. Almost instantly, Noelle became my second skin. Hours passed. The rat didn't move; neither did Noelle or me. The dog was still tied outside and the cat could be anywhere. We remained immobile--all three of us--until the boys came home. Mike grabbed his BB gun and started shooting. He missed the rat as it scurried into the dining room, but managed to hit the stove. The BB ricocheted off the stove and lodged in my Norman Rockwell print. Dante chased the rat with a baseball bat, swinging in every direction, a fruitless effort since the rat was long gone. So was my favorite lamp.

Butch walked into the house and found it in an uproar. "Why can't that darn cat earn its keep?" he asked, after hearing of our ordeal. "Cats are supposed to kill rats."

Cleo appeared out of nowhere, gave him a disdainful glance, and left the room. I made a note to buy some rat poison squares the next day.

I placed the poison around the house in places safe from the dog and cat, but accessible to the rats. It worked quickly, but at a great emotional toll to us. One by one, the family of rats, mostly babies, ingested the poison and went to their demise; but not gracefully. Each one staged a performance that would have done Shakespeare proud. The poison made them thirsty. They crawled out of their various hiding places, rolled over a few times, gasped, grabbed at their light gray throats with their little pink paws and died. I felt like a murderer.

Just as Nicole attracted rats, Noelle seemed to draw bats. I was hanging curtains above the window seat, admiring the hand carved lattice work that enhanced the windows, when all six kids came rushing down the stairs. Noelle was in the lead, screaming. "There's a flying mouse after me."

I was out the front door before any of them reached it. Where bats were concerned, it was every man for himself. I'd always thought I'd be the type of mother who would run into a burning house to save her children. My bat reaction made me rethink that. We sat on the front porch until after sunset, terrified of going back inside. Michael sneaked into the foyer and grabbed our coats off the stand right next to the door, just as the winged marauder swooped down at him. Mike nearly flew out the door; sadly the bat did not follow. Butch found us there, shivering, hungry and tired. He shook his head in disbelief and walked right into the house. None of us followed. We watched him through the window, battling the bat with a tennis racket, much of his bravado gone as the bat held its own. A little later, he walked out in triumph with the horrid creature splayed between the racket strings. We ventured back inside, tentatively, hoping the bat was a bachelor. We were about to discover that more than wildlife inhabited our home.

~

Vermin would not be the major problem while living in our antiquated farmhouse. At first Butch and I were too busy fixing up the house and adjusting to a new environment to be aware of the subtleties going on around us. The kids kept trying to tell us that strange things happened in the house, especially the attic. I dismissed it as overactive imaginations; after all, the house was over a hundred years old with probably a rich history behind it. I grew to love the house more every day, feeling secure, protected, and at peace.

The kids insisted it wasn't them when all the kitchen cabinets kept opening. I didn't buy it. Teens had huge appetites and someone was always in the kitchen; and when did any of them ever clean up after themselves? Or close cabinet doors?

"Mom," Kelly said, one afternoon while eating her after school snack. "My bed shakes at night."

"Mine too," Kim and Noelle both said at once. After school was a pleasant, if hectic time. When it neared three o'clock, I dreaded the onslaught of six hungry kids descending upon me at once, with six different sets of stories to relate and problems for me to solve.

"What makes your beds shake like that is the rumbling of the big trucks driving down this road at night, that's all," I said. "It's happened to me now and then, too."

"Then how come we never hear any truck noises?" Noelle asked.

"Because you're in an enclosed attic and up high. I can hear the trucks go by," I said, grabbing the last Twinkie just as Dante reached for it.

"Yeah, and what about the spinning balloon, Ma?" Kim asked. "And that icy cold spot in the middle of the floor between our two rooms?"

The girls had hung a red "hot lips" balloon from their ceiling, but every time they called me up to watch this phenomenon, it hung perfectly still. Even the attic wasn't drafty enough to spin a balloon that size. I blamed it on their hormones. One could blame half the world's problems on hormones.

"Ma, I saw the balloon move, too," Dante said, watching to see if I was really going to eat that last Twinkie. "What I hate is the footsteps pounding halfway up the steps and then back down. I can't get any sleep."

"Ma," Kim asked, "when are you going admit this house is haunted? I have the same dream each night, where I see a burned man, all bloody, holding something that looks like charred wood in his arms."

"Yeah, and I keep telling you every time I go up there to study, the door slams shut on me and locks. Why can't you believe us, Mom?" Kelly asked, indicating a snit fit was on the way.

This was impossible, I gently assured her, because the door was made of vertical slats with a crossbar and a latch for a lock. It was difficult to open and close the door due to its weight and the warped floor--closing on its own just couldn't happen. The girls had hung a curtain in front of the door just so they wouldn't have to struggle to open and close it.

"Hey, Kel, Mom's never gonna believe us about 'Orville,'" Noelle said, grinning.

"Orville?"

"Noelle, that's supposed to be a secret." Kelly scowled at her sister.

"Kelly saw a blurred profile of a bald man's head floating across the attic room yesterday, Ma," Kim explained. "So we named him Orville. It's really cool to have our own ghost."

She went on to say that the outline of a man came through the curtain and into the room, moving the curtain as if walking into it, not pushing it aside. The balloon started spinning and the cold spot became frigid.

Mike walked into the kitchen and opened the fridge. "You guys still talking about your ghosts that don't exist?" he said, smirking. "They just don't get it, Mom. There's no such thing as ghosts."

"Michael, you don't know everything. I see stuff in my room, too. I see movies on my windows of kids that wear funny clothes," Nicole added to the conversation.

Hmm, I thought. Another reason for her sleeping in her parents' room each night. Mike and I were pragmatic. We saw nothing, heard nothing and slept soundly. It was a wonderful house. Haunted? Of course not. They tried to bolster their proof with stories from the neighbors confirming ghosts, but I shrugged it off as rumors. I was basically a coward and if things were going bump in the night, I would be the first to know about it. With five out of six kids in their teens, I figured the ghostly activity, if it existed at all, might be poltergeist activity--especially since so many of them had fair to strong ESP (extra sensory perception). The kids shared knowing glances and went off to do their homework.

~

When November rolled around, we were invited to Butch's brother Don's wedding. We had met his girlfriend the last year we'd lived on Long Island, but hadn't seen her since. Beezy was perfect for Donald. She was pretty, always laughing and upbeat, the opposite of Donald, who was laid back and a little reserved. Because her family lived only an hour's drive from us, we were able to attend their wedding. After the honeymoon, they moved to Pittsburgh, where Don lived and worked as a draftsman for a railroad company.

~

A week before Thanksgiving, my realtor called, reminding me that she'd promised a fully cooked holiday meal as a housewarming present. It had slipped my mind and I'd never expected her to really do it. Thanksgiving day she arrived and dropped off everything from a large turkey to pumpkin pie. It was wonderful not to have to cook, since Butch was working at the hotel and it would just be the kids and me. He did get off early enough to grab some delicious leftovers. While it couldn't match my turkey dinners, it was a treat.

~

Our first Christmas was wonderful. The turn of the century country home exuded enchantment, radiating warmth and hominess. The old house seemed made for Christmas. A cheery fire glowed in the Franklin stove, stockings hung around the window seat and mistletoe garnished the doorways. The smell of a freshly-cut pine tree permeated the air. It was covered with ornaments that had crossed country twice and remained intact. I had a hard time finding the ingredients for my Italian recipes in Williamsport; but I made do with what I found. The Christmas repast laid out on the round oak table with parquet squares, handmade by Butch so many years before, was filled with our favorite foods, eggnog and desserts. A few neighbors and co-workers from the hotel visited. It was a lovely evening, almost like a Christmas back home on Long Island. After everyone left, the kids ran upstairs in anticipation of opening their gifts stacked under the tall, pungent tree. Butch, following a new family tradition that had begun in Las Vegas, took out his shotgun and at one minute before midnight, fired upon Santa's sleigh. As usual, he missed, but claimed that this time he got a tuft of fur from Rudolph's tail. The kids came running down the steps, on cue, Noelle and Nicole shrieking, as they dived into the pile of presents.

The only damper to a perfect holiday was the Ouija board I gave the girls as a present. I figured they might have some fun with it, talking to their imaginary ghost. The girls loved the board and played with it immediately. When they asked the board a question it always spelled out the same answer--GET MOM. They got hysterical, cried and went to bed, except for Kim, who stayed behind to tell me that the house wanted me and intended to harm me.

"Okay then, Kim," I said. "I'll be sure to watch my back. Or maybe you can get Orville to protect me."

"Fine," she said, skulking off to the attic bedrooms. "Don't say I didn't warn you."

During the Christmas break from school, we were lucky to have a few feet of snow. The kids had a great time sledding down the hill that was our back yard. They liked to slide all the way down under the electrified fence that kept the cows from entering our property, and right onto the frozen pond. During winter the fence was turned off.

The girls talked Kim into coming out and sledding with them. When she got on the round, plastic sled, she said, "Wait, I'm not ready." Kelly somehow translated that to "Push me," which she did, and off Kim soared. Her six-foot-one frame did not make it under the fence; instead she slammed into a tree. She was hurt and not moving. The boys pushed her up the hill on the sled, telling Kelly to run and get me. Kelly ran into the house screaming, "Kim's been hurt bad."

I grabbed my boots, threw on my coat and followed Kelly, but by then the boys had Kim up to the front porch. We lifted her up and she half walked, was half carried into the living room where we laid her on the couch. I was going to make her some tea, but she refused it. Thank God she did.

"Ma," she said, barely above a whisper. "I hurt bad. Something's really wrong."

I grabbed the phone and called Butch at work. He was home in less than ten minutes, and I wrapped Kim in a dry coat and blanket. Every move she made was sheer agony. We drove her to the emergency room and the doctor took x-rays of her stomach.

"Her spleen is ruptured," the doctor told us after checking her x-rays. "She needs immediate surgery. It's good she didn't eat or drink anything."

"How immediate?" Butch asked.

"As in right now or this could get very serious. Her bleeding spleen could kill her."

We were stunned as we gave our permission for the surgery and called Mom and Dad. They were on their way. They got to us a little after midnight. Kim was still waiting to go into surgery. The first thing Mom did was get the hospital priest to give Kim last rites before the surgery. I was angry. *Kim can't die*, I kept praying. But my faith was not as strong as my fear. Butch and I stayed all night while his parents went back to our house to watch the kids. Finally, near dawn, the doctor walked over to us and removed his surgical mask.

"She's fine," he said, smiling. "Everything went well, but we did have to remove her spleen. The damage was too severe to repair. A few days in recovery and she'll be good as new."

"What does this mean?" Butch asked.

"Nothing, really. She can live without a spleen, but she will need to get yearly pneumonia shots, because her spleen gives immunities to diseases, which she'll be missing."

New Year's Eve fell on the day before Kim was scheduled to be released. I let myself be coerced into going to the Genetti Hotel and keeping Butch company while he worked. I put on the gold lamé pantsuit I had sewed for our fifteenth anniversary, threatened the kids to behave themselves, and drove to the restaurant. I only stayed an hour. My heart just wasn't in it. This was the third time one of my kids endured a major life-threatening surgery. I just couldn't take any more. I thanked God for saving Kim and asked, as always, that He keep my children safe from harm; my only request. I needed to be home with my kids. The next day we brought Kim home to recuperate. It was new Year's Day. I hoped the new year would bring happier times.

~ *Thirty Five* ~

August 28, 1981

My insurance agent, Lynn Burkey, calls to ask if we need anything. He tells me he's been reading the account of the accident in the Williamsport Sun-Gazette.

"You do realize your daughter is covered by your auto insurance as a pedestrian?" he asked.

"No," I said.

"Just tell me what you need and I'll see that you get it," he added.

"Really? I didn't know she was covered. I never gave it a thought. I do know the drunk driver has only the minimum insurance."

"Not to worry," Lynn said. "Whatever his policy doesn't cover, ours will. We'll get you a nurse to stay with the family as a grief counselor and we'll fly in a specialist from anywhere in the country for a second opinion, if you want one."

"Oh, that will be wonderful. I have only the opinions of the doctors here and they've already been wrong on so many issues. We're hoping to call the surgeon that operated on our other kids and get his opinion" I say, feeling a deep sense of relief.

"Okay, then. I'll have a nurse contact you as soon as possible to make arrangements. And Micki, your family and Noelle are in my prayers."

I thank him and hurry to tell Butch this good news. He looks drawn and tired; and so lost. The news cheers him a little.

"Let's call Dr. Bronster right away," I tell him. Dr. Bronster, the large bear of a man who saved Kelly's life when her appendix ruptured, is sorry to hear of Noelle's injuries.

"I know a doctor in Philadelphia, the best in the country," he says. "I'll call him myself and tell him to await your call. If this man can't help you, no one can. Please keep me posted on what he tells you."

Hope pushes up through despair. Butch and I feel optimistic. Maybe Noelle can be helped.

I call my insurance agent back after the specialist speaks to us. This doctor tells me time is crucial and insists upon seeing Noelle as soon as possible. Lynn Burkey arranges a private jet and the doctor lands in the small airport just outside Williamsport. A taxi brings him to the hospital where he goes directly to the ICU to examine Noelle. Hours pass. Butch and I sit side by side, waiting and praying for good news. Our feelings are ambivalent--excitement that Noelle is being seen by the best spinal cord expert in the country--fearful of what he may tell us. Hope and despair wage a war within our hearts. We are one in this.

The specialist walks down the long corridor toward us. He is a tall, handsome man with a kind face. His gentle manner puts me at ease. Again, hope flickers like candlelight bent by a breeze. We rise to greet him. Whatever we hear this day may decide Noelle's future--or lack of one.

He introduces himself, but his name rolls right out of my memory.

"Mr. and Mrs. Peluso." He smiles and reaches out to shake our hands. "Let's step into a private room to talk."

He sits behind a dark wooden desk and leans back in his chair. Butch and I sit on the edge of our seats facing of him.

"I have examined Noelle at great length, ran my own tests, and I am afraid the prognosis is not good."

I feel faint. Butch squeezes my hand so hard I nearly cry out. It is a reflex on his part as our world comes crashing down.

"But doctor," I say, my voice barely audible. "She responds to me. She can hear me. She's not comatose."

"Is there no hope at all, doctor?" Butch asks.

"I realize that," he says to me. "And no, sadly there is no hope whatsoever for a severed spinal cord injury of this severity. She will have no life worth living. Nothing is left but a pair of eyes that can barely see, ears that can hear, a perfect mind that cannot communicate--and a body that will never breathe, eat, or move on its own. Infections will set in, but she can't tell you her symptoms and they will become fatal. Do you really want this prison for your daughter? If so, you do her a great injustice."

We shake our heads, numb beyond reason.

"Then it is my recommendation that all life support be removed as soon as you feel comfortable with it. The sooner the better for her sake."

He shakes Butch's hand and looking into my eyes, he hugs me--and we both know I am not going to do it. I sense his empathy, his sadness. He rises to leave and flies back to Philadelphia, having confirmed our greatest fear.

Butch and I look at each other; pain mirrored in our eyes. He reaches for my hand as we walk slowly back to the ICU waiting room.

"I'm not doing it," I said.

"I know," he said. "I know."

The kids are in the waiting room, except for Nicole. We try to keep her away from the hospital as much as possible. She goes, with much protest, to school each day with her friend Gina, and stays at the Steiger's house until someone comes to take her home.

"What'd the doctor say?" Kim asks.

"Nothing much," I lie. "He says we have to wait and see, but it's very serious."

Kim understands. The other kids take my words literally. Mom just keeps praying . . . Noelle's only hope.

Butch and I go in to be with Noelle. A young, perky nurse smiles and says, "She's been awake again and opening her eyes. It's so amazing."

Yes, I think, *it is amazing and that is the horror of it.* I smooth Noelle's forehead, wanting so badly to hug her close, but the life support machines keep us apart. She had a small incision cut into her brain to drain the excess fluid today and seems tired. Noelle slips back into that place between life and death . . . in a holding pattern. Butch leaves--it rips him apart to see her this way. I stay a little while, praying and willing her to live--just to live, until my God and Savior fixes all this.

~

August 30, 1981

Jeanie calls me the next day from Easton telling me that a mutual friend from high school, Maureen Holmes, heard about the accident and wants to send a Catholic charismatic healing group to pray over Noelle. I tell her that will be wonderful and to thank Maureen for me. The healing team of about ten people arrives the next day, a little past noon. An aura of warmth and love emanates from them. It envelops me like a warm blanket and I feel the tension drain from my body for the first time since this nightmare overtook my life. I feel the power of their prayers as they stand around Noelle's bed, some holding hands, others placing one hand upon

Noelle. The air is charged with an electric intensity. Something otherworldly is happening. I grow hopeful. Yet deep within my soul...I know a healing is not to be.

The leader of the prayer group calls me at home, late in the evening.

"We are praying hard for your daughter," he says.

"Yes, I know and I'm so grateful. I feel the power of the prayers pouring forth from all of you. But I need for you to know that your prayers will not be answered. I have prayed as well. God is determined to take her home."

"I believe you. That's why I'm calling. We have all sensed, like you, that Noelle is meant to go home. I am so very sorry," he says.

"Yes," I whisper, barely able to speak. "Thank you all. I will never forget what you tried to do."

"We will keep you and your family in our prayers," he promises. "And if you need anything, please call me."

I hang up the phone and lean against the kitchen wall, slowly sliding to the floor. All energy drains from my body. The time has come. I know what I have to do now. I will never disconnect Noelle. No, never. What I must do is the hardest thing I have ever had to do in my entire life. God help me.

~ *Thirty Six* ~

Springtime in Williamsport burst forth from the cold snowy winter, with flowers and songbirds. The melted snow ran down the mountain behind our home, overflowing the small creek that rushed past our house. Dante, Kelly, Noelle and Nicole loved to perch over the rocks of the cold stream and capture the tiny minnows as the fish zipped through the water. They always let them go. White bee hive houses spaced at intervals buzzed with activity as the worker bees began their tireless search for nectar from blossoming bushes and flowers. The neighborhood kids were amazed at the things that captured our kids' attention since it was the norm for them. The twins, Mick and Mark, sent Dante on many a wild goose chase for unusual "critters" that didn't exist. Of course, Dante swore he found them all, but then they got away.

Nicole was happy in school except for the indignity of taking daily speech therapy classes. She begged me to talk to her speech teacher and get her out of it.

I made an appointment to speak to the speech therapist, who, in my opinion, didn't speak correctly himself, with his Pennsylvania Dutch dialect.

"Nicole really doesn't have a speech problem," I told him. "That's the way Long Islanders in New York speak."

He wasn't buying it. "Sorry kiddo," I told Nicole after school during snack time. "I tried my best, but you're stuck in speech class. Maybe if you practice the 'r's' and say 'car' instead of 'cah', it might help."

Nicole sulked and headed outside to the backyard playhouse, muttering as she left, probably mispronouncing her 'r's'.

~

As the weather warmed, I was able to see more of my neighbors. Carmella and Sam Aloisio lived next to me down the road (about half a block away in New York distance). The pond in the back was their property. Carmella's daughter was Kelly's age, but her boys were younger than my kids.

Carole's house was high on a hill directly across the road from us. She had a large round above ground pond with an attached patio. Her home was a ranch style house that her husband had built to his own design. I also met the twins' mom, Jane, who lived farther down the road toward town.

Butch fell back into working long hours at the hotel, going in early and returning late. He couldn't live with himself if he didn't do his absolute best in any endeavor he began. He increased productivity at the hotel, improved service and food for the same pay as if he put in his eight hours and left. Gus made a deal with Butch that he would increase his pay after one year-- almost double his present salary--if he could revitalize the hotel's restaurant. I knew now it was not just Benny who kept him working long hours; it was his own demon of perfectionism. I made up my mind then to accept this. There was no more fight left in me. Butch loved his family more than his life, but somehow his workaholic genes pressed him to put his personal achievements first. And now Gus put an incentive in front of him that he felt compelled to accept; plus we needed the money. No wonder Benny tried to hold on to Butch. In the end Benny and I both lost him.

~

School let out in early June and it was fun to have the kids around all day instead of bombarding me all at once, at three o'clock in the afternoon, hungry and with piles of homework and projects. Kim graduated high school and got her driver's license. I had sewn her prom dress. She was beautiful--tall and slim, with long, wavy, raven-black hair. She was only allowed to stay out until three a.m. which made her mad, but her father wouldn't budge. Kim graduated school and went out with a bang. She had walked into that country high school in high leather and fur boots, cowboy hat, shawl and jeans; head held high with the confidence she had gained from living in Las Vegas, where her height and beauty had been admired. She soon won over even the snobs with her poems and songs, and often sang on the stage in the auditorium. I had a feeling Michael would go out the next year with a bang of a different nature. He and his brother were constantly getting into mischief, bringing letters home from their teachers.

~

The younger kids couldn't wait until we opened the pool, which had been winterized and covered when we bought the house.

"Oh no," Nicole said when Butch removed the pool cover. "Where's the water?"

"Better question, where's the liner and pump?" Butch said. What we had was a large round sand box. The kids were disappointed, but they were often invited to swim at the Steiger's pool. We left the pool as it was, in hopes of fixing it when we had the extra money.

The kids were happy. Between so much open land, pond and creek to explore and the neighbor's pool, I rarely saw them all day. Our property was a haven for a variety of birds as well as a flock of mallard and drake ducks that lived on the pond. There were robins, cardinals, speckled starlings, crows, sparrows and more, but Noelle's favorite, was a bird she called "Theodore." This bird had a lovely three syllable song that sounded just like that name. To Nicole, the bird sounded like "Perkiness." It was nocturnal and sang from dusk through to around midnight. The bird showed up in April or May singing its joyous announcement of spring. I once asked Carole's husband, Gene, what type of bird it was. "A whippoorwill," he said. "It only stays until fall."

We looked it up and the book said the whippoorwill had two songs-- one happy, lilting song for spring, followed by a guttural tune of deep sadness as autumn approached and the bird was replaced by the winter wren. One English legend stated that the whippoorwill senses when a soul is about to leave a body and it grabs it, helping it on its eternal journey. Noelle searched and searched, but never found the mysterious whippoorwill, only teased by its constant call, "Theodore, Theodore." The quality of its song was as elusive as the bird itself.

~

Butch's mom called frantically one evening. His sister, Gerry was still married and lived in Los Angeles. Mom wanted Butch to fly out and bring her home. Her husband Oliver, had called to say that Gerry had stopped taking her meds and regressed into a serious schizophrenic relapse. He could not handle her and asked for help. I was so saddened by this news.

Butch flew out within a few days and collected his sister, who was in a highly delusional state, and hostile. My mother-in-law was grateful to have her home again, but I felt sorrow. The disease, which is a chemical imbalance in the brain, was robbing a beautiful young woman of the best years of her life. I doubted her future would be much different, as each psychotic episode caused more damage to her brain, which in turn caused more episodes. It was a sad waste of a life, and a frightening delusional world that, to Gerry, was the only reality she knew.

~

Kim moved into her own apartment with her friend, Judi, in September. She was still hanging out with the motorcycle gang she met at the gas station near the Genetti. Now that she was eighteen, I had little control over her actions--which with Kim, was worrisome. Butch had taught her to drive, both stick shift and standard, but she had nothing to drive--except for the motorcycles of her friends; which resulted in a fall that injured her ankle. Now I could worry without the authority to prevent her headstrong activities.

Mike had his driver's permit and wanted lessons, too.

"I taught Kim," Butch said. "Mike's all yours."

Great, I thought. *I don't like being a passenger in a car with a person who knows how to drive.*

"Let's go, Mike," I said one day as they all piled off the bus. "Let's get this over with before I lose my nerve."

Mike grinned. I drove to a nearby neighborhood with lots of streets where he could practice his turns and parking. I pulled over and he got out. I slid over to the passenger's side. Mike got in and turned on the ignition. He started off slowly and all went well for a block or two.

"Turn right at the next corner," I said. I didn't add the obvious, "slow down and stop at the stop sign."

Mike took the turn way too wide, narrowly missing a telephone pole, and almost sideswiped a parked car. He hadn't shut the passenger door completely and in the midst of his wild careening, the door flew open and I nearly fell out.

"Michael, get out of the driver's seat."

"Why? What'd I do?"

When I could catch my breath, I said, "You better find someone else to teach you to drive. I am never getting in a car with you again."

The drive home was silent. I was traumatized and Mike was sullen. The rest of the kids thought his lesson was hilarious. I would not survive teaching them to drive.

~

Butch approached Gus in September, just over a year after he'd started working for him. Gus reneged on his promise to double his salary unless Butch agreed to be an executive chef and hire someone to replace himself as general manager. Butch refused. Neither would budge. Butch made Gus fire him so he could collect unemployment between jobs. With him leaving, Kim lost her kitchen job, and Michael lost his new job as a busboy.

Butch, home and jobless, was a new experience--a first in our married life. It could have been bliss, or at the least, a short vacation. Instead it was a nightmare. He fell into a depressed state after one job lead after another fell through. My neighbor, Carmella, had a cousin, also named Carmella, who, with her husband Donny, owned The Villa, a popular Italian restaurant at the other end of Loyalsock Township, a few miles past the kids' schools. Carmella needed help for her mother, called "Aunt Mary" by everyone, who helped her with the food prep--all homemade. I had to be at work at 8:30 in the morning, before the kids even left for school. The jolt to my system was brutal. I worked until two in the afternoon and got home before the kids. It was hard, tedious work--molding hundreds of meatballs, cutting and filling never-ending batches of ravioli dough, plus gnocchi, little shell-like pasta made with flour and mashed potato dough; each one rolled by hand.

I had hopes of Butch taking over at home, fixing meals and doing housework, but that never happened. Kim soon joined me at The Villa as kitchen prep worker. She'd recently moved home again. Kelly was old enough to babysit for Carmella's six small children while Carmella was at the restaurant. Soon, I added two weekend nights and some "all you can eat" Sundays to my schedule. Working as dinner cook was hot, fast moving and exhausting. Forty hour work weeks came to about forty dollars or less for a week's work. But it was something.

Butch found a job opportunity in the town of Clayton, New Jersey at "Nick's Pizzeria Steak House" which meant he was out of town all week, sleeping in the back of the pickup camper, and home on weekends. He made a little more money, but with six kids home, it was still tight. The cost of living index in Williamsport was as high as New York, except for the price of houses. With Butch gone all week the onus of carrying the household was all on me.

~

Christmas was special that year. My mother-in-law, upset that we no longer spent the holiday with her, sent us a huge six-foot artificial blue spruce tree as a family present. It was so full you couldn't see through its branches. It was perfect in the room with the Franklin stove; and all our antique and homemade ornaments enhanced its beauty. Carole and I had enrolled in a ceramics class and we now had oven-fired and hand-painted ornaments to add to our collection. The kids, especially Noelle, were in high spirits. She was ten years old before she realized that the song, "The First Noelle," wasn't written for her. We had lots of snow that year, something I dreaded when driving to work. My Vista Cruiser plowed steadily through foot high snow drifts, passing jeeps and trucks that were stuck. The pond froze solid and the kids, along with the Steiger girls, loved to skate on the pond. Noelle was an excellent skater, whether on roller skates or ice skates.

Carmella and Sam moved from next door to a house farther into Loyalsock and less rural. New neighbors, the Berkheisers, Rick and Linda, moved in with their four kids. Tyler was Nicole's age and looked like a "Tom Sawyer," with his straw-colored hair and blue eyes. His brother Brian was a few years older and had darker hair. They had adopted two little Vietnamese girls, about three and four years old, named Tara and Kimmy. Rick kept the pond cleared and slick with his tractor, which thrilled the kids, who were used to taking flying leaps and falls over random chunks of ice and piles of snow. They'd all come in through the basement door, leaving boots and coats behind, and climb the steps into the kitchen, drawn by the aroma of hot cocoa and marshmallows.

That Christmas Eve the table was laden with our regular holiday goodies. Kelly and Noelle sampled the eggnog which had a touch of rum in it--not meant for the kids, who had their own eggnog. Kelly only took a sip, but Noelle drank enough to make her tipsy. She was giggling and flying around the round oak table, arms spread, pretending to be an airplane when her father walked into the room. Her evening was cut short as he sternly banished her to her room where she fell asleep until midnight. She was not so perky on Christmas Day, as her stomach reeled and her head throbbed. Needless to say, she never tried that again.

~ *Thirty Seven* ~

We managed pretty well with Butch gone during the week. We kept to a set routine. I worked at The Villa, often doing double shifts, as morning prep and night cook. I assumed my kids were mature and old enough to take care of themselves. Mike was eighteen and Dante was sixteen. However, the stories from Kelly, Noelle and Nicole regarding their brothers' antics were hair-raising. Kelly tried to stop them and even threatened to call the police, but they were out of control. Nicole always hid until I got home, unless her brothers tired of teasing and harassing them and went to bed. I often got calls at work in the middle of the dinner rush. Butch put a stop to some of it, but the boys threatened the girls if they told on them. To think at one time I had wanted all boys.

Michael was growing what I was pretty sure was marijuana in a potted plant in his attic den. He denied it, saying he just wanted some fresh plants for his room--for decoration. I waited until the plants grew to about four feet tall, nearly ready for cultivation. I'd slip up to the attic whenever he was out of the house and pour straight white vinegar into the plant, causing it to wilt almost immediately. Mike would re-plant; I would re-pour. This went on for the summer months until I mentioned to him one day that he seemed to lack a "green thumb." He was not amused.

As promised, Kim filled her back pack, took her guitar and rode a Greyhound bus to Ohio, where she then hitchhiked to Los Angeles, California. She'd planned to go right after graduation, but my pleas had kept her home for a while longer. Butch, fed up with the oddball friends she kept and her late hours, got into a heated argument with her, ending in her leaving and him throwing her out in mutual agreement.

"I'm so furious with you, Butch, I could scream. What good did making her leave do, except send her off alone across the country? Anything that happens to her is on your head."

He didn't answer me. It couldn't be undone; too much anger on both their parts.

Kim wrote me letters when she reached L.A. None allayed my fears. She slept on the beaches, played her guitar and sang, as beachgoers tossed money into her cowgirl hat. She sang in coffee houses and finally got a job as a car wash attendant. Each letter was more bad news. She hooked up with the owner of the car wash, moved in with him and took care of his two small children. Suddenly, life was no longer exciting to her. I wrote back, pointing out that she'd chosen to make her decisions and I couldn't help her now. But each letter she wrote that year broke my heart. My little girl was beginning to grow up and realize that life was not a game. But would it be too late?

~

Meanwhile, life continued on Bloomingrove Road. Dante, who was as mischievous as ever, announced he was "Captain Bligh" and ordered the younger girls to walk the plank off the raft he'd built in the pond. They screamed and plopped into the murky waters of the pond, inhabited by the ducks, bullfrogs, catfish, golden carp--and occasional visits by a small herd of black angus steers, grazing in the farm pasture on the other side of our property. The bottom of the pond was slimy, like a mixture of quicksand, algae and mud. They sunk to their knees and got stuck. The girls were all bathed in bleach and water and Dante grounded--again. Kelly was convinced she would get polio like Franklin Roosevelt. Her knowledge of history, at least, was improving.

Dante was accused of tying the cat to an umbrella and dropping him from the attic window to see if he could make a parachute. The Engler twins were in on this caper. Cleo did not waft gently down with the umbrella, but plummeted at a high rate of speed to the ground. The cat, using up another life, landed on his feet unhurt. Dante denied this, but Kelly saw the umbrella with Cleo attached, fly past her window.

I think the most appalling thing he did that summer was catch four frogs; crucify one on a homemade cross, and nail the other three in kneeling positions in front of the cross. He swore the frogs were already dead when he found them. I needed badly to believe that. It cost him a month's grounding, which only tortured me more as he blasted his music from his room. I heard enough Elvis to become an impersonator myself.

My days after work were spent lounging with Carole by her pool. I sewed bathing suits and bikinis for myself and the girls. All my kids were proud of my sewing endeavors, except Nicole. She wanted "store bought" clothes and was ashamed to wear home-sewn clothing; although my work surpassed most store-bought apparel.

"Nicole, sometimes I think they either switched babies at the hospital or else you were born into the wrong family," I told her.

I felt that Nicole agreed.

"Why can't I have name brand clothes like my friends?" she asked. "I always look different." Her big brown eyes narrowed and her lips were drawn into a thin line, as her jaw jutted forward.

"Are you sure you're my child? You're nine years old. You have a lifetime ahead for wearing what you want. You better start thinking about getting a job."

"I'm too young."

"My point, exactly; and too young to be complaining over what you wear."

Nicole sighed heavily and stomped upstairs to her room. The fact that she was ashamed to wear the clothes I sewed insulted me.

"Mom," Noelle said, hugging me when she saw my sad face. "Don't worry about Nicole. We all love your clothes. She's just a little spoiled."

"Yes, and thanks for spoiling her. I warned you all when she was born that one day it would backfire."

"She'll grow out of it, Mom," Kelly added, coming into the living room after hearing most of the conversation.

"I don't think so," I said. "Nicole is who she is."

~

I drove home from work one day. No one was home. When I went inside it was eerily quiet. Sheba was tied outside by her doghouse. A recent encounter with a skunk, not helped much by many tomato juice baths, made her an outcast until the odious smell was gone. Cleo didn't come meowing to greet me, which was odd. I called him, to no avail, figuring he must have slipped outside.

When I went upstairs to change from my work clothes, I found him in the center hallway, beaten up and bleeding. He lay still, too weak to cry out to me. I left a quick note for the kids; carefully wrapped him in a towel and put him in a cardboard box. The veterinarian's office was fifteen minutes away.

"In all my years of practice, I've never seen an animal in a state like this," the vet said. He wore a face mask, because he was allergic to animals--an irony, I'd often thought.

"What happened to him? You could take a cat and throw him across the room, full force into a brick wall and not do this kind of damage."

"He was home alone all day, while I was at work. I found him like this."

He shook his head as if he didn't believe me.

"All you can do is keep him warm and hydrated. I gave him a shot to make him sleep, a rabies booster and an antibiotic shot. If he lives through the night, he might make it."

The girls were crushed when they wandered in from swimming and playing pool at the Steiger's house. Later the boys followed. They said they were playing baseball with their friends. One never knew with those two.

"Dante, do you know anything about this?"

"Mom," Dante said, angrily. "Why do you always blame me for everything?"

"Because it's usually you who does everything."

"I wasn't home all day, swear to God. Ask the Englers."

"Oh yes, good character references there," I said.

Cleo slept through to the next morning and slowly recovered.

"Mom," Kelly said, "we keep telling you the ghosts do bad things. When will you believe us?"

"I'm beginning to," I said. "But Cleo loves to prowl the attic. He may have fallen from the widow's walk or had an encounter with a bat."

"I don't want to meet the bat that did this," Noelle added, walking up behind us, tripping over air and stumbling into Kelly. She had entered a stage where she was so clumsy that nothing was safe anywhere near her. Her head was in the clouds as she went through the house like "Mr. Magoo," taxing my patience. It was bad enough having two clumsy teenage boys whose feet grew three sizes a year, along with the sickening odor of athlete's foot permeating the house.

"You notice Sheba never goes into the attic, Mom," Kelly went on. "She knows something's up there and it scares her."

~

Besides me, Michael was also pragmatic about the alleged spectral happenings in the house.

"There's no such thing as ghosts," he told Nicole, as she begged to sleep in his room that night.

"Then how come nothing ever lives very long in your room, Mike?" Kelly asked, like the attorney she hoped to become one day.

This was true. His canary died within a week after he bought it, as did the parakeet that took its place. His guinea pig was found feet up in its cage. I interrupted their conversation to point out that due to the condition of Mike's room, it was a wonder he could live in it. Mike didn't see the humor.

"Well, what about the flies buzzing around his windows?" Noelle chipped in, "and all the dead ones on his windowsill?" She'd just come home from swimming and was sunburned.

Noelle was paranoid about bugs. Wasps got into the attic, which often forced her to vacate her room and sleep on the living room couch, her face covered with a sheet.

"If he didn't keep food in his room, he wouldn't have flies," I said and left them to continue the argument among themselves. Their constant assertions of ghosts and hauntings wearied me.

That Friday night, Butch came home late for the weekend and warned Nicole that his bed would only have two people in it and one of them had better not be her.

That night, after we had fallen into a deep sleep, around four o'clock in the morning I woke to the sound of heavy breathing. And it wasn't coming from my husband or Sheba. Nicole heeded her dad's warning and was not on the floor by our bed. I nudged him awake.

"Do you hear that?" I whispered. "Do you think it's the bear?" I knew there was a bear that came down the mountain and through our driveway to raid the garbage. The bear would then cross the country road on his journey to the woods and mountains behind Carole's house.

"No," he said. "It's the house breathing."

"I don't believe you said that."

"Well, it does--every night around this time, the house breathes. It seems to come from the corner next to the window. I told you this is an evil house."

He turned his back to me and went back to sleep. I certainly wasn't about to sleep after digesting that information. As I lay awake, I glanced across the hall into Nicole's room, which faced ours. As I grew drowsy, I noticed shadows moving in her room. Soon, blurred visions of young children from years past began changing into their old-fashioned nightclothes; then climbing into their beds. There were two or three of them. Their ages appeared to range between four and six years old. As I watched, I was too transfixed to be frightened; just curious. I fell asleep. The next morning the apparitions were still clear in my mind. I owed my kids an apology. This house *was* haunted. But they were not evil. I felt only benevolence and calmness in this house.

~

Mike graduated in June and as I predicted, went out with a bang. He set off a few cherry bombs in the boys' bathroom a week before his big day. It made quite an impression on his peers, but the principal was furious.

"Mike, whatever made you do such a stupid thing?"

"It was no big deal, Ma," he said, his head down. "It was just a loud bang and a little smoke."

"Who put you up to this?"

He refused to answer.

"Fine, don't rat out your friends, but remember they will be going to their graduation ceremony and the principal has banned you. You're lucky he's letting you graduate at all."

Mike said nothing.

"Just leave me alone for awhile, Mike. I'm so disappointed in you."

Butch was angry when he heard about Mike's ban from his graduation ceremony.

"Mike," he said. "Since you're not going to college, think about joining the armed forces or finding a technical school. Otherwise, you have no future."

Within weeks, Michael joined the Army Reserves and headed off to boot camp in Fort Benning, Georgia, for six weeks of training. When his training was completed, the Army Reserves would fly him to Germany for a few weeks, and then back home.

~

In late summer, we were having a barbeque in our back yard. Butch was home for the weekend and tried to fill in as much family fun as he could. Kim was still miserable in L.A. and Mike was finding out that boot camp was no vacation. Dante was off somewhere, no doubt with the twins.

Noelle helped gather up the remains of our dinner, being no help at all, as usual. She often talked about helping with chores, even said she did chores, while managing to look busy without actually doing anything. Nicole helped Butch put out the fire in the barbeque pit. Kelly left to change her clothes for a date with Nate, a school friend. We heard her scream and raced to the attic.

What we saw was mind-boggling. Every panel of wallboard in the dormered attic was pushed out and lying on the floor. More astounding, all the red clothes in the girls' closet had been neatly placed on their beds, as if ceremoniously. Only red clothing.

Dante had come home and joined us.

"Wow," he said. "What happened in here?"

"You tell me," I said. "This sure looks like your work."

"Mom, I've been with Mick and Mark all day, skateboarding. I just got home now. Honest."

The girls stood close together in the middle of the mess, shaking.

"Mick," Butch said. "This is really strange. These nails are perfectly straight. Something from inside the walls had to push out these panels."

"Maybe Dante found another secret passage around to their room."

"Mom!" Dante objected.

The old house had several secret stairways. One led from the center hall closet, down behind the kitchen. There was another short flight of steps off the smaller bedroom leading nowhere, blocked by a ceiling. Both had been covered up and not easily found.

"Mom," Noelle said, hardly above a whisper. "Why just red clothes? This is getting scary now."

"I don't know, honey. Your ghosts seem to be trying to tell us something."

Kelly and Noelle moved downstairs for awhile. With Kim gone and now Michael, they felt unprotected.

~

Kim wrote me a heart-wrenching letter, begging me to help her come home. I scraped up as much money as I could and sent it to her. She rode all the way home on a bus. My story about the Las Vegas madman who had picked up a hitchhiker, raped her and cut off her arms, leaving her for dead, deterred her from hitching rides. Kim moved back into her room in September, just before school started. She bought a 1977 black Dodge van after working a few months for the Red Giant Rental Co., owned by Scientologists. Their brainwashing techniques were subtle, beginning with insisting Kim work twelve to fourteen hour days, six days a week while only paying her for forty hours. Kim was smart enough after a few months to realize they were taking advantage of her and she quit. The girls had fun being together again, with Kim strumming her guitar and all of them singing their favorite hit songs. Sometimes, I would join them, singing the hits and some classics from the 60's. We sang Terry Jack's "Seasons in the Sun," and "Teen Angel" by Mark Dinning, always causing us to cry-- yet we loved to sing those songs.

~

School started and fall, as always, descended upon us at once, mourned again by the whippoorwills, which had to migrate to warmer lands. I had come to grips with the ghosts; whether true ghosts or poltergeist activity by my wacky teenagers. The house blew a lot of fuses that strangely, flew clear across the large basement, a good thirty feet, which baffled Butch. It happened mostly on weekends when he was home to change the fuses and always in the middle of a good television show.

Butch had traded the white pickup truck, aka camper, for a ridiculous looking UPS truck, painted a bright orange. Inside, it was nicely furnished as a large camper, with a kitchen, bed and bath. It had two comfortable, large swivel chairs in front which made for comfortable driving. He'd had enough of New Jersey and took a job in Massapequa, Long island, working for a Ground Round Restaurant, as general manager. It was about an hour and a half from our old home in Island Park, Long, Island. Our friend, Danny, from Benny's, had also moved back to New York and told him about the job. The traveling time was longer than from New Jersey, but Butch was more comfortable and loved the job. It was similar to what he did at Benny's, except more a family style restaurant--a cross between fast food and fine dining.

That Sunday he left early for his long ride back. The younger girls and I were all home watching the movie, "Halloween," when we heard odd thumping sounds from the basement. The ghosts never appeared there, and I feared an intruder had come in through the unlocked basement door. I grabbed the shotgun and put a shell into it, hoping not to have to use it and break my shoulder or hip. I peeled Nicole off me, who had wrapped herself around my legs to keep me from going downstairs, and made her sit down and be quiet. I snapped my fingers for Sheba to follow me downstairs, although the usually good watchdog hadn't barked at the noise. I quietly opened the door to the basement, warning all the kids to stay on the couch. They actually obeyed. Maybe it was the sight of me brandishing a shotgun. Sheba stayed behind me, brave dog that she was-- watching my back, I supposed. I tiptoed down the steps, scanning the basement, shotgun ready to fire, when I saw a large potato at the bottom of the steps. I held my fire. The menacing spud had fallen off the pantry shelf and thumped down the basement steps. I tried to bribe the kids to secrecy, but never lived down the story of the night that Mom nearly shot an Idaho potato.

~ *Thirty Eight* ~

March 1980

Kelly and I caught a viral mouth infection, diagnosed as thrush. We were put on antibiotics because we ran fevers. Kelly recovered quickly, but I developed a violent reaction to the medicine, causing my fever to soar over 101 degrees. Kim was home and took care of me through my delirium and weakness. I stopped the medicines and the fever left; tried them again and the fever climbed. The doctor finally believed I was allergic to the drug. The virus triggered a six month illness that kept me homebound and on the couch. All medical tests proved negative and since I looked healthy, neither doctors nor family believed I could be so sick. I took a leave of absence from The Villa, as weakness, anxiety and panic attacks descended upon me. My neighbor, Carole, gave me a book on how to deal with agoraphobia--fear of open spaces.

"I know someone who has this," Carole said. "And your symptoms seem to fit."

After further research, I felt it was CFS, Chronic Fatigue Syndrome, a fairly unknown disorder, thought to be caused by a virus--although there were as many reasons postured as there were symptoms. Whatever it was, it took me down hard and kept me there.

"Told you the house wants Mom," Noelle told Kelly after school.

"Maybe," Kelly said. "She never wants to leave the house anymore. Even Dad's worried. We should ask Kim."

Kim had moved into another apartment with a new girlfriend. She was working full time as a bartender at the Holiday Inn down the highway from The Villa. She stopped by the house often in her black van, now equipped as a camper. She often camped out with whichever boyfriend was in her favor. Sometimes, I thought that girl was trying to give her father heart failure.

"It could be," she told her sisters on one of her visits. "We know the house loves and wants Mom for some reason."

"Maybe it's because she has the same name as that girl that lived here so long ago," Kelly said, remembering one of the many haunted rumors that neighbors told us regarding the house.

"But," Kim added, "Mom's strong. She'll get better and the house will lose its hold on her."

My doctor gave me valium to take the edge off the panic attacks and anxiety. My prescription ran out, so I called his office for a refill. My doctor was on vacation so the receptionist connected me with the covering doctor. Just as the doctor came on the phone, a bat flew out from behind the brick facade, diving and swooping through the living room. Noelle, who'd conned me into letting her stay home from school--supposedly too sick--screamed. Kim, who had dropped by for a visit, was running around the room, long arms flailing, until she dove her six foot one body under the kitchen table, curling herself into a ball and not budging an inch to let me join her. In desperation, I grabbed the afghan blanket and covered up on the corner of the living room couch, while still holding on to the phone for dear life.

"Sorry doctor," I said. "It's noisy here because a bat is attacking my daughters and me. I just need you to order a refill for my valium prescription."

"Arrggh!" I yelled, as the bat brushed close to my face, even under the blanket. Noelle was still screaming.

There was a long silence on the phone. Then . . .

"Lady, I'm sorry, but I don't know you well enough to give you valium." Click. He hung up the phone. I sat in stunned silence until the confusion roused me back to the task at hand--bat deflection! By now Kim and Noelle were battering me more than the bat, while trying to get under my afghan. That wasn't happening. When it came to bats, the rule was clear; every man for himself. The bat eventually decided to leave us alone and disappeared. I found out later that Kelly had met the fanged fiend prior to going to school that morning. She'd watched it try to climb out of the fake brick wall. She'd pulled a chair up to the wall and smashed it in the face with a broom. Then she caught the bus and went safely off to school, not mentioning that she'd left us with a rather disgruntled winged tormentor.

~

I rallied enough to take Nicole to her Little League baseball practices and games. She played catcher and looked cute in her green and white uniform, even with body armor and mask covering her pretty face. She was an excellent catcher.

Noelle played basketball for her school team, so adeptly that she moved up to the varsity team. She also played the trumpet in the school band.

"Hey Mom! Wanna hear my new song?" Noelle asked one afternoon.

"Sure, do you know the song, 'Long, Long Ago?'"

"Yeah, I just learned it!" she said.

"Good, go play it far, far away."

"Mom!" she said, pretending to be insulted.

She was a natural musician like Kim and Dante. I loved watching her and Kathy play duets, sitting up in front of the band, looking so cute in their band uniforms. Noelle was also proving to be a delightful writer. Noelle and Dante were alike in that they were both artistic, but Dante far surpassed all his siblings with his amazing talent. His art work was displayed all over his school walls. This was another reason the faculty refused to believe such a gifted boy was dyslexic.

Kelly sang in the choir and ran long distance track like her brother Mike, had before her. I summoned strength to drive her to practices and meets. The team ran laps around the school track and then on neighborhood streets around the school to get in practice going up and down hills. Kelly was a strong and fast runner, but she had a terrible sense of direction. She pulled a hamstring and fell behind her group. Soon she was completely lost. It was well over an hour before she limped home. I had no idea that anything was wrong. I just figured her practice ran late that day.

Noelle became furious and the next day in school, she found the strict, stern track coach during her lunch hour and reamed him out for losing her sister and not even noticing she was gone, or looking out for her. The coach walked over to Kelly during practice and told her about Noelle yelling at him. Kelly was sitting out practice, still in pain. She thought the coach would be mad, but he thought it was so cute and noble of Noelle to defend her sister that he laughed as he told Kelly how bravely she'd stood up to him. So as much as I wanted to collapse on the couch, the kids' activities curtailed that. With Butch still working in Long Island, running the household fell to me.

~

Late May brought two events. John Andrew, Ann Eunice's son, was visiting his sisters in New York and they drove him to Williamsport to stay with us for six weeks. He was just in time for the second event. Noelle's Holy Confirmation. Dante, who missed his Confirmation during our moves, was receiving the Sacrament with the adults that same day. Noelle looked lovely in a long pink filmy gown. Dante, after suffering through puberty where he was mostly nose, was now handsome in his new slacks and crisp white shirt. At eighteen, he was not just handsome, but "cool" and never short of dates.

John Andrew was twelve years old, still blond with dark blue, devilish eyes. I was getting my strength back and had prepared a huge amount of food. Grandma baked a large sheet cake that felt like it weighed thirty pounds. Lynn and Bob came up with their kids. Besides Mark, who was six months older than Nicole, Lynn had Courtenay, who at five years old resembled Noelle. Lynn's youngest child, Michael, was an impish three-year-old. I invited co-workers from The Villa, who wanted to know when I was returning to work. "Soon," I told them, hoping it would be true.

~

During the summer on weekends, we took the kids to Rock Run, a veritable paradise north of Williamsport, nestled in the mountains next to a crystal clear icy stream that flowed to a water fall before dropping into a deep body of water. Kim came with us. We'd packed food and drinks, later grilled hot dogs and told all the kids to watch out for rattlesnakes.

"Rattlesnakes!" John Andrew spoke up. "You're kidding me, right?"

"Nope," Butch said, "why do you think I'm carrying my shotgun?"

John Andrew stayed real close to Butch after that. My kids loved swimming in the icy water. The rocks formed a completely smooth, narrow water slide straight down a ten foot drop to a crisp, clear pool of water at the bottom. The pool was so clear that although it was about thirty feet deep it appeared shallow, the giant rocks seeming close enough to touch. The kids were sliding down the rock slide and splashing into the pool below, and diving off jutting cliffs at the top. John Andrew, after fifteen minutes or so, began swelling up like a giant puffer fish. I realized it must be some kind of allergic reaction and instinctively fed him sweet drinks. It seemed to help. We quickly packed up and drove the twenty minute ride home. I called Ann Eunice and she confirmed that in cold water he sometimes swelled up.

"Would have been nice to know that before we threw him into an icy stream," I told her.

"Just give him some antihistamines like Benadryl and he'll be okay," Ann Eunice assured me.

He blew up a little while swimming in the Steiger's pool, becoming quite an attraction to neighborhood kids who'd never seen a skinny young boy suddenly puff up like a balloon. In mid-July John Andrew went back to New York and then flew back to his new home in Arizona. We missed him.

Butch bought a bright red canoe that summer. Since working out of state, we did more family things than when he'd worked in town. He tied the canoe to the top of the station wagon. I packed an ice chest of picnic food and blankets, and off we headed to the Susquehanna River. The boys explored the woods while I dangled my feet off the small pier on the river bank. The girls, afraid of fish nibbling at their toes, passed on that. Butch managed to convince me to take a ride with him across the width of the river. I couldn't swim and we had no life jackets. I climbed into the tippy canoe as he paddled across, the canoe rocking from side to side. The river whispered a serenity which belied its treacherous steep drops and swirling eddies. One trip was enough for me. Some experiences don't warrant repeating.

Butch and the boys paddled all the way to the rapids near the bridge. I paced the riverbank watching for their safe return.

He then took the three girls out, but stayed close to the shoreline. Butch was calling out to those paddling, "stroke, stroke," when Noelle decided she wanted to stand up.

"No," her dad said. "You can't stand up in a canoe."

"Yeah, I can. Watch me," Noelle said.

I stood on the pier, horrified, watching as the canoe capsized and they all went under. All I could see was splashing around the overturned canoe--and then a small figure literally "walking on water" as fast as her legs could carry her to shore. I only knew of one other being that walked on water, but that day, I swear that Nicole was upright all the way 'til she reached land.

Kelly and Noelle insisted they could climb back into the canoe that Butch had righted.

"You'll never be able to climb back into a canoe from deep water," he told them.

Noelle felt a fish brush her backside. Then Kelly felt something touch her legs. They both screamed and launched themselves back into the canoe. The biggest calamity of the day, besides aging me ten years, was the loss of Noelle's cool new sunglasses.

"Wanna take another ride with me?" Butch asked.

"Yeah, that might happen," I said, moving away from him.

~

In late July, Kelly and Noelle were the next in line to go on one of Grandma's religious excursions. This time it was a trip to Quebec, Canada. They were so excited. Kim and Michael had gone with Grandma to Sainte Anne de Beaupre, the famous Canadian shrine. Kelly and Noelle were nervous, but elated about riding a bus to Canada. After they arrived and brought in their luggage, Noelle was wild with pent-up energy. My mother-in-law told me later that they'd no sooner put down the luggage, than Noelle opened a window and was standing two stories up on the fire escape roof outside the window. She laughed at Kelly and Grandma's stern pleading to come back in. There were no gates or fences--just a nice long drop. They'd no sooner pulled Noelle back inside when she spied the newly made bed and began jumping up and down, sneakers on, all 5'6" of her. Grandma and Kelly broke out laughing. There was clearly no controlling Noelle until she tired herself out.

The next day at a café with waiters speaking very formal French, Noelle struck again. They all ordered tea served formally with cup and saucer, lemon, creamers and sugars. Noelle and Kelly were used to fast food places. Noelle spent a lot of time fixing her tea with everything the waiter offered, in order to savor the full experience. It became obvious to all, including the waiter, that she should have chosen either lemon or cream but not both. The waiter removed the curdled cup of tea and replaced it with a fresh one while Grandma and Kelly tried to recover from another bout of laughter at Noelle's whimsical antics. It was difficult for anyone to keep a straight face while in Noelle's company. Kelly and Noelle returned at the end of July refreshed and happy from their vacation. Their grandma took a well-earned rest.

Noelle kept us constantly in stitches with her comedic antics and comedy routines. She did an impersonation of Robert Klein's stand-up comedy act "I can't stop my leg" which was hysterical. She also mimicked the TV commercial, "We're teasing Mrs. Bearnowski--we're going to take away her Tide.... She did a perfect rendition of the Saturday Night Live skit, "Mr. Bill"--we would double up laughing, listening to her falsetto voice saying, "Oh no! Mr. Bill."

It was impossible to stay mad at Noelle. The moodiness of early puberty was long gone. She delighted in life, doing cartwheels in piles of autumn leaves, or trying to please Kelly by running up and down Bloomingrove Road to keep her company. Kelly would walk in the door, barely winded, while Noelle collapsed on the foyer floor, arms spread eagle, moaning and refusing to move. She'd do her comical stints as her sisters did the chores, never realizing that while Noelle was amusing them, she deftly avoided doing any of her share of the work. Her one-liners, never remembered for long, were so funny that none of us could stay mad at her for long. If she pushed too far and angered someone, she'd rest her arm lazily on their shoulder, grin and ask, "You're not mad at me, are you?"

~

Mike took a bus to Tennessee in August for a nine month course in automobile welding. He was as handsome a young man as he was a beautiful child. And sweet-natured. He called home often, lonely and miserable. The calls were mostly one-sided, as I gave him news of family events.

Dante was out of school, working part-time for a neighbor who was in construction work. He wanted to save money for a car. I was well enough to go back to work at The Villa. We had a heat wave that August that lasted for two weeks. Kim had left her apartment and temporarily moved home until she found something better. The old farmhouse was chilly in the winter, but also cool in the summers. It took at least a week of intense heat for the house to heat up. When it did, it held that heat. I hung sheets and blankets to block the sun in an attempt to cool the house. It was sultry, with the high humidity making it feel even hotter. We swam in Carole's pool during the days, but the steamy evenings made sleeping difficult, especially in the attic.

The heat wave peaked on a Friday night. I worked the dinner shift as cook at The Villa, leaving Kelly and Noelle to babysit Nicole. Noelle was cranky from sun poisoning on both her shoulders. At thirteen, Noelle, like all teens, was suddenly smarter than me and not afraid to tell me. We argued constantly that summer. She was still comical, but now she was also mouthy. I wished she was more like Kelly, who still stomped off to her room when angered or upset. Not Noelle. She had to wear me down with constant arguments. Now that she babysat for Carmella with Kelly, I had some peace although Nicole, going on ten years old, was getting sassy herself. At least the boys were always out of the house, wreaking havoc on the neighborhood, instead of me.

Anyway, I went to work that Friday night and manned the salad station, grateful to be away from the hot grill and large pots of boiling water for pasta. Not paying enough attention, I sliced through the tips of three of my fingers while prepping the salad vegetables. I bled all over the cutting board. One of the other cooks called Donny, the owner, into the kitchen. He checked out my bloody fingers and left, returning with a roll of black electrical tape. He handed it to me and left again. I guessed I wasn't going to be able to leave work. I pressed the flaps of skin to my fingers and clumsily wound the black tape around them.

Donny stuck his head into the kitchen.

"Micki, work the other end of the kitchen so you don't handle raw food," he said and went back to tending bar. *All heart*, I thought. This station entailed being a "gofer" and getting steaks, bread, and other staples from the back supply room, as well as the cold walk-in fridge that held all the pre-made food. It was also my job to microwave the lobster tails and other entrees. I thought the night would never end.

Wild thunderstorms struck right before my shift ended, which slowed business for a few hours. I was allowed to leave early. The storms had passed before I drove home, but streets were flooded in spots.

I walked into the house, anxious to collapse on the couch with a cold drink and ice on my throbbing fingers. Instead chaos greeted me with a myriad of calamities--none good. Nicole was throwing up from heat sickness and a migraine headache.

"Girls," I said to Kelly and Noelle. "Didn't I tell you to keep her out of the sun?"

"We thought she was in her room," Kelly said, and Noelle agreed.

"Great. Now she's going to be up all night in pain."

"There's more bad news, Mom," Noelle said. "Kelly left Kim's rabbit outside in the sand in the empty pool. We think he got struck by lightening. Come see."

Puff, a sweet little white rabbit, housebroken to a litter box, was Kim's latest pet. He had the run of the house which delighted Sheba, who loved to chase him; never able to catch the quick-footed "waskily wabbit."

"Mom, Kim's going to kill me. It was storming something awful when I remembered Puff was outside. He was screaming and running in circles and now he won't move. I think he's dead." Kelly started crying.

I knew rabbits only screamed when in pain or dying. I cradled Puff in my arms. He seemed to be in shock and barely alive. I tried putting drops of warm sweet tea into his mouth and then drops of whiskey. Nothing worked.

Kim walked into the house, also home early from work, just in time to see Puff go into a seizure and scream one last time as he took his final breath. We all cried.

Dante came home and suggested we lay him on a work table in the basement until we could bury him in daylight.

Near midnight, as the heat was still intense, the girls and I sat side by side on the sectional sofa. Butch came home after a long drive, through erratic bands of thunderstorms.

He was used to Nicole running up to him yelling, "Daddy!" while he answered, "Baby!" as he swung her up and into his arms--a really corny scene as far as the rest of us were concerned, but it was their ritual. And then Noelle would be next, holding out a cake made from scratch that she had baked just for him, and making some comical remark or antic to make him laugh. Kelly tried to follow Noelle's example, but her cakes were grayish thin pancakes that her father didn't even try to sample.

It was a sad, sorry bunch, who greeted him that night. As we related our saga of heat and heartache, he said "hang on a minute," and headed for the kitchen. He came back with a salt shaker.

"Oh no, you don't," I said, backing into the corner of the couch.

"It has to be done or you'll get an infection," he said, ripping the tape from my fingers in one quick swipe.

The tips that I'd so carefully adhered to my fingers came off with the tape. Butch grabbed my hand and shook salt into the open wounds. The kids were appalled, but not surprised--this was their father's solution to healing all wounds. At the moment, he was a heel I wanted to wound. But I was too overcome by the pulsing flare up of fiery hot pain to speak. Nor would I give him the satisfaction of crying out. But I vowed he would pay for this somehow, someday--as soon as I could come up with a payback equal to it. Needless to say, his weekend home was not a pleasant one.

~ *Thirty Nine* ~

August 31, 1981

It is the ninth day since Noelle was snatched away from us--ripped violently from a happy teenage life; a time of change and new beginnings. She will never experience them now. Her life and dreams snapped, the day a drunk driver broke her neck and severed her spinal cord. My shock and denial change to deep, deep sorrow for all the "might have beens."

One of her regular doctors comes to see me in the waiting lounge. This is it, I thought. He's going to insist we disconnect her or move her to some other facility.

"We can't go on like this," he said. "Not you, not me, not the nurses caring for Noelle. It's too big for any of us to handle. I go home at night and hug my children." He shifted in his seat, as if unable to get comfortable.

I want to embrace this man. The raw emotion in his eyes speaks to my heart. I realize now that it is not easy for all those tending to Noelle. They have come to care for her in spite of their training in non-involvement with patients. They already are. This is the first time since the accident that any of the local doctors have spoken with any degree of humanity--yet the entire ICU staff is deeply affected by Noelle's situation.

"What are you saying?" I ask.

"I believe, like you, that whatever happens to Noelle must happen naturally. The responsibility for her death can't be decided by any one of us. It's too hard a decision. I also think that she won't last much longer."

He lets out a long breath, as if grateful to blurt out all his feelings.

Relief overwhelms me as I relate the doctor's words to Butch, who agrees that Noelle cannot hold on much longer. I know, too, that what I must do may hasten her death.

~

Noelle's first love, Chuck, often comes to the waiting room, usually sitting off by himself, his sweet boyish face masked by confusion and deep sadness. I take him to the cafeteria for a soda and a talk.

"Chuck, I need to know what you want. You have choices. I can take you in to see Noelle or you can go alone. Or you can choose to remember her as she was the last time you were together."

His face twists, looking physically pained by my questions. His body trembles; he looks down at the floor and speaks in a barely audible voice.

"I think I want to remember Noelle as she was."

I hold him in my arms, briefly. "Noelle would have wanted that," I whisper in his ear.

~

Butch, Kim and I stand by Noelle's bed that evening. I will never get used to the whirr of the machines keeping her alive, or the bell tones that sound like utility trucks backing up. There is also a smell I cannot identify, but it permeates my very being. I fear it is the smell of death. I massage legs that can't feel my touch, because I need to…it soothes me. We look at her face, behind the tube breathing for her and all the bandages, and watch as a tear forms, then slowly slides down her cheeks.

The male nurse caring for her says, softly, "She's crying."

"No," I say, feeling my heart jump. "The day nurse assures us that it's the medication they put in her eyes to keep them moist."

"No," he says. His face holds a gentle, yet knowing look. "She really is crying."

I know in my heart that his words ring true, but I want to believe the lie. This is more than I can bear--my daughter, lost and alone--now crying. I lean against Butch for support.

"Let's get out of here," he says.

~

As always, Butch, Mom and Kim stay the night. I return home, spend time comforting Nicole, tend to household things; and hope to sleep. Michael is home. I slip out of my light jacket and shoes, and then pour a copious amount of red wine.

"Michael, she's crying." I can say no more. He holds me as I sob and sob until my tears run dry. He says nothing as his tears intermingle with mine. I go to bed, hoping the next day will not dawn. It does, and the nightmare waxes on.

September 1, 1981

Butch needs to drive back to his job in New Jersey to check on a few things. He asks the doctor if Noelle will be stable for the time he'll be gone.

"There's no way to tell," the doctor answers. "But most likely her condition will remain the same for a while yet."

Butch leaves that same morning, hoping to return as quickly as possible. When I arrive at the hospital, my mother-in-law goes home to my house with Kim, to rest, go to mass, and feed the constant flow of relatives that come and go.

My friends, Jeanie and Pamela come again, but their visits are hazy, as days and nights seem to merge into one long trip to Hell. Anita calls from Las Vegas, but I still can't talk to her or to Ann Eunice, who can barely speak to me. Carmella pops in and out when the restaurant is slow, as do neighbors and friends. I have times when I feel so rational that I amaze myself; other times it seems surreal. The nurse offered by my insurance company drops by every day. She tries to communicate with us, but it isn't possible. We cannot be counseled or consoled. So she does the only thing she can; offers support by being there with us.

~

It is evening. I stand by my daughter's bed. I watch as her eyes open and dart about, sensing my presence before I speak. I lean over and kiss her forehead, remembering it is the only place that she can feel sensation. I stroke her hair--hair she took such care in styling just right. Its richness and burnished color ripple through my fingers. It is time.

I reach for Noelle's hand. *Damn! When will I realize she can't feel my touch?* Nevertheless, it is me who needs to feel her. *Oh my God, help me in this. Do not let me falter. I know Your will now and must fulfill it. This is so hard, Lord. Heal her, so I don't have to do this.* He does not answer, but His presence surrounds Noelle and me. It is now or never.

"Noelle," I whisper close to her ear. "I love you so much and always will. But it's okay, baby, to go toward that beautiful light you see."

Noelle's eyes stop darting about and she seems to relax a little.

"Sweetie, I want you to know that it's okay for you to go whenever you choose and if you choose. Everything you need or want awaits you."

I remember Nicole's tunnel dreams and I am certain now that it was Noelle in the tunnel, searching for the bright light of Heaven. As I watch her slip away from me, I no longer see my daughter trapped in her broken body.

I envision her running like the wind down the basketball court, blowing her hair out of her eyes, as she shoots for the basket and scores the winning point for her Loyalsock team. I see her ice skating on the frozen pond, gliding in perfect rhythm to the music within her soul. I hear her sweet voice as we all hang out in the attic singing to the strumming of Kim's guitar--Ed Cobb's "Tainted Love," and "Stairway to Heaven," by Led Zeppelin. We laugh and cry but we can't stop singing them over and over.

I recall her smiling face, when she came home from school one day and told us that her teacher said that day that there was one person in the class who was special and would do wonderful things with their life. After class, he called Noelle up to his desk and told her that she was the one that was so special. It made Noelle feel so proud and "special."

What could be special about dying at fourteen? I wondered. *Had she done what she was meant to do on the earth already? So many forebodings. And I never noticed.*

"I promise," I tell Noelle, "that somehow the world will know who you are and what you meant to those who loved you."

Noelle's eyes focus directly upon mine, and then close as she slips back into a coma. I collapse against her bed, cursing myself for what I have done--telling my daughter to die, to let go of hope.

I cry a river of remorse. Grief and loss will be my companions for the rest of my life. Back in the recesses of my mind, I hear a soft voice . . . *You did right.*

Whether I did or not, I cannot know. It is a burden I will carry the rest of my life. I let my daughter go Home. It is done.

~ *Forty* ~

March, 1981

Kim met a young man named Kyle at The White Horse, a rock bar, and fell in love yet again. He had long, wavy, unkempt, dark brown hair, velvety dark brown eyes. He sported a beard and mustache, looking as if he'd just stepped out of the Woodstock era from twenty years past. Kyle also had an affinity for marijuana and was always half stoned. This was the man Kim wanted to marry. Sometimes I thought Butch had the best job--working out of town all week, leaving me to deal with six kids. Kim had turned twenty-one in February, an adult now. I no longer had control over her choices. In retrospect, I realize I never really did.

She moved into Kyle's home in the mountains of Montoursville, a small town next to Williamsport. For reasons I couldn't fathom, she took in a goat named Max, who had the run of their house.

"Why did you take in a goat?" I asked, perplexed.

"Well I'm gonna milk it. You always told me you loved goat milk when you were little."

The first time she tried to milk the goat was a disaster. "It kicked and all I got was this nasty, sticky thick white stuff that didn't look anything like milk. And the goat was indignant and refused to let me try again! Kyle came home and I told him about my problem milking the stupid goat and he said, laughing, 'You idiot! Why would you try to milk a male goat?'"

Apparently Kim couldn't tell one udder from another.

~

Oddly, Noelle and Kelly liked Kyle and Nicole thought he was "cool." Even I had to admit he was likeable, if a bit maniacal. After meeting him once, Butch just shook his head. I think he was at a loss for words. "They better not breed," I thought I heard him mumble.

~

Noelle was fourteen that summer and had changed dramatically. I was watching her and Nicole roller-skating at the Montoursville indoor rink, their favorite hangout. I looked at Noelle, as if a stranger. *She is beautiful, I said to myself, and is becoming a stunning young woman. When did the clumsiness disappear, when she would walk into a spacious room and trip over air? When did her pouting mouth, always turned down at the corners, become so sensuous?*

Her boyish, lithe figure, kept slim from bicycling, swimming and roller-skating, was curvaceous, with firm, rounded hips meeting long, tanned, shapely legs.

Even her demeanor had changed, subtly, but surely, and I marveled at the lilt to her previously husky tomboy voice.

Noelle had changed that summer, from a gangly teenager, to a lovely, confident young woman. She had just succumbed to her first love; and I had nearly missed the magical transformation of a young girl's journey into womanhood.

She met a cute boy named Chuck Bowman. He had sandy-colored, shaggy hair and twinkling large brown eyes with long eyelashes. Noelle would ask me for permission to walk to Brandon Park at the end of Bloomingrove Road, to sit and read her Harlequin Romance books. I found out later that she was meeting Chuck there. I said nothing, remembering my own first love at her age. And I knew I could trust Noelle.

One late spring evening, Noelle was off work from babysitting for Carmella. She begged me to let her go into the Center City with a few friends to see a movie. I'd never let her out at night before, but she wore me down with her pleas, promising that Wendy's mom would drive them back.

"Be home no later than eleven o'clock," I told her.

By midnight, I was frantic. I called all her friends and no one knew where they were or why they were so late. I called Kim, who was off work, and she raced over, searching the streets between Center City and our house. I was certain Noelle was killed or hurt. When she walked in the door, I exploded.

"Where have you been?" I said, loud enough to wake the neighborhood.

"Wendy's mom was late picking us up and then we got lost dropping off one of my friends," she started, surprised by my violent reaction.

I ranted at her for a good fifteen minutes, not giving her time to defend herself. Then, as I noticed her shoulders shaking and tears running down her face, I said in a calmer voice, "Noelle, don't you know that if anything happened to you I couldn't live?" I led her to the couch where she fell into my arms, sobbing.

"I'm so sorry, Mom. I didn't realize how late it was and then I didn't know what to do."

"Just don't ever scare me like that again," I said, holding her close and stroking her hair.

~

In mid-summer my friend Anita flew out for a visit, on her way to her yearly trip back home in Sweden. Butch had left the Ground Round Restaurant in Long Island to open a new one in New Brunswick, NJ. Anita and I wanted to drive back to Long Beach and see some old friends. I was leery of leaving the kids alone for three days, but Kelly insisted that she and Noelle could handle things. Dante was home too, not necessarily a good thing.

"We'll be fine," Kelly said. "The Steigers are right here if we need them."

Kelly, at seventeen, was gorgeous. She had long, sun-streaked brown hair and large yellow- flecked brown eyes. While puberty had not been gentle with her, the result was stunning. She was medium height, with a curvaceous body that kept her busy with dates. She was still a highly moral and spiritual young woman, and I knew I could always depend upon Kelly to do the right thing.

"Dante," I said, calling him up to my room while I packed for the trip. "If I hear one, just one thing you do to annoy or hurt your sisters, I will make you rue the day you were born. Got that?"

"C'mon Mom, I'm not a kid anymore."

"Thanks for the reminder, but somehow that doesn't reassure me much. And none of your friends are to step foot in this house while I'm gone."

"Fine," he said and walked out of the house to go meet the twins.

~

Anita and I set off for Long Island the next day. It was a three hour trip, but the day was balmy and not too hot. She drove through my old neighborhood and the house I'd lived in for six fun-filled years. Only Rosie Miranda still lived in her house by one of the canals.

"Guys," Rosie said, running up to hug us. "So glad you stopped by. You both look great."

"You too Rosie, but you're still short, especially next to us two Amazons."

She chuckled and poured us a glass of wine. We caught up on old news and current happenings. Anita called the number we had for Cathy Scott, but it was disconnected. She had divorced Scotty and moved back to Island Park, into a small apartment, according to Rosie.

"I think she's moved out to the Rockaway's," Rosie said. "She got sick with a thyroid problem and cut ties with all her old friends."

We left Rosie and drove into Long Beach to see Benny's. Most of the help we knew had retired, died or moved on. Benny came up and hugged Anita, all smiles, as we sat at the bar having a drink--not on the house. He ignored me as much as possible. That was fine with me, although I had enough manners to be cordial to him. Since we were hungry and Benny didn't offer us dinner, we said goodbye and left.

"I was sure he would feed us," Anita said, in a fit. "What a cheapskate."

"He would have fed you. It's me he hates."

"Jah, I should have left you in the car and brought you a doggy bag."

"Very funny. Where should we have dinner?" I asked.

"How about our old haunt, The Mariner's Harbor? I'm dying for their lobster."

"Sounds good, if we can afford it. Everything's changed so much. It's like our past never happened," I noted.

"Jah, I know," Anita said. "It's eerie. I expected it to be the same--it's only been six years."

The lobster was as superb as I'd remembered, but the restaurant was staffed with people we didn't know. Nick, our piano bar player and singer no longer worked there. We stopped by a few other restaurants and lounges, but it was the same. We'd moved on and so had everyone we'd known.

"Well," Anita said. "At least we don't need to miss this place. It's not ours anymore."

"Yeah, you're right. Might as well look for a hotel before it gets too much later."

Anita hadn't changed from our trip west when it came to finding cheap lodging. She drove to at least six motels and hotels and they were either booked up--since it was summer tourist time--or too expensive. We ended up ala Anita style, in a rather shabby motel at the end of Long Beach Road. It sat across the highway from a Greek diner.

"Hmm, if we don't get mugged or murdered in our sleep, we can have breakfast there before we head for New Jersey for Butch's grand opening."

"You worry too much," Anita said. But I knew she was a little nervous when we had to find our room. Two seedy, quiet men appraised us and watched as we entered our room.

We lived to greet another day, grabbed an omelet brunch at the diner and headed for New Brunswick--late as usual. Butch would be mad if we missed his opening. We arrived just in time to change our clothes in the orange camper. The restaurant was stunning, its décor eye-catching, yet cozy. Ground Round Restaurants are family-oriented, catering to children. This gives parents and caretakers time to enjoy their meals at fast food prices. For the opening, Butch hired a few clowns and a band. Anita and I found Kim and Kyle, who'd driven from Williamsport for the opening, and we sat together at one table. It was great--Butch had done a wonderful job.

Kyle managed to behave himself until after dinner. He was drunk, stoned, or both, by then.

Butch needed for Kim to leave her car there for him. Anita and I drove the three hour trip back to Williamsport with a very happy, boisterous drunk in the back. Kim seemed embarrassed for once, and furious. With any luck, she would soon realize that she had no future with this man.

~

The next day we drove Anita to the small Williamsport Airport. She'd fly to Kennedy Airport on Long Island, then continue on to Sweden for her yearly visit. Carole walked over for a cup of tea. She had a deep tan from sunning each day at her pool, which made her blue eyes brighter and blond hair streaked with gold. I was afraid to ask what had gone on while I was gone.

"Oh, Micki," she said. "You should be so proud of Noelle. She took wonderful care of Nicole and played outside with her almost the entire day."

"Good to hear," I said. "And thanks for keeping an eye on the kids. I was worried about being so far away from them."

"One night I did see someone inside the house, charging back and forth across the living room windows, brandishing what looked like a sword. The girls were running and screaming."

"That sounds like Dante. I'm going to kill that boy one of these days."

~

I saw a woman walking by my house. She stopped and stared at it.

"Can I help you?" I asked.

"No, I just love your house. How are you managing with the ghosts?" she asked.

"You know about them?"

"Oh yes, the legend is that the man who built the house left for twenty years, came back and forced his two sisters to live in the attic."

"I've heard that story," I said.

"Rumor has it that he killed his sisters and buried them somewhere behind the house, in the woods," the woman added.

"So there are two ghosts?"

"According to the legend," she said.

She started to move on and waved goodbye.

"Thanks for the information," I called out after her.

She turned back, smiled and kept walking.

I mentioned this to the kids.

"Looks like you named your ghost wrong. Its two ghosts and they're sisters."

"Figures," said Dante. "Girls are always a pain."

I pondered this information for a while, then got an idea. I waited for a day when Kelly and I were alone in the house.

"Kel, since you and me have no ESP, we should be safe from the Ouija Board. Want to help me send these sister ghosts home? They've been lost and stuck here for more than half a century."

"Okay, Mom. I'm scared, but they need to find the light and go to Heaven."

"Let's hope it's Heaven," I said, grinning.

We worked the Ouija Board for about fifteen minutes, asking questions. The board confirmed the rumor. Two sisters were killed by their brother and haunted the house. We asked them if they wanted to go to the light. The answer was 'yes.' We told them to look for a bright light and it would take them home. There was no movement for a few minutes, then our fingers touching the planchette swept to the bottom of the board-- where the word, GOODBYE was spelled out.

"Wow!" Kelly said.

"I wonder if they really left?" I asked. "Guess we'll know soon enough."

And we did. The rest of the kids were skeptical, but even Butch agreed that the house felt different. It had an emptiness to it. No bumps and thumps in the night, no dark shadows passing through rooms. The cold spot in the attic was gone. The house no longer breathed. It was an odd feeling after so many years of sharing their house. I found I missed them.

~

I drove Kelly and Noelle to a nearby field and stayed with them to watch Dante and his friends play baseball. His friend Tim Hamilton, who'd moved away, was back for a visit and staying with us. Tim caught poison ivy from the plants near the field and puffed up. I drove him to the emergency room for a shot and bought him an oatmeal bath for the itching. He refused to leave the house until he was presentable.

~

Kelly and Noelle were becoming closer again. For a while, their activities sent them in different directions. Kelly had spent her mid-teen years in her bedroom, shunning everyone.

"Why won't she come out of her room, Mom?" Noelle had always asked.

"Honey, it's a good thing. When she does come out, she's a grump. This will pass soon and she'll be her old self."

By the time Kelly navigated her way through puberty, Noelle entered it, but didn't hide in her room. She preferred to torture all of us. Now both girls had leveled out emotionally and re-bonded with each other. Nicole was mad over this, since she'd had Noelle to herself for a while and now felt like an only child. She played with Gina and read her Nancy Drew mysteries while her sisters hung out together.

Kelly and Noelle both still babysat for Carmella and sometimes the Berkeisers, next door. I drove them to Fashion Bug where they spent hours buying new clothes--Noelle actually, since she could never decide what to buy. They carted their treasures up to the attic and came downstairs, announcing they were going for a bike ride.

"Okay," I said, "but not too long. Supper's almost ready."

I happened to hear their conversation in the foyer.

"Noelle, what are you doing? How many outfits are you wearing at one time?"

"I couldn't figure out which one to wear first so I'm wearing them all," Noelle answered.

"But you have on a bathing suit, shorts and two shirts. You're crazy!"

"Maybe," Noelle said, "but you only live once."

Kelly sighed. "I have all my new clothes neatly folded or on hangers. I'm not wearing them except for a special occasion."

"I think a bike ride is special enough," Noelle said, laughing.

I was in the kitchen trying to restrain my own laughter.

Mike was home again, having completed his auto course, but due to leave soon for Fort Jackson, South Carolina, for his annual two weeks of Reserves training. Dante was out, dating or with his friends. So in effect, Nicole was becoming an only child.

~

An intense heat wave struck in the middle of August, although not as hot as the one the year before. Carole had taught me how to can vegetables. I chose tomatoes and pickled cucumbers, vegetables less likely to kill anyone, due to their high acid content. I didn't trust the seals on the canning jars and botulism was a real threat--especially if you canned something wrong and it was low acid, like string beans. Besides, pickles were one of Noelle's favorite things and I could use tomatoes for spaghetti sauce. Kathy Steiger and Noelle's new friend, Wendy, helped me.

Noelle did her usual act of looking busy while doing nothing. The kitchen became a sauna with pots of boiling water to sterilize the canning jars.

The process took the whole day. I had a dozen jars of tomatoes and almost as many pickles. I felt that was an achievement--one I wouldn't attempt again--at least not in ninety degree weather. As her friends helped me clean up the kitchen, Noelle did a dance with the broom she was supposed to use to sweep the floor. She stuck a large dill pickle into her mouth and did a "Groucho Marx" imitation. She was impossible. We laughed too hard to stay mad at her.

~

Kelly came home from work at her new job at the Williamsport Hospital cafeteria. Noelle couldn't wait to tell her about Chuck Bowman. Kelly later told me Noelle had experienced her first kiss. She hugged Noelle and they vowed to share all their secrets and keep each other updated on their lives. Kelly was dating several nice boys, but not in love with any of them. The girls made plans to go to Brandon Park the next evening after Kelly got home from work. Noelle could bring Wendy, Kelly would bring her new friend from work, Erin, and they could meet there. Noelle doubted I would let her go to the park at night, but Kelly insisted she try.

"Mom lets you get away with more than the rest of us," Kelly had said. "So just tell her you're a teenager now and I'll watch out for you."

"Okay, I'll try," Noelle had said.

Kelly left for work and Noelle went off to pick out an outfit in case I agreed to let her go.

~

August 23, 1981

The next day the heat wave broke and the crisp, cool dryness that foretells the coming of fall, was in the air. Noelle bounced through the doorway, high-spirited from the drop in humidity, the only thing that could flag her antics, and announced she was bored.

"Hmmm," I said. "Maybe you can help me with dinner. Tim and the twins will be here, so I could use some help."

"Sure Mom, I'd love to."

"Really?" I said. "Since when?"

"Well there's this concert at Brandon Park tonight and Wendy's mom says she can go. Kelly's gonna meet us there after work with her new friend, Erin."

"Let me think about it," I said.

The large round table was filled with hungry boys, myself, and Nicole and Noelle. I served all their favorites--roasted chicken, corn, potatoes, salad and Noelle's personal favorites--mushrooms and string beans. The boys gulped down their dinner then left to play baseball, except for Tim, who still refused to go out in public.

"All right, Noelle," I said, as she and Nicole helped me clear the table. "You can go to the Henry Mancini concert in the park."

"Yea! You're the best, Mom," Noelle said, jumping up and down and hugging me.

"I'll pick you up at ten p.m. at the entrance to the park. You'd better be there."

"Great, will you do the dishes for me? I don't want to be late."

"Not likely," I said. "Don't push your luck."

When she offered me in pseudo-humbleness, the sum of one dollar, I laughingly agreed, knowing full well I had succumbed to her winsome guiles once more.

Her last words as she rushed out the front door, too exuberant to remember to give me a hug, were…"Bye, Mom."

~ *Forty One* ~

September 2, 1981

The waiting room was quiet and nearly empty. Kim and Grandma left to rest and change clothes. Kelly was working downstairs in the cafeteria. Butch got back from New Jersey early that morning and sat beside me. Michael sat across from us, his eyes closed. Nicole was home, as was Dante. It was better that way.

~

Today was Wednesday. Monday evening, after I told Noelle she could go toward the light, she started to go rapidly downhill. I wondered if she'd heard me and decided to stop struggling so hard to live. She'd begun running a high temperature. Her eyes no longer opened as she sank into a deep coma.

We had agreed with the doctors and nurses that while nothing would be done to advance her death, we would do nothing to prolong her life. Yet as her fever soared, the nurses gave her aspirin and extra fluids to bring it down. I was grateful. I couldn't watch my child suffer and do nothing to alleviate her pain. She could be having terrible headaches, for all anyone knew. It was the tenth day since the accident.

The doctor told us Noelle could go anytime now. Her kidneys and other organs were failing. I didn't think it was a good idea to call the other kids and Butch's mother back to the hospital. I was going to have my hands full as it was, when the time came.

The nurse called Butch and I inside the ICU. Noelle had been taken off all machines, except the respirator and was moved to a gurney. We stood by her side, silent. She looked so gray. It was clear that she was dying.

"Do you want to stay with her until she passes?" the nurse asked, her face filled with concern. I saw the stricken look on Butch's face, felt his body stiffen, as my own soul ripped to shreds.

"No," I said, softly. "No, we'll wait outside."

I could not bear to watch the last flicker of life slip from Noelle. I grabbed Butch's hand and we turned to leave.

"It will be about twenty minutes," the nurse said, "I'll let you know when she's gone."

We nodded and went back to the waiting room.

Butch asked the nurse to page Kelly in the cafeteria. She needed to be here.

Kelly came up right away.

"What's wrong, Mom?"

"Sit down, Kelly. Noelle's not going to last more than a few more minutes. Wait with us."

"Can I go see her?"

"No sweetie, I really don't think you should."

Kelly was numb with shock. Mike's eyes were still closed, but he heard me. Tears slipped from his long lashes as he faked sleep.

The room was so silent, I could hear the ticking of a clock, or someone's watch. Or maybe the beating of my broken heart. I felt guilty allowing Noelle to die alone even knowing she was already far away, deep in a coma. When the actuality of her death arrived, I couldn't watch it rob me of my child. Yet I knew I would regret leaving her alone for the rest of my life.

The door to the ICU swung open. The nurse looked at us, but didn't have to speak. She nodded. We knew. I hugged Kelly close to me as Butch grabbed Michael. We rose in unison and walked out, leaving behind the one we so loved. It was over.

~

Butch drove us home. None of us said a word. We could not even cry. Before we entered the house, Butch told us to wait a few minutes. He went around to all the family cars and removed the distributor caps. I wondered what he was doing, but didn't care enough to ask.

We walked into the house. Dante was in the living room, along with relatives and friends.

I told Dante to get Kim and Nicole.

"Mom wants everybody downstairs," he called up to Kim.

Kim ran down the stairs and asked, "What happened? What happened?" Her voice rose in panic.

When all the kids were gathered in the living room, I said, "She's gone."

"Gone? What do you mean gone? Gone where?" Dante asked.

Then he realized what I meant and chaos broke out. It took three men to hold Dante down. Kim grabbed her purse and ran for her car. Kelly flew upstairs to barricade herself in the hidden staircase in her room. Michael headed for the door, flushed with anger, seething with vengeance. His father assumed he was going after the drunk driver that killed his sister-- Butch blocked the door--holding Michael close against him, refusing to let go. Nicole screamed and ran out the back door. I let her go, knowing she was heading out to her clubhouse to be alone.

I stood in the midst of this storm of madness which swirled about me-- a tornado--touching down and destroying all in its path.

What is wrong with this family? I thought, too numb to move or stop them. I realized now, why Butch made sure no one's car would be operational, except for his. My mother-in-law got past us somehow and a neighbor phoned, telling us that she'd seen an older woman running down the road. Butch and his brother Don got into our car and tried to find her. She was heading toward the Catholic Church about three miles down the road.

It was more than I could handle. I wanted to go to bed and never wake up. I left the crazy scene in my house and went upstairs to escape into sleep.

Later, I would hear that Butch and Don nearly got arrested by police officers, who'd gotten a call from a concerned bystander saying that two men were abducting an old woman and forcing her into their car. The police called my house. Kim had answered the phone. They told her they had stopped two men on Market Street, trying to force an elderly woman into their vehicle. They asked if this woman might possibly be related to us? Kim told me that she'd confirmed that it was probably her grandmother.

The police, knowing of our situation, said, "We're so sorry for your loss--if there's anything we can do...."

At last the house emptied of relatives and friends. The house was finally quiet.

Relatives made the long ride home, only to return the next day for the funeral. There would be no viewing. I felt that the last ten agonizing days were Noelle's viewing; and I insisted upon a closed coffin. Butch agreed and the kids were too much in shock to care.

My mother-in-law was completely distraught. She insisted she must rush home (a three hour trip) and sew a white dress for Noelle to wear because she was now the bride of Christ.

"What are you talking about, Mom?" I asked. I just wanted everyone to go away and leave me alone.

"Micki, the last thing Noelle said to me this summer, when I was in the car getting ready to drive home, was 'Gram, when I get married, will you sew my wedding dress?'"

"I said, 'Sure I will, Noelle,' wondering why she'd asked me that question. Now I must do as she asked." On that note, she left. She never made the dress--there was no time.

~

When the house was empty--the kids all off by themselves--I laid on the couch, hoping to fall into a dreamless sleep. I awoke a few hours later to hear two of my neighbors arguing over which one should vacuum my living room rug. Whoever won the argument began to vacuum around me as I feigned sleep. I could never repay them for the ten days in which they cleaned my home and filled my refrigerator with food, but enough was enough. They left, still arguing, and the house fell silent again. Not for long.

Butch came back with Kim, who had needed to go to her house and get clothes for the funeral.

"Mick," Butch said, shaking my shoulder gently. "Do you want to come help me pick out a casket?"

"No," I said. "Go away."

"Well, what kind should I get?"

"I don't care. Wood, I guess. Make sure it stays closed."

"What do you want her to wear?"

I sat up, rubbed my eyes. "I want her in her new jeans and blue silk shirt she just bought with her babysitting money."

"I'll go find them, Mom," Kim said, and went upstairs.

"You sure you won't come with me?" Butch asked again.

"I can't. I just can't. Take Kim."

He looked so lost, but I knew he functioned better when busy. I had been stoic during the past ten days and now needed to just sink into oblivion. If I could just get through tomorrow….

~

I stood in the small church, supported by the prayers of loved ones, mantled with the soulful whine of the church organ playing its dirge of death. I felt a separation of mind and body. Someone was standing here, but it couldn't be me. The smell of incense permeated my senses, overwhelming with its cloying scent. Next to me, covered with a shroud, stood the casket of my child. I would not look at it; could not.

The words of the priest droned on and on, but I was lost in a sea of unrelated thoughts. I heard nothing, I felt nothing, except a desire to be done with this, to be free to face my grief alone.

The priest had been asked to keep the funeral mass as short as possible. He glanced over at me as if remembering our request and saw my face. He must have sensed I was near the end of my endurance and went directly to the celebration of the Eucharist. I took Communion, something I never did, because the Church insisted upon confession and I didn't believe I needed to confess to priests. I was taught as a Baptist, that it was a commemoration of the body and blood, not an actual transformation. The moment I accepted the wafer, it attached to the roof of my mouth. My body relaxed at once, calmness fell over me like a soft blanket and I was able to withstand the rest of mass. I knew then that the body of Christ was truly within me, guiding me through this ordeal.

It was over at last. We stood and turned as Noelle's casket was picked up by the pallbearers, made up of her family and friends. Loyalsock High School allowed her entire grade to take off from school for the funeral. We walked down the endless aisle of grieving, tear-streaked faces, united in a mélange of emotion, following the one who would never again walk among us. Then out into the overcast day, whose sun had the dignity not to shine; we entered the limousines and headed for the cemetery to say our final goodbye.

The ride to the cemetery was torturously slow. We climbed the long winding mountain road to the top of the cemetery, surrounded by grotesquely beautiful tombstones, the only proof of former lives.

Surely this was just a dream. I would awaken soon and rebuke the nightmare that enveloped my senses, sighing with relief. *Oh God, please let this be a dream.* But no, the grass was too lushly green. Tear-shaped droplets of rain hung precariously from misted, succulent leaves. The dark gray clouds swirling in anger as the sun tried vainly to push them aside in a futile effort to dominate the day, were too real. Yes, this was actually happening.

There were over a hundred people standing behind me; their silence bearing down upon me like the crush of ocean waves. I fought the compulsion to slide into oblivion and let this travesty proceed without me. The Communion wafer stayed intact within my mouth.

There was a small crucifix on top of the darkly ominous box which was now my daughter's residence. I tried to focus on that one object in an effort to retain my sanity. The voice of the priest, overflowing with empathy, broke the silence with, I was told later, a moving and beautiful eulogy. His words rained down on me, covering me with a compassionate warmth, but I comprehended no meaning. Closing my mind to everything around me, the box and I stood alone together in the macabre stillness of a lonely mountain top whose residents, except for birds and trees, were all stone-cold and unfeeling.

There was no life here, not even serenity, just the vacuous emptiness of space and time, devoid of animation. What a cruel, unlikely place to leave one who was so vivacious, so seething with spirit, so very much alive. I had to leave this place. My daughter was not here.

~

We drove back to the house in limousines, followed by lines of cars with relatives and loved ones. While we were gone, Dave Mealy from the Hillside Restaurant, had a buffet set up at the house to feed everyone. I had no idea what was serve, but heard that it was magnificent. Flowers were being delivered every few minutes, as they had been for two days, even though we'd requested no flowers in her obituary.

My friends and co-workers from The Villa were there, neighbors, all our relatives from New Jersey, Butch's whole family and our friends. I spotted my brother Stevie and rose to hug him. He'd reached the funeral late, hitting traffic as he drove up from Allentown, where he now owned his own hair salon. My brother Billy had walked out on his wife Pat and their daughter, Susan, several years before and no one knew his whereabouts. My step-father had dropped out of my life since we'd left New York and I'd never thought to call him. I hadn't the strength to deal with my mother yet, nor the desire.

My mother-in-law was too distraught to remain, said a quick goodbye and headed for Easton with my father-in-law driving. Gradually, the crowds dispersed and we were alone at long last. The solitude I craved was now frightening. Our support group had left and we were on our own. None of us spoke. Kids went to their rooms and I lay down on the couch. I had no idea where Butch was, and didn't really care. I wanted to die.

The next day and for many days to follow, flowers were delivered to our door, casseroles arrived, given by neighbors and strangers, and letters and cards piled on my desk. All offered heart-felt condolences; some included money. It seemed as if the entire city of Williamsport shared in our grief.

~ Forty Two ~

The day after the funeral, the house was silent, a silence coveted for so long. Now it descended upon me as if I were in a vacuum; I felt so alone. The onslaught of friends and relatives, while wearing me down had also kept me from facing the grim realty of Noelle's death.

Jeanie drove up the next day. She claimed she waited to come alone and go to Noelle's gravesite without people around. I had not planned on returning to the cemetery for a long time. We drove up the winding mountain road. Jeanie placed yellow roses upon the gravesite. I just wanted to leave. I hated this place; could not bear the thought of my child lying beneath the ground, all alone.

Jeanie left for home and I thought maybe now I could collapse and lie down on the red velvet couch and close my eyes forever.

I had yet to make the phone call to tell my mother that Noelle had been killed. I couldn't take her histrionics during the ten day ordeal, nor could I bear it during or right after the funeral. It had to be done, so I called her and told her as quickly and succinctly as possible.

"How could you not call me, Micki?" she started, sobbing and wailing. "I would have come right away."

She wouldn't have come and we both knew it, but I couldn't take that chance. I had way too much to deal with--my mother would have put me over the edge.

"I didn't want you to come and get upset, so I waited until it was over, for your sake," I lied.

She accepted that as a viable reason and said she had to hang up--she was too upset to speak.

~

Most of the kids left me alone. Kelly spent her time in her room, door closed. Dante was never home. Nicole was off in the woods behind the house or in her room. Kim left and went back to her own apartment. Butch did what he always did in a crisis--turned to work. Butch worked with Dave Mealy, who had worked with him at the Genetti Hotel, and now owned the Hillside Restaurant. He took the job change to be with us. But he was not with us; he receded into an unreachable place. He would not speak of Noelle. Five years would pass before he would even be able to say her name. He was sure Noelle would have lived if he were home. That made me feel even guiltier. If I had driven her to the concert that night, instead of letting her walk the half-mile, she would be alive. I was to pick up her and her friends, at ten o'clock. Why didn't I just drive her there as well? It was irrational thinking because we all walked the six-foot gravel berm along that road or rode our bikes each day. Still, remorse fell upon me like a heavy weight. I would never get out from under it.

Mike was the most annoying. Each day as I slept on the couch, he would ask when I was making supper. *Supper? I lose my sweet daughter and Michael wants supper?* "Go away, Mike," I said. "Find something to eat and leave me alone."

"Mom, the kids and I are hungry. Are you going to make supper or not?"

"Damn!" I rose from my stupor on the couch and stormed into the kitchen, slamming pots and pans, and cooking whatever I could find.

"There! Supper's made! Call whoever's hungry and leave me alone!"

He would not. Finally, I got up, faced my responsibilities and began functioning as a mother again.

Daytime, I saw that the children's needs were met. Evenings, when the household was asleep, I vented my rage against my Creator.

I screamed into the night. *"My God, how could you take my child? I have suffered enough. I want her back. I want her back now!"*

No answer came, or comfort that I could hold onto--if God was guiding me through the worst Hell I had ever known, He hid it well.

My mother's birthday fell on September 22nd, twenty days after Noelle died. In my despair, I had forgotten to send her a card or call her. She sent me a long and hateful letter, for missing her birthday. Some things just never changed.

~

Noelle died on September 2, 1981 and I turned forty years old on October 25th. Normally, forty would be a milestone birthday. Not now. Pamela and Danny drove out to be with us. She brought a casserole of chicken, broccoli, cheese, and mayo, topped with breadcrumbs. It was delicious, even to me. I ate to live; I didn't live to eat. They spent the night and cheered us somewhat. Old friends had held a raffle and sent us the winning basket full of various goodies and alcohol, as well as a check for a thousand dollars.

Carmella came over and made me write out the thank you notes. I dreaded this chore but it had to be done. And there were so many to thank.

Oddly, all the ducks in the backyard pond came waddling up to the back of the house. They had never, ever done that before. I remembered Noelle's love for birds, especially doves, and wondered why they'd come, while tossing them bread. They waddled up to the back porch and stayed there for hours every day, for a full week after Noelle died. Never in the five years we'd lived there had they strayed so far from the pond. It was as if they were paying their final respects to Noelle.

I thought Sheba was dying. She lay limp and dejected, refusing food and only drinking water. I had no inclination to worry or care about the dog. It was much later that I realized that she was deeply grieving.

The elusive whippoorwill swooped down from the mountains and through the trees; heard but never seen. Through the night and into the dawn it sang its haunting song of another summer's loss, as I cried mine.

~

The kids were suffering acutely and I was unable to ease their pain, too ensconced by my own. Kelly became bulimic and suicidal for a while. Kim dropped by often, but she could not handle her grief while overcome by ours. Dante raced his car in an effort to tempt death to take him, too. Michael was silent, but filled with rage. He stormed out of the house one day heading in the direction of the drunk driver's home with murder in his eyes. I quickly called Dante and his friends, who went after him and after a struggle, brought him home. Nicole slept in our bed again, and when chased off, lay on the floor next to the bed.

She experienced severe anxiety and panic attacks, which I knew so well. I was helpless to console her. We were lost souls, suffering alone, not able to comfort each other or unite as a family. It was then I began to write down my thoughts.

Nicole turned eleven on November 30th. It was a subdued celebration as was mine. I insisted she have her pizza party at the Great Skate rink. She had looked forward to it before Noelle's accident. It was painful to be there and I could barely wait for the party to end. As the last song played, I glanced over at the rink, while Nicole and her friends were eating pizza. I saw a vision of Noelle, skating gracefully across the rink. I blinked and the vision was gone, but I heard a line from the stereo playing the song "American Pie," by Don Mclean--"The Day the Music Died."

~

Christmas was coming--Noelle's favorite holiday. What were we to do? We wanted to forget it, ignore it; not acknowledge it. But it was Noelle's favorite holiday.

Somehow, we gathered the strength to make the decision to create this Christmas in Noelle's honor. It was beyond difficult, but it was something we all knew would please Noelle.

Each time the radio played "The First Noel," it was like a knife in our guts. I was positive that the song played more than usual that year.

I baked cookies, made all the traditional foods, shopped for presents and put up the six-foot blue spruce Christmas tree that had shared our lives each Christmas since 1977. I invited friends and neighbors, and shed a few tears as I placed Mr. Bill on the stately tree, or remembered the few years before when Noelle and Kelly got into the rum-spiked eggnog meant for adults and Noelle got tipsy.

The pond was frozen and enough snow had fallen to cover the landscape in a pillow of white, bringing memories of the girls' skating on the pond and sleighing down the backyard slope. The memories were cherished and painful at the same time.

We pulled it off. That first Christmas without Noelle would have made her happy. We felt her presence among us. The following Christmases would be so bleak, so hard to bear.

~

As January of 1982 rolled around, the trial was nearing for the man who drove drunk and killed Noelle. I could, but will not, mention his name. I will not give him recognition in this saga of love and loss. I never hated the man, only the act. Not out of benevolence--I just had no room in my heart for hatred. Grief filled every space where hatred might have taken root. Except in my dreams. The dream was always the same.

A soft tapping at my door . . . I am alone. I know before I open it who is standing there. My shotgun is loaded and ready to fire. I let him in.

He steps into my carpeted foyer, stops beneath the chestnut archway. Each detail of the room is seared into my mind. Except for him. It is silent as we stare at each other, his face hidden by his bowed head. Cleo, the orange tabby cat, leaps up and catches a fly on the wall. The crunching of his prey breaks the silence.

"Ma'am, won't you please forgive me this time? I can't go on living without it."

"Don't worry, you won't." My voice is flat, emotionless.

This drunk--this loser--took my sweet Noelle's life. Fate screwed up, leaving this child/woman with her life before her, paralyzed and comatose. His pleas fall upon deaf ears. He is alive, Noelle is dead.

He slumps to the floor, as I recoil from the impact of the weapon.

I awoke in a sweat, feeling a rage that tore through my body like a thing alive. I would have preferred to break his neck, letting him suffer her loss; nothing left but eyes not quite seeing, distant, and yet a perfect, sound mind. Shooting him was too easy, too merciful--and something he preferred.

His teenage years were troubled, I heard. A tour in Vietnam pushed him into a life of alcohol and drugs. I contemplated the irony. My husband, brothers, sons, and relatives were all spared from serving in Vietnam. Yet this senseless "police action" took the life of my daughter twenty years later. A stranger, so affected by that conflict, destroyed my daughter . . . and himself as well.

Awake, I forgave him--grief and sorrow saturated my soul, leaving no room for hate. Yes, I forgave him, except in my dreams. This killer came again and again, knocking at my door. I shot him again and again. I prayed that one day, anger would give way to true forgiveness, setting us both free.

~

I found the strength to write editorials, one of which was read on a local TV station. Noelle's accident was constantly reported in the Williamsport Sun-Gazette during the entire ten days leading to her death and again as the trial of her killer drew near.

I wrote petitions to the judge to come down hard on this man who, by his negligence and drunkenness, took the life of a budding, bright girl who would have given much to the world had she lived. Kim and I drove to the malls and food stores, stood outside K-Mart, and got my petition signed by hundreds of caring people. The judge assigned to the case was so inundated by calls and letters, he almost had to recuse himself from the trial. But he didn't.

~

The trial took place on April 8th, 1982. I refused to go, as did Kelly, but the rest of the family went, except for Nicole, whom I felt was too young to go through such an experience. I had never seen the face of the man who took away my child and I never would. I refused to have a face to hate. Kelly felt the same. I did the groundwork that helped get him sentenced for two and a half to six years in a state prison, a first in Pennsylvania history for a DWI (driving while impaired) offense.

Butch wrote the following statement and read it in front of the packed court room and judge, at the end of the trial:

"Your Honor, I am addressing the court today in response to a particular case and also on behalf of a grave, general problem. Drunk driving has been considered a minor offense, something to joke about back at the neighborhood bar. In most cases there is no real penalty, only a small fine and a mark on the driver's license.

"Because the punishment is so lenient, the offense is therefore considered minor. Because of this attitude by society and the courts, my lovely young daughter is dead. The man before you has an appalling record of alcohol abuse, public drunkenness and drunk driving, yet he has repeatedly been turned loose on society because the offense was only minor. Murder is not minor. This man murdered Noelle just as surely as if he'd taken a gun and shot her. It would have more merciful if he had shot and killed her--she wouldn't have lingered and suffered for ten ungodly days. I realize that nothing can be done to repair the damage caused, but this court can ensure that he takes no more lives.

"You have, your Honor, an obligation inherent in your position, to protect the lives of the citizens of this town. I am asking you to do everything in your power to prevent this man from causing more pain and anguish than he has already done. He has demonstrated repeatedly that he will not respect the law or conventions of society. He has demonstrated that he will not be rehabilitated. Therefore, I am asking that the maximum penalty be imposed and at least, for a time, he will be unable to cause harm. Thank you."

As he sentenced him, the judge said: "It's very obvious from the pre-sentence investigation that you have little or no respect for the law . . . You have repeatedly been in court on alcohol-related offenses and have shown no motivation to rehabilitate yourself."

Judge Smith said his sentence would not be based on "public opinion and public pressure" despite a flood of mail he had received during the last three weeks. The judge said letters and petitions containing nearly seven hundred names had been received either at his home or office.

As a result, the drunk driver received the maximum sentence for this offense. The maximum penalty had never been imposed for vehicular manslaughter in Pennsylvania history at that time.

Years later, we would find out that due to an over-crowded state prison, he was sent to a county jail for part of a year; then a halfway house, free on weekends. He never served one day in the state prison.

I suggested suing the City of Williamsport for allowing a known drunk to continue to wreak havoc upon society. No one listened. Years later, a woman in New England did sue, and won her case.

While we sued both restaurants which had served him when he was obviously inebriated, the restaurants quickly filed chapter 11 bankruptcies and reopened under other names. Technically, we won $100,000 lawsuit, but it was paper money due to the bankruptcies.

On the up side, the paper ran the story as a $100,000 win in court, so perhaps other lives might be saved. The people reading the paper--and hopefully, restaurants and bars--would believe we really received the money and refrain from serving drunks, in the future. Creating and/or allowing drunken situations that would cost them financially, or shut them down were powerful deterrents. The money, had we been able to collect it, meant nothing to us--it was the message we were trying to send: If you help people drink, drive, and kill, you'll pay. Hopefully, it helped.

~

1982

By late spring, the headstone was ready for Noelle's gravesite. Kim, Kelly, Nicole and I made a pilgrimage to the cemetery--we had not been there since right after the funeral. It was too painful. I'd designed the headstone for Noelle's grave. It showed a white dove in flight, holding a red rose in its mouth. From the rose, several tear-shaped droplets fell. Her epitaph read:

There Were Only Those Who Loved her,
And Those Who Never Knew Her.

Butch had written it, plagiarizing a bit from the book, "The World According to Garp." I doubted the author, John Irving, would mind. The stone was set, and I needed to make sure it had been done correctly.

As we drove up the winding road to the top of the cemetery, we couldn't remember where she was buried. The cemetery was huge, with both Catholic and Protestant sections. We drove up, down and around, several times, but couldn't find her.

Kim slowed the car to ask a middle-aged man walking his dog, for help. Before she could say a word, the man asked, "You're looking for Noelle? She's right over there, under the large oak tree." He pointed toward a side road, no more than a few yards away. We thanked him and he smiled widely, waving at us as he continued on his way.

Sure enough, Noelle's headstone lay beneath a large oak tree, exactly where the man had directed. Her headstone was lovely--exactly as I'd planned it. It was also heart-wrenching and none of us could bear to stay more than a few minutes, unable to stem the rush of tears blurring our vision.

Kim drove back down the mountain road, but we never saw the man and his dog, even though there was only one way down and we had all been at the very top of the cemetery.

"Who was that man?" I asked Kim.

"I don't know, Mom. I thought you knew him."

"Kelly, have you ever seen him on your runs through the cemetery?"

"No Mom, I thought you knew him, too. He seemed like he knew all of us."

"Well, I never saw him in my whole life," Nicole added.

We drove home in silence, each of us pondering the events of the day. It seemed apparent to all of us that somehow, some way, we had met an "angel unaware" who had pointed us in the direction of Noelle's grave.

~

By summer, Butch couldn't take anymore. Driving down Bloomingrove Road past the spot where the truck struck Noelle was too hard. There was a dark blood-red stain where she was struck, that almost a year of rain, ice, and snow had not washed away. He had seen the pieces of broken mirror on the road and berm, where no skid marks were ever found at the scene. It tortured him, it haunted him--it was more than he could bear.

~

I rebelled against moving so soon. I knew it was not good to add the stress of moving to our suffering. It was evident that if we did not move away from Williamsport, Butch was going to lose his grip. Against my better judgment, I began to pack. We gave the house I loved so dearly to Kim. She had fallen in love with a nice young man named Michael Bower and they planned to marry in November.

Dante chose to stay with Kim in Williamsport. Only Mike, Kelly, Nicole and our dog Sheba would be moving with us. I felt I was losing more children and the "empty nest syndrome" hit me hard.

~ *Forty Two* ~

Butch was offered a job as general manager for a Ground Round restaurant in the mall in Staten Island, New York. His friend Danny was already working there. Pam and Danny had an apartment in Staten Island. He started the job at once while I finished packing up the house. In early September we made the move to New York. Butch had already picked out a new house in a new development on the south end of Staten Island. The girls and I had driven down one weekend in a heat wave, but hadn't seen anything we liked. I told Butch he'd have to find us something himself. He did. The girls and I hated the Island on sight, especially the stifling heat and humidity, which made the fumes from the Fresh Kills Landfill even more potent. It was an ugly place. Kelly enrolled in Tottenville High school, with a graduating class of a thousand kids. Nicole went to the intermediate school a few miles farther down the same road.

Our rented home was a beautiful, brand new house, but I missed my old, familiar farmhouse. Michael took over the family room in the new house and it was soon a pigsty. I wasn't sure whether the fumes were from the dump or the family room.

Staten Island, a borough of New York City, is made up of many small towns and villages. Tottenville was one of them. We lived in Huguenot. Nicole had a beautiful, large room that she decorated herself. She took "I Love NY" bumper stickers with the red heart under "love" and crossed it out, and wrote in "hate," instead. None of us were happy here.

The highlight was helping Kim plan her wedding in November. Butch booked the Hillside Restaurant for her reception, knowing his friend, Dave Mealy, would make it memorable. Kim's biggest problem was finding a dress long enough--Grandma refused to sew her gown because she wasn't getting married in a Catholic church. Grandma boycotted the wedding entirely.

Kim's godmother, Marie, along with her friend Judi were her matron and maid of honor. Kathy Steiger and Kelly were Kim's bride's maids. Seeing Kathy walk down the aisle in Noelle's place nearly broke my heart. They looked so much alike. Dante and Michael, along with Mike Bower's brothers, were ushers. Butch walked Kim down the aisle and the two of them strutted like stars on the red carpet. She was smiling, tears glistening in her eyes as her father kissed her cheek and handed her over to the man who would soon be her husband. Without Noelle, her joy and ours was bittersweet.

Anita and George flew in for the wedding, and Danny and Pam drove from Staten Island. Relatives, neighbors and friends made the wedding memorable. The sting of the one not there was temporarily eased. We drove back home afterward, while Kim and Mike went to scenic Danville, Pennsylvania--thirty miles away. Later she told me that her honeymoon suite was much like the one Butch and I had shared on our wedding night--I had described our elopement and honeymoon to her many times. She said she found a two-inch long cockroach in the bathroom. I smiled, remembering my own bug-infested entrance into matrimony.

~

In the following year we had all come along a path etched with tribulation, fear and the ever-present reality that Noelle was no longer with us. Noelle would have hated to see us react as we did, but we had no rules or standards for handling the death of a loved one. We did the best we could. Each of us walked through our own valley of the shadow of death to find our peace. We had to grapple with individual sorrow before we could reunite as a family, perhaps not the best way of dealing with the situation, but it was the only way we knew. We had never met grief like this before and were learning daily of its many facets and its endless depths. Sometimes there was a near blissful numbness; other times, if a friend or stranger spoke of the tragedy, their words struck like a lightning bolt of pain coursing through our bodies. Yet in other instances words could soothe for a time and bring passing relief.

We had made strides toward a healthy mentality, becoming a family capable of feeling and sharing; a unit instead of seven lost, bewildered souls, wandering in chaotic misery. There were sleepless nights and nights when we slept like the dead; and other nights pulsating with intense nightmares. Once in a while, I would dream of Noelle, see her so clearly, talk to her, and awaken with a sense of quiet peace; expecting to see her alive and all that had transpired was just a bad dream. Oddly enough, we all seemed to miss her at the same times, unbeknownst to each other.

Emotions surged, intertwined and merged with reckless abandon; rage, anger, hatred for her killer, depression, love and helplessness. Tempers were short. Passions fluctuated between intense feeling and utter lethargy.

Our lives moved on, steadily, seemingly without compassion for our thoughts and feelings, as if the regularity of a daily routine would somehow set things right. It was the routine of everyday life that pushed us forward and kept us going. The anguish was a black hole we needed to pass through, however long, to reach recovery. It would take many shapes and forms along the way, sometimes separating us, sometimes uniting us, but with us always. Grief had not only taken over our lives, it became our lives, until we were almost comfortable living with it; and many years would pass before we would be able or willing to put our heartache aside. . . .and then the miracle happened.

~

Kim called to tell us she was pregnant. She had a wonderful pregnancy until her labor began early. She was due to have the baby on September 9, 1983, but she went into labor in the early morning hours of August 30th. I had come up the week before to stay with her in the last weeks of her pregnancy, and we were both glad that I had. Kim labored through the day, pains coming every ten minutes, then every five minutes. I had the television on to try and distract her from her discomfort; soap operas and game shows that just seemed to annoy her.

The baby didn't come that day. The next day, the news interrupted our favorite soap opera, "General Hospital," to report that some kind of strange, unidentified disease was killing nurses and hospital workers at Divine Providence Hospital--the very hospital where Kim was due to go deliver her baby.

"Well, Kim," I said. "This will surely be a good entry for the baby book."

"I'm not going to that hospital!" Kim yelled from the couch, struggling to raise her bulky body.

"Don't panic, I'm sure it's nothing," I said with a huge, fake smile.

"It's nothing?" she said. "You go have the baby there then--there are three dead nurses and they don't know what's killing them."

Kim called Doctor Kolb, a Mennonite and homeopathic family doctor, who assured her that she and her baby would be fine and that he would be with her every moment.

The soap opera was interrupted by a special news broadcast--an airliner had been shot out of the sky over the USSR. No one survived. Korean Passenger Airline KAL 007, carrying two hundred sixty-nine people, had accidentally crossed into Soviet air space and Viktor Chebrikov gave the order to shoot them down, assuming they were spying. The plane went down in the cold waters off Russia's east coast.

"What?" Kim asked, trying to get her bulk up off the couch.

"Wow," I said, "This is going to be something you can put in the baby's book, that's for sure."

Kim didn't look pleased. Her face tightened with the arrival of another labor pain.

Early in the day, on September 1st, her labor pains became stronger and her doctor told her to come to the hospital immediately.

Butch, the girls and Michael drove up from Staten Island and took up their posts in the waiting room. Except for Kelly. She was so terrified that Kim would die that she couldn't go to the hospital. She stayed at Kim's house and prayed. Kim and the father-to-be were in a birthing room because they wanted natural childbirth. Hours passed. Kim's labor was not progressing. I was able to be with her often--and she called for me many times, throwing her husband out and threatening his life. More hours went by. Kim was encouraged to walk up and down the halls, to no avail. Twenty-four hours after admittance, Kim was still not dilated. The baby was in distress. Her doctor told her that the baby was stuck in the birth canal, the cord around his neck. It was too late for the caesarian section that had been set up in the room in the event she needed it. Her doctor sat on the bed, rubbing her back; nurses aides cried at the foot of the bed as Kim writhed in agony. I was made aware that Kim and the baby were in mortal danger. Her husband, Michael, was warned that the baby would not survive the birth, and that Kim might not make it either.

Kelly, Nicole and I prayed constantly. Butch, Michael and Dante paced. The doctor finally walked through the door. We were afraid to hear what he had to say.

"You have a grandson. It was touch and go for a while but they both made it through okay." He looked exhausted. We were all exhausted. We went back to Kim's house to get some sleep.

The next day, we got to see Kim and the baby, who had passed the APGAR test with scores of eight and ten--amazing, since he'd been without oxygen for eight minutes. Kim held the baby close in the cheery room.

"Oh Mom, I'm so sorry." She cried out, "I didn't realize--I didn't think . . . he wasn't due 'til next week. It's the second. It's September 2nd." She started sobbing.

None of us had realized what day it was, except for Kelly. We were too worried about the safety of Kim and baby Ian. Kim was so upset and while we didn't tell her, so were the rest of us.

During the next two years the tragic day that claimed the life of Noelle became, instead, the birthday of a beautiful little boy. Noelle had somehow sent us the gift of healing. Today, as we continue to celebrate that day, our grief is temporarily put aside, and the memories of Noelle have become sweet, bittersweet, yet softened by the little boy born on the date she died. This, we believe, was Noelle's way of assuring us that her soul was alive and well, her way of easing our grief--her legacy of love.

Sometimes we can remember something Noelle did, delighting in the memory of her, and the sharp pain in the pits of our stomachs fades to a dull ache.

And sometimes we can think of her and smile.

The End

Aftermath

Noelle was never far from us--part of her was interspersed among her ten nieces and nephews. Like their parents, many were psychic or tuned into Noelle in some way.

She spoke to me through automatic writing. Noelle predicted the sex of my first two grandchildren, noting that "Ian" would know her. He was Kimber's first child and being born on September 2nd, seemed to have a special affinity with Noelle. They were alike in personality as well. At two years old, Ian told his mother that Noelle did not jump out in front of the truck, something that had always haunted me. No one asked him--he just blurted it out. He said that when he grew up and "became Noelle," the truck would miss him. This prophesy came true. At the age of 14, again on September 2nd, Ian was in Rome with his grandmother as guests of the Vatican. A close friend of my mother-in-law's family was about to be canonized. Later, in a narrow alleyway, a truck zipped by and the side view mirror missed Ian by inches.

Noelle came to her father as I lay dying from back to back heart attacks, too unstable for the by-pass I would need. She stood at the end of his bed and smiled, and winked. I lived.

Kelly's son, Brandon, saw spirits before he could even speak, pointing and babbling baby talk to the ceilings and walls. Later, like his cousins, he proved psychic to an even greater degree; seeing Noelle in the clouds and on streets or in the car right next to his mother, Noelle's sister.

Nicole's son, Nicholas, was barely talking when he told his mother that Noelle was in the room with them. It was on September 2nd, as usual.

Dante's wife, Kerry, felt her second child, Mackie, jump in her womb on another September 2nd. Twenty-five years have passed since she left us physically, yet she is a strong presence among us. She offers protection, often giving warnings, like the day she warned Brandon not to play in the street. Her love still envelops us softly, taking away the scorpion-like sting of her passing.

Perhaps, one day she will pass on to a higher realm and leave us. But for now, her love remains among us, consoling us with the truth of eternal life. She will know when it is time to leave us . . . and we will miss her. But, we will be ready at long last, to let her go.

Noelle would have loved being among her ten nephews and nieces. She will be a guardian angel for them as she has been for all of us. We have not really lost Noelle . . . her life, her love, her hopes and dreams beat on in the hearts of those who loved her. She left a legacy of love, never to be forgotten.

On days when I miss her most, I can hear her happy, bright voice calling out to me.

"Bye, Mom!"

"Bye, Noelle," . . . for now.

~

Noelle,

You were the glitter in our lives, the foil to our temper-- the giggle to our tension. You were the thread that ran through our family and drew it together. Noelle, your voice was the firebrand of conscience and the iconoclast of convention. When a new school rule forbade smoking or swearing on or near the school grounds, you erupted in umbrage. You neither smoked, nor swore, but denied the school's right to manage your mores. You are forever in my heart.

Love,
Dad

Authors Note

Each year the lives of children, teenagers and young adults are lost through alcohol and drug related deaths-- most often by drunk drivers. Each one of them was special to those who loved them and to society at large. Each one deserves to be remembered. This book was written for each of them.

Micki Peluso

September 2, 2007

Epilogue

Kimber had two sons, Ian and Jesse, who could see and speak to spirits until they outgrew it. She divorced and moved to New York near us and later remarried and had a third son, Benjamin. She married again, to Al, a retired NYPD Detective, and lives in upstate New York. Her talents as a songwriter, singer, poet, guitar and classical piano player and writer matched her skills as executive assistant for a major computer company. Recently, she battled lymphoma cancer and beat it.

Michael became an amateur photographer, then a sous chef, after years of working in the restaurants for his father. He is now head chef for a major NYC restaurant, The Marina Cafe.

Dante still excels in artistry of all forms, plays musical instruments by ear, and is a noted architect, working and living in New Jersey. He married his soul mate, Kerry, an accountant, who works as an executive at Penn State University. They have two children, Samantha and Mackie.

Kelly kept her promise to Noelle and became the lawyer that Noelle had hoped to become. She passed the bar exam for both New York and New Jersey at the same time, on her first try. She runs her own real estate law office. She married Keith Wren, a banking, insurance and financial advisor, and bore three sons, Christopher, Brandon and Tyler.

Nicole still has trouble speaking about the loss of Noelle. She married Scott, a New York City ESU/EMT, who teaches search and rescue teams. She has two children, Nicholas and Bailey Rose, and is a title closer for real estate transactions, and a financial advisor.

Anita and George lost their son, Steven, to brain cancer. He was twenty-eight years old. He had worked as a grip in the movies and as a stagehand for Local 720. His last big jobs were "Leaving Las Vegas," "The Stand," and "Casino."

Printed in the United States
89095LV00003B/88-135/A